Wild Island Love

The Steeles at Silver Island

Love in Bloom Series

Melissa Foster

Leni & Raz

A Note from Melissa

I had so much fun writing about Duncan "Raz" Raznick and Leni Steele. Neither is looking for love, much less expecting their initial fake date to turn into more. Their banter is hilarious, their chemistry is off the charts, and their stubbornness makes their happily ever after that much sweeter. Leni needed someone who wouldn't try to change her but who could weasel his way into her heart without her realizing it, and Duncan did not disappoint. I hope you love them, the epic pranks, and their families as much as I do. All Love in Bloom stories are written to stand alone or to be enjoyed as part of the larger series, so dive right in and enjoy the funny, steamy, and deeply emotional ride.

If you're an avid reader of the Love in Bloom series, you'll be happy to see cameos from Abby de Messiéres (MAYBE WE WILL, Silver Harbor), Jake Braden and Fiona Steele (CRASHING INTO LOVE, The Bradens at Trusty), Mason Swift and Remi Divine (THIS IS LOVE, Harmony Pointe), and I hope you enjoy learning more about Shea Steele. Yes, she will be getting her own book!

I have many more steamy love stories coming soon. Be sure to sign up for my newsletter so you don't miss them.
www.MelissaFoster.com/Newsletter

Free Love in Bloom Reader Goodies

If you love funny, sexy, heartfelt stories, be sure to check out the rest of the Love in Bloom big-family romance collection and download your free reader goodies, including publication schedules, series checklists, family trees, and more.
www.MelissaFoster.com/RG

Bookmark my freebies page for periodic first-in-series free ebooks and other great offers.
www.MelissaFoster.com/LIBFree

Be sure to check out my online bookstore for pre-orders, early releases, bundles, and exclusive discounts on ebooks, print, and audiobooks. Ebooks can be sent to the e-reader of your choice and audiobooks can be listened to on the free and easy-to-use BookFunnel app. Shop my store:
shop.melissafoster.com

SILVER ISLAND

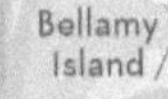

SILVER ISLAND FAMILY TREE

Extended families not noted

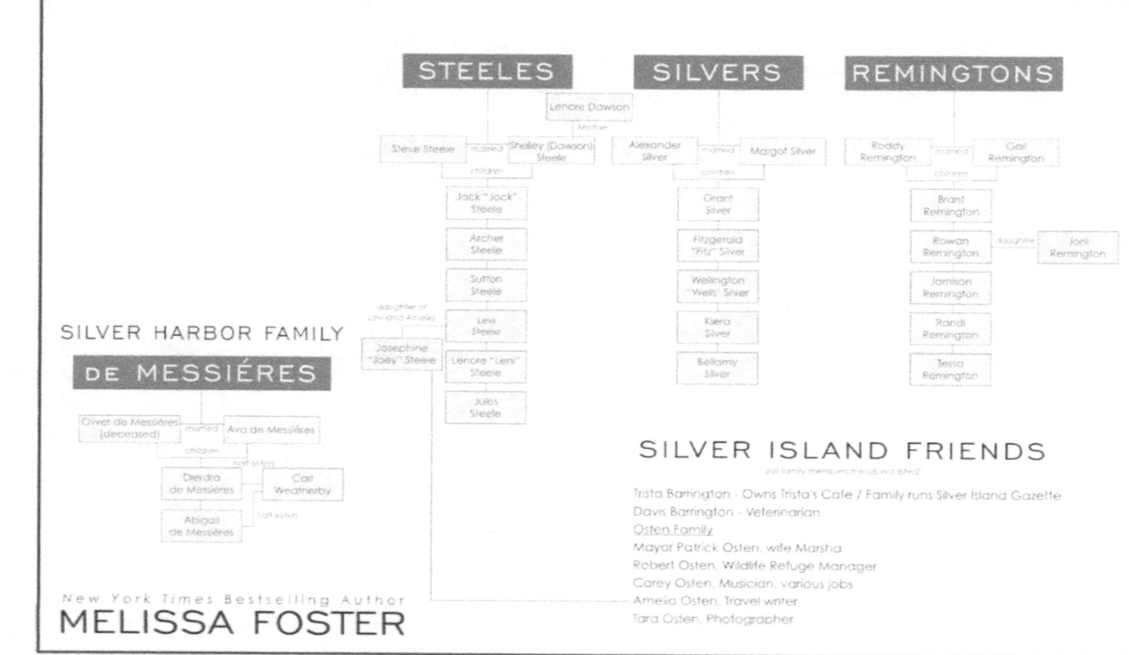

New York Times Bestselling Author
MELISSA FOSTER

Playlist

"The Night We Met" by Lord Huron, Phoebe Bridgers

"Craving You" by Thomas Rhett, Maren Morris

"Consequences" by Camila Cabello

"Lottery" by Latto, LU KALA

"A Safe Place to Land" by Sara Bareilles, John Legend

"I Can't Fall in Love Without You" by Zara Larsson

"Almost Lover" by A Fine Frenzy

"Kindly Calm Me Down" by Meghan Trainor

"Back to You" by Selena Gomez

"Just Want You to Know" by Backstreet Boys

"Love Me Like You Do" by Ellie Goulding

"Running Back" by Ashley Cooke

"Quit Playing Games (With My Heart)" by Backstreet Boys

"Never Really Over" by Katy Perry

"Hurt No More" by Chase Wright

"This Feeling" by the Chainsmokers, Kelsea Ballerini

"Vindicated" by Dashboard Confessional

"What If I Never Get Over You" by Lady A

"Die from a Broken Heart" by Maddie & Tae

"When You're Gone" by Shawn Mendes

"Still Falling For You" by Ellie Goulding

"Run to You" by Lea Michele

"Ruin My Life" by Zara Larsson

"I Believe You" by Fletcher

One

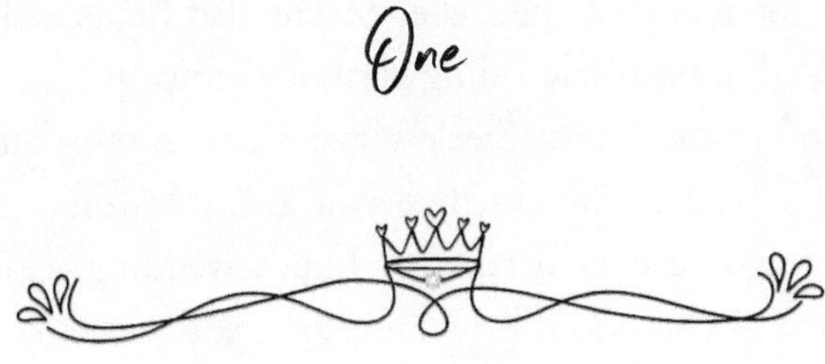

LENI STEELE ENDED the call to her favorite Thai restaurant, musing about how the people who worked there probably thought she lived in her Manhattan office. The fact that working on a Friday night gave her more satisfaction than the last several dates she'd been on had to say something about the male species. Or did it say something about her? She'd never had much patience for bullshit and putting on airs, but she didn't let that hinder her love for her job as a marketing and public relations manager for Steele Marketing & Media Solutions. She'd simply honed her ability to be hardnosed and to cut to the chase, and she excelled at it.

Her thoughts were interrupted as her cousin and boss, Shea Steele, walked into her office looking as sharp as ever. Her blond hair fell like spun gold over the shoulders of her fitted white blouse, a Chanel tote hung from her arm, and her cell phone was glued to her hand, as usual. Leni's mentor had built her business on sheer determination and grace, the latter of which was not in Leni's repertoire. Leni eyed her curiously. Her cousin's smile told her she was excited about wherever she was going, but that could mean business or pleasure. "Where are you off to?"

"I'm meeting Hawk for a drink. Do you want to come?" Hawk Pennington was a highly-sought-after photographer who worked with many of their clients. He also happened to be a tall, tattooed, motorcycle-riding glass of champagne.

"I don't think I'm the Steele Hawk wants *coming* tonight."

"That's a tasty thought, but you know I won't cross that line. We're going over details for Jules's wedding. Come with me. Take a night off. It'll be fun, and you never know who you'll meet." Jules was Leni's youngest sister. She was getting married in December, and as a wedding gift, Shea had hired Hawk to photograph her big day.

"You and I both know what's out there, and none of it equates to a bigger temptation than the Thai food I just ordered for delivery and the Mets game I'm going to watch while I'm working." Leni was done with wishy-washy men who didn't know how to handle a strong woman in or out of the bedroom or men who couldn't hold a conversation unless it was about themselves.

"I hear you, but I'm not giving up on finding my Mr. Right," Shea said cheerily. "If you change your mind, we'll be at NightCaps."

As Shea left her office, Leni went back to work. A few minutes later she heard Shea stomping back down the hall, tension rising in her voice. The life of a marketing and PR rep was riddled with urgency, and they both thrived on it.

Shea stormed in, poking at her phone. "It turns out you do need to work tonight." She put her phone to her ear. "You need to go to the ARTS gala with Raz."

Leni's head snapped up. She was *not* going anywhere with Shea's most difficult client, A-list actor Duncan "Raz" Raznick, who went by the stage name Duncan Raz, or simply Raz. "You *can't* be serious."

Shea held up her finger and spoke into her phone. "Yes, this is Shea Steele. I need to change the pickup for the ARTS gala tonight." She gave them the office address.

Leni pushed to her feet, fuming as Shea ended the call. "*What* is going on?"

"You know how the paparazzi are all over Raz again now that Jacinda and Rafe have signed on to make another movie together and pictures of them making out are all over social media." Raz had dated actress Jacinda Carr for several months. They broke up right before summer, after she cheated on him with her costar Rafe Jenson. "You've seen the stories about how Raz isn't over her. That one photographer, Ken Singer, is *always* stalking him. I'm worried about the bad press he's getting, so I set him up with an actress for the gala to give them something else to write about, but she broke her tooth and can't go."

"Can't he go alone?" Leni knew arguing was pointless. If Raz was her client, she'd make damn sure he had a woman on his arm, but that didn't lessen her hatred of the idea of going to a gala, much less going to one with an arrogant actor.

"That's not going to help the media see that he's over Jacinda."

"You're asking me to help the guy who royally screwed over my client for a big cologne campaign. Rugged for Men? Remember that? You were right there in the office when he told me to schedule it with his assistant, and then the week before the shoot, he claimed the timing didn't work. And let's not forget that he went through two other PR companies after leaving the one that repped him for years. He's become a problem child, Shea, and you know it."

"So what? He's not the first difficult client we've worked

with, and he won't be the last."

"But he's the first you're asking me to go out with. You *know* I hate being in the spotlight. Why don't you go as his PR rep and make a statement?"

"I can't. It'll look planned and manipulative."

Leni deadpanned. "I work for you. Isn't that the same thing?"

"*No.* You guys are going on a fake date, not making a statement."

"So now you're pimping me out?" Leni arched a brow. "Sorry, Shea, but I can't go. I'm working on marketing plans for the launch of Sterling Silver's new jewelry line and for Alyssa Braden, the director of the Sweet 'n Savory Dessert Festival. I'm trying to close those deals in the next four weeks."

"I'll work on them while you're with Raz if you go."

"You're meeting Hawk, remember? Can't Raz just no-show? Celebs do it all the time."

"*Shit.* Hawk." She began thumbing out a text. "Raz won't no-show. It's a fundraiser he believes in. He goes every year, and the guest list has been out there for weeks. His presence carries weight and helps the foundation get more donations." The ARTS foundation helped fund arts programs in New York City schools.

A cocky asshole with a heart. How unique.

"*Please.*" Shea's brow knitted. "I know he's not easy, and I hate asking you to do this, but I'm out of options. The gala starts in an hour and a half, and the media will eat him alive if he crosses that red carpet alone."

Leni huffed out a breath. "It's a good thing I love you, but we still have a problem. I don't have a dress fancy enough for a gala."

"You know I do!" Shea didn't have an office. She had a suite, complete with a full bath and a closet loaded with outfits, from casual to black-tie, accessories, and heels.

"You are annoyingly overprepared for everything."

"Thank God I am," Shea said excitedly. "I owe you one."

"You owe me a hell of a lot more than *one*." Leni pushed to her feet. "Wait. What am I supposed to tell my family? They'll see the pictures, and you know how Jules is." Jules was a bundle of unending optimism and the unofficial spreader of good cheer on Silver Island, where Leni and her five siblings had grown up.

"Well, you can't tell them it's a setup. If someone slipped and word got out, it would be even worse for Raz. Just say you went on one date and decided there were no sparks."

"I hate lying."

"It's not really lying. It *is* one date. It just happens to be a fake date, and with how difficult Raz is, if there are sparks, they'll be of the hateful kind. Come on. We're running out of time." She took Leni by the wrist, pulling her down the hall toward her office. "If anyone asks, you met Raz in the office and hit it off, so he asked you to go with him. Easy peasy."

"You mean I can't say I'm there against my will and would rather be shot out of a cannon than walk down a red carpet?"

AN HOUR LATER Leni was sitting in the back of a limousine parked in front of Raz's building, wearing a black Jillian Braden original gown with a sequined bodice, three-quarter sleeves, a cinched waist, and a puffy satin A-line skirt with a slit from floor to midthigh. It was a beautiful gown, and the least revealing of all the available options, although you wouldn't know it by the wide-plunging neckline that went nearly to her belly button, showing an uncomfortable amount of cleavage. The Manolo Blahnik ankle-wrap sandals and the sliver of diamonds around her neck added another level of elegance she wasn't used to. Thanks to one of Leni's longtime besties, Indi Oliver, a makeup artist and skincare boutique owner who also happened to be her older brother Archer's fiancée, Leni was able to create perfect smoky eyes and plump up her too-thin lips, which she'd always been a little self-conscious about. Shea had worked magic with a curling iron, all the while reminding her to act like she wanted to be there with Raz.

How long did it take for a guy to get ready?

She glanced at her phone, answered an email, and when she looked up, Raz was walking out of the building. She was used to handsome men, but she was thankful for the tinted windows as she drank in the square-jawed, chisel-faced actor. Tall and broad-shouldered, he wore the hell out of his tuxedo as he strode toward the limousine with an air of authority. His brown hair was short, his cheeks perfectly peppered with scruff, and *damn*. No wonder he'd been named *People*'s Sexiest Man Alive two years in a row.

Too bad he was as difficult as they came.

The driver opened the door for Raz, and he slid into the seat beside her, bringing a woodsy, spicy scent with him. Their eyes met, and his narrowed. "You're not an actress."

"Well, hello, Mr. Charming. Thanks for bursting my bubble. Here I thought I'd found a new career. Your other fake date broke her tooth and couldn't make it."

He flashed his pearly whites. "Aw, were you girls fighting over me?"

"You wish. I'm here as a favor to Shea."

"I guess thanks are in order, but I'm not sure why she bothered lining up a date."

"Because she cares about your image, like any good PR rep would." Leni's protective claws were coming out for her cousin and her industry.

He held her gaze, a challenge burning in his piercing blue eyes. "I guess it's good someone does."

"Don't you care about the bad press you're getting?"

"Not really," he said casually. "Fuck 'em if they don't want to watch my movies."

And there it was. The infuriating arrogance so many celebrities possessed. It wasn't so different from how Leni would react if people talked shit about her. But she knew better than to announce that to the world.

"Then why did you hire Shea?"

A slow smile crept across his face. "So I could get a date with her knockout marketing rep, obviously."

"You're a piece of work. Without good PR and marketing, you would have been just another pretty face."

"I knew you liked my face. I felt you staring at me through the tinted windows."

"You did *not*."

"See?" He arched a brow. "You *were* staring."

Leni sighed. "I can see this is going to be an exhausting night."

"I don't know what Shea led you to believe, but just because we're on a fake date doesn't mean I'll sleep with you. I'm *not* that guy."

He said it so seriously, she felt the need to clarify what she meant, but before she could get a word out, his lips quirked, and he said, "But I am a runner, and I have incredible stamina, so if we *were* to hook up, you'd definitely need to sleep in tomorrow."

She glowered at him. "Please stop talking."

He held his hands up in surrender, a playful grin lingering on his lips.

"You can act. I'll give you that," Leni conceded. "But you had solid reps helping you find every rung of the ladder you climbed, and now the career you worked so hard to achieve is being torn down, one inflammatory article at a time. Shea is working her ass off to turn things around for you. You should be grateful she's staying on top of your public image."

"I am grateful, but that doesn't mean I have to enjoy playing the game," he said coldly. "I care about this charity, which is why I'm here instead of watching the Mets game, but I don't give a damn if the media says I'll never work again. They don't hold all the cards."

"Not all the cards, but they do carry a lot of weight, and as your public image dwindles, so will your worth. Is that why you backed out of the Rugged for Men cologne campaign? Because you didn't give a damn?"

He shrugged. "So what if it was?"

"That's my client you screwed over," she fumed. "You know what? If you don't care about your reputation, then I have better things to do, and the Thai food I ordered won't go to waste." She reached for the button to speak to the driver, and he snagged her hand.

"You got all dolled up. You're not cutting out now. We're in this together."

"There is no *we*."

"Sure there is," he said as they pulled up in front of Lincoln Center, where the gala was being held. "You wouldn't want to disappoint Shea, would you?"

Two

BEYOND HER REPUTATION for being a pit bull and having stopped him in his tracks the first time he'd seen her in her office, Raz knew very little about the feisty porcelain-skinned beauty sitting beside him. But he knew one thing for sure. Tonight was going to be a hell of a lot more fun with Leni than it would have been with some starry-eyed actress. He couldn't remember the last time anyone had challenged him. Pushing her buttons was going to be fun.

Turning on the charm, he said, "Ready to show the world how much you love me?"

Those incredibly gorgeous *and* wicked green eyes narrowed. "I don't fake love, but don't worry. I'll make you look good."

His gaze slid from her eyes to her sexily bowed lips, down the sculpted auburn curls tumbling over her shoulders to the tempting path of flawless skin between her breasts, lingering there, feeling—and enjoying—the heat of her annoyance. Only then did he follow the curves of her body down to the slit in her skirt, admiring her long, lean legs. When he finally met her gaze, she was shooting him daggers. "In that dress, you can't help but make me look good."

The greeter opened his door, and through a camera-ready

smile, she said, "I'd make you look good if I were wearing rags."

Fuck yeah, you would.

He climbed out, and as cameras flashed and paparazzi shouted, he gave them what they needed to get off his ass, flashing a proud smile as he helped Leni to her feet. He put a hand on her lower back and leaned in closer, whispering, "Let's sell the hell out of this. Try to look like a well-satisfied woman."

With a dazzling smile in place, she put a hand on his chest, gazing adoringly up at him like a pro. "Won't that tip them off that this is fake?"

Why did he find her snark so sexy? As they made their way up the red carpet, he said, "It seems you've been sorely misinformed."

"Says the man who needed a fake date."

Someone shouted, "Who are you wearing?"

Leni looked at him expectantly.

"They're talking to you, beautiful."

"Oh, *right*." She beamed at the photographers. "Jillian Braden."

Once inside, Raz played up the dog and pony show, introducing Leni to the hosts of the event and other attendees, mingling like he loved these types of events. Leni was gracious and played the part of his adoring date perfectly.

As they headed into the ballroom, she said, "I need a drink," at the same time he said, "Let's hit the bar." She laughed, and it was a surprisingly sweet sound.

"Looks like we have one thing in common." Raz kept his hand on her back as they made their way toward the bar. "I should know what you're drinking, so I can order it for you."

"I guess it would be inappropriate to order tequila shots before the event even starts."

He chuckled. "Not in my book, but unfortunately, I think some of the guests might frown on that."

"Then I'll go with whiskey. Neat."

"Interesting choice."

"Why?" she asked with a hint of annoyance.

"Most women prefer wine or champagne."

"Yeah? Well, most men don't need fake dates, so how about you try being a little less judgy and a little more appreciative?" She straightened his bow tie, feigning a killer smile.

"Someone's sensitive."

"Not at all. I simply don't enjoy having my choices questioned."

He had a feeling there was more fueling that statement than just her annoyance at being stuck there with him for the evening. "I wasn't questioning your choice. I said it was interesting. It sets you apart from others, and that's never a bad thing."

"Unless you're a single celebrity after a breakup attending an event," she said thoughtfully.

Her change in tone caught him off guard. He knew better than to try to figure out what game she was playing and headed up to the bar to get their drinks.

THEY SURVIVED COCKTAIL hour, and as the night wore on, he couldn't take his eyes off Leni, with that thick auburn hair and those cupid lips. She had dainty features—catlike eyes with impossibly long lashes, a slim, upturned nose, high cheekbones, and a slightly pointy chin. That delicate femininity contrasted with the strength she exuded with every sharp-tongued sentence. She was by far the most beautiful woman in the room, and that smart mouth of hers was proving to be a hell of a lot of fun. She appeared captivated by the presentations and chatted amiably with other guests during dinner, though Raz noticed her leg bouncing impatiently under the table. That impatience went hand in hand with the whispered snark they'd volleyed all evening. Yet another thing no one else seemed to notice. Leni Steele would have made a damn good actress.

After their plates were cleared and people began moving to the dance floor, Leni whispered, "How long do we have to stay? If I have to listen to one more story about this woman's pet poodle, I might lose it."

He was sick of being there, too, but he was curious about what she would rather be doing. "Do you have something better in mind?"

"*Yes*," she hissed. "I'm missing the Mets game, too."

The man across the table glanced over, so Raz put his arm around her, nuzzling her neck, trying to ignore her sweet and all too tempting scent, a mix of honeysuckle and warm caramel, as he whispered, "A little late to try to get on my good side, isn't it?"

She must have noticed their watcher, too, because she put on the charm. "You know I like all your sides. Good, bad, and *especially* naughty."

She'd piqued his interest, proving it had been too damn long since he'd been with a woman. He wondered what she'd be like if this were a real date. "I need you in my arms, sweetheart." He pushed to his feet, bringing her up beside him, and guided her to the dance floor.

"What are you doing?" she asked as he swept her into his

arms.

"Getting us out of here." He twirled her, inching toward the service door he'd spotted the waitstaff using. "There's a hole-in-the-wall pub a few blocks away where we can catch the highlights of the game." That earned him a smile.

"Won't you get mobbed by paparazzi or fans at the pub?"

"With you in that dress, nobody's going to be looking at me." Another two twirls, and he took her hand, making a beeline through the door. She giggled, holding tight as they weaved around the kitchen staff. He nodded to the chef as they hurried past. "Exceptional dinner, thank you."

When they reached the back door, there was a Mets cap hanging on a hook with a jacket. He snagged the hat and put it on. "They'll be looking at you, but it won't hurt to keep my face shielded."

"You're stealing it?"

"I'm not classless." He whipped out his wallet and shoved a hundred-dollar bill into the pocket of the jacket. "Come on." They blew through the back door and hurried down the street. "Any lingering paparazzi are out front. Hopefully they won't catch wind of us."

"My bag is in the limo, and isn't that the point of me being here? So the media will see us together?"

"The driver will keep your bag safe, and the photogs already got what they needed." He shrugged off his tuxedo jacket and untied his bow tie. "I've had enough of the limelight for one night." He unbuttoned the top two buttons of his dress shirt, and her gaze followed. "Want me to keep going?"

Her eyes snapped up. "Get over yourself. I was just lost in thought."

"About my body? It's all natural, and yes, the nine-inch

rumor is true."

"I was *not* thinking about you. Believe it or not, the female world does not revolve around the male anatomy."

"I hear what you're saying, but those rosy cheeks say otherwise."

AS THEY MADE their way down the long city blocks to the pub, Leni didn't know what was more irritating. Getting caught staring at Raz's chest, or the fact that she'd looked in the first place. She told herself that it was simply refreshing to see chest hair because so many men waxed their entire bodies these days. But she'd had the urge to run her fingers through the dusting of hair on his chest and over the scar cutting through it. He'd been shirtless in plenty of movies, but he'd never had chest hair, and she'd never seen the scar. For some stupid reason, she couldn't stop thinking about it.

"Still thinking about my body?" he asked as he opened the door to the pub.

"Yes, as a matter of fact. I'm trying to figure out how deep a hole I need to dig in order to hide it." She heard him chuckling as he followed her inside. He was infuriatingly fun to toss barbs with, which bothered her because he had no regard for how important or difficult Shea's job was—and in turn, how important and difficult *her* job was. Catching the game highlights would be a good distraction from that annoyance.

The pub was deep and narrow, with wood-covered walls, seventies-style stained-glass lights hanging from the ceiling, and three big-screen televisions behind the bar. *Perfect.* There were only a handful of people at the tables and bar. They gave Leni and Raz once-overs as they headed for the bar, but they didn't stare or act impressed, which was a relief. She'd had her fill of pomp and circumstance.

The silver-haired bartender lifted his chin in Leni and Raz's direction, his warm smile drawing a genuine one from Raz, noticeably different from the cocksure grins he'd been flashing all evening. "I see we have Raz with us tonight."

"You know me better than that. It's always Duncan around here." He pulled out a high-backed stool for Leni. "Dave, this is my beautiful date, Leni Steele. Leni, this is my buddy, and the owner of the pub, Dave Wichard."

"It's nice to meet you, Dave." Leni thrust a hand across the bar, and he shook it.

"You, too. Where did you kids get off to tonight?"

Raz hung his jacket on the back of a chair, and as they sat down, he said, "A charity function."

"Why am I not surprised?" Dave said teasingly. "What can I get you to drink? Duncan, your regular? Fat Tire?"

"Are you a beer snob who drinks only your favorites?" Leni asked.

"You know how we celebrities are, but no beer tonight, Dave." Raz's gaze turned rascally, and it was a good look on him. "What do you say, Leni? Think we earned a few shots of Patrón?"

"I know I did."

As Dave got their shots, Leni watched the game highlights. The Mets had won seven to three, but they hadn't caught up until the eighth inning. "The *eighth* inning? What is wrong with them? Thank God I didn't watch the game. I would've gnawed off my fingernails."

Raz lifted her hand, arching a brow. "You wouldn't waste your perfect manicure."

"Of course not, but I would have cursed a blue streak."

His lips quirked. "Good to know."

"Do you blame me? Did you see that hit?" She pointed at the television. "It was perfect. Right *over* the wall and freaking spider arms caught it. That should've been a home run. And what the hell was wrong with Sharpe tonight? He's the number-one pitcher in the league, and he couldn't strike those guys out sooner?"

"Man, you are harsh," Raz said. "Give the guy a break. He's having an off night."

"Then he shouldn't be out there," Leni said as Dave set the shot glasses in front of them. "Thank you, Dave." She picked up a glass. "Here's to ending on a win."

Raz clinked glasses with her, and they downed the tequila.

"Where'd you meet this one? I like her." Dave refilled their glasses.

"Do you want to tell him, or shall I?" Leni cocked her head, wondering if he'd admit to being on a fake date.

He put his hand on her thigh, giving it a squeeze, and kept it there, a glint of playfulness rising in his eyes. "I've got it, sweetheart."

What are you up to?

"It was incredibly serendipitous," he said. "I was meeting with my PR rep, Shea, and I saw this auburn-haired knockout in black slacks that hugged her curves strutting down the hall on mile-high heels, focused on whatever she was thumbing out on her phone. I swear, Dave, it was one of those heart-stopping moments you see in movies, where the whole world stops. I saw her moving in slow motion, hair blowing over her shoulders, every sway of her hips pronounced. The whole shebang. And then she looked up from her phone, and our eyes connected." He put his other hand over his heart. "I kid you not, a bolt of lightning shot through me. She must have felt it, too, because she stumbled, and I caught her around the waist, and when those evergreen eyes found mine, I was *done*. Putty in her hands. I think I fell for her right then and there."

He turned those piercing blue eyes on Leni, and her pulse quickened. Damn him. He was so good at acting, *she* almost believed the story.

He tightened his hand on her leg. "Right, sweetheart?"

"That's right. Talk about falling head over heels." She laughed softly, playing along.

"I'll never forget what you said as I steadied you on your feet."

This was a guy who obviously liked to push limits, and she pushed right back. "I believe it was, *A little handsy for a first meeting, don't you think?*"

A slow grin lifted his cheeks. "See, Dave? You know how I love a challenge." His eyes never left hers. "That was the best moment of my life."

"He's obviously led a very boring life," Leni teased.

"Come on, baby girl. You know that's not true."

She scowled, remembered she shouldn't, and softened her expression. "What did I tell you about calling me baby girl?"

"Sorry. I forgot." He lowered his voice. "Only in the bedroom."

She had a feeling he'd push limits there, too, and tried not to let that idea entice her. "Careful telling all our secrets. You know I'm a private person." She tossed back another shot and set down her glass. "Hit me again, Dave."

"You're driving the girl to drink, Duncan." Dave refilled her glass.

She drank the shot, needing it to quell the interest simmering inside her. "Better than driving me into the arms of another man." She regretted it the second it came out of her mouth.

"*Ouch*. Cheap shot, baby." Raz sat back, taking his hand with him.

"I'm sorry. I shouldn't have said that."

"It's okay. It's not like it isn't true." He drank his shot and glanced at Dave. "You'd better leave us the bottle."

Dave chuckled and set the bottle on the bar. As he went to help another customer, Leni said, "Seriously, Raz. I can be a little unfiltered. That was inappropriate. I know what it feels like to be cheated on, and it's not funny. I'm sorry."

"Well, in this case it is *kind of* funny." He refilled their glasses. "I think I dodged a bullet. I don't even know who the woman that's out there sucking face with Rafe all over the media is, but it's not the Jacinda I knew." He lifted his glass. "Here's to shitty relationships."

"To being *over* shitty relationships." They clinked glasses and drank. "I'm done with men."

"Because of the guy who cheated on you?"

"No, because I've done the whole dating thing, and it's a waste of time. Ninety-nine percent of men don't even make it past coffee."

"Coffee?"

"Yeah. I prescreen my dates, and don't give me shit about it. I get enough of that from my girlfriends."

"Prescreen?" He arched a brow. "What do you mean?"

"If a guy passes the talking stage, which usually lasts a couple of weeks, I'll meet them for coffee. It's quick, noncommittal, and on neutral territory. I don't have time to spend an entire evening with someone I don't connect with."

"That's actually kind of brilliant."

"It's called time management." She picked up the bottle to refill their glasses.

"You're a tiny thing. You sure you can handle more?"

"I might be petite," she said as she poured. "But I've got my big panties on."

"Really?" He laughed.

She realized her mistake, and her eyes widened. "*Shit*. That came out wrong. They're not big. They're barely there, and lacy, and…" She took a deep breath. "Why are we talking about this?"

"I don't know, but now I'm thinking about your barely there panties." He knocked back another shot.

And now I'm thinking about you thinking about them. Ugh! "*Stop* thinking about them. Don't think about them ever again."

He leaned closer, his leg brushing hers. "Sorry, sweetheart, but what's done is done."

She rolled her eyes, futilely trying not to let that thought turn her on.

"Tell me about the idiot who cheated on you." His voice was hushed, intimate.

"Why?"

He covered her hand that was resting on her thigh with his. "Because tonight I'm your boyfriend, and I'm curious."

"*Fake* boyfriend. It happened a long time ago."

He brushed his thumb over her wrist. "In college?"

"High school." She must be high from the tequila, because his touch was enticing, the slow strokes, mesmerizing.

"Hold on." He got a faraway look in his eyes and bit his lower lip. "*Mm-mm.* Okay. I'm ready."

"What was *that?*" she asked with a laugh.

"I had to picture high school Leni, but don't worry. I reverted to high school Duncan when I did it, so it wasn't creepy."

"Ohmygod. What did you picture?"

"A mouthy sprite with freckles across the bridge of her nose, gloss on those pixie lips, and an attitude twice her size, who was just starting to learn how to use her skinny little body to her advantage."

He wasn't wrong with his assessment, but she'd been covering up those freckles for years. "What makes you think I have freckles?"

"Oh, I don't think. I *know.*" He lifted her hand, brushing his fingers over the freckles on her forearm. There weren't many, and they were so fair, she was surprised he'd noticed. Holding her gaze, he swiveled her stool, bringing her knees between his legs, so she was facing him. "And these." He ran his index finger along the ridge of her shoulder bared by the dress. "And then there are these beauties." His fingers trailed down her breastbone light as feathers all the way to the crest of her breast.

She moved his hand, steeling herself against the lingering prickles of heat they'd left in their wake. "What were you doing, studying me all night?"

"Admiring you. You *are* my date."

She reached for the shot glass, but he covered her hand with his, stopping her. Her heart beat faster. She couldn't remember the last time she'd reacted to a man or his simple touch this way. She tried to yank her hand away, but he held tight.

She met his steady gaze. "*Excuse* me."

"Tell me I'm right."

"About *what*?"

"The freckles," he said with an arrogant grin.

How had she forgotten *that* so fast? "I'm not telling you all my secrets."

"You just did." He let go of her hand, their gazes holding for a few torturous, silent beats. "So, we're in high school, and you're dating…what's his name?"

It took her a second to remember they were talking about cheating exes. "Wells."

"Great name. Too bad he's a douche."

"Don't say that. Only *I'm* allowed to call him that."

"Ah, do we have leftover feelings for Wellsy?"

"No." Geez, this guy.

"Okay, sorry. I thought I picked up on something. So you and Wells. Give me a visual. What did he look like back then?"

"Are you always this nosy?"

His brow furrowed. "No, actually. But what the hell. I'm going with it, so paint the picture."

She knew he wouldn't let it go until she did. "He's always been good-looking—you know, tall, dark, and cocky, and he was funny and popular."

"As I'm sure you were, too. Popular, I mean."

She shrugged. "I guess. Anyway, I have very protective older brothers, and I grew up in a close-knit community. All the kids, the families really, were protective of each other, and Wells was kind of a player in high school, but we were friends. Until the night he kissed me, when we turned into more. But because of his reputation, he thought we should keep it between us. We secretly dated, and at his suggestion, I made the mistake of not even telling my best friend, Abby. After a few months of sneaking around, I was so happy with him, I couldn't hold it in any longer. I told her I'd been seeing him, and she burst into tears. It turned out that he'd been secretly seeing *her* for two weeks and had convinced her not to tell anyone, either."

"Oh man. What about you? Did you get your teenage heart crushed, too?"

"*No.* I was pissed. He made my best friend cry. He was lucky he didn't sleep with her, or he wouldn't be alive today and I'd probably still be locked up."

He chuckled. "So I guess he wasn't your first love?"

"Nope. I never had one of those." It wasn't exactly true, but she knew better than to bare her soul to anyone other than her twin, Levi.

"That's surprising," he said thoughtfully.

"Why? Not everyone exists to fall in love. Some of us aren't cut out for it." She wasn't one of those people who didn't believe in love. But she knew how it felt to be hurt by someone she loved, and that was enough to keep that particular emotion off her to-do list.

"I'm not sure I'm buying that. Did he at least apologize?"

"I wasn't about to let him soothe his sorry soul with an apology. I didn't want to hear his rationalizations."

"Damn. You are tough. What happened with you and Abby?"

"We ditched his cheating ass and made a chicks-before-dicks pact."

He laughed. "I love it. Are you still friends?"

"It would take a lot more than a guy to break our bond. She's one of my closest friends. She's getting married in November, and I'm going to be in the wedding."

"That's great. What about Wells? What's he up to now?"

"He's still single and lives in our hometown. He owns a restaurant there and does well for himself."

"I actually meant, is he still that thing I'm not allowed to call him?"

"*Oh.*" She wondered why he was so curious about the one guy she didn't want to talk about. "I don't follow his personal life, but he's a good guy."

"Do you ever see him?"

"Every time I go home. Our families are still close."

His brows knit again. "What's that like for you?"

"I don't know. He's just Wells. Can we *not* talk about him?"

"Interesting."

"You use that word a lot."

"It's not that often I meet a smart woman who can talk baseball and has sworn off an entire gender."

She scoffed. "I'm sure there are plenty of us out there. Now it's your turn. I know what the media says happened between you and Jacinda, but I want to know what really happened."

"There's not much to tell," he said tightly. "We were seeing each other, and I thought things were going okay. We weren't soul mates, but we were having a good enough time, and then she started shooting that movie. The next thing I knew, there were pictures of her and Rafe all over social media."

"That's how you found out? You didn't have a fight or see it coming?"

"Nope."

Leni felt bad for him, but she was also feeling the effects of the tequila—warm, tipsy, and a little looser lipped than usual. "Well, speaking as a girl with three brothers, I can tell you on good authority that guys can be clueless about such matters. So maybe you were on the outs, and you didn't realize it."

He waggled his finger at her. "You might be onto something. Or maybe that's just Hollywood for ya."

"It's not just Hollywood. It's people everywhere. I'm sorry you went through that. That must have hurt."

"It didn't feel great, and I'm not going to lie. My ego took a beating at first, and like you, when she wanted to explain, I didn't want to hear it. But like I said, I dodged a bullet. She obviously wasn't the person she pretended to be with me."

"Why do people do that? Is it so hard to be authentic?"

"I don't know why or how, but I'm so over all the shit that went down and the media being up my ass. I'm done with dating drama. In fact, maybe I'll take a page from your script and give up women altogether."

"That's what I'm talking about. Who needs the headaches?"

"Not me. But let me ask you something."

"As if you haven't been asking me things all evening?" she teased.

"Like I said, you're interesting, and I'm curious. How long has it been since you've gone out on a real date? I mean *beyond* coffee?"

"Several months."

He leaned in so close, she saw starbursts in his irises. "What about sex?" His voice was low and seductive. "Don't you get lonely? It's been several months for me, too, and I'm starting to miss human touch."

"Human touch? What's that?"

They both laughed.

He began rolling up his sleeves, exposing thick, muscular forearms. She felt a tug low in her belly. Why did she have to have a thing for forearms? And why were his so damn perfect?

He cleared his throat, and her eyes snapped up, catching his smirk.

"Lost in thought again?"

She lifted her chin. "I happen to have a very busy brain."

"I bet you do," he said coyly. "Seriously, though, you haven't swiped right or left or whatever it is to scratch that itch?"

"Nope. When I get tempted, I just remember how disappointed I'd be during *and* after."

"Well, there is *that*. But you might be missing out on the one guy who can blow your mind."

"Trust me, I'm *not*."

He grabbed his glass, sliding the other closer to her, and lowered his voice. "Here's to fake dates, where we can just be ourselves because we don't give a damn what the other person thinks."

"Now you're talking my language." They clinked glasses a little too hard, and tequila splashed over the rim of her shot glass. They laughed, and she licked the liquid off her fingers, enjoying every second of his heated stare.

Three

WHEN THEY FINALLY left the bar, they were buzzed and cracking up as they tried to one-up each other with their bad-date stories. "He asked if he could suck your toes while you were having coffee?" Raz barely got the words out past his laughter.

"*Yes*. In the first five minutes after I met him." Leni hadn't had this much fun in so long, she wasn't ready for the night to end, but she had to get out of her heels. "Come here." She tugged him over by his sleeve and leaned on his shoulder as she took off her heels. "That's *so* much better."

He gazed down at her, looking bigger and broader now that she was barefoot. "I didn't think it was possible for you to get cuter than you were when you were all riled up, but all that fierceness in such a petite package? You're a hell of a mighty sprite, Leni Steele."

"Shut up, or I'll get some woman to say she wants to suck your toes."

"You little temptress." He waggled his brows, making them both laugh again.

She shivered against the cold air.

He took off his jacket. "Here, put this on."

"It's okay. I'm fine."

"Leni, put the damn jacket on." He helped her put it on. "I'll call the limo driver."

"*Ugh*. Boring. Wouldn't you rather walk?"

"Yes, but I figured you wouldn't."

"Why? I love walking. I walk all over this city. I could out-walk you."

She started walking, and he grabbed her wrist, pulling her back. He looked at the heels dangling from her fingers. "Are you going to put those back on? Because I'm not letting you walk these sidewalks barefoot."

"Heck no."

"All right, then you leave me no choice." He took off his baseball cap and put it on her. "Well, damn, that's even more adorable."

"I'm a grown woman. I'm not adorable."

He scoffed. "Fucking adorable." He turned around and crouched. "Hop on."

"I'm *not* getting on your back."

He looked over his shoulder, flashing that devastating grin. "If you want us to walk back to Lincoln Center, you'll hop on. Otherwise I'm calling the limo or putting your ass in a cab."

"*Raz.*"

He backed up and tried to grab her legs.

She squealed, swatting at his hands. "Stop. What are you doing?"

"Move all that fabric so I can get to you." He scooted backward, grabbing at her legs.

"Ohmygod." She swatted at his hands again, laughing. "Stop twerking! I'll do it."

That playful glimmer shone in his eyes. "Good girl."

She glowered at him.

"Oh, sorry. Is that only to be said in the bedroom, too? Got it."

She crossed her arms, stifling a laugh. "You have one second to look straight ahead and shut your mouth." He looked straight ahead, laughing, and she tried to gather her skirt in her arms. "There's too much skirt."

"I prefer you without a skirt, too."

She dropped the skirt, loving his playfulness, and grabbed his shoulders. "You're too big."

He eyed her over his shoulder. "I hear that a lot."

She tried to deadpan, and burst out laughing, high from the tequila. "Get lower and shut up." She grabbed his shoulders, bracing herself to jump onto his back. "I can't believe I'm doing this."

"Plenty of women would pay good money to climb all over me."

"Yeah, yeah, yeah." She hoisted herself up, and he reached back, grabbing her ass and lifting her as he rose to his full height. A gasp of surprise escaped, and she hung on for all she was worth. His muscles flexed against her chest and thighs as he carried her down the sidewalk, and even through her gown she could feel his big hands clutching her ass. "You can let go of my butt now."

"I've been thinking about those lace panties all night. If you think I'm going to let go, you're crazy."

"Is that why you insisted I climb onto your back?"

"No. It's just an added bonus."

Oh yeah? Well, two can play that game. She slid her hand into his open shirt.

"Hey now, I'm not here for your cheap thrills," he said

teasingly.

"Fair's fair." She ran her fingers through his chest hair and over the smooth scar that tugged at her thoughts.

"I knew you were still thinking about my body."

"Don't get too excited. It's a side effect of sex deprivation."

"Damn, woman. You won't even let me enjoy a simple ego stroke, will you?"

"Your hands are on my ass and my body is plastered to your back. Take that as a win. You beat out most of my coffee dates."

"I hope you don't expect me to suck on your toes."

"You're ridiculous." Leni laughed, and watched their reflection in the windows as they passed. He was smiling, and hell if she wasn't, too. She didn't recognize herself. Jules was the carefree type to ride on someone's back, not her. Leni had always been firmly grounded and an expert at keeping men at arm's length. But she couldn't try to pick it apart right then, because it would only piss her off, and she was having too much fun. "If you ever stop acting, you can always become a professional piggyback giver."

"Nah. I save the cheap thrills for my fake dates."

"Smart. You don't want to water down your brand."

"Four shots and you're *still* talking shop?"

"I talk shop in my sleep."

"Someone's not keeping your mouth busy enough."

She giggled, feeling high, and rested her cheek on his head. His hair was soft and thick and smelled like him. "Why do you have to smell so good?"

"Why do you have to *feel* so good?"

"It's a curse."

The walk back to Lincoln Center was a mix of quiet contentment and fun banter. When she slid off his back, she stumbled, and he wrapped an arm around her, drawing her against him.

"Is the paparazzi still here?" She looked around for photographers.

"Not that I can see, but that was the most action I've gotten in a long time, and I'm a snuggler, so…" He embraced her.

"I'm *not* a snuggler."

He tightened his grip. "You owe me, Steele. Just go with it."

She laughed softly. She'd met few men who could keep up with her, and as much as she loved it, she reminded herself he was an actor who could probably pull off anything. But that didn't stop her from nestling against his broad chest. She breathed him in, letting her hands roam up his back, feeling his muscles flexing and his heart beating steadily against her cheek. She'd forgotten how good it felt to be held and reveled in the feel of his strong arms around her, his big hands splayed across her back. He tightened his hold on her, one hand pushing beneath her hair, his fingers threading through it. She closed her eyes, desire clawing at her. God, she'd missed the luxurious sensation of wanting a man. A low growl left his lips. She knew she should pull away, but she wanted to climb him like a tree and feel those hot hands all over her body.

He fisted his hand in her hair, tugging her head back, sending shocks of painful pleasure flaming through her. His eyes blazed into hers, fierce and hungry. His jaw clenched, and he gritted out, "Fucking fake date," and he released her, taking a step back and digging his phone out of his pocket.

Leni could do little more than stare at the man who had left her reeling after only a single embrace.

LENI WAS GLAD she'd given Raz back his jacket before getting into the limo, because the ride to her place was riddled with heart-pounding tension, the rising temperature threatening spontaneous combustion. He clutched his jacket in one fist like his life depended on it. His other hand rested on the seat between them, their pinkies grazing with every bump in the road. She was wound too tight, hyperaware of how close they were sitting, the silence pulsing between them, and the rigid set of his jaw. Was he fighting whatever devilish temptation this was, too?

When they finally pulled up in front of her building, she reached for her bag, and he turned to her, eyes dark as midnight, his tight smile making it hard for her to breathe. "I'll walk you up."

She should nip this in the bud, douse the wildfire they'd started. She opened her mouth to tell him she was perfectly capable of walking herself up, but "*Great*," came out. *What the hell?*

He helped her out of the limo and went to talk to the driver. A minute later his hand took up residence on her lower back again, stoking those flames as they headed inside and across the marble lobby to the elevator. "Classy building, close to your office. Very *you*."

"Why do you say that?" They stepped into the elevator, and she pushed the button for her floor. Her heart hammered against her ribs as the doors closed, and he stepped closer.

He ran his index finger along the diamond necklace she wore. "*Classy* needs no explanation." His voice was low and seductive. "You could have picked a building with a view, but you went for location because time is always of the essence for the woman who barely has time for coffee."

She swallowed against her mounting desire, trying to diffuse the ache growing inside her. "So you *were* listening." The elevator doors opened on her floor, and she fished out her keys, focusing on that instead of the heat wafting off him as they walked down the hall.

"I was having a good time. I listened to every snarky word that came out of that sexy mouth of yours."

"What is it with you and my mouth?" *Shit.* She hadn't meant to say that out loud. She unlocked her door and pushed it open, dropping her bag and heels just inside before turning around. He was *right there*, big, broad, and so alluring, her loneliest parts pleaded for his touch.

"Don't play me, Steele." He leaned in so close, his breath warmed her lips. "You know *exactly* how tempting your mouth is."

She didn't know, but he made her want to believe him. He made her want to *use* it. "My mouth has been called a lot of things but never tempting."

His eyes held her captive as he cupped her cheek and brushed his thumb over her lower lip. "Then you've been dating the wrong guys, because I've spent the entire evening fantasizing about all the dirty things I want to do to your mouth *after* I use mine to make you forget those other assholes."

Her entire body clenched in anticipation. "That's awfully big talk for a fake date."

He slid his hand to the nape of her neck, dipping his face so close, she thought he was going to kiss her, and she desperately wanted him to.

"One night with me, and you won't be faking a damn thing."

His voice was low and gruff, and her restraint snapped. "*One* night. Don't make me regret this."

She grabbed him by the collar, tugging him through the door as his lips came down over hers, rough and demanding. Their kisses were fierce and urgent, both of them groping greedily. He unzipped her dress and shoved it to the floor, leaving her in only her panties. She had a fleeting thought about the fact that he was Shea's client, but she was too far gone, too in need of everything he was willing to give to care. She stepped out of her dress and fumbled with the buttons on his shirt. He grabbed her by the wrists, backing her up against the wall, and pinned her hands above her head, holding them there with one of his hands. This was what she needed, what she craved. One night with a man who knew what he was doing to satiate that dull ache she tried so hard to deny.

His eyes bored into her as his free hand skimmed down her chest, fondling her breast. He raked his gaze down the length of her. "You're so fucking beautiful."

As much as she craved his taking what he wanted, she felt unexpectedly vulnerable, and that was something she wasn't used to. Trying to reclaim the upper hand, she demanded, "Kiss me."

A wicked glimmer shone in his eyes. "I'll kiss you when I'm damn good and ready."

His hungry eyes followed his hand as he took her nipple between his finger and thumb, squeezing hard enough for her to feel it between her legs. She bowed off the wall with a moan. He growled and dipped his head to slick his tongue over her taut nipple. She inhaled sharply, aching for more. He dragged his fingers along the waist of her panties, and she rocked her hips, craning to capture his lips, but he was just out of reach. "I said when I'm ready," he gritted out, and cupped her through her panties, rubbing his fingers and palm in slow circles as he brushed his lips over hers. "I fucking love lace."

"That makes two of us."

He rubbed her faster through her panties, and she moaned.

"So wet for me." He reclaimed her mouth, kissing her hard and deep, and pushed his hand into her panties, both of them moaning as his thick fingers slid through her wetness. "Fuck." He tore his mouth away, and a whimper escaped her lungs as he dragged his tongue around the shell of her ear, his fingers moving forward and back through her arousal, without entering her, driving her out of her freaking mind. "I'm going to ruin you for all other men," he growled huskily into her ear.

As thrilling as his words were, she wouldn't give him that power. "One night. That's *all* this is," she panted out.

"That's all I need." He bit her earlobe and pushed his fingers inside her. She cried out at the agonizing pleasure searing through her. "That's what I like to hear." He fucked her with his fingers, just rough enough to let her know he was in control, stroking over that hidden spot with perfection. "But next time say my name." Before she could respond, his thumb pressed down on her clit, and she shot up on her toes, biting back a cry of pleasure, unwilling to give him the satisfaction. "Is that how you want to play this, sweetheart?"

He withdrew his fingers, and she gasped. She narrowed her eyes. "If you're going to stop there, you might as well leave."

"Who said anything about stopping? I'm just not playing by your rules." His eyes remained trained on hers as he teased her clit. He quickened his efforts, and she struggled to maintain control. "You're going to come on my hand, and you're going to say my name." He pushed his fingers inside her again, using his thumb on those oversensitive nerves. Lust coiled low in her belly, tight as a viper ready to strike, stealing her ability to speak. "Then you're going to come on my mouth, and you're going to say my name again." His dirty promises heightened her desire. "Then you're going to wrap those pretty little lips around my cock, and if you're as good as I think you're going to be, you'll get to hear me say *your* name." He pressed harder with his thumb, pumping his fingers faster. She was trembling, her every muscle taut, need pulsing through her veins. She closed her eyes, gritting her teeth.

"Come on, sweetheart," he urged. "Say Duncan."

She opened her eyes at the unfamiliar name and saw he wanted—*needed?*—to hear it as much as she needed what he was giving her. He sealed his mouth over her neck, biting down, and "*Duncan*—" shot from her lungs, loud and untethered as pleasure engulfed her. He released her hands and crushed his mouth to hers. She hung on to his strong frame to combat her weak knees as he fucked her mouth with his tongue to the same wild pace as he was fucking her body with his fingers. She was lost in wave after unstoppable wave of pleasure, which went on and on like a surging sea. Just as she started coming down from the peak, he quickened his efforts again, sending her spiraling into the torrent of ecstasy.

When she finally collapsed against him, breathless and shaking, he lifted her into his arms, heading for the bedroom. Through the haze of lust, she said, "You don't have to carry—"

He silenced her with a soul-searing kiss and laid her on the bed. She stayed there, drunk on him as he took off his shoes, socks, and shirt. *Yum!* He came down over her, and she ran her hands up his arms and along his chest, enjoying the feel of his hard muscles and the nearly silent *hiss* he made as her fingers brushed his nipples. When she touched the scar on his chest, he pulled back and said, "My turn."

He began kissing his way down her body, murmuring against her skin, "So sexy…so soft and feminine…fucking perfect."

Every touch of his lips caused a sharp inhalation. She closed her eyes, reveling in the feel of his hands groping and caressing, his teeth grazing, tongue licking as he peeled off her panties. How many times had she wished for a man who could satisfy her like this?

He slicked his tongue along her center, sending electricity arcing through her. She fisted her hands in her blanket, and he pressed a kiss to the apex of her sex. "Bold and beautiful on the outside, sweet and tangy on the inside." His tongue slid over her clit as his thumb teased between her legs in a mesmerizing pattern. "I can't wait to fuck this sweet pussy."

Leni was not easily embarrassed, and this was the type of dirty talk she craved, but she felt her cheeks flame, and that made her feel vulnerable again. "Then do it," she challenged.

"There's no way I'm rushing this night away, so lie back and enjoy the ride, princess."

"Don't call me—"

Her words were lost to the feel of his glorious mouth between her legs, licking, sucking, *devouring*, while one hand wreaked havoc with her clit and the other gripped her ass *hard*, sending sparks skittering through her. She writhed and moaned, fisting her hands in his hair, rocking against his mouth as he feasted on her with reckless abandon. He reached up with one hand, taking her nipple between his finger and thumb, and squeezed, sending a flurry of sensations raining down on her. She dug her heels into the blanket, prickling heat consuming her.

She *had* to see him devouring her, to remember every second of this wicked night so she could draw upon it during the long, lonely months ahead. She grabbed a pillow and shoved it under her head. Their eyes connected with the heat of a fire and an underlying hum of something dark and dangerous.

He cocked a brow. "Enjoying the show?"

"I will be when you stop talking and get busy again."

He grinned and nipped at her inner thigh with his teeth. God, that felt good. He lowered his mouth to her clit, taking it between his teeth as his fingers entered her, stroking quick, with deadly precision. She was moaning, begging, enraptured by his touch, his tongue, his teeth. *"Duncan…Oh God."* He did something with his fingers and mouth, catapulting her into ecstasy.

RAZ SAVORED EVERY pulse of her climax, the sound of his name streaming from her lips, and the tug of her fists in his hair. When she sank into the mattress, boneless and breathless, he kissed his way up her body, slowing to enjoy the curve of her hips, the swell of her breasts, and her sweet sounds of satisfaction ringing in his ears. He gazed down at her, glossy auburn hair strewn across the pillow, lips parted, and those evergreen eyes drenched with desire. He felt a tug deep in his chest. He was dying to be buried deep inside her. To feel this strong, capable, sexy woman wrapped around him. If this wasn't a one-night thing, he'd forgo taking advantage of that luscious mouth and fuck them both senseless. But he wasn't making the mistake of getting in deep with another woman. Not when the media got off on making his life hell. *No.* Tonight was about satiating a need, and nothing else.

"You're insanely good at that," she said huskily.

"We're not nearly done, princess."

Her eyes narrowed. "I told you not to call me that."

That's it, sweetheart, let your claws out. "What did I tell you about not playing by your rules?"

She reached for the button on his pants. "That all you got?"

"Don't worry, there's plenty more where that came from." He pushed off the bed. "But first I want to fuck that pretty mouth of yours."

Her eyes remained trained on him as he stripped off his slacks and boxer briefs. Appreciation shimmered in her eyes as they trailed down his body to his erection, and she licked her lips.

"I'm glad to see the rumors are true."

He grinned and fisted his cock, giving it a few tight strokes. "Get your sexy little ass over here." She smirked as she got up on all fours, crawling like a cat on the prowl to the edge of the bed. "Christ, you're sexy." He gave his cock another tug, and she started to get off the bed. "No. Stay right there, but get up on your knees."

She rose onto her knees. "You do like control."

"You have no idea." He took her in an excruciatingly deep kiss, using his hand between her legs again, earning the sexiest moan. When he tore his mouth away, they were both breathing hard. "Now, hands and knees, sweetheart."

She flipped her hair over one shoulder, looking sexy as sin, and did as he asked.

"Good girl."

"You have no idea," she parroted with enough snark to take down an army. "*Don't* be gentle."

His cock jerked at her demand. "I wasn't planning on it. I want you needy as fuck by the time I get inside you." He guided his thick length into her mouth, and holy fuck, she took him deep. He pumped his hips slowly at first, letting her get used to his size as he gathered her hair in his fist. Her eyes held as much challenge as desire, spurring him on. He thrust faster, and she sucked harder, rocking with him. When she drew back and slicked her tongue over the head, her eyes remained trained on him, and he just about lost it. She took him deep again and reached up with one hand to cup his balls. *"Fuuck."*

She moaned, and the vibration nearly pulled him over the edge. But her hot, willing mouth felt too good. He wasn't ready for it to end. "I need my hands on you. Sit on the edge of the bed."

She was quick to comply, eager for more, and reached for him as he drove into her mouth again. He used one hand on her breast, the other between her legs, teasing and taunting, taking her right up to the edge with him. Her jaw went slack, and she stopped sucking.

"Suck my cock, you sexy thing, or I won't let you finish."

Her eyes blazed into his, and she drew back. "*Listen*, bossy. It's been a really long time since I've felt this good. Take it as a compliment and just keep doing what you're doing, and I'll *try* to return the favor."

He threaded his fingers into her hair, tugging her head back, and lowered his smiling lips a whisper away from hers. "Glad we're on the same page."

"Stop talking and kiss me."

He kissed her slow and deep, torturing them both. "Your mouth is addicting."

"Then make better use of it," she challenged, wrapping her hand around his dick.

Damn, she was his every fantasy come true. She stroked and sucked, tight and swift, as he worked her clit. "That's it...*Fuck yeah.*" He felt her muscles tense and knew she was close. "Don't stop," he warned. "Keep sucking as you come. I want to feel your pleasure everywhere."

She squeezed her thighs together.

"Open your legs. I want to see it, too," he growled. She opened her legs, showing him her glistening sex. "That's it. So damn hot." He quickened his efforts between her legs, and she grabbed his ass with both hands, moving his hips faster, taking him impossibly deeper, sending them both over the edge. Her eyes slammed shut, sex clenching, fingernails digging into his ass cheeks as his release spilled down her throat. "Fuck, Leni. *Fuuck.*"

When the last of it left his body, he pulled out of her mouth, shuddering as the sensitive head brushed her lips. "Jesus." He rubbed her jaw, kissing her cheek, neck, and shoulder. "So damn good."

"You weren't bad, either." She flopped onto her back with a sigh and put her hand over her heart, looking like a sinful angel with her tousled hair, flushed cheeks, and sweet, sated, half-mast eyes.

He lay beside her. "This is a good look for you."

"Naked?"

"Sexually satisfied."

"Mm." She closed her eyes.

His gaze skirted around the tidy bedroom, getting a sense of her. The off-white furniture was elegant and feminine, like her. A black silk robe lay over the back of an upholstered chair by the closet. Ah yes, black for the secret vixen she was. Her hand slid from her chest to the mattress between them, and he couldn't resist covering it with his. Her eyes opened, the air between them humming with a deeper connection. Her brows knitted, as if she felt the shift, too, and she pushed to her feet. He snagged her hand, sitting up. "Where do you think you're going? We're not done yet."

"I'll decide when I'm done." There was the snark that he found so damn appealing. "I need a drink, and maybe some ice cream. If you're lucky, I might share it with you."

Leni Steele à la mode sounded perfect to him.

He pulled on his boxer briefs as she put on the short silk robe, tying it around her waist. "Aren't you a sexy thing? I like this." He touched the end of the tie.

"Play your cards right, and maybe I'll let you use it." She turned on her heels and strutted out of the bedroom as if she hadn't left him with that erection-inducing thought.

Four

RAZ FOLLOWED HER out of the bedroom, catching a glimpse of the living room. Like the bedroom, it was neat and tidy. The pale gray corner couch with peach, gray, and black-and-white accent pillows, off-white tufted chair and footstool, and marble coffee table were classy and feminine. A cozy-looking blanket was folded over one end of the couch, and he wondered if that was where she cuddled up to watch television or read. There were a few elegantly framed pictures of what he guessed were friends and family on end tables and on a glass bookshelf, and a large painting of a beach hung over the couch. He saw another room with a desk in it. On the desk was a picture of several people. Her apartment felt warm and homey, unlike his massive house in LA.

"That's a nice painting over the couch. I didn't peg you as a beach girl," he said as they headed into the kitchen, which was as clean as the living room. Although the front of the refrigerator was littered with pictures held in place by magnets with sarcastic sayings on them, like *My dentist said I need a crown. I was like, I know, right?* and *I'm not bossy. I just know what everyone else should be doing.* He was curious about who the people in the picture were, especially the tatted guy with his arm around Leni.

"I grew up at the beach. That's Silver Island, where I'm from. My sister Jules's fiancé, Grant Silver, painted it."

"Silver Island, really? My buddy Beau's brother Zev is a treasure hunter, and he recently unearthed a massive pirate ship with tons of artifacts off the shores of Silver Island."

"Zev Braden? He was all over the news there. My friend Randi Remington dives with him. You probably know their sister is Jillian, the fashion designer whose gown I wore tonight."

"Small world. I know Jilly. We all grew up together. Beau's been my best friend for years."

"Really? My sister Jules loves that movie you were in, *Anything for Love*, which I think is about Beau and his wife, right?"

"Yeah, Charlotte, Beau's wife, wrote the story the year they met." He didn't want to talk about Beau, because Beau had dated his sister, Tory, whom they'd lost years ago. That was not a topic up for discussion, especially with a one-night stand, no matter how much they were connecting. He leaned out of the entry to the kitchen and glanced at the painting again. "Your friend Grant is very talented. He's a Silver from Silver Island? Sounds like your sister snagged a wealthy one." He leaned against the counter, watching her. She was an intoxicating sight, padding around in that skimpy robe.

"You wouldn't know it if you met him, and Jules doesn't care about money. She owns a gift shop and does well on her own. You know how they say some people are fated to be together? That's Jules and Grant. An unlikely but perfect couple. They're getting married in December." She withdrew a glass from a cabinet and began filling it with water from the dispenser on the front of the refrigerator.

"Why unlikely?"

"Because Jules is as sweet as sugar and as peppy as a cheerleader, and Grant is her total opposite. He was in the Special Forces, and he's tough as nails. He calls her Pixie, which is perfect for her because she flits about spreading happiness and helping others."

"She sounds great."

"She is, although her positivity can be a bit overwhelming if you're in a bad mood. And she sings *all* the time, but she never gets the lyrics right. It's hilarious." She was quiet for a moment as she filled her glass. "Do you want some water?"

"Sure."

She eyed the glass, and a small smile appeared before she handed it to him.

"Thanks." As she filled another glass, he said, "You considered telling me to get my own glass, didn't you?"

"Only for a second." She took a drink and set her glass on the counter. "But you're technically a guest. My mother taught me to be gracious to guests, and I'm feeling pretty gracious tonight." She grabbed a spoon from a drawer and got a pint of strawberry ice cream out of the freezer.

A woman who was snarky, owned her sexuality, and was honest despite how the truth made her look? That was an alluring and rare combination. "Your mother would be very proud of you."

Leni opened the container and ate a spoonful of ice cream. "Mm. Now, that hits the spot."

"I seem to remember hitting several *spots* for you."

She pointed the spoon at him. "You certainly did. I think you earned some ice cream." She dug out another spoonful and held it out toward him.

He closed the distance between them and ate it without taking the spoon. "That's tasty, but not nearly as tasty as you are." He put a hand on her hip and leaned in to kiss her.

"Good to know," she said adorably.

He went to check out the pictures on the fridge. It was nice seeing her smiling, laughing, and making silly faces. But there was one picture that caught his eye. She was sitting on the sand by a bonfire with a young honey-haired girl on her lap, gazing out at the ocean with a thoughtful expression. "Your place is so organized, but it looks like your camera exploded over here."

"Can't a girl love her family and friends?" She ate another spoonful and went to stand beside him. "What's on your fridge?"

"Nothing." Family was everything to him, and he'd learned over the years that how a person spoke about their family told him more than pointed questions ever could. But he'd never decorated his place in LA with family photos, because even after all these years, it didn't feel like home. "So, who's who?"

She filled the spoon with ice cream and fed him another bite. "These are mostly pictures of my siblings." She stuck the spoon in the container and pointed to a picture of two athletic-looking men, one with dark hair and a friendly smile, the other with a serious face and massive muscles, and a beautiful, tall, thin blonde with a smile similar to Leni's. "This is Jock."

"Jock or Jack?"

"His real name is Jack, but he goes by Jock because an old friend of his called him that. He's an amazing thriller writer. He recently got married and moved back to the island with his wife, Daphne, and her daughter, Hadley, who just turned four. Jock adopted Hadley after they were married. She's so stinking cute." She pointed to a pretty, thick-waisted blonde holding a little girl with wispy blond hair. "That's them."

"Nice family."

"They are." She pointed to the first picture again. "And this stocky creature is Jock's twin, Archer, who is engaged to my friend Indi. Archer is an award-winning vintner and runs our family winery. He and Jock are the oldest, and they're nothing alike."

"How do they differ?"

"Jock is thoughtful and careful with his words, which I guess comes from being a writer, and Archer is even more unfiltered than me. He's tough, but he has a big heart. When I came here for college, Archer came out and showed me all around the city to make sure I knew how to use the subway and how to hail a cab and get to different places."

"That makes sense. You said your brothers are protective of you."

"Archer takes it to the extreme. I was glad he came out. I loved being in the city, but it was a little intimidating at first. Their taste in women is also different. Daphne is super sweet, and Indi, Archer's fiancée, is as much of a smart-ass as I am."

"Poor guy," he teased. "Is that Indi in the picture with Jock and Archer?"

"No, that's my older sister, Sutton."

"Another snarky Steele? She looks familiar."

"She's sweeter than I am, but she's got her own edge to her. She lives in Upstate New York and is faking her way through a job as a reporter on the *World Discovery Hour* show."

"That's where I recognize her from. I've seen a few episodes. She didn't look like she was faking her way through it."

"She's learning as she goes. But her boss is trying to get her fired, the jerk."

"You sound like you'd like to give him hell."

"I do, but Sutton won't let me. Anyway, moving on." She pointed to the picture of herself and the tattooed guy. "And this handsome devil is my twin, Levi."

"You're a twin, too? Two sets in one family? Your parents must have had their hands full. Is he a smart-ass, too?"

"He can be, but I'm better at it. Levi had to grow up really fast. He became a father at twenty." She pointed to the picture of herself and the little girl by the bonfire. "This is his daughter, my adorable niece, Joey. He's an amazing father, and she's a great kid. She's totally into skateboarding right now."

"What about Joey's mother? Is she in the picture?"

"She's a wicked bitch."

"Don't cushion the blow or anything," he teased.

"If you knew the story, you'd say the same thing. Levi was raising Joey alone, but now he's engaged to—pay attention—Joey's mother's younger sister, Tara, and they've just moved back to the island."

"Whoa. That sounds complicated." He scooped some ice cream onto the spoon and fed it to her, enjoying the trip down Steele Family Lane.

"I know, but unlike her sister, Tara has always been in his and Joey's life. She's loved them both forever. I'm really happy for all three of them." She pointed to another picture of a young, pretty blonde holding hands with Levi. "That's Tara." She pointed to another picture, of an attractive young woman with golden-brown hair sprouting from a ponytail on top of her head and a handsome guy with longish brown hair and a beard standing in front of a sign that read SILVER LININGS FOUNDATION, RESOURCES FOR AMPUTEES. "And this is Jules and Grant the day he started his foundation."

"They look really happy."

"They are. And these are my parents," she said proudly, pointing to a picture of a big, beautiful woman with long auburn hair, bangs, and a bright smile, in the arms of a thick-chested, salt-and-pepper-haired man with a neatly trimmed beard. "They're sickeningly in love. We're always catching them making out."

He laughed. "That's great."

"Depends on what stage of making out they're in."

"Oh, yeah. I could see that being uncomfortable. You look like your mom."

"Thanks. I think she's beautiful."

"Like I said, you look like her." He cleared his throat. "It sounds like you're close to your family."

"We're pretty close." Her brows knitted, and she got a faraway look in her eyes for a second. "Anyway, this is my grandmother, and these are my besties…"

She pointed out her friends between bites of ice cream, revealing a snippet of information about each of them as enthusiastically as she had about her family. Raz wanted to know more about her relationship with her parents and siblings, why she'd left the island, and what was behind that faraway look in her eyes he'd caught a glimpse of. But those were things you asked a person you were actually dating.

He needed to redirect his thoughts, and with the gorgeous woman in front of him digging out another spoonful of ice cream as she finished showing off her friends, it wasn't difficult. He set the pint of ice cream on the counter as she ate the spoonful, then took the spoon and placed it beside the carton.

Her brow furrowed. "You don't want any more?"

"I want a hell of a lot more." He dipped his finger into the ice cream container and painted the cold sweet treat over her lips. He backed her up against the counter, boxing her in with one hand on either side, and slid his tongue along her lower lip. "Now, that's sweet." He held her gaze as he untied her robe, ran his hand down her side, and palmed her ass. "I want to see this fine ass as I take you from behind." He covered her mouth with his, kissing her deeply and sensually, until she moaned and rubbed her body against him. "Those sexy noises make me crazy. This has to go." He slid her robe off her shoulders, and it puddled at her feet.

He nipped at her lower lip, dipping his finger into the container again, and dragged his finger down the center of her chest, painted both nipples, then went back for more. This time he wet several fingers with the sweet treat, using it to blaze a path down her stomach and across her ribs, earning a ragged gasp. He went back a third time and used those sticky fingers to paint her inner thighs and pussy. Her eyes turned dark and lustful. He brought the fingers he'd used to her lips. "Open that sexy mouth." She did, and he put two fingers in. "Suck them like they're my cock." She closed her lips around them and sucked. "God, Leni. I could come just watching you."

She stroked him through his boxer briefs. He growled and withdrew his fingers from her mouth. "Lick the rest while I lick you." He held his fingers in front of her mouth, and felt every slick of her tongue as if it were on his cock as he tasted and sucked his way down her body. When he sucked her nipple to the roof of his mouth, she cried out and clawed at his shoulders. "That's it, baby. Dig those nails in." He gave her other breast the same attention and used his teeth on her nipple.

"Oh *God.*"

"Like that, sweetheart?" He did it again.

She went up on her toes. "Yes—"

He continued taunting and teasing, slowly tasting his way

down her body, devouring all the ice cream with nips, sucks, and bites. Her every sinful sound got him harder, until his dick throbbed. He sank to his knees and pushed her legs apart. She watched him suck her inner thighs clean, whimpering and moaning. He sucked hard enough to leave a mark, her pleasure-filled sounds spurring him on. They might have only one night, but he wasn't about to let her forget who made her feel so good.

He guided her hand between her legs, and she narrowed her eyes.

"I'm sure you can make yourself come in seconds, but I can make you come *harder*, and together we're going to blow your mind." He licked her fingers, which were on her clit, applying pressure. She gasped and began stroking herself while he licked her fingers again. When he moved lower, devouring her pussy and fucking her with his tongue, she grabbed his hair with her other hand, sending a sting of pleasure and pain straight to his cock.

He grabbed her ass with both hands. "I need more of you. Straddle my face and don't stop touching yourself." He took her hand as he lay on the floor, bringing her sweet, hot center down over his mouth, and feasted on her. He gripped her hips, feeling her tremble, her thighs tightening around his head.

"Ohgod...*Duncan...Oh...*"

He fucked her with his tongue and reached around her back, grabbing her hair, and tugging it, catapulting her into orgasm. "*Duncan—*" flew from her lips as she rode his mouth, her pussy throbbing, cries of pleasure echoing off the walls. Her hand stilled as she came down from the peak, and he pushed it out of the way, taking over and sending her reeling again.

Her body quaked and quivered, and he stayed with her, tasting every last pulse of her pleasure. She went up on her knees, but she was trembling so hard, he knew she couldn't climb off, so he helped her. He pushed to his feet and lifted her into his arms. "I want your mouth."

She lowered her mouth to his in an excruciatingly sensual kiss as he carried her to the bedroom. She didn't flinch at the taste of herself, as he'd known she wouldn't. This incredible woman had a dark side, which he wanted to explore, and he knew extinguishing that desire was going to be hell.

He lowered her to the bed and pushed off his boxer briefs, gazing into her trusting eyes as he came down over her, and realized he'd made a big fucking mistake. "*Shit*. Leni, I wasn't prepared for this. I don't have protection."

Her brows knitted. "*Oh*. God. How did *I* forget that? You don't have a condom?"

"No. I wasn't planning on sleeping with my fake date."

Her eyes lit up. "Wait. I have some!" She wiggled out from under him and ran into her closet. She came out with a beach bag and dumped it on the floor, dropping to her knees and digging through towels, sunscreen, bathing suits, and a whole bunch of other shit.

"I guess I know what you do at the beach."

"I do *not*. My grandmother runs the Bra Brigade, and the last time we sunbathed with them, they gave out strips of condoms to all the girls."

"Bra Brigade?"

"Aha!" She held up a strip of condoms and ran to the bed, landing on her knees, grinning like she'd won the lottery.

He laughed and tackled her to her back. "First of all. I'm going to need to know more about this condom-distributing Bra Brigade, and second of all, that was the cutest thing I've ever seen."

"Later," she said with a giggle. "I seem to remember you promising to ruin me for all other men."

"I'll ruin you, all right, you greedy little thing." He kissed her then, long and slow, but slow lasted only a minute. They both went a little wild, and he reluctantly tore his mouth away, grabbing the strip of condoms. "Only four? I need to have a talk with Grandma."

Her smile grew as he sheathed his length. "Just promise me one thing," he said as he aligned their bodies.

"Do fake dates get real promises?" she asked.

"Tonight they do. The media is already all over me. So, weeks from now, when you're still glowing, and people ask who fucked you so thoroughly that you can't get him out of your head, for Pete's sake, don't say my name. I can just see the headlines. *Actor goes from heartbreak to breaking mattresses.*"

She laughed. "I should have brought duct tape to bed. You talk way too much." She pulled his mouth to her soft, warm lips.

He tried to take it slow, but she tasted too sweet and felt too good with all her soft curves pressed against him. He sank into her, savoring every inch as their bodies became one. She felt like heaven, tight and hot, and tasted like happiness and sin. She pressed on his lower back, urging him deeper. He lifted her knees, driving in until electricity seared through him.

They both gasped and stilled. Their eyes connected. Overwhelming need and want stared back at him. *Do you feel that?* was on the tip of his tongue, but he locked it down, shoring up his walls.

He lowered his mouth to hers, and she returned his efforts hungrily, kissing him harder as he rocked and thrust with an animalistic fervor unlike anything he'd ever felt before. She was right there with him, holding him tight, wrapping her legs around him, taking and giving as desperately as he was. *Fuuck.* She was too good. Too addicting. He tore his mouth away, gritting out, "Hands and knees," and didn't wait for her to comply. He flipped her over and lifted her hips, driving into her again, trying to fuck those unwanted emotions away.

She clutched the blanket and looked over her shoulder at him, her hair tumbling over one side of her face as she demanded, "*Harder.*"

This woman was going to do him in. He pounded into her, her tight pussy and sensual sounds blurring his thoughts. He reached around her waist, using his fingers where she needed them most. "*Yes,* don't stop," she pleaded. "So good. Harder…faster…*Ohmygodohmygod. Ohhh*—" Her pussy clenched tight as a vise as she surrendered to her climax. He continued pounding into her, gritting his teeth against the urge to come, trying to escape how incredibly perfect she felt. When she sank to her elbows, panting for air, he had a dire need, an urgency, to see her beautiful face. To be on top of her and kiss her luscious mouth.

He pulled out and not so gently rolled her onto her back. As he came down over her, her sweet smile glimmered in her eyes, tugging at someplace dark and deep inside him. "Still with me, sweetheart?"

"I'm not ruined yet," she whispered, wrapping her arms around his neck and craning up to kiss him. "Again."

He didn't know if she meant the kiss or an orgasm, so he gave her both. Their mouths fused together as their bodies became one, and they moved in perfect sync, to a fast and fierce rhythm. He found himself memorizing the feel of her body, her breasts against his chest, the tightness of her pussy around his cock, the taste of her mouth, the scent of her arousal. They grew slick as they groped and kissed, bit and clawed. She was as eager as he was, grabbing every inch within reach and begging for more, her pleas driving him wilder. He wrapped her legs around his waist, driving in deeper, pounding faster. He broke their kiss to look at her, enraptured by him. Her eyes were closed tight, brows knitted, as she whispered, *"Yes, yes, yes."* He was captivated by the sight of her so lost in him—in *them.*

He kissed her jaw. "That's it, sweetheart, come for me."

She opened her eyes, and the emotions swimming in them stole his breath.

"Come with me," she pleaded, sweet, sensual, and a little desperate, obliterating his control. He crushed his mouth to hers, thrusting and gyrating, until they spiraled over the edge together, their mingled cries filling the air as the world spun away, and pleasure consumed him.

When she went boneless beneath him, he gathered her in his arms.

"Well," she panted out. "That was pretty mediocre."

He laughed against her neck. "Where have you been all my life?" The question came out of nowhere, shocking him, and he scrambled for something to say. Anything to take it back, but before he could form a sentence, she spoke.

"I get that a lot," she said teasingly.

Jealousy clawed at him, an emotion he wasn't familiar with or comfortable with. He hadn't ever been jealous over Jacinda. Pissed when she'd cheated, yes, but not jealous. But then he remembered what little Miss Mouthy had said about her coffee dates. "From all the guys who didn't make it past coffee?"

"No, from my other boyfriends. You know, the battery-operated ones."

He chuckled, and that uneasy feeling dissipated, but not quite as quickly as it had come. "I hate to tell you this, sweetheart, but we're going to be at this all night, and we might have to have a threesome with one of those boyfriends."

"I would be disappointed if we didn't."

LENI WAS USUALLY up before the sun, but this morning she blinked against the light streaming through her curtains and stretched like a lazy cat, wincing at the soreness of her muscles. It was exquisite pain, worth every twinge and pang. Everything hurt. Her arms, hands, and back ached from holding Raz so tight. Her legs, thighs, and even her stomach and butt cheeks were sore. He'd held her ass so tight, she probably had handprints on it. But the warm body that had been wrapped around her as they'd fallen asleep was gone. She listened for the shower and was met with silence. Pushing up on her elbow, she scanned the floor. His clothes were gone, and her gown was on a hanger on the back of the closet door.

Duncan Raz is a sexual god and a gentleman?

That couldn't be the same man who fought Shea on every little thing. She should have tried to get him to comply with Shea last night, but that would have required thinking about work, and she'd had too good a time joking around and screwing him senseless to think about anything else.

She threw her blankets off and sat up, surprised to see hickeys on her thighs. Memories of his talented mouth bringing her all sorts of pleasure floated in, warming her all over as she climbed out of bed and put on her robe. She scanned the room for the silk tie he'd used to bind her wrists and found it on the floor between the bed and the nightstand. Snagging it, she put it on and headed into the kitchen to see if he was there. She didn't usually bring men home, but then again, Duncan Raz wasn't just any man. The A-lister showed her exactly how well he could act, because she'd never felt so wanted. Bravo, Raz. *Bravo.*

He wasn't in the kitchen. She tried to ignore the disappointment tiptoeing in.

He'd done her a favor. She'd have kicked him out anyway, which would have been awkward. She was sure she'd find the ice cream melted all over the counter, but it wasn't there, and neither was the spoon. She opened the trash and found the carton of ice cream. She opened the dishwasher, but it was empty. He must have washed the spoon and put it away.

Leni had always been a good sleeper, but to sleep through a man moving around her apartment? Dressing and doing dishes? He must have really worn her out. There was a note tucked beneath a magnet on the fridge. As she reached for it, she remembered their conversation about her family and felt a pang of regret. It was no secret that Raz had lost his younger sister, Tory, in a car accident when she was eighteen. How could she have been so thoughtless?

Reality came rushing in. She clearly hadn't used her head last night in many areas. She had to tell Shea she'd slept with her client, and her cousin would be well within her rights to fire her. But gushing about her family to a man who had lost his only sibling felt worse than losing the job she loved.

She read the note. *SA, I'll never look at strawberry ice cream the same again. Duncan.*

SA? What the hell is that? And why did he sign it Duncan

instead of Raz? His voice whispered through her mind. *Come on, sweetheart. Say Duncan.* Her stupid body heated again. She must be delirious, because Leni Steele did not get warm and fuzzy over any man. She needed sleep. Stalking back to her bedroom, she flopped onto the bed and pulled the sheets up, but they smelled like him. She smelled like him.

Oh God, what have I done?

She bolted out of bed and stripped off the linens, grabbed her panties from last night out of her laundry basket—*thank you, Raz*—and headed directly to the laundry room. She tossed her robe in, too. Needing to get thoughts of sex with Raz off her mind *and* her body, she showered, scrubbing so hard she felt every tender spot he'd left behind.

As she dried off, she noticed more colorful remnants of their night of debauchery on her neck and breasts. She turned around and glanced at her butt in the mirror. Sure enough, there were finger-shaped bruises and a hickey on one of her ass cheeks. Why did that particular man have to bring her darkest fantasies to life? Sure, he was fun, and they'd had quite a bit of tequila, but this was *not* who she was. She didn't sleep with clients of the firm.

She saw the lie in her eyes.

She might not sleep with clients, but how she acted last night was *exactly* who she'd always been. She just hadn't let anyone see that side of her since she'd first realized she liked things rougher and dirtier than her friends did. She was usually careful about who she shared her body with, and she was *always* the one in control. She never went down on guys, much less swallowed. And she didn't think she could have stopped herself last night if she'd wanted to. The need to possess him had been too big, too primal to turn off.

Angry with herself, she dressed and went to get her phone out of her bag and check social media. Hopefully there were enough photos from the event to get the media off Raz's back. At least then she'd be armed with something positive when she confessed her sluttery to Shea, and maybe she wouldn't fire her.

She grabbed her phone and saw two missed calls from Shea, a text from Indi, and several missed group texts from her family. Jules was the queen of group texts and a social media hound. Taking that as a good sign, Leni started with Indi's text.

Indi: *You and Raz? How am I the last to know?! I thought you swore off actors after Kip.*

The name sent a ripple of regret through Leni, and she steeled herself against it. Thankfully, the only one who knew how she really felt about Kip Jones was Levi. To Indi, Kip was just a guy Leni dated for a while before he made it big as an actor.

Leni: *It was one date. There's nothing to tell. I'm jumping over to the group text.* Jules had added Indi to the family group texts when Indi and Archer had gotten engaged.

She opened her family's text thread, and a bunch of messages popped up. She started at the top, with a screenshot of *E! News*'s social media page, which showed a picture of her and Raz on the red carpet, along with the caption RAZ STEPS OUT WITH A DAZZLING NEW LADY.

Jules: *Looks like my big sis has a hot new boyfriend! Yay! Leni + Raz.* She added three heart emojis.

Levi: *Leni doesn't do boyfriends.*

Sutton: *Levi, how do you know about her sex life?*

Levi: *I meant she doesn't long-term date!*

Sutton: *I thought Raz was an arrogant ass?!* A thinking emoji popped up.

Daphne: *Go Leni! You look amazing. Jock says he's happy for you and he wants to meet him.*

Archer: *What the hell? It's 7am. Some people have sex lives.*

Sutton: *TMI Archer!*

Levi sent three flame emojis.

Indi: *Ignore Archer!*

A devil emoji popped up from Archer.

Jules: *Can we focus on Leni and Raz?*

Leni: *It was one date. I met him at work. We hit it off and decided to go to the event together. No big deal.*

Another group of screenshots popped up from Jules. Leni quickly scrolled through the pictures of her and Raz walking into the bar, of the two of them walking out, and of Leni leaning on his shoulder, her heels dangling from her fingers, a goofy smile playing on her lips. The next picture was of Leni climbing onto Raz's back. Leni's stomach pitched. *There goes my hard-nosed reputation.*

Levi: *You could've fooled me. That looks like a pretty big deal to me.*

Sutton: *Maybe she was drunk.*

Indi: *A piggyback! Hahaha! She had to be drunk!*

Daphne: *Happy looks good on you, Leni.*

More screenshots popped up from Jules, of Leni, still on Raz's back, her cheek resting on his head and a smile of sheer contentment on her lips, and—*Oh God*—one of the two of them walking into her building, with his hand on her back. *Shitshitshit.* Fucking paparazzi. How did they even get those pictures? She hadn't seen anyone around. But then again, she hadn't been looking.

Levi: *I didn't need to see that last one.*

Leni: *Relax. We had some tequila, and he walked me to my*

door.

Archer: *I don't trust anyone who pretends to be other people for a living.*

Several more images appeared of Raz walking out of her building wearing his tuxedo from last night and a big-ass satisfied grin. The last of which was Raz climbing into a cab. *Fuck.* They were all time-stamped between 5:40 and 5:48 a.m.

Archer sent an angry emoji.

Leni: *Chill, Archer. It was one date. Can we please move on now? I have work to do.*

A text from Abby appeared. *You and Raz?! Call me!*

Leni quickly thumbed out a response to her. *It was nothing. I'll call you later.*

Her phone rang, and Shea's name appeared on the screen as more texts rolled in. She gulped a breath and straightened her spine. Time to face the music. She paced the living room as she answered. "Hi, Shea. Please don't fire me. I know I crossed a line, and I can explain."

"This ought to be good. Go for it."

"We had too much tequila, and he wasn't an arrogant jerk last night. He doesn't have the highest regard for our profession, which pissed me off. But he didn't disparage us, and don't worry, I gave him hell for it anyway." Her words flew fast and vehement. "He doesn't get how important it is to have good press. But he was funny and charming, and *ohmygod*, I'm so sorry. I can't believe I crossed such a horrific line. I'm so embarrassed. I saw the pictures, and my reputation as a badass is shot to hell. I never should've slept with him, but if you think about it, it's your fault, too. You're the one who pimped me out, and if you fire me, you have to take over my clients. You're already overloaded, so can't we just write it off to both of us having bad judgment and not fire me?"

Shea laughed. "That last part was genius."

Leni exhaled with relief. "I'm pretty good at spinning things. I learned from the best. I really am sorry, Shea. I'll understand if you feel the need to let me go."

"Leni, he's my client, not yours, and the media is eating you guys up."

We were eating each other up last night.

"And as far as your reputation as a badass goes, you went home with an A-list actor. The media is already printing the scoop about Raz's new girl, *cutthroat publicist and marketing guru Leni Steele.*"

"Thank God. Now we can let them sit with it for a few days, and then they'll move on to the next couple, and we can all go back to our lives."

"Well…"

"Well *what?*"

"I think we need to keep this up, or we're basically feeding him to the wolves again."

"*No.* I'm sorry. I know I screwed up, but no way. Last night was a onetime thing. I don't want more."

"Was he *that* bad in bed?"

"No, he was great in bed, but I'm not interested in being his fuck buddy."

"I never said you had to sleep with him in the first place, much less *again.* He leaves to film his next movie in a month. Just be seen in public together a few times until then. A couple of lunches, maybe a dinner here and there."

She couldn't do that. He'd try to get her into bed again, and as much as she enjoyed it, she had never been, and didn't intend to ever be, anyone's fuck buddy. "*No.* Let them assume we're too busy having sex to be seen."

"You know how this works, Leni."

Damn it. How am I going to get out of this? As soon as the question appeared in her mind, the answer showed itself. "Have you talked to Raz about this? He'll never agree to it, either. He hates the paparazzi."

"No. I wanted to speak with you first."

"Go ahead. Get him on the phone. He doesn't even care if people watch his movies."

"That's not true. He cares a lot. He's just overwhelmed by the attention about the breakup."

She was probably right, but still. Leni was sure she'd found her golden ticket. "Maybe you're right, but I know how he feels about the media. Get him on the line so we can put this issue to bed."

"I'm pretty sure you already did that. Hold on." The line went silent, and a minute later Shea said, "Leni, I have Raz on the line. Are you there?"

"Yes, I'm here."

"Looks like we nailed our fake date," Raz said.

Leni rolled her eyes, unwilling to respond.

"I take it you've seen the pictures," Shea interjected.

"I did. Sorry about that, Leni. The photog who's been on my ass since I started in the business is the one who got the pictures. I should've been more diligent, but I was *distracted*."

"What's done is done," Leni said as professionally as she could.

"Raz," Shea said, sounding much less annoyed than Leni. "Since the media is loving you two as a couple, I strongly suggest we continue the ruse, just until you film your next movie. Then we can announce a quiet breakup."

"Sounds good to me," he said without hesitation.

"*What?* You fight Shea on everything, and on this you're all *sounds good to me*? No. No way. If you're hoping I'll jump into bed with you again, you're wrong."

"I never said *I'd* sleep with *you* again," he said in a serious tone, making her feel ridiculous. "But I think it's a good idea to give the media what they want so they stay off my back. Shea has me scheduled for some publicity events, but I can work around them."

"Excuse me," Leni said. "But I have a life to live and my own reputation to uphold. What would I tell my family and friends?"

"As I pointed out earlier, your rep is in excellent shape," Shea said. "And this is business, Leni. You and Raz can't tell your family or anyone else the truth. After we announce the breakup, you can confide in your family if you really feel the need to, and I'm sure they'll understand. Your family is all about pranks. This is just like another prank. But as you well know, something like this is best kept under wraps, or it can backfire on both of you."

"Patch knows you set me up with someone else for the event," Raz interjected.

Patch Carver was his assistant. Patch was based in LA, but Leni had met him a few times when he'd worked for another actor. She knew him to be efficient and professional. Although with his laid-back attitude, colorful tattoo sleeves, shaggy brown hair, and penchant for concert tees and worn jeans, he looked more like he followed a band around the country than kept actors organized.

"Right, so tell him she didn't show and you decided to ask Leni," Shea said. "I just don't think it's worth the risk of someone slipping up and all this blowing up in our faces."

Jesus Christ. Was she in the twilight zone? "In what world is this okay? Shea, you and I are all about authenticity. This is anything *but* authentic."

"You make it sound like you don't like me at all," Raz said. "I think we both know that's not true. Come on, Len. I'd do it for you."

Does a last-minute cancellation of a cologne commercial ring a bell? "You would not. You're too self-centered."

"Should I remind you just how generous I was last night?" he asked.

"We are *not* talking about last night," she fumed.

"Maybe we should," he said lightly. "I feel like if you don't agree to this, I might have loose lips."

"You wouldn't dare," Leni said through gritted teeth.

"Okay, you two, back to your corners," Shea said. "Leni, all I'm asking for is three or four dates over the next month. I don't care if you sit on a park bench and eat ice cream together."

"No ice cream," Leni and Raz said in unison.

"Wow, okay, no ice cream," Shea said. "This can really turn things around for Raz, and, Leni, you were so cute in the pictures, getting a piggyback ride and resting your cheek on his head like a lovestruck girl. If it ends now, I'm afraid it might look like last night was a setup."

"I can't believe this." Leni sat on the couch and rubbed an ache in her temple.

"What do you say, sweetheart? Think you can be my girl for a while?" Raz asked.

"You mean your *fake* girl." Other than their one night of debauchery, Leni had always remained professional around clients of the firm. Whether she liked it or not, she *should* do this for Shea. She just needed to remain clearheaded, which wouldn't be an issue. No more tequila. "I'm swamped with new client meetings and client dinners this month. I don't think I have much free time."

"You're going to the Mets game Wednesday night," Shea reminded her. "That's a perfect public date."

"I'm down for a game," Raz said.

"Fine," Leni relented.

"I have to work around the podcasts, interviews, and photo shoots Shea set up, but I have that restaurant opening coming up," Raz said. "We could go to that together."

"That's right. The opening for Seth Braden and Jared Stone's restaurant. Leni handles all their marketing. She's going to it anyway, so that's another easy date," Shea suggested. "Does that work for you, Leni?"

Do I have a choice? "I suppose it will have to."

"Excellent," Shea said. "What about after that?"

"I'm going home for a weekend to see my parents, and I've got Jay Gold's wedding after that," Raz said. Jay Gold was one of the top movie producers in the industry. He was marrying Naomi Turner, a stunning black model.

"I'll take the wedding. No tequila," Leni said.

"We have Jules's bridal shower that weekend," Shea reminded her.

Shea and her older sister, Fiona, and their mother would be at the shower. "I know. I'll come back Sunday morning to go to the wedding with Raz. But after that I'm all work and no play until I go home for the Field of Screams at Halloween." Field of Screams was her family's annual Halloween event at the winery.

"Field of Screams? I'm in," Raz said. "That sounds fun."

"*No,*" Leni said flatly.

Raz laughed. "I'm heading back to LA for filming the next day anyway."

"I think that's enough for now," Shea said. "If we need an extra outing or two before Raz leaves town, I'm sure you can come up with something. So, do we have a deal?"

Leni closed her eyes. "I still can't believe I'm doing this, but yes."

"Don't worry, Leni," Raz said. "I'll make it worth your time."

Why did she feel like she'd made a deal with the dirty devil himself?

Six

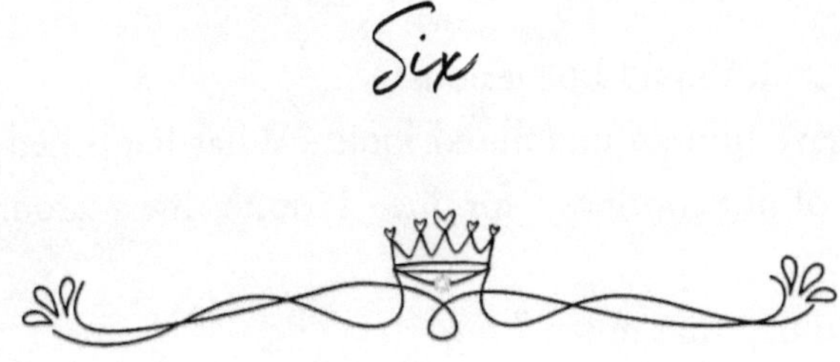

LENI WAS DETERMINED to treat her time with Raz like a job and not get carried away, but by Wednesday evening she was already sick of paparazzi trailing her, hoping for a comment or a sighting of her and Raz together. She was trying to grin and bear it, telling herself she could do anything for a few weeks, but between her typical overloaded schedule, trying to convince certain family members and friends not to get carried away, and avoiding Raz's texts, she was fit to be tied.

"Are you going to tell me why you didn't answer my texts?" Raz asked.

They were being driven to the game, sitting in the back of the sedan. She looked at him in his stolen Mets cap, gray Henley, and jeans, and *boy* did he look delicious. Memories of their steamy night together tugged at her, but she couldn't make that mistake again.

"I was tied up."

He cocked a brow, a grin tugging at his lips. "Should I be jealous?"

"I meant with clients," she said as professionally as she could, though that devious glint in his eyes made her want to bring back the bad-boy dirty talker who had left her in a sex coma.

No sex comas. No dirty talking. No anything but fake for the cameras.

"As I said, should I be jealous?"

She gave him an unamused look. "What happened with us was out of the ordinary for me. I don't mess around with clients."

"I assumed that much."

"Then *why* are you pushing me?"

His grin broke free. "Because you're cute when you're irritated."

She rolled her eyes at the infuriating sex god. Nobody had called her *cute* for years, and now she was too aware of him thinking she was cute when she was irritated, which was annoying in and of itself. "Why did you agree to this arrangement?"

"To get myself out of a bad situation with the media."

"But you made it clear that you don't care about the media."

"True, but I seemed to offend you when I made that comment, and you made it clear that I should care. This is me, caring." He put his hand on hers. "See? I'm not only an attentive fake boyfriend. I'm also a good listener."

She tried to pull her hand away, but he tightened his grip.

"Getting more time with the feisty woman I enjoyed spending a night with isn't a hardship."

She yanked her hand away. "We're *not* sleeping together again."

"You've made that very clear. I don't like jumping through hoops any more than you do, but like I said, you spoke, I listened, and I realized you were right. I hired Shea for a reason, and I wouldn't have hired her if I didn't think she could fix the media nightmare that damn breakup created."

"It wasn't just the breakup. You went from being the affable actor who took the photographers in stride to disappearing from life for six weeks, and when you returned, it was as a disgruntled, angry ex who scowled at the cameras instead of smiling, or worse, covered his face. You looked and acted torn apart from the breakup. All they did was post the pictures."

His jaw tightened, and he looked away.

"It's okay if Jacinda broke you."

He met her gaze with icy eyes. "Do you really think a woman like Jacinda could break me?"

"How should I know? I barely know you."

"Right. But you're smart enough to see that Jacinda was with me because of what my status could do for her. She wanted *Raz* for the weight that name carried, not *Duncan* for the man I am. That's part of life as a celebrity. I know what I signed up for. That's why I rarely date. So, yeah, I dodged the cameras as best I could, hoping the media circus would die down so I could go home to see my family in peace on the anniversary of my sister's death. When that didn't happen, you're damn right I was angry."

That took the starch right out of her. "Oh, Raz, I'm so sorry, and I'm sorry for going on about my family last Friday night. I wasn't thinking straight."

His tone softened. "Yes, you were. You love your family, and that's a beautiful thing. Don't ever let anyone make you feel like your family needs to be pushed aside. Once you start putting them last, reality can slip away real quick, and before you know it, you're alone with your ghosts instead of surrounded by the people who love you."

He said it like he'd done just that himself, and she wondered if something had happened after his sister died, but she felt an empathetic part of her opening up that she might have trouble closing. So she circled back to her safety zone. *Work.* "Why didn't you have Shea handle that situation for you instead of fighting her on every public appearance? She could have made a statement asking for privacy. She had no idea what she was up against, and she can't help you in the best way possible unless you're honest with her."

"You know as well as I do that no matter what Shea said to the media, there was no *handling* that situation. They were already claiming that I was heartbroken. Tory's death would have become another thing for the fucking photographers to make shit up about. I know that Singer asshole who was stalking us and got the pictures of me leaving your place would have been all over my family that weekend. I wasn't about to let that happen. My parents stopped reading gossip rags a decade ago. They don't know about any of the bullshit I deal with, and if I can help it, they never will. I don't get angry often, but that was the first and only time I wasn't with my family on that anniversary, and it hurt more than any breakup ever will. So forgive me if I begrudge the people who held me back."

If she'd been standing up, she was sure she'd have stumbled backward by the sheer force of the pain and anger radiating off him. It was so strong, *she* ached with it, and it was no wonder. This media circus that had been following him had stolen his most treasured time. Time he could never get back, and they didn't just steal it from him but from his family as well. That pissed her off on his behalf, because she knew what it was like to know her family was hurting and being unable to fix it. "There's nothing to forgive. You don't owe me or anyone else anything."

"That's what I was trying to say last night. *Fuck 'em*. But if this diversion is going to work, we need to call a truce, or those daggers shooting from your eyes will spark new headlines about a rift between us before we're ready for it."

Given what he was dealing with, she didn't want to make things harder for him, but she needed to stand her ground, too. "Who says I'm not ready for it?"

"You certainly *didn't*." He smiled. "But I can tell you're not ready for a rift. I can feel it."

"No, you can't. That's wishful thinking. You just want more sex."

"Sex with you was off the charts, and now I know you've spent the last few nights thinking about how good we were together."

Why was volleying barbs with him as much fun as sex?

She had tried not to think about how good they were together, but she'd made the mistake of telling Indi how great their night was. She'd wanted to tell her about the ruse, but she hadn't, and since Indi assumed this was the potential start of a real relationship, she'd tried to convince Leni to have as many sexual trysts with Raz as possible, stockpiling orgasms to hold her over when he eventually left to film his movie. Leni had immediately booted Indi's idea to the curb, because after only one night, she'd done everything she could to distract herself from thoughts of Raz, and the harder she'd tried, the more prominent the sinful memories became. His naked body was etched into her brain, the feel of his hands and mouth had seared into her memory banks, and his dirty talk had been playing on repeat at the most inopportune times. Which was why she'd had trouble concentrating during client meetings and why she'd woken up hot and bothered every morning since their sexy night together.

But she'd be damned if she'd let Raz know that. She lifted her chin in defiance. "You're projecting."

"Is that what you're going with?" he asked incredulously. "Whatever it takes, right?"

It was a good thing she'd only sworn off tequila. If she was going to survive this evening, she definitely needed alcohol.

RAZ HAD NEVER been out with a woman who didn't enjoy being the focus of attention, but it was easy to see that Leni wasn't comfortable being the target of eager fans taking pictures and videos of them on their way into the stadium. She hid it fairly well, but he noticed the tighter smile, the way her eyes skated nervously around them, taking everyone in. He felt protective of her in a way he hadn't toward anyone else and kept her close until they reached their seats.

They'd been there for forty minutes, and she was finally letting her guard down. He enjoyed watching her cheer and holler at the players, commenting on plays to the older couple beside her as if she were an authority on baseball. An alluring authority, in a tan sweater that clung to her curves with shoulder cutouts that made him want to get his mouth on her silky skin again, black skinny jeans that accentuated her gorgeous ass, and tan sneakers. How she managed to look classy in sneakers was beyond him, but he had a feeling she could make rags look classy. But she was still a little stiff with him. If he could just tap into their synergy again, they'd pull this off with flying colors.

Ramsey "Razor" Sharpe hit the ball out of the park, and the fans went wild, including the feisty sprite pushing to her feet beside him. "Did you see that?" she exclaimed. "Razor's got his mojo back."

She beamed at him, lighting him up in the same way her snark and touch had brought something new and edgy to life within him the other night. He slid his hand around her waist, pulling her closer, and felt her tense up. He lowered his face beside hers, whispering in her ear, "Why are you uneasy with me?"

She grabbed his shirt and sat down, bringing him down to his seat. When she leaned closer, he did, too, allowing her to speak for his ears only. "I'm not used to being under a microscope. People are watching our every move."

He glanced around them, noticing a couple of people with their phones aimed at them. "They're just fans."

"The photogs are down there, too." She tilted her head, her eyes shifting to the right.

He looked in that direction and saw fucking Ken Singer with his camera lens aimed directly at them.

"And fans are everywhere," she whispered. "Three seats down from you, a woman's been taking pictures every time I look at you, and there are two girls who keep coming up the steps, taking pictures, then going back to their seats." She surprised him by putting her hand on his chest. He knew the gesture was for the photographers' benefit just like her smile, but he missed real intimacy enough to appreciate the fake. "Now I understand why it annoys you so much."

"You weren't this bothered by the cameras at the event Friday night." He tucked her hair behind one ear and ran his fingers through the thick waves, remembering the way tugging it had made her entire being flame.

"That was different. It was a onetime thing, and short-lived. They're *not* stopping. This puts us out there like a real couple, and I'm trying, but I'm not a big PDA girl."

"I get it. You like to be as in control as I do. I've never been big on PDAs, either, but we need to give them something more than two people sitting next to each other." He'd learned many things about Leni the other night and drew upon the one that could help them through this. When he was kissing her, she was solely focused on how good it felt. "Let me help you forget about them."

Throwing caution to the wind, he took her face between his hands, and in the split second before their lips touched, he saw a warning, and heat, in her eyes. But she didn't pull away. She surrendered her sweet, luscious mouth to him, and the inferno that ignited every time they kissed scorched through her tension. He pushed his hand beneath her hair, angling her mouth beneath his as he deepened the kiss. She grabbed his shirt, tugged him closer, *taking* more. He wanted to lift her onto his lap and explore this otherworldly connection that held power beyond anything he'd ever felt. But he was too well practiced at being in the limelight, and after Saturday morning's debacle, he wasn't about to let Leni become the talk of the tabloids for being *too* eager.

Fucking fine lines.

He drew back, drinking in the lust in her eyes. "Welcome back, sweetheart. Now we can enjoy the game."

She blinked several times, the lust subsiding slightly as her eyes narrowed. "That was sneaky."

"My girl likes sneaky." He laced their fingers together, brought her hand to his lips, and kissed the back of it.

"Your *fake* girl," she said sweetly. "And for the record, I'm trying to forget how much I liked *sneaky* with you."

"That's a futile effort if I've ever heard one." He stole a quick kiss, and she stole his baseball cap, settling it on her head with a challenging lift of her chin. "Adorable."

"Women aren't *adorable*. We're...something else."

"You sure are, SA."

"What does that even mean?"

He whispered, "Sinful angel."

Her cheeks pinked up, and she glowered, as if she hadn't been exactly that and so much more. "Don't call me that."

"Only in the bedroom, like the others? Got it, princess."

She swatted him, but she was laughing as he caught her hand, pulling her close again. "You know you're into it."

"I know my fist will be into you if you call me SA again." She flashed a camera-ready grin. "Now, how about being a good boyfriend and getting us some beer and hot dogs?"

"Hot dogs? Really? They have all kinds of vendors here."

"Don't be a snob. Hot dogs are an essential part of baseball games."

"In that case, it would be my pleasure to service you." He smirked.

She gave him an imploring look and tilted her head toward the older couple sitting beside her.

"*Serve.* Sorry. My bad." He didn't want to leave her. He was having too much fun, but he pushed to his feet, adding one last barb. "I'll miss you while I'm gone, princess."

She surprised him again by grabbing his hand and standing, speaking quietly. "You'll probably get hung up with fans. Do you want me to go instead?"

Look at you, thinking about me even as you try not to. "Don't you know there's nothing I won't do for you?"

"I'm serious, Raz. I know it bothers you."

He liked knowing she cared, and as he gazed into her eyes, he saw that it wasn't feigned for their audience. "I have a better idea. How about if we go together? That way nobody will be tempted to corner me."

"Okay."

He held her hand as they headed down to get their food, and kept hold of it as they waited in line. "How often do you come to games?"

"All the time. I have season tickets."

"Really? Who did I boot out of a seat?"

"Nobody. I usually take a client to give them a perk, or go alone, which is what I prefer, so I can focus on the game."

"Maybe I shouldn't have dragged you with me to get food. You're missing the game."

"No, I'm not." She squeezed his hand. *"Looklooklook!"*

He turned just in time to see the Mets hit a home run on the mounted television screen. They cheered, and she launched herself into his arms, feet dangling off the ground, both of them laughing. Their eyes connected, hers twinkling with joy, and electricity crackled between them.

She fell silent and must have realized how easily she'd leapt into his arms, because she whispered, "Hope that was a good one for the cameras," and slid down to her feet, as if it were all for show.

He knew better. Their dates might be fake, with a foreseeable, and desirable, end date, but there was no faking their chemistry. He was pretty sure the entire stadium had vibrated with it.

He cleared his throat, reaching for a safe subject to get his mind off how incredibly good she'd felt in his arms. "How'd you become such an avid baseball fan?"

"My brothers and father used to watch together, and when Jock and Archer were around fifteen, they started going to their friends' houses to watch, and they'd leave Levi behind, because we're five years younger than they are. I get that they didn't want their younger brother hanging around all the time, but they did so much without him, I felt bad. It was bad enough that they were always pranking everyone, and Levi was often the focus of those pranks since he was an easy target. He was a good kid and he trusted them. Anyway, I didn't want Levi to feel left out, and since we all ran in packs back then, I'd grab Wells and Abby, and we'd watch the games with him. I ended up really enjoying it."

He was glad she was focused on talking with him, instead of the few fans he saw taking pictures of them. "That was thoughtful of you."

"Yeah, well, he's always been there for me."

"So you hung out a lot with Wells and Abby, together?"

"Mm-hm."

"That must have made the breakup even harder."

"He broke my trust, Raz. How much harder does it need to get?" she said as they stepped up to the counter to get their snacks.

They got their beer and hot dogs, and Leni tried one of his favorite beers, New Belgium's Fat Tire, which she determined was *not bad*. As they made their way back to their seats, she said, "There's another reason I love baseball. You know how I said all the families I grew up with were close?"

"Yeah."

"Well, we used to do everything together—fishing, boating,

picnics, and even sports like baseball and touch football. I'm a *tad* competitive, and I was really good at it."

"You are a force to be reckoned with." He imagined her hollering at her siblings and friends with the same vehemence as she hollered at the players. "I bet you're good at everything you set your mind to."

"Pretty much." She grinned and took a bite of her hot dog. "*Mm.* This is the best thing I've eaten all week."

He arched a brow.

"Get your mind out of the gutter. We're talking about family."

"Family. *Right.* The way you described your family reminds me of Beau's family."

"Did you know he and Seth are related?"

"Yeah, second or third cousins or something. There are dozens of Bradens out there. Beau and I grew up together."

"There are dozens of Steeles, too. What was it like growing up with them?"

"Their family is big, like yours, and there was always something going on over there. The same way you ran in packs with the other families, Tory and I were always at the Bradens'. Zev and his wife, Carly, were childhood sweethearts, and Tory was Carly's best friend. Hell, everyone loved Tory." He didn't trust most people enough to talk about Tory, and he wasn't sure why he was talking about her with Leni. But she was looking at him without that wariness in her eyes, which made him want to share more. "Tory and Beau were madly in love, and then we lost her, and all our lives changed."

Leni was quiet for a minute as they climbed the steps to their seats. "Does it bother you, talking about her here?"

"I'm talking to *you*, not feeding her to the media hounds. I love talking about Tory. I miss her every day, and the only people I can really talk to about her are my parents or relatives."

"It must be awful not having anyone to share those feelings with."

"You get used to it."

Her brows knitted, her gaze empathetic. "I don't know if I believe that. How can you get used to holding in feelings about someone you love?"

"I don't know. You just do."

"Well, I like hearing about Tory, so feel free to talk about her when you're with me."

The sincerity in her voice told him it wasn't an empty offer. "Thanks. Maybe I will."

They settled into their seats, focusing on the game and lighter, more jovial conversation as they ate their hot dogs and drank their beers. Raz didn't know exactly what had changed, but Leni was more relaxed and feistier, the way she'd been Friday night. Acting like they were friends instead of stressed about who was watching them and what they were supposed to be portraying. They had a great time cheering on their team, joking around, and talking with the people sitting nearby like he wasn't a celebrity and she wasn't his fake date. She didn't even make a snarky comment when Beau texted and he put his arm around her for a selfie to send to him, or when he held her hand, or any one of the many times he couldn't resist kissing her.

In an effort to miss the stampede, they left the stadium shortly before the end of the game and made their way to their waiting car. "I'm telling you, I'm the team's good luck charm," Raz said as they climbed into the back seat.

She looked amused. "How do you figure?"

"Think about it. They didn't play well the other night because I missed the game."

"That ego of yours needs a seat of its own. How often do you go to games?"

"Almost never."

"Then it's not *you*." She laughed, bumping him with her shoulder as they were driven out of the parking lot.

"Ah, that's the thing about me. I don't have to be present for others to feel my power, as I'm sure you can attest to." He held her gaze. "I won't ask how many times you've thought about me in your bed since Friday night."

Heat rose in her eyes.

"That many, huh?"

"Don't flatter yourself," she said flatly, but her eyes betrayed her. "You have no power over me or the Mets."

"Okay, let's say you haven't thought about me, which I don't believe, but we can pretend. I usually watch the games, but as you'll recall, I was tied up Friday night, and they had an off night."

"I believe *I* was the one tied up." She arched a brow.

Loving her need to challenge, and the sinful scene it brought back, he said, "Now you're just trying to get me hot, thinking about you naked, wrists bound, eyes pleading for more."

She swallowed hard. "I was only stating a fact."

"Mm-hm." He put his hand on her thigh, and she breathed a little harder. "So you weren't thinking about how good it felt to have my mouth between your legs or how hard you came while I was inside you?"

She tilted her head, smiling so sweetly, she *almost* looked innocent, but that sinful angel in her was too strong to deny. "Sorry, but no."

LENI HEARD THE lie in her own voice and hoped he hadn't heard it, too. Why had their night together had to have been so damn hot? She was enjoying getting to know him. There was more to Duncan Raz than the shallow actor she'd pegged him to be. That made her want to know more about him, and his family, and *hell yes*, she wanted to get him naked again, but she had to be careful. This wasn't real, and Raz had a way of getting under her skin. Opening herself up to him had heartbreak written all over it, and she was not going there.

"Uh-huh," he said like he wasn't buying her response either. "You weren't wondering what it would be like to tie me up and have your way with me?"

She tried to fight the heat of his hand spreading up her thigh, but she was getting even hotter at the thought of tying him up. "I don't need to wonder. I know exactly what it would be like."

He cocked a grin. "Do tell."

Oh, the things she could say. *Excruciatingly erotic* and *fun* topped the list, but she kept that to herself and she managed a scoff. "I don't think so."

"Why not? Afraid of wanting me too much?"

Yes. "No. We just pulled up to my building."

"Perfect. I'll walk you up."

He helped her out of the car, the thrum of desire coiling around them like a snake as he pulled her into a long, slow kiss on the sidewalk. She tried not to give in to it, but it felt too good. *He* felt good, all hard-bodied male, sexuality oozing from his pores, and she melted like butter in his arms.

Wait. What was she doing?

No. Nonono. This was not happening again.

She forced her brain into gear and realized they must have been followed by the paparazzi. She eased away from his tempting lips, but he pulled her right back into another toe-curling kiss. Sweet baby Jesus, the man could kiss the life out of her right there on the sidewalk.

When they finally parted, she blinked several times, trying to bring the rest of the world back into focus, and looked around. "Did photographers tail us?"

"No." He gazed deeply into her eyes. "I've just been dying to do that all night."

She tried to steel herself against the *want* billowing inside her, but it was like trying to forget her own name, and that pissed her off. "This is *fake*, Raz. You don't have to say things like that. Nobody can hear us."

"Who are you trying to convince? Me or you?" he asked on the way up to the entrance to her building.

"I don't need convincing. I'm just reminding you."

He brushed her hair off her shoulder, and it felt tender and intimate. "Is it so awful that I want to kiss you?"

He reached for the door, but she blocked his way, putting a hand on his chest. "This is as far as you get."

"What's the matter, princess?" His eyes were as amused as his voice was seductive. "Afraid you'll fall for me if we get naked again?"

"*Hardly.* We had a great time tonight, and I'm sure pictures of us are all over social media. But that's all this is. I've done my job, and now I'm going to say good night and you're going to leave."

His jaw tightened. "Right. Your job."

Why did he sound hurt? "That's right."

He stepped closer. "This *job* was a lot more fun when you let yourself take what you wanted."

No kidding. "That's what got me into this situation. But I'm smart enough to learn from my mistakes."

"We both know it wasn't a mistake."

"Maybe our tryst wasn't, but getting caught was. I'll see you next week for the restaurant opening."

"Why don't we do something this weekend?" he suggested. "It can't hurt to give the media more of what they want."

She wondered what he had in mind, and for that matter, what he did for fun, but she wasn't going there, either. "I can't, sorry. I'm busy."

"Busy?"

"Yes. I do have a life, you know."

His jaw ticked again. "You can't date anyone else while we're seeing each other. You know that, right?"

"Trust me. One man in my life is more than enough."

"I'll take that as a compliment." He leaned in and kissed her again.

She pushed at his chest playfully. "Get outta here."

"Is that any way to treat the love of your life? You never know who's watching."

She rolled her eyes, but for the sake of the press, she grabbed the front of his shirt, tugging him down as she went up on her toes, and said, "Goodbye, you handsome devil. I won't dream about you." She pressed her lips to his, then escaped into her building before he could see the lie in her eyes.

Seven

LENI GLANCED OUT the window on her way into her home office late Saturday morning, and Raz's voice came back to her. *Time is always of the essence for the woman who barely has time for coffee.* Why did he act like he knew her so well, when they'd only just met?

She sipped her coffee and set the cup on her desk as she sat down, excited to get some planning done for her newest campaigns. She fired up her laptop, and as she waited for it to go through whatever technical dance it had to in order to do her heavy lifting, her mind returned to Raz. It hadn't strayed far since she'd seen him Wednesday night.

How could it when he'd texted each day, claiming it was what boyfriends did and he didn't half-ass his acting jobs. The brawny brat made it impossible *not* to think about him. She scrolled back to read the texts he'd sent last night.

Raz: *Remember what we were doing last week at this time?*

Leni: *Nope.*

Raz: *Do you think the paparazzi will notice your nose has grown after that lie?*

Her phone rang, startling her, and she nearly dropped it. Sutton's name appeared on the screen. Sutton was doing a story about an archaeological dig site and had been working on location in Portugal for the past week. Leni had just spoken to her a few days ago, and Sutton wasn't a frequent caller, which made her worry that something was wrong. She wiped the silly grin off her face and answered the call. "Hey, Sut. Is everything okay? How's filming going?"

"It's going well. They made a huge discovery about—get this—what Neanderthals ate. They found ninety-thousand-year-old remains of a brown crab. How cool is that?"

"It would be cooler if someone cooked me crab. What's going on? Is fine-ass Flynn lightening up at all?" Her boss, Flynn Braden, was Seth Braden's brother. But while Seth was one of the easiest clients Leni had ever worked with, according to Sutton, Flynn was his polar opposite. He was hard on her and thought she was too green for the job. Maybe she was, since she'd been unable to find a reporting job right out of college and had spent several years as a fashion editor for LWW Enterprises. When the reporting job opened in another division, they gave her a shot. She was smart, researched the hell out of every project, was great on camera, and was always on point. Flynn needed to chill and realize he had a gold mine in her, even if it took her longer to get up to speed.

"*No.* Apparently I'm getting on his last nerve, and this place is super remote, so if I don't come back, you know where to look for my body."

"Sutton, do you hear yourself? You work your ass off for him. You need to stand your ground or he'll never give you the respect you deserve. Or, now that you've got some experience, you could find another job. He'll be sorry he lost you when your ratings blow his away."

"With my luck, he'd get in front of the camera and millions

of women would flock to watch him."

"He doesn't report. He runs the freaking show."

Sutton didn't respond, but Leni heard her breathing.

"Sutton?" Answered with silence, she looked at the phone to see if she'd accidentally muted herself, then tried one more time. "Hello, are you there?"

"Yeah, sorry."

"What happened?"

"Nothing," Sutton said guiltily.

"Ohmygod. You were ogling him again, weren't you?"

"Shut up. I can't help it. He lifted his shirt to wipe the sweat from his face with it, and holy shit, Leni. There's a lot of man under there. Too bad he's such a dick."

Why did that make her think of Raz? Raz wasn't a dick.

But I thought he was.

What am I doing? Why am I thinking about him again? Leni squeezed her eyes shut for a second, forcing him out of her head. "Are you going to be back in time for Jules's bridal shower?"

"Yeah. I'll be back next week. I saw some pretty cozy pictures from what I assume was date number two. Did Raz get a home run?"

"*No.* I told you that was a onetime thing."

"I know, but come on, Leni. You also said it was the best sex of your life. Who wouldn't go back for seconds?"

"Me, that's who. We had seconds, thirds, and more last Friday night. I had my fun, and now I'm just"—*completing my assignment*—"seeing where it goes outside the bedroom. By the way, if Archer asks, *please* tell him what I said. He's driving me nuts, texting about all the pictures and wanting to meet Raz. Indi is trying to get him off my back, but—"

"He's Archer," they said at the same time, and laughed.

"Has Levi cornered you yet?"

"He called after that group text last weekend, and he understood that I'm allowed to have fun with a guy, although he's so glad to be back on Silver Island and with Tara, I highly doubt he's spending time worrying about my sex life. I think he just wants me to know that he's there if I need him."

"Yeah, probably. So…Does Raz know about your secret movie addiction?"

"*No*, and he never will. I never should have admitted that to you." Leni had watched *Anything for Love*, the romcom Raz had starred in, with Sutton and Jules when it first came out. Mainly because they'd made her, but she'd liked it so much, she'd watched it after every disappointing coffee date to cheer herself up.

A knock sounded at her door, and Leni got up to answer it. "Hold on. Someone's at the door."

"Are your neighbor's deliveries still coming to your place?"

"Not as often. One sec." She opened the door and found Raz looking delicious in black running shorts, a gray T-shirt, and the stolen Mets cap, carrying a black duffel bag over his shoulder.

He cocked a grin. "Hello, sweetheart."

"What are you doing here?"

"Picking up my girlfriend to go for a run. I'm no spring chicken. I've got to keep this bod in tip-top shape."

"I'm *not* your girlfriend," she hissed quietly so Sutton wouldn't hear her. "And I told you I was busy."

"Yes, but I had lunch with Shea yesterday, and she said you usually work on the weekends and that you could use a break. She loves the idea of us being seen together as much as possible, and, well, she already tipped off the press." He held out his hands. "We've got no choice."

"*What?*" Leni fumed. "Now you're in cahoots with my cousin?" She put the phone to her ear. "Sutton, I have to go."

"Hi, Sutton, sorry your boss is a jerk," Raz called out as he strode past Leni into her living room.

"Is that Raz?" Sutton asked.

"Yes, and apparently he's lost his mind." She glowered at him.

"He's pushy. No wonder you had so much fun with him," Sutton said with amusement. "Does he know you don't run?"

"Not yet, but he's about to find out. I'll talk to you later." She ended the call and planted a hand on her hip. "You can't just come in here and expect me to drop everything and go out with you."

"You're right." He dropped the duffel bag and sat on the couch, languidly stretching his arm across the back of it. "Take your time and finish whatever you were doing. I can wait."

"*Raz*," she warned.

"I really wish you'd call me Duncan." He pushed to his feet, sauntering over with a coy expression. "Come on, Leni. What's more fun on a sunny day? Sitting at your desk working, or hanging out with me? No ulterior motives. I'm not going to try to wrangle you into getting naked." He took her hand, pulling her closer. "It's a couple of hours of your time, that's all, and if we don't show up, who knows what they'll print about us."

She groaned and looked up at the ceiling. "*Why* are you doing this to me?"

"Because you work too much, and before this little arrangement arose, I was about a week away from becoming a hermit."

She sighed.

"I like hanging out with you, and I think you like hanging with me, too. So let's make the most of it and have a great day. Don't worry. I brought a change of clothes so I won't stink after our run."

Damn it to hell, he had the puppy-dog eyes down pat. "Don't look at me like that."

His eyes narrowed, and a wicked grin appeared, making her stomach flip-flop.

"*Jesus*. Don't look at me at all." She turned away and covered her face so he wouldn't see her smile.

He pried her hands away. "How long has it been since a guy has made you laugh as often as I do? Be honest."

She rolled her eyes, not about to answer that question. "I don't run."

"We'll jog."

"I'll slow you down."

"I like slow." He lifted his brow playfully.

"I hate you right now."

"That fire in your belly is lust, not hate." He patted her ass. "Go change into sexy little shorts."

She crossed her arms, scowling. "Don't touch my ass, and don't tell me what to do."

"Okay." In the space of a second, he bent at the waist, leaned his shoulder into her stomach, and tossed her over his shoulder like a sack of potatoes.

She shrieked, and he carried her down the hall. "*Raz!* Put me down!" She couldn't help but laugh.

He tossed her onto her back on the bed and crawled over her. His body heat seeped through her clothes, scorching her skin. She could practically hear her body cheering, *Raz! Raz!*

He's our man!

"The way I see it, you've got two choices, princess. Get changed to go running." Raz rubbed his nose along her cheek. "Or maybe you'd prefer to get naked, and the photogs can catch me walking out looking freshly fucked in a few hours."

"As enticing as getting naked with you sounds, I have *many* more choices than that. For example, I could knee you in the balls right now."

He laughed, which made her laugh. "Do you know how badly I want to kiss you right now?"

"Stop with the flattery, and get out of my bedroom. I need to get changed." She pushed him off and sat up.

He tugged her back down beside him. "It's not flattery. I really *do* want to kiss you, and I think you want to kiss me, too."

"*Raz.*"

"Tell me I'm wrong."

"You're wrong."

His brows knitted. "I'm disappointed. Texting a lie is one thing, but lying to my face?" He pushed to his feet and strode out of the room, calling over his shoulder, "We leave in five, Steele."

RAZ HAD THOUGHT long and hard about going to see Leni before he'd shown up. In fact, he'd thought of nothing *but* seeing her for the past few days. He'd worried that he was misreading the heat between them, and she might slam the door in his face. When she didn't, he knew their flame hadn't dwindled for her, either, despite her ranting at him. And now here she was, twenty minutes into their jog through Central Park, huffing and puffing and cute as could be with her ponytail threaded through the back of a Mets cap, wearing black spandex running shorts and a white tank top with a red sports bra peeking out from beneath it.

"Tell me again why we're running?" she panted out.

"It's good for us."

"So is sunbathing. It gives you vitamin D, but it also gives you cancer."

"And yet you sunbathe with the condom-distributing Bra Brigade, which I still need details on."

"No, you don't."

"Don't make me call Grandma Lenore."

Her head snapped toward him. "How do you know my grandmother's name?"

"A gentleman never gives out his sources."

"I'm going to have a long talk with Shea."

"It wasn't Shea. I do have connections, you know. I'm a pretty big deal."

"*Whatever.* Don't you dare call her."

He chuckled. "Then spill the beans about the best-kept secret on Silver Island."

"It's hardly a secret," she said as they jogged around a bend. "My grandmother and her friends started sunbathing in their bras when they were teenagers, and they never stopped."

"So you're telling me there are sunbathing grannies in their bras all over Silver Island?"

"Not *all over*. They find a secluded spot and do it there."

"And you do it, too, in that lacy lingerie?"

"We all do. My mom, my sisters, our friends. It's tradition."

"I bet Wells loves that," he said more to himself than to her.

"*Wells?*" She looked perplexed. "All the guys I grew up with have run into the original Bra Brigaders sunbathing at least once, and they've gone to great lengths to avoid running into them again."

"Maybe so, but if I grew up there, and I knew you sunbathed in a lacy bra, I'd be out there like Dora the Explorer every damn time."

She laughed. "Dora, huh?"

"Damn right. Backpack and all."

As they jogged through the park, they made small talk, and Leni gave him a hard time every chance she could. She was funny, sassy, and kept up with him fairly well.

"How long have we been running? Eighteen hours?" she panted out. "How can it still be daylight?"

"It's only been about forty minutes."

"That's a lifetime. Oh, thank God. *Water.*" She pointed to a vendor cart up ahead and sprinted toward it.

He caught up to her and smacked her ass, earning a scowl as he bolted past. She ran faster and poked his side. When he caught up, she grabbed his arm, holding on as she bent at the waist, gulping for air.

"You've been holding back on me. You can run like the wind."

"Only when there's something I want in front of me."

"I'll be sure to run ahead of you from now on."

She straightened and stretched, giving him that adorable don't-flatter-yourself look. "Please tell me you brought money."

He arched a brow. "It'll cost you."

She looked around, and he knew she was looking for paparazzi.

"Stop looking for reasons, and give yourself over to the role." He tugged her into a kiss and kept her close. "You might as well enjoy these lips while you can."

"I'm not an actress."

"Like hell you're not. You just don't own it. You play a role every time you meet with a client, or go on a date, or say you don't like to kiss me." He slung his arm around her.

"We're sweaty."

He held her tighter. "I like us sweaty, remember?" He headed to the vendor cart. "Water, right?"

"Yes, please, and a soft pretzel," she said, smiling at the vendor.

"We've still got to jog back."

"No, we don't. We're walking." She looked over the pictures on the front of the cart. "They have strawberry shortcake bars. I'll take one of those, too, please. I'm starved."

He raised his brows. "You know how I like strawberry ice cream à la Leni."

She stifled a smile. "Since you're not getting *that*, you might as well enjoy *this* on the way back." She looked at the vendor. "He'll take the same, please."

He paid the vendor, and they ate their ice cream as they headed back to her place. He liked the way she nibbled around all the edges first, then worked through the crunchy outside before eating the rest. "You're in great shape. I can't believe you don't work out."

"I never said I don't work out. I said I don't run. I walk everywhere and take spin classes a few times each week. I also hit the golf range to relieve stress."

"You play golf?" he asked incredulously.

"*Yes.*" She sounded annoyed by the question. "I have clients

who play. It's good for networking and strengthening relationships."

"So you take clients to baseball games, and your other fun
activity is basically a networking function?" That certainly
backed up what else he'd learned about Little Miss Workaholic.

"It's called multitasking and effective time management."

"That's not exactly fun, but who am I to judge? I'm having
a hard time picturing you playing a tame sport like golf. Why
do I think you'd curse at the ball when it falls short."

She smirked. "It doesn't fall short. I'm good at it."

"I know what we're doing after this."

"After this?"

"Yup. Today is boyfriend-girlfriend day. Didn't you get the
memo? Work can wait. I've got to see you hit a golf ball and
make sure you're not embarrassing yourself with clients."

"Are you kidding? Do you even play?"

"A little. My father taught me when I was eight, and I'm
sure I can teach you a thing or two."

She scoffed. "Dream on. I'm bringing my A game."

He had a feeling she always brought her A game. "What else
do you do for fun?"

"When I have a night off, I binge some of my favorite shows
and pig out on junk food."

"Now, that sounds like fun. What kind of shows?"

"Right now I'm rewatching *The Walking Dead* and *Supernatural*."

"Whoa, my girl's a horror fanatic? I wouldn't have guessed
that." She was even tougher than he'd thought.

"I'm not your girl, and yes, I am. Jock and Archer have
always loved horror movies. The scarier the better, and they
used to try to scare me and my sisters all the time. I guess I got

used to the thrill of it. What about you? You like to run, and you play a little golf. What else do you like to do?"

He cocked a brow. "You."

She said, "*Cheesy*," but she was still smiling as she ate her ice cream. "Come on. I want to know."

"I act a little."

"So I've heard. Now, stop messing around and tell me what you like to do for fun."

"This is an honest answer, so don't give me shit. Lately, I like spending time with you."

"Can you back that up with something more than because it might be a prelude to sex?"

He sure liked her no-bullshit attitude. "Of course I can. You're fun, Leni. You're smart, and you've got a great personality. You're also sexy as sin, but you know that."

She eyed him as if weighing his answer.

"What?"

"You're a good actor, that's what. Can't you just tell me what you do for fun *without* trying to distract me?"

"Why do you think it's a distraction? You've got to know you're beautiful."

"I also know I say what I feel, and that's hard for guys to deal with." They tossed the sticks from their ice creams into a trash bin.

"Not for me. I welcome your challenges."

She took a bite of her pretzel. "So you're a masochist?"

He grinned. "I just know something special when I see it."

She was quiet for a minute, picking at her pretzel. "And for fun?"

"There isn't much I don't like to do, except the club scene. I'm over that. I like seeing my family, and when I'm home I hike and bike and hang out with my old friends if they're around."

They left the park, heading down the busy sidewalk and enjoying their pretzels. "How often do you go home?"

"As often as I can. Sometimes I'll go for a couple of weeks or a weekend. How about you?"

"Once a month or so, depending on what's going on. But we keep in touch. Mostly by text."

"It's only me and my parents, and they aren't big texters."

"Neither are mine. My mother says she'd rather hear her kids' voices than read our cryptic texts. You live in LA most of the time, right?"

"Yeah. I'm only in New York for the month to carry out a few obligations Shea has arranged."

"Do you bike and hike in LA, too?"

"Sometimes, but I prefer Maryland."

"Why? I would think California would be ideal for anything outdoors."

"LA has beautiful places to hike, but it's not an easy place for me to relax. I've been contemplating moving away from there."

"Where would you go? Maryland?" She popped a piece of pretzel into her mouth.

"I'm not sure. I'd like to settle down somewhere near my parents, maybe have a family one day, far away from the LA scene. But in light of the recent media headaches, I'm not sure I want to risk introducing any of that to my parents' quiet lives. What about you? Why did you move away from the island?"

"To get a life of my own, away from the prying eyes of everyone who has known me since I was in diapers." She wiped the salt off her hands and guzzled water.

"Is New York all you'd hoped it would be?"

A tease rose in her eyes. "With the exception of the male species? Yes, it is."

"Careful now."

She laughed softly.

He liked having time to get to know her without the pressure of stress and obligations. "How about your job? Do you like it? It seems like you spend your days putting out fires and scheduling events."

"There's a lot of that, but that's just one piece of a really great puzzle, and even though it can be like wrangling toddlers from time to time, I love what I do. Every aspect of it, from negotiating contracts and creating marketing concepts to bringing all the elements together and watching brands soar because of my efforts. It's not an easy job or one for thin-skinned people. You always have to be more creative than the competition and anticipate reactions and stumbling blocks. And even if you think you have a perfect plan, the client might not like it and can send you right back to the drawing board."

"Now I feel bad for giving Shea a hard time."

"You should." They waited for a light to change, then crossed the street.

"Don't you get frustrated?"

"I have my moments, but I can't let that get to me or it'll kill my creativity. I use it to feed my competitive side instead. Every day there's a new mountain to climb, so I pull on my Louboutin boots, grab those thingies that you hook into the sides of mountains, and scale the hell out of it."

"Those *thingies*?" He laughed. "I'll add mountain climbing to the list of things I need to do with you."

She shook her head. "I like my feet on the ground, thank

you very much."

"You are quite grounded. How'd you get into that line of work?"

"When I first came here for school, Shea was already out of college and had been working for a few years for another PR company. We used to get together every couple of weeks, and she'd tell me all about the work she was doing. Sometimes we'd brainstorm, and I loved it. My brain doesn't slow down, and in marketing and PR, it's go-go-go all the time. She opened her company during my junior year and hired me as an intern. I've worked with her ever since."

He tried to ignore the curious glances aimed their way as they crossed another street. "Sounds like you found your calling."

"I think so. What about you? Why acting? Did you always want to see your name on the big screen?"

"Wouldn't everyone like to see their name on the big screen?"

"Not me. I'm perfectly happy behind the scenes, promoting the people who like the limelight."

"I get that, but you shine on camera."

"Thanks." She smiled appreciatively. "But I can't wait to be done with *that*."

"Done with me, too?"

"We were talking about how you got into acting, not me, or us, or this. Was it the thrill of it all? Is that why you went into acting?"

Her redirection was impressive. "There is an undeniable thrill knowing I can bring a story to life and make the people feel like they're right there in the movie with me. But that's not why I started to act. It was because of my sister. We got into an argument when I was in high school. She was two years younger than me, and the sweetest person you'd ever met. But when you pissed her off, she could be feisty."

"Sounds like Jules."

"Grant's Pixie? The spreader of happiness?"

"Yes. Jules was diagnosed with cancer when she was three. Thankfully, she beat it, which is why she always finds a silver lining in everything."

"She was so young. I can't imagine how scary that was for your family." They turned onto Leni's street.

"It was," she said thoughtfully. "But she's healthy now, and like Tory, when Jules is mad, that innocence can cut you to shreds."

"That was Tory to a T. I remember this one time, when football practice ran late, and I was supposed to take her and her friends to the mall. By the time I got home, her friends had left, and she was furious. She called me a stupid jock, and when I tried to explain that I couldn't just leave practice, she said not to act like I cared."

"That sounds like a familiar argument. I think all younger sisters have them with their older brothers."

"Maybe, but the truth is, at that time, I *was* a stupid jock acting like I cared. I was a self-centered teenager, all about sports and friends. I loved Tory so much, but at times like that, all I saw was my little sister pitching a fit. When I pleaded my case, she said I couldn't act worth shit, and we got into it again. Somehow it ended with her daring me to audition for the high school musical. I auditioned to prove a point and landed the lead role, which pissed off the theater kids who really wanted it. But I couldn't back out. I had to prove myself to Tory. I did a hell of a job and ended up with new friends and a passion for acting and everything that came with it." His chest constricted as they climbed the steps to Leni's building. "I'd give anything to live that afternoon over again and leave practice on time."

He looked up as they stepped onto the landing. The emotions in Leni's eyes nearly bowled him over as she wrapped her arms around him, speaking softly. "She knew you loved her."

He embraced her, thankful for the comfort and feeling like he'd just found a chink in her armor. What part of this strong woman's heart had been touched by loss? She'd probably kick him in the balls for thinking he'd seen the pain in her eyes, but he knew camouflage when he saw it. "I hope she did."

Leni looked up, those evergreen wells of emotions tweaking his heartstrings. She blinked several times, squaring her shoulders as she stepped back, slipping into the armor she wore so well. "Trust me. As a younger sister, I know how our minds work. I bet she came to you a million times after that when she was sad or troubled about something."

"She did. How'd you know?"

"Because calling your older sibling a stupid *anything* is a rite of passage. Tory probably bragged to her friends about how great you were, and then you made a liar out of her and let her down. But you were just being a kid, and so was she."

He opened the door, and they headed inside. "I didn't think about it that way."

"Of course not. Kids have their own agendas, especially as teens. There's so much going on at that age. Older siblings have so much power, and even though I'm sure they know it on some level, they probably don't think about it in the same way their younger brothers and sisters do."

"What do you mean by power?" He pressed the button for the elevator, and they stepped in when the doors opened.

"They can drive and stay out late, and they know how to act cool when the younger ones are still in that awkward stage. And older siblings know things the younger ones haven't learned yet. It's like they can share knowing glances with their friends and parents, and that's frustrating for younger kids. It makes them feel left out. But unless you were a total asshole, I'd bet Tory idolized you and was proud watching you in that musical."

"She was. She brought all her friends and stayed for the cast party afterward. It sounds like you've gone through being let down by your older siblings, too."

"I might've been there a few times," she said coolly.

"Care to share?"

"Not even a little." The elevator doors opened, and she walked out.

As they made their way to her apartment, he wanted to pull her close again, to gaze into those *actress* eyes and get another glimpse of that squishy heart of hers. But without the threat of cameras, he was liable to draw fire, and he was looking forward to spending the rest of the day with the most complicated woman he'd ever met.

Eight

LENI COULDN'T HELP the laughter slipping out as Raz swung at the golf ball and missed *again*. They'd been at the Chelsea Piers golf range for twenty minutes, and he had yet to hit a solid one. He either whiffed it or made a lousy shot. At least his butt looked great in those jeans, and his body was drool-worthy with that T-shirt clinging to his broad, muscular back. He owed her the eye candy after chasing her around the apartment, trying to convince her that showering together was the best way to save water. She had *not* given in, but she'd gotten a good laugh out of the comments he'd shouted through the door while she showered.

He glanced over his shoulder. "I'm glad this is amusing to you, because it's pissing me off."

"I'm sorry. I know I should feel bad for you, but you're such a big talker, I expected you to be serious competition. I thought your father taught you to play when you were eight."

"He did, and I sucked then, too, which is why it was the last time I played. I figured since I kick ass at other sports, I'd be great at golf by now. And you're over here like some kind of pro. What'd you do, study under Tiger Woods?"

"Tiger and I are tight." She laughed. "Golf isn't the kind of sport you can just jump into and be good at. It takes patience and practice."

"I've been practicing this whole time, and I swear the damn tee is crooked or something."

She set her club down and went to him. "You're not even holding the club right. Let me show you how." She took his club. "Watch where I put my hands." She quickly walked him through how to grip the club.

"Yeah, yeah, give me that." He grabbed it from her and held it like a bat. "I've got it, right?"

"That would be great if we were playing baseball. You can't manhandle it. You need a lighter grip. Here, let me show you this way." She moved behind him and reached around to adjust his hands.

He wiggled his ass against her, grabbed her hand, and pressed it to his chest. "All right. *Now* I'm getting it."

She pinched his nipple.

"*Ow*, Jesus." He spun around, rubbing his chest. "That was cruel."

Barely stifling a laugh, she planted a hand on her hip. "You're the one who wanted to golf. We don't have to do this."

"Yes, we do. I need to beat you at it."

"There's no *beating me* at a golf range. It's not like you get points."

"Well, I need to hit it better than you. Show me how. I promise to behave." He drew an X over his heart.

She rolled her eyes, doubting he even knew what the word meant. "Get behind me, and we can do it that way."

"Now we're talking." He sauntered behind her and wrapped his arms around her waist, grinding against her ass. "Oh yeah. I could definitely get it in the hole from here."

Trying not to laugh, or enjoy the feel of his strong arms around her and the heat of his body against hers, she pried his fingers off and held his left hand out. "Pay attention. I'm only going to show you once, and if I feel anything against my ass, this pole will go up yours."

"*Mm*. Kinky."

A laugh tumbled out. "*Why* am I doing this again?"

"Because it's way more fun than working."

"Isn't this work?"

Ouch. That stung, but it was true. "Yeah, yeah. Are you going to show me how to hold the club, or are you just going to stand there enjoying the feel of my body? I'm starting to feel objectified."

"Shut up, or I'm going to tell Shea no more dates unless they include a muzzle." They both laughed, and she guided his left hand to the club. "Think you can stop acting like a kid and pay attention?"

"I hate to tell you this, but that's all your fault, sweetheart. You bring out the kid in me."

"Then maybe we need a muzzle *and* a paddle to keep you in line."

"There you go again, luring me in with kink."

She'd walked right into that one.

"For the record. I prefer a bare-handed slap," he whispered, low and gravelly in her ear. "I'm sure you will, too."

She closed her eyes against the warmth climbing up her core.

"Having trouble concentrating?"

Her eyes flew open. "*No*. I was trying to delete the image you made me conjure of Jacinda slapping your bare ass."

"Jealous?"

"Hardly."

"Well, she never slapped my ass. No woman has, at least not in that way. But I'd welcome it from you."

"Please stop talking" came out irritatingly breathy. "Can we just focus on your grip?"

"I thought you'd never ask." He squeezed her against him.

"Your grip on the club!" She pried his hands off again. "God, you're frustrating. This is your last chance."

"Okay. I promise, no more funny talk."

Why did that make her smile?

It took far too much effort to redirect her focus back to showing him how to grip the club, but she managed. "You want to align your left hand so the grip runs from the edge of your pinkie, where it meets your palm, to the middle of your index finger, and wrap your hand around the shaft."

"I can attest to the fact that you're very good at that."

"Hush." She couldn't stop grinning as she moved his left hand into position. "Don't hold it too tight, and your thumb goes on top."

As she aligned his thumb, he said, "You can't even call this thing a shaft. It's more like a toothpick."

She laughed. "Pay attention." She showed him how to angle the club. "Now bring your right hand over." She guided his right hand into place. "You want to grip it so the fat part of your palm is on top of your other thumb."

"Did you just palm shame me?"

She laughed. "How does it feel?"

"Palm shaming? It feels bad, actually. You should never do that again, to anyone."

"Raz!"

"I wish you'd call me Duncan."

Come on, sweetheart. Say Duncan, burned through her thoughts, sending a shudder of heat through her. "Can you *please* concentrate? How does it feel?"

"You feel good." He pressed his warm lips to her cheek, whispering, "Never know who's watching."

She ached to turn into that kiss and taste his lips as she had the other night, but he was too easy to get carried away with. "Do you see any photographers?"

"I don't know. The only thing I'm looking at is the view down your body and your hands on mine. Although I'm wishing your hands were on my shaft, not that one."

Holy smokes.

She broke his grip and stepped aside, hating the rush of cooler air on her back. But if she was going to get through this without tearing his clothes off, she needed space. "Okay, you do it."

He looked down at his zipper and arched a brow. "Here?"

"*Raz.*" Great. Now she was thinking about getting naked with him in public, and for some crazy reason, it turned her on. This guy was his own brand of tequila. His words went down easy, but they stacked up, chipping away at her resolve one seductive sentence at a time. "Grip the damn club, and don't say a word." When he did, she adjusted his hands. "Okay, take a few practice swings, and *no* dirty talk."

The bastard didn't say a word, but he dragged those electric-blue eyes down the length of her and licked his lips, making her pulse quicken. She pressed her lips together, motioning for him to practice, and folded her arms over her chest. After a few practice swings, she taught him how to hit the ball, and he was just as playful during that lesson.

By the time she went back to her own area, she could barely

concentrate.

Luckily, she didn't have to concentrate for long, because Raz said, "I give up."

Finally. Now she could end this playful torture, go home, and get her head on straight.

They returned the clubs, and he pulled out his phone, scrolling through it. "Great. They have bowling. Let's go."

"Bowling? I thought we were done."

"Nope. I've got to be better than you at something. My male ego is fragile."

She didn't know how much more of his charm or this fun she could take. Why couldn't he just be the arrogant jerk she'd thought he was? "Seriously. We can *say* you were better than me."

He stopped walking, his expression serious. "So you can tell Shea and your besties that you kicked my ass? No way. I'm great at bowling. We're going."

RAZ TURNED OUT to be a damn good bowler, but Leni refused to be one-upped by him. She challenged him to laser tag, and when she blew him away, he dared her to play one-on-one basketball. After *that* losing fiasco, she dared him to play arcade games and won four out of five. She was feeling pretty sassy about it until he dragged her to the batting cages. She did great, but not as great as Mr. Grand Slam.

Nearly three hours after heading to the bowling alley, they stumbled out of the rock-wall area in fits of laughter. "I was *this close* to beating you up that last wall," he insisted, and hooked an arm around her neck, pulling her against his side. "Let me guess, your family used to scale the cliffs on Silver Island."

"No, we did *not*. I told you I was scrappy." She'd stopped fighting his hand-holding, arms around her, and stolen kisses in the arcade. It was a losing battle anyway. The more she'd fought, the more aggressively he'd taunted her with dirty talk. The guy was determined to make everyone around them believe they were a couple, and he was so good at it, she had to remind herself it was fake. "You know what this means, don't you?"

"That I should have done more digging about your athletic abilities before today?"

"Live and learn," she teased. "Now you have to feed me, and as the overall winner, I get to choose the place."

"All right. What are you thinking?"

"You'll see." She was actually looking forward to a fun night with him.

"Do we need to change our clothes?"

"And expend more calories being chased around my apartment? I don't think so."

"So I guess you weren't thinking about *Chez Leni*. I hear the breakfast-in-bed option is unforgettable."

If he only knew how right he was. "Come on, dreamer. Let's get a cab and lose whoever's been taking our pictures."

She hadn't seen a single photographer, but she'd received several texts from family and friends with pictures of her and Raz throughout the day. There was a picture of her leaning on him in Central Park, of them eating ice cream, and of them laughing on the piers. There was even a series of pictures from the batting cages, with Raz crooking his finger, like he was going to tell her a secret, and another of Leni putting her ear to the net. They caught her gleeful surprise when he'd grabbed her through the net and kissed the living daylights out of her. Shea had texted, saying she loved how natural they looked together, and Jules had sparked a slew of group family texts by sending a number of the photos and several smiling emojis with hearts around them, which prompted private messages from Indi, Levi, and Archer.

An hour later they were exiting an elevator at Skyline Six, an open-rooftop pub surrounded by glass panels, with stone planters overflowing with autumn blooms and twinkling lights overhead. Raz stopped cold, his arm tightening around her waist. "We're on the roof."

"I know. Isn't it cool? They have the best pizza, and we got here just in time. Look." She pointed to a poster announcing tonight's comedy show. "It's seat yourself, but let's check out the view before we sit down."

"Nah. If you've seen it once, you've seen it a million times. Let's grab a table in the middle." He guided her toward a table.

"You've been here before?" She was disappointed. He'd surprised her with so many fun things today, she was hoping to show him something new and exciting, too.

"No."

"Then you've got to see the view. It's incredible, and it'll give you a whole new appreciation for the city."

"You're the only view I need." He wasn't even looking at her. His eyes were downcast.

"Are you okay?" She lowered her voice. "Is there someone here you want to avoid?" She looked around, but she didn't see anyone taking pictures or staring at them.

"I'm fine. I'm just hungry, and the show's about to start." He finally met her gaze, but the jovial light in his eyes she'd gotten used to seeing was gone.

"Okay, let's sit down and get some pizza. Are you one of those people who get cranky when they don't eat? Archer is like that, too. I get it."

He didn't respond, but they found a table and ordered a mushroom pizza and drinks. The drinks arrived quickly, and Raz scooted his chair closer to Leni, draping an arm around her as they chatted about their day. He gloated about his wins, and she teased him, and when she gloated, he toasted her. Their pizza arrived at the same time as the comedy show began. When the applause died down, the comedian, a thin, bearded man with a youthful face said, "How's everyone doing tonight?"

People called out, "Great!" "Fine!" "I suck!"

"You suck, huh?" The comedian laughed. "Hey, ladies, you looking for an honest man? Or maybe he's into dudes. Check him out, guys, he *sucks*." Laughter rang out, and he paced the stage. "I tried to get my wife to come with me tonight, but last time she was at a show, she got jealous that I lasted more than three minutes." More chuckles ensued. "So here we are in the Big Apple. Who's from the city?"

Hands shot up, and whistles and applause sounded.

"How many of you who *didn't* raise your hand got mugged today?" There was a rumble of laughter. "I'm just a small-town farm boy, and I've gotta be honest, city people scare me. Half of y'all are talking into earpieces, and I swear this is what comes to mind." He puts his hand on his ear, like he's talking into a headset, and lowered his voice. "I've got the one in the black jacket. You bump into him, and I'll swipe his wallet." He waggled his finger at the crowd. "That's why I keep my wallet in my underwear. Ain't nobody going after that. Hell, my wife hasn't been in there in years."

Leni and Raz laughed along with the crowd.

"Now I know why this is the city that never sleeps. Everyone's afraid to close their eyes," the comedian said. "I couldn't get by on no sleep. I'm getting up there in age. I'm thirty-eight, but I'm proud to say I'm finally working on bettering myself. Anyone else in therapy?" There were a few mumbles from the crowd. He lowered his voice. "Yeah, yeah, I know. The rest of y'all are in therapy, too, but don't worry. I won't out you." Then, louder, he said, "My therapist says I need to practice more self-love, but I've already got calluses on both hands. What does she want from me?"

He went on, earning laughs, a few heckles, and giving it right back to the crowd. The pizza must have done the trick, because Raz was all smiles.

"I'm digging this rooftop venue. How about you?" the comedian asked. People clapped and cheered. "Anyone afraid of heights?"

Leni noticed Raz looking down again, almost like he wished he could disappear. The pieces started falling into place. She touched his leg. "Are you afraid of heights?"

He winced and held up his finger and thumb about an inch apart. "A little bit."

"Ohmygod. Why didn't you tell—"

"Here we go, ladies and gents." The comedian looked directly at Raz. "We've got a big handsome guy over here who is afraid of heights."

Leni's stomach clenched.

"Dude, you're not just handsome. I'd switch teams for this guy. Look at him," the comedian said. "It's no wonder he's got the hottest babe in here. Wait, you look familiar. Do I know you?"

Leni covered Raz's hand with hers, squeezing it apologetically, wishing she hadn't said anything.

"That's Raz, the actor!" a woman shouted from across the room, and out came the cell phones, pointing at them as murmurs of "*Raz*," moved through the crowd.

Raz gave a winning smile and waved at the gawkers. Then he looked at Leni and lifted her hand, pressing a kiss to the back of it. Damn, he knew how to play the game.

"Are there any stuntmen here in need of a job?" the comedian called out. "We all know this guy doesn't do his own stunts." Chuckles rose around them. "Let me ask you something, Raz. Does fear of heights carry over to the bedroom? I guess the BDSM swing is out of the question."

The crowd howled with laughter, and Raz seemed to take it in stride, laughing along with them. But Leni's protective urges surged. He was *her* fake boyfriend, damn it, and even though it went against everything she knew she should do, she wanted to cut the comedian off at the knees and couldn't stop herself from saying, "Who needs a BDSM swing when this man knows his way around silk ties?"

Raz turned a scorching gaze on her as the crowd hooted and hollered. He leaned closer, said, "That was the sexiest damn thing I've ever heard," and kissed her.

The crowd went wild, and the comedian called out, "Damn, I'm trading in my swing for silk ties!" causing more applause and shouts.

The show was great, and afterward, Raz signed autographs and graciously allowed fans to take pictures with him. Although he didn't let Leni escape the cameras, keeping her by his side for every photo. She played along, and it was strange how she wasn't getting used to having her picture taken, but she *was* getting used to being by Raz's side. She hadn't thought she was capable of putting work out of her mind and just enjoying herself. She couldn't remember the last time she'd done that. But they'd had so much fun together, she hadn't thought about work even once.

But she wasn't really doing that, was she?

He was an assignment, after all, and despite his comments about kissing her and how much he enjoyed hanging out with her, she knew exactly how this would go. He was just making the best of a situation, too, and once he left to film his new movie, she'd be a mere blip on his radar, easily forgotten, while thoughts of him had already taken root.

"I REALLY AM sorry for outing your fear of heights," Leni said for the millionth time as they walked into her apartment. Indi had texted her on the cab ride home, telling her to check social media and that she was glad Archer didn't have social accounts. Leni and Raz had briefly scrolled through a few sites on the cab ride home, and they'd seen dozens of pictures of them, a video of the comedian making jokes about Raz's fear of heights, and a video of Leni coming to his defense. She'd sparked a media frenzy about the two of them using silk ties. One she was sure she'd have a hard time getting out from under. She could handle that. She didn't live in the spotlight like Raz did, and *that* was what she worried about.

"Don't give it another thought," he said. "I told you I don't give a damn what strangers think of me."

"If you didn't, then we wouldn't need to keep up this ruse."

He drew her into his arms, gazing happily into her eyes. "Are you going to tell me you didn't have fun today?"

"No. I enjoyed kicking your ass."

He laughed. "But you didn't enjoy the kisses, or holding my hand, or laughing like you didn't have a care in the world?"

I loved it all, and I like the way you're looking at me right now, which is why you need to leave. There was only one other guy she could ever remember having that much fun with, and he'd crushed her. That wasn't a heartache she was ever going to open herself up to again. Lifting her chin with resolve, she said, "Those things were okay, too."

"You are a stubborn girl."

"I just don't fawn over guys." She stepped out of his arms.

"You went to bat for me, sweetheart. I can't remember the last time a woman stood up in my defense. You know what that means?"

She arched a brow. "That I'm a loyal employee who won't let Shea's client be publicly put down?"

"As true as that probably is, I doubt it extends only to work relationships. I bet you gave Wells a verbal lashing for hurting Abby."

"So? That's what friends are for."

"Exactly, which is why I don't believe what you did was only out of obligation. That sweet heart of yours cares about me."

She rolled her eyes and went to get his bag from beside the couch before he had a chance to further analyze her. "My heart is anything but sweet, and you know that."

"You're wrong. I think your heart has a tender side that you keep very well hidden."

Time to shore up those walls before X-ray vision over here saw even more of her. "You must be confusing me with someone else." She dropped his bag at his feet. "I guess I'll see you next week at the restaurant opening."

"You can't just throw me to the wolves," he said with a laugh. "If I leave now, they'll think I'm not getting any, and you know the media will have a field day with that after your silk-tie comment."

She crossed her arms against the truth of his assessment. Why did she have to come to his defense? "*Fine.* But you're sleeping on the couch." She stalked to the linen closet, wondering how the hell she was supposed to keep things in perspective if he was in the same frigging apartment. Grabbing linens and a pillow, she tossed them on the couch. "I'm going to get changed."

She closed the bedroom door and headed into the bathroom. As she pinned up her hair, chiding herself for agreeing to let him stay, she heard the shower in the other bathroom running. She tried not to think about him naked, just on the other side of that drywall. Images flew into her mind of his big hand stroking his cock as he thought of her, gritting his teeth as he brought himself to orgasm, growling out her name. She shook her head, angry with herself, and turned on the cold water in the shower.

She stepped beneath the frigid spray and rinsed off her makeup and the grime of the city, trying to distract herself from thoughts of him jerking off. But she was too needy for him. Even the cold water wasn't dousing the flames. Giving in, she turned on the hot water, and as it warmed, she closed her eyes, envisioning his hand around his cock, and slid her hand between her legs. She was already slick, and she didn't have to reach far for memories of their night together or the feel of his hands on her breasts, his mouth on her pussy. She moaned, her legs flexing. She was close. *So close.* She imagined his cock buried deep inside her and thrust two fingers into her pussy, using her other hand on her swollen clit, working herself into a thrusting, moaning frenzy. Her orgasm barreled toward her, and Raz's voice growled in her ear, *Say my name, sweetheart. Say*

Duncan. She clamped her mouth shut, silently shouting, *Duncan, Duncan, Duncan* in her mind.

She leaned against the wet tiles, trying to catch her breath. That took the edge off, but she desperately wanted another night of scorching-hot sex with the only man who had ever fully satisfied her. But after the effect *one* night with him had had on her and how she'd felt when the comedian had joked about him, she knew sex with Raz would be a tightrope, and she couldn't chance falling off the wrong side.

She finished showering and changed into sweats and a baggy T-shirt, leaving her hair up in a messy bun, and glanced in the mirror. There was nothing sexy about what she had on, and without makeup, her fair skin made her look a little washed out, like a faded photograph.

The perfect man deterrent.

She grabbed the extra blanket from the foot of her bed and headed out of the bedroom.

Raz was sitting in his boxer briefs, one arm stretched across the back of the couch, feet propped on the coffee table, crossed at the ankle. She heard the television and wondered what he was watching. But he wore a ridiculously sexy grin, and his eyes were trained on her and full of dirty promises that made her feel like he could read the thoughts she was working so hard to keep at bay. She tried to ignore the flutter in her chest, but as she passed the hall bath, she caught a whiff of his body wash. *Jesus, what's that scent? Potent Male? Guaranteed to melt panties with a single sniff?*

"Well, that's hardly fair," he said as she handed him the blanket.

"What? It's a great blanket."

"Not that." He motioned toward her. "You're just trying to

turn me on with that fresh-faced, adorably freckle-nosed girl-next-door look."

"Yeah, *right*. I'm going to get some ice cream, and then I'll be out of your hair."

"Strawberry?" He licked his lips, raising his brows.

She knew how lethal that tongue was to her willpower. "Definitely not." She sauntered into the kitchen and took a pint of chocolate chip ice cream out of the freezer. She grabbed a spoon and leaned against the doorframe, watching the highlights of the Mets game.

"Come watch with me." He patted the cushion beside him.

"I'm good over here."

He grinned. "Afraid to get too close? I am pretty irresistible."

"*No*. I'm going to bed."

"After you eat, right?" He crooked his finger and patted the cushion again.

She relented and plopped down beside him. He put his arm around her, pulling her against his side.

"There are no cameras in here," she pointed out.

"I don't want to fall out of practice. Are you going to share that, or what?"

She held up her spoon without looking at him, and as he took it and scooped out ice cream, she said, "The Mets played great today. Guess they didn't need their lucky charm after all."

"I was thinking of them. They felt my mojo."

"You have an answer for everything."

"I'm like Yoda," he said in a low, serious voice. "Very wise."

"Wiseass maybe."

They shared the ice cream as they watched the rest of the highlights and talked about the game. Leni had plenty of male friends she could watch a game with or eat ice cream with, but she'd never had this type of easy camaraderie with a man she wanted to get naked with. She and Wells had been friends when they were together, but not like this. They were teenagers with teenage issues, not adults with jobs and stresses to manage. They were still friends, but he'd soiled her trust, and their friendship would always carry an edge because of it. Then there was Kip…

But that hadn't been real, either.

She'd just found out too late.

At least this time she was prepared. She knew that while the friendship she and Raz were developing might be real, and the sex was out of this world, anything more was not possible or wanted.

He scooped out the last of the ice cream and held the spoon out for her.

"Don't you want it?" she asked.

"A gentleman only takes the last bite in bed."

His smoldering look had her contemplating letting him do just that, but her previous thought barged in, tamping down that impetuous desire. "Why do you have to be so good at this fake boyfriend thing?" She ate the last bite, pushed to her feet, and carried the empty container into the kitchen.

"Want to watch a movie?"

That sounded like fun, and she wasn't tired, but fun with Raz was dangerous. "No thanks. I'm going to bed." *Before I lose my ability to resist you.* She tossed the spoon into the sink with a loud *clank* and threw out the container. "See you in the morning." She didn't look back as she marched down the hall and into her bedroom. She went to close the door, then hesitated. Was it rude to close the door all the way? Would it look like she didn't trust him if she left it open?

Why was this so complicated?

She trusted him a lot more than she trusted herself with him.

She left the door ajar, turned off the light, and climbed into bed. She closed her eyes, but their day played like a movie in flashes of them laughing, hitting baseballs, climbing the rock wall, and egging each other on at the arcade. She saw him pulling her into his arms for kiss after kiss and remembered exactly how good and right each one felt.

With a huff, she squeezed her eyes shut, trying to block out the images, and heard Raz walking down the hall. Her eyes flew open, and she froze. The hall bathroom door closed, and a minute later she heard the toilet flushing and the sink running. When the bathroom door opened, she heard him step into the hall and saw his shadow, just standing there. She held her breath, the vixen on her shoulder hoping he'd come into her room, the rational-thinking girl on the other shoulder willing him away.

His footsteps retreated to the living room, and she breathed a sigh of relief but couldn't deny the burn in the pit of her stomach.

RAZ LAY ON the couch, amused by his current situation. Who would believe one of Hollywood's hottest actors was being forced to spend a night on the couch pretending to have slept with a woman for the paparazzi's sake? He could hardly believe it himself, and he sure as hell wouldn't have stuck around for anyone else, but he and Leni had a connection that went far beyond sexual attraction, and he liked being in her orbit. But he didn't understand why she was trying to deny it. She was a realist. She knew what this was, just as he did. So why didn't she just give in to it and accept that it had a termination date? Most women would jump at the chance to be with him, even if temporary. He understood protecting her heart, but they could have fun without hurting each other. Hell, his walls were as thick as bricks, but she was slithering between them, and he was enjoying it for what it was. A few weeks of happiness before diving back into the acting scene? He'd take it.

His phone vibrated on the coffee table. He snagged it and opened the text from Beau, wishing he could tell him about his situation. They'd have a good laugh over it.

Beau: *Char is threatening to kill me if I don't find out what's going on with you and your new girl.*

Raz: *Tell Char I said she can't put these details in a book.*

Beau: *Already did.*

Raz: *Tell her one date turned into more, and we'll see where it goes.*

Beau: *Got it. You okay? You want to talk?*

Raz: *No. I'm good. I'm with Leni now. How are you?*

Beau: *Never better. Go have fun. We'll catch up another time.*

His friendship with Beau had been shattered after Tory had died, and Raz had wondered if they'd ever get it back. They'd crossed paths a few years ago and had lain all their painful cards on the table. It hadn't been easy to mend their broken fences, but friendships like theirs were once-in-a-lifetime, and they'd both finally gotten their heads out of their asses and had fought for it.

Raz scrolled through the pictures of Leni he'd taken that afternoon. She was so damn adorable with her brows pinched in concentration as she swung at the baseball, and her eyes lit up when she threw her arms in the air after getting a solid hit. He just wanted to be near her, even if it led nowhere. He wanted to soak her up from dusk until dawn, her energy, her challenge, that smile that held a world of snark and seduction. He ached for her company, and that was something he'd never experienced before. He'd thought he'd be able to stop thinking about her after she went to bed, but that was almost an hour ago, and his thoughts were still circling her.

Was she thinking about him, too?

He looked down the hall at her bedroom door, which was ajar. "Hey, princess, you awake?" he called out in a hushed voice.

"I'm not a princess."

He grinned at her attitude. She wasn't a princess in the sense that she expected people to bow at her feet. But she carried herself with a rare mix of self-respect, confidence, and class that demanded attention and that he found painfully attractive. "What are you doing?" he called out.

"Trying to sleep. What do you think I'm doing?"

He could think of a few things he'd like to *see* her doing. "Are you tired?"

A long silence stretched between them. "Not really."

Well, damn, no need to suffer alone. He had an idea, but he needed something to strengthen his case. He headed into the kitchen to raid her pantry. But a quick scan of the shelves gave up nothing. He'd worked on enough movie sets with women to know they all hid their favorite snacks. He had a feeling Leni would keep them close to where she spent most of her time.

He circled back through the living room and headed for her office. He felt a little guilty opening the desk drawers but told himself it was for good reason. *Bingo.* He grabbed the box of Cheez-Its and his pillow from the couch, snagged a bottle of water from the fridge, and headed down the hall to her bedroom.

When he peered in, she lifted her head from the pillow and said, "What are you doing?"

"It's lonely out there."

She sighed. "Don't you sleep alone every night?"

"Not on a strange couch with a woman I enjoy being with right down the hall." He walked closer to the bed. "I thought we could have a slumber party. I brought snacks, and I promise to keep my hands to myself."

"Are those my Cheez-Its?" She sat up, looking at him with shock and irritation. "I did *not* invite you to snoop through my drawers and steal my snacks." She reached for the box.

He pulled it back. "Is that a yes to the slumber party? Or am I taking these back to my couch?"

Her eyes narrowed.

"Okay. I guess I'll just…" He opened the box, purposely rustling around in it as he turned to leave.

"*Fine*, you can stay, but give me my snacks." She reached for the box again, and he handed it to her. She closed it and stuffed it into her nightstand, mumbling, "You don't mess with a woman's Cheez-Its."

He chuckled as he went to the other side of the bed and threw back the blanket.

"Stay on your side of the bed, and sleep on *top* of the blanket." She put a pillow between them.

He lay on top of the blanket and tucked a hand behind his head. "You don't trust yourself, do you?"

She rolled onto her side with her back to him. "No comment."

Good to know.

He lay next to her, grinning up at the ceiling. "Thanks for hanging with me today. It's been a long time since I've had that much fun."

"Mm-hm."

"It reminded me of when I was a kid and it seemed like the days were endless. It must've been like that for you, too, with such a big circle of family and friends."

"Pretty much."

"God, I miss it, you know? Not having to worry about what other people think every time I open my mouth."

Her phone vibrated on the nightstand. She grabbed it and rolled onto her back as she read the text.

"Booty call?"

"*No.* It's Jules. My parents are watching Joey, so she and Grant are out with Tara and Levi and Indi and Archer." She held up the phone, showing him a picture of the girls, Grant, and Levi squished together, smiling, and Archer, standing behind them, his face serious. The caption said, *Look who we got to come out with us tonight! Mom's watching Joey!*

"Send them a picture of us."

"*Us?* Now?"

"Hell yes. You don't want them to think you don't know how to have fun." He leaned his elbow on her pillow. "Come on. I'll take it. My arm is longer."

"Fine." She handed him the phone and leaned closer, giving him bunny ears, as he took the picture, then immediately snagged her phone back, thumbing out a message.

"What are you writing?"

"Why do you care, nosy?"

"Just curious."

"I said I wished I were there, too, but I was busy working." Her phone vibrated, and another text popped up from Jules, with an eggplant emoji, a peach, and a flame.

"Is that what they think you do for work? Well, I sure had the wrong impression."

She pushed his chest. "Stop reading my texts, and get back to your side of the bed so I can set her straight."

He moved to his side and leaned on his elbow, watching her.

"I'm turning my phone off or she'll go on all night." She set her phone on the nightstand and lay on her back.

"Archer didn't look thrilled to be out."

"He likes going out and being with friends, but he always looks like that unless he's looking at Indi."

"That says a lot about his love for her. He's the tough, big-hearted brother who showed you around the city, right?"

"Yeah."

Raz thought about their conversations and circled back to one of the things he'd been wondering about. "You alluded to having been let down by your older siblings. Has he ever let you down?"

She went quiet again.

"I don't mean to be nosy. It helped to hear your view on being a younger sister, and I was just thinking maybe I could do the same for you."

"He has let me down," she said softly.

"In the same way I let Tory down?"

"I wish it were only that, but it was worse. It wasn't only him, and I wasn't the only one who suffered."

"I'm sorry to hear that. Are things better now?"

"Yes, but getting there was awful." She was quiet again for a few minutes, and when she spoke, her voice was soft, thoughtful. "Archer lost his best friend, Kayla, and blamed Jock for it. But it wasn't Jock's fault. Jock loved her, too. We all did. She was a special person. But that blame he placed on Jock led to a rift that kept Jock away from the island and turned Archer into a different person. The rift lasted for a decade, but it felt like a lifetime."

Her pain was so raw, he wanted to pull her into his arms and soothe it, but he knew he shouldn't. "Loss changes people, and when you're grieving, you can say all sorts of things you don't mean. It can go a hundred different ways, and none of them are easy."

She rolled onto her side, her sad eyes meeting his. "It was the worst thing I've ever gone through."

"What happened?"

"Jock and Kayla were living together here in the city, and they were in a car accident. She was thirty-four weeks pregnant. Kayla didn't survive, and their baby took his last breath in Jock's arms." A tear slipped down her cheek.

"Fucking car accidents. Come here, sweetheart." He tore the damn pillow out from between them and threw it to the floor, pulling her into his arms. "I'm sorry you had to go through that." He stroked her back, his heart breaking for her, and the pain from the stormy night Tory was killed rushed in. "How long ago did it happen?"

"I was still in high school, and my whole family was falling apart. I was mad at Archer for blaming Jock and at Jock for abandoning us, and I didn't understand why my parents couldn't make them fix it."

Gutted, he held her tighter. No wonder she protected herself with everything she had. She was so young to have lost not only a friend she cared about but the brothers she knew and loved and the stability of the very foundation on which she relied. Pile Wells's betrayal on top of that, and it was a wonder she trusted at all. How much heartache could one teenage girl take?

"They probably couldn't have fixed it. That's a lot of grief for everyone to process, including them. And it's not only grief but survivor's guilt, too. It's a bitch. If you were in high school, your brothers were, what? In their early twenties?"

She nodded, sniffling.

"They were young men, babe, making their own decisions and mistakes and, I'd imagine, battling overwhelming grief over losing each other, too. If it's true what they say about the bond between twins, then cutting ties and walking away couldn't have happened without its own pain."

"I know. It just sucked. Everyone on the island was grieving for Kayla and the baby, and Archer was pissed at the world, and Jock basically disappeared. My whole family was on edge, trying to figure out how to deal with the loss and the wreckage of our family. We were so close, and all of a sudden Archer was still there on the island, but he wasn't really there, and we almost never saw Jock. When we did, Archer couldn't be around him without wanting to kill him. We were all trying not to pick sides and, at the same time, feeling like if we were with one or the other of them, we *were* picking sides, so it added all this guilt and even more anger."

His chest constricted. "I can only imagine how awful that was." He kissed the top of her head. "It must have been devastating to see two brothers who you probably thought were too strong to ever falter fall apart and know they were unable to protect themselves from that pain. You said you felt abandoned by Jock, but while Archer stayed on the island, it sounds like he emotionally abandoned everyone, too."

She looked up at him, glassy-eyed. "You sound like a therapist."

He wiped her tears with the pad of his thumb, glad she wasn't pulling away. "I paid good money to my therapist. I hope I learned something." That earned a small smile. "I know how much it hurts to have someone you love *choose* to disappear from your life. It's a different type of pain than losing someone to death, but it's just as real."

"Did someone do that to you?"

"Yeah. When we lost Tory, Beau took off without so much as a goodbye. I was devastated. I can't remember a time that he and I weren't as thick as thieves. We were always there for each other, and then he was just…gone."

"You were abandoned by your best friend when you needed him most?"

"Yeah, so I get it. I didn't have any other siblings, but I could always count on Beau, and if not him, then his family. But they were also falling apart. Zev broke it off with Carly and then he disappeared, too."

"Did they at least go together?"

"No. They headed in different directions, for different reasons."

"That's awful for them, and for you. I would have been lost without Levi and my sisters. How did you deal with that?"

"The only way I could. I had graduated from college and was in Maryland figuring out my next step when the accident happened. I stuck around for my parents as long as I could, but there were too many memories of Tory everywhere. We didn't know she was flying in. She called me to pick her up from the airport, but I was on a date and didn't answer the call. I found out later that she'd called all of us—my parents, Beau, Carly— and no one answered. That's why she'd taken a cab." His throat thickened with emotion. "I would have sold my soul to change places with her, and that made it harder for my parents, but I couldn't get my arms around it. I fought going to therapy, because…well, survivor's guilt. One day my mother told me to go live out my dreams because Tory couldn't and that's what she'd want. I'll never forget the determination in my mother's voice or the single confirmatory nod from my father. I think they needed me to leave and not wallow my life away as much as they knew I needed that. Eventually I went to LA and buried myself in auditions and work, but I was still lost. At the suggestion of my agent, I got a good therapist, and she helped me realize that those memories that hurt so badly were the very things I needed to be grateful for."

"Boy, isn't that the truth. Have you and Beau seen each other since then?"

"We didn't for many years, but I ran into him in Maryland a few years ago, and we finally talked about everything. Grief can bury a person, and that's what it did to him, until he met Charlotte, and she somehow saved him from it." He hadn't talked like this with anyone, ever, and he paused to pull himself together. "Have you talked with your brothers about how things went down and how you felt about it?"

"Do I seem like the kind of person who can keep my thoughts to myself?"

"Definitely not." He laughed softly, glad for the reprieve. "How'd that work out for you?"

"For *me* it was a relief, but Archer might feel differently. It wasn't exactly a onetime event. Every time I tried to talk to him about what happened, he refused, and that made me even madder. I gave him hell dozens of times, hit him a few times, and cussed him out a few hundred times. He took it but refused to engage, which was *infuriating*. His silence fueled my rage. I felt like he was denying the position he put everyone in, but no matter how much hell I brought down on him, every single time I walked away, he'd called after me, saying he loved me." Teary-eyed again, she wiped them dry. "The arrogant jerk."

Raz smiled and hugged her against him.

"I know now that Archer didn't know how to deal with his own emotions, much less mine, but even if I'd known that back then, it wouldn't have stopped me. I was too upset."

"That's understandable. And with Jock?"

"It was different with him. He was just as broken as Archer, but when I talked, he listened and heard everything I said. It didn't bring him back home over the years, but there was no need to yell, because, for Jock, words were everything. They held weight, and I could see their impact. He didn't talk about what happened either, but he said he was sorry and that he couldn't come back, because he saw the island as Archer's home after the fight, and he'd caused him enough pain." She rested her head on his shoulder.

"Like I said, survivor's guilt is a bitch. I'm glad things are better now."

"I can't believe I cried in front of you."

"I hate to tell you this, beautiful, but you're only human after all."

"If you tell anyone, I'll have to kill you." She was quiet for a few minutes. "Hey, Raz?" she whispered sleepily.

"Yeah."

"I've never told anyone outside my family any of those things."

Her trust made that tug he'd felt in his chest even more prominent. "I've never told anyone but Beau how much his leaving hurt, either. Your secrets are safe with me."

Taking her hand, he pressed a kiss to her palm and placed it on his chest, covering it with his own. He lay listening to the even cadence of her breathing, thinking about how much of herself she'd shared with him and how good it felt to be there for her and share his own secrets. He was starting to understand why she said she wasn't built for love, and it was painfully similar to the way he felt. He had never met anyone who truly understood what it felt like to not only lose his sister but his best friend, too.

He stroked a hand down her back and threaded his fingers into the ends of her hair, putting the pieces of the sweet, sensual tigress in his arms together. As she dozed off, her body melted against him. He closed his eyes, soaking in the feel of her, and whispered, "You're something special, princess, and I'm really glad you're in my life."

Ten

LENI AWOKE TO the feel of a warm hand beneath her sweats, resting on her ass, and her body draped over Raz like a blanket. Her face was tucked into the crook of his neck, her arm lay across his stomach, fingers resting on his nipple. Her leg was stretched over both of his, her thigh balancing on his morning wood. Warmth spread through her core with that realization. He smelled incredible and felt even better. She didn't want to move, and at the same time, she knew every second she spent enjoying this man took her deeper down the Duncan Raz rabbit hole.

He stretched, squeezing her butt, his other arm wrapping firmly around her, trapping her in place. He kissed her forehead and said, "Morning, princess," gravelly and lazy, like it was the most natural thing in the world to wake up together.

"Sorry for sleeping all over you." She tried to move, but he didn't let her.

"That was the best sleep I've ever had. You are the cashmere of human blankets."

It was the best she'd slept, too, but she kept that to herself as he shifted onto his side, keeping their bodies flush. He withdrew his hand from within her sweats and positioned his arm so she could use it as a pillow. *Thoughtful.* His other hand was quick to sneak beneath her sweats and palm her butt. He pressed his lips to hers, and she closed her eyes, enjoying the praise, the kiss, and the feel of his hard length against her. What could it hurt to allow herself a little pleasure from this man who not only knew how to bring it but who had the unusual ability to make her forget her responsibilities and have fun?

She arched against him, and he took the hint, holding her tighter as he deepened the kiss. He pushed his knee between her legs, rubbing her neediest parts. She moaned, craving the friction. He rolled her onto her back, grinding his cock against her center.

"More," she pleaded against his lips.

He shifted his big body, moving his hand from her ass to between her legs. "You're so wet for me. I've missed touching you," he said gruffly, taking her in another mind-numbing kiss as he teased her into a moaning, rocking frenzy of desire. She clawed at his back, grabbing his ass as they devoured each other's mouths. When he pushed his fingers inside her, shocks of pleasure ricocheted through her. He was rough and sweet and oh so perfect. He crooked his fingers, using his thumb on her clit, and she tore her mouth away with a gasp.

"Don't stop."

He pushed up her shirt and lowered his mouth to her breast, sucking and taunting as he worked his magic between her legs, making her want and need and beg until she could barely breathe. She fisted her hands in his hair. *"Ohgodohgodohgod."* Her body was on fire, desire stacking up inside her, pulsing and begging for release. A hard *rap* on the apartment door sounded, and her eyes flew open, both of them going still. His eyes met hers, brows knitted.

"Don't you dare stop," she warned. "It's probably my neighbor's groceries."

He grinned and slicked his tongue over her sensitive nipple. She sucked in air between clenched teeth, bowing off the bed.

A pounding on the door rang out. "Open the fucking door, Leni!"

She froze. "*Crap*. It's Archer! I'm going to kill him. Stay here." She ran to the bathroom, quickly cleaned up, and stalked through the living room as he pounded on the door again. She threw it open, and Archer pushed past her, his work boots clomping on the hardwood floor, massive chest and arms straining the fabric of his shirt.

"Where is he?" He scanned the living room, the veins in his neck bulging.

"I'm sorry!" Indi said, rushing in after him, long blond hair bouncing over the shoulders of her sweater. "I tried to stop him! He wanted to come last night."

Leni crossed her arms. "What the hell do you think you're doing, Archer?"

"Stopping an asshole from taking advantage of you," he fumed.

"Have you lost your mind?" Leni bit out. "I'm thirty years old. *I* decide what goes on in my life, not you."

"Think I give a shit how old you are?" Archer bit out. "He could be *using* you."

"How do you know *I'm* not using *him*?"

He made a disgusted face.

"Get over yourself," Leni seethed. "Raz isn't even *here*."

"Yes, I am."

Leni spun around and saw him sauntering down the hall in his boxer briefs, with a fucking rascally look in his eyes. *Shit.*

He pushed a hand through his tousled hair. "What's all the commotion, Len Bug?"

"*You*," Archer seethed, hands fisting as he closed the distance between them.

Leni jumped into her brother's path and held up her hand. "*Stop!* Indi, control your beast. Raz, put on your frigging pants."

Raz grabbed his jeans from his bag.

"Sorry, Raz. I tried to thwart this, but at least I brought pastries to soften the blow." With an apologetic expression, Indi held up a pink box from the Sweet Barista.

"I like pastries," Raz said casually as he buttoned his jeans, as if he wasn't the least bit fazed by Archer, standing before him like a bull ready to charge. "You must be Archer. Dude, it's a little early to be pounding on doors, but it's still a pleasure to meet you." He held out his hand. "Duncan Raznick."

Archer ignored his hand, gritting out, "You and I need to talk."

"Sure. We can talk while I whip up some eggs to go with the pastries. Princess, you have eggs, right?"

Before she could respond, Archer grabbed him by the arm, dragging him toward the kitchen. Raz wrenched his arm free, flashing a cool grin. "I doubt Mama Steele forgot to teach you manners." Those eyes narrowed with warning. "You should have paid attention." He tossed Leni a wink. "Have a nice visit with Indi, baby. I'll let you know when the eggs are ready." He strode casually into the kitchen with Archer breathing fire on his heels.

Leni stalked behind them, but Indi grabbed her hand, pulling her toward the office. "Let them have it out."

"Why is he poking the bear? Archer is going to kill him!" Leni snapped.

"No, he's not." Indi closed the office door behind them. "He's much calmer since we got together."

"Did that smoke coming out of his ears look *calm* to you? Archer can tear a man apart in seconds, and Raz makes a living with his face."

"Don't worry. I told Archer if he touched Raz's pretty face, I'd withhold sex for a month."

Leni breathed a sigh of relief. "Thank you, but what the hell? Why didn't you warn me?"

"Have you checked your phone? I called and texted a hundred times, but you were obviously a little busy with your new boy toy. What is up with you two? When you answered the door, you looked like we interrupted you mid—"

"You *did*. I finally give myself permission to enjoy that delicious orgasm master of a man, and now I'll probably have PTSD and freak out every time we're alone. Fucking Archer. Give me one of those." She reached into the box of pastries and took a bite of something chocolaty and doughy. "How did Archer even know he was here?"

"Did you look at the selfie you sent last night? You both look way too happy, and you can clearly see you're in bed together."

"Shit." She took another angry bite and leaned against the windowsill. "We didn't even fool around last night. We stayed up talking and then fell asleep."

"Really?" Indi leaned on the sill beside her. "Why?"

"Because he's *dangerous*, Indi. I didn't think about work *once* yesterday while we were out acting like kids."

"You looked happy."

"I was. He's different than I thought. He's surprisingly fun and annoyingly sexy, and a freaking gentleman to boot. You should hear the cheesy things he says."

Indi raised her brows. "Princess?"

"I know, right?" She couldn't stop her smile. "It's ridiculous, but it's better than what he tried to call me. *Sinful angel.*"

Indi cracked up. "Sounds like he knows you well."

"He does *not*. I'm not a princess, much less an angel." She finished her pastry. "I'm a badass businesswoman."

"Yes, but you could *also* be a princess if you ever let a guy treat you like one."

Leni rolled her eyes. "Like I need *that* nonsense in my life?"

"Why not? You said you like him."

"I do, in the same way I like a new project. He's fun and exciting, but"—*this is all fake*—"he's only here for a few weeks, and we're not like you and Archer. You guys have *more*."

"But you could have more if you wanted it. He seems unflappable. Most guys would've taken one look at Archer's murderous expression and hightailed it out of here."

"Raz is an *actor*. He can fake anything." A good reminder that she couldn't trust the things he said either, because Duncan Raz had mastered the art of pretending. "We should go save him."

As they left the office, Leni heard Raz and Archer arguing but couldn't make out what they were saying. "That can't be good."

"I don't hear any bodies being thrown against a wall," Indi said.

Their voices became clearer as they neared the kitchen. "You're wrong, man," Raz insisted. "I've seen cooking shows, and all the pros say to take the pan off the burner, let the eggs cook for a few seconds, and then put it back on."

"That's bullshit. Fluffiness has nothing to do with that. It has to do with how you whisk the eggs and using milk instead of water. I've watched my mom do it a million times."

Leni and Indi exchanged incredulous glances.

"So it's not just manners you failed to pay attention to? If Mama Steele is as good a cook as you say, there's no way she'd make that mistake. Everyone knows water equals fluff and milk makes eggs creamier."

Leni peered into the kitchen and saw Archer hulking over Raz by the stove.

"Dude, *don't* question my mother or I will slaughter you," Archer warned.

Raz scoffed. "Get your head out of the jungle, King Kong. I'm saying *you're* wrong, not her."

"What the hell…?" Leni asked.

The guys looked over their shoulders, and a sexy grin climbed across Raz's face. "Hey, sweetheart. I'm just setting this silver-backed gorilla straight."

"Fuck off," Archer snapped. "He doesn't know shit about cooking."

"Looks like the orgasm master is a beast tamer, too," Indi whispered as the guys turned back to the stove.

THEY SAID GOODBYE to Archer and Indi an hour later. Leni was still baffled by what had transpired in her kitchen. Archer and Raz had refused to clue her and Indi in over breakfast. Instead, Raz had peppered Indi and Archer with questions about Silver Island, and Archer had invited him to come by to tour the vineyard. Leni had no idea who this version of her brother was.

She closed the door behind them and looked at Raz. "Are you going to spill the beans and tell me how much you paid him or what you promised him in exchange for your life?"

He shrugged. "I have no idea what you're talking about. We talked. We're cool."

"Archer doesn't *talk*."

"I don't know what to tell you, sweetheart." He drew her into his arms and brushed a kiss to her lips. "Feel like finishing what we started before we were so rudely interrupted?"

Yes. But she'd come to her senses and realized how bad an idea it was to dip her toes in Raz's naughty sandbox again. "*No*. You're leaving, too. And don't use the paparazzi as an excuse. If any are lingering outside, they'll think you had a fantastic night."

"You're throwing me out?" He gave her those puppy-dog eyes.

"Yes. Now take last night as a win, grab your bag, and get out of here." *Before I change my mind.*

"You sure that's what you want?" he asked seductively.

"Do you want me to get Archer back here and tell him you're being pushy?"

He looked at her like she'd lost her mind. "I'm not afraid of him."

She opened the door and stuck her head out, spotting Archer and Indi walking into the elevator. "Hey, Archer!"

Archer's hand shot out, holding the doors open. He lifted his chin in question.

"*Okay, okay. I'll go*," Raz whispered urgently.

"Tell Mom and Dad I said hi!" Leni called down the hall. Still holding the door open, she met Raz's gaze. "Guess the acting only goes so far."

He picked up his bag, arrogance replacing the puppy-dog eyes. "You'll miss me when I walk out that door."

"I'll survive, and I'll see you at the restaurant opening later this week."

He hooked an arm around her waist, hauling her into a deep, penetrating kiss that had her knees weakening. She pushed away and nudged him toward the door. "*Go*, please."

He chuckled as he walked out. "I'll miss you too, princess."

She closed the door and leaned her back against it, breathing a sigh of relief. Why was he so hard to resist? She pictured him coming out of the bedroom with his messy hair and sleepy eyes and thought about the way he'd handled Archer without a hint of trepidation. She'd never seen *anyone* handle her brother like that. Was Raz *that* good of an actor, or was he truly unfazed? It bothered her that he wouldn't tell her what had happened between them in the kitchen.

She headed into her bedroom and saw that Raz had made the bed. Memories of yesterday's fun brought a smile, and thoughts of last night's sharing of secrets brought warmth to her chest. *Ugh*. What was wrong with her? She was thinking about him too much again. Where was her willpower? She considered stripping off the sheets to get rid of any lingering scents of him and felt a dull ache deep inside her.

Damn it.

The cocky bastard was right. She did miss him. Thank God for that knock on the door. It had saved her from herself.

Saved by a knock. Ruined by an actor.
What the hell is wrong with me?

Eleven

BEFORE HEADING OUT for his run Tuesday morning, Raz texted Leni to see if she'd join him, just as he had the day before. Yesterday she'd responded with, *I don't run, and even if I did, I wouldn't. Food vendors aren't up this early.* She added a smirking emoji. He'd responded with, *I have something you can eat,* and a devil emoji. Her reply had made him laugh. *Let me know if your penis learns how to emit ice cream or brownies. Until then, keep it in your pants.*

But he wasn't laughing at this morning's shutdown. *I don't run. Heading into my office early.* No cute emojis, no fun banter. The fact that he was bothered by it annoyed the hell out of him.

He must be losing his mind, because it had only been two days since he'd seen her, and he fucking missed her. He and Jacinda had spent weeks thousands of miles apart, and he couldn't remember ever missing her, or any other women he'd dated, like he missed his feisty *fake* girlfriend.

And he didn't just miss her. He missed her with an intensity that had made it difficult for him to concentrate on the script he should be memorizing the last two days. He wanted to hear her laugh, to see that challenge brewing in her eyes, and the seductive sensuality simmering there when he talked dirty to her. He wanted to make her moan and beg and cry out his name as he fucked her six ways to Sunday, and once he'd pleasured the challenge out of her, he wanted to sleep with her in his arms, draped over his body like she was *his*.

That was precisely why, as he jogged down her street, he knew he couldn't stop to see her. If he saw her beautiful face and she laid that ever-ready snark on him, it would be too damn tempting to convince her to finish what they'd started the other morning.

Forcing himself to continue running past her building, he swore he saw that damn photographer/stalker lurking across the street. Did that mean Leni *hadn't* gone to work early? Or had fuckface shown up after she'd already left and not realized it?

Raz jogged down the next block and around the corner, wondering if running past Leni's apartment building and not stopping would fuel that jackass to spin something derogatory about their relationship to gossip sites. It was one thing to write shit about him, but he couldn't stomach reading negative shit about Leni.

He picked up his pace, irritated with the idea.

Leni had seemed to take the silk-tie bullshit in stride, joking that maybe it would help her dating profile. Raz had gritted his teeth against the discomfort *that* had brought. He just had to make it through a few more weeks, and then she'd be free to do whatever she wanted, and he'd be too busy filming to care.

Even so, if that asshole's pictures sparked anything that hurt Leni, he'd tear him apart.

He could hear Leni chiding him for the thought, saying he'd only make things worse. Maybe he could use this situation to his advantage and get some extra time with his wall-building partner in crime.

SHORTLY BEFORE NOON, Raz walked out of the restaurant and climbed into his waiting car. He gave the driver the address to his next destination and thumbed out a text to Leni.

Raz: *Miss me?*

Leni: A GIF popped up of a woman drinking water and spitting it out with a laugh.

Raz chuckled, thumbing out, *I miss you, too. How's my princess?*

Leni: *I'm not your princess, and I'm busy.*

Raz: *How busy? Can I take you to lunch?*

Leni: *I'm working through lunch.* Another message popped up. *Sorry.*

Finally, a crack in her armor. Raz gave the driver new instructions and made a phone call before replying to Leni's text.

Raz: *Dinner tonight?*

Leni: *I'm having dinner with a client.*

Raz: *Drinks afterward?*

Leni: *Sorry, I'll be busy strategizing ways to clear up my reputation from the silk-tie vixen the world believes me to be.*

Raz: *I look forward to proving that reputation correct again very soon. Here's to a brighter day, sweetheart.*

His phone rang, and Patch's name appeared on the screen. "Hey, Patch. What's up?"

"I want to go over your schedule, but did you hear the news about Johnny Bad?" Johnny Bad was a rock star.

"No. I've been busy. Why?"

"His life blew up yesterday. It's all over the media. Apparently he's got a teenage daughter, and the baby mama leaked the story to TMZ after abandoning the kid."

"What a nightmare." Raz was glad he'd always been selective about who he shared a bed with. He wanted kids but sure as hell not like that. "That poor kid. This'll follow her forever."

"No shit. I thought the story might take the heat off you, but he took off in a helicopter and nobody knows where he went."

"That must be why that asshole Singer was in front of Leni's building again this morning."

"That guy has been capitalizing on you forever. We can get some extra security for Leni if you're worried."

"Thanks, but she'd hate that."

"Yeah, she's a tough one. I bet Shea is going crazy. She reps Johnny, you know."

"I didn't know that." But it might explain Leni blowing him off this morning. Although he had a feeling she'd have blown him off anyway.

"I just wanted to make sure you knew what was going down. Did you get the script changes I emailed this morning?"

"Yeah, thanks."

"And you're set for your four o'clock interview with *Men's Fitness.*"

"Yes. Did Shea give you any idea about what they're going to ask?"

"No, but she said it might be helpful if you mentioned how much you enjoy exercising with Leni, now that you two are the new It Couple. I assume your new leading lady will visit you on set next month. Do you want me to make any arrangements?"

The idea of Leni visiting him on set and staying for a few sexy nights was highly appealing. But that wasn't what this was. "Nah, we're just hanging out, having fun. It's not serious."

"Really? I've worked for you for almost three years, and I've never seen the look in your eyes that I see in every picture of the two of you."

Raz gazed out the window. He was trying to keep his emotions in check where Leni was concerned, but she was damn fun to be around. "That's why they pay me the big bucks. I'm an excellent actor."

"Are you shitting me? Those smiles were all fake?"

"No, of course not, but I know how to play it up for the cameras."

"Man, I wish I had that skill. The chicks I go out with would melt at my feet if I looked at them the way you're looking at Leni in most of those pictures. You two look like you've known each other forever."

That was the strange thing about them. She was the most complicated woman he'd ever met, and yet he felt more comfortable around her than he did with anyone else.

As Patch went over Raz's schedule and other business, Raz *wished* he'd known Leni forever. Maybe he could have kept her from going out with Wells, preventing that asshole from breaking her heart, and talked some sense into Archer so she'd never know the pain of her family coming apart at the seams.

"NO COMMENT." LENI hung up on the reporter, cursing under her breath. Shea represented rock star Johnny Bad, whose life just went off the rails. People were coming out of the woodwork trying to gain inside information, and the entire administrative, marketing, and PR staff were picking up the slack for Shea's other clients.

Leni pushed the button that rang her assistant. "Meg?"

"Yeah."

"That last guy you put through wasn't who he said he was. He was a reporter. From now on, if they're not a legitimate, paying client on our current client list, they don't get through. Anyone else, take a message. Try to verify phone numbers before handing them off to me, and I'll get back to everyone as I have time."

"Okay, got it."

"Thank you. I'm knee-deep in prepping for my one thirty meeting and forgot to order lunch. Would you mind ordering me a sandwich?"

"Will do."

"Thanks." Leni ended the call and got back to work, only to be interrupted a few minutes later by a knock at her door. "Yeah?"

Raz strode into her office carrying two enormous bags. His warm smile was a surprisingly nice sight on her chaotic morning. She tucked that thought down deep. "Raz? How did you get past Meg?"

"It's good to see you too, princess." He kissed her cheek. "Don't be mad at Meg. She couldn't help giving in to my charms."

Like every other woman who walks this earth. "What are you doing here?"

"Brightening your day." He carried the bags to the table by the window.

"That's really nice of you, but I don't have time to chat. One of Shea's clients had an emergency, and we're all picking up the slack."

"I know she reps Johnny Bad, and I heard about what happened. I'm not going to stick around, but you still have to eat." He pulled a glass vase with a vibrant bouquet of sunflowers, yellow lilies, orange roses, and other fall blooms out of one of the bags and set it on the table.

She melted a little inside. "You got those beautiful flowers for me?"

"Not a bad fake boyfriend, huh? I know how hard you work, and I also know you rarely take time to enjoy your surroundings. In case you didn't realize it, it's the first week of October, and fall blooms are everywhere. I didn't want you to miss out, so I brought the view to you."

Her thoughts stumbled.

"And since you missed eating Thai food to accompany me to the charity event, I brought your favorite lunch." He reached into the other bag and withdrew a smaller bag from her favorite Thai restaurant. "You can thank Meg for cluing me into your favorite dish, and since we both know you're an ice cream fiend..." He pulled out another bag, this one from Surreal Creamery, one of the best ice cream parlors around. "I know you love strawberry, but I figured with the hellish things you're probably dealing with, Nom Nom Cookie sundae might be a welcome distraction."

Her mouth watered as he set a mason jar full of ice cream on the table.

"This has Monster Cookie ice cream, chocolate crunch, chocolate syrup, Cookie Crisp cereal, marshmallows, and Oreos. It should satisfy your cravings. Well, of the food variety anyway." He winked. "I wasn't sure if you were a whipped cream fan or not, but I am, so I took a shot." He set a can of whipped cream on the table.

Leni could barely breathe for the emotions billowing inside her. Nobody had ever done anything like this for her. "You did this…just because?"

"That depends on what *just because* means to you." He closed the distance between them, looking like he walked out of a dream in jeans and a denim-blue button-down, untucked, sleeves rolled up, exposing those sexy forearms. "I did it because I wanted to see you, and you tried to blow me off." He placed his hands on her hips. "I liked it much better when you were actually blowing me."

She laughed and swatted him, her eyes darting toward her office door.

"Don't worry, princess. That wasn't loud. It just rang some intriguing bells in your mind, so it felt loud."

"In your dreams."

"Fantasies, babe. Dark, *dirty* fantasies."

She laughed softly, shaking her head.

"Seriously, though, consider lunch a thank-you for finding time to help me fix my reputation while you're so busy."

It took everything she had not to say it wasn't a hardship. "Just doing my job."

"You do it well, and as far as the flowers go, try to take some time to enjoy them. As capable as you are, I'm not sure you're taking care of yourself in the ways that matter, or with the same careful care you give your clients."

Everyone knew how hard she worked, and while her family told her she should give herself a break more often, nobody had ever mentioned the little things she'd been missing. She noticed the scenery every time she went home to the island, but in the city, her life was a blur and the scenery, white noise. How a man who had known her on a personal level for only a couple of weeks could see that so clearly was beyond her.

"I've already taken up too much of your time, so I'll get out of your hair," he said. "But you should know one more thing."

She raised her brows in question, afraid if she spoke, she'd tell him not to leave, and she really needed to get back to work.

"That asshole photographer was outside your building when I ran by this morning. He saw me, and I don't know if they'll post something about me running alone or not."

"They already did."

"You saw it?"

"It's my job and my life they're screwing with. Of course I keep tabs on that."

"And?"

"It was nothing. A fluff piece about if you're running from me or if our sexy Saturday—their words, not mine—wore me out."

He grinned. "I'd like to make door number two come true, please."

"And on *that* note, you need to go. Thank you for brightening my day. I will enjoy everything you brought."

"Save some whipped cream for us." He turned to leave and walked right into Shea. "Whoa. Sorry, Shea. I was just leaving."

"Everything okay?" Shea asked.

"Couldn't be better." He winked at Leni and walked out the door.

Shea looked curiously happy. "He's in a good mood."

"Isn't he always?" Leni headed straight for the ice cream and shoveled a spoonful of chocolate into her mouth. "*Mm.* Taste this orgasmic creation." She held a spoonful out for Shea.

"Did he bring you all this?" She ate a bite, delight showing in her smile.

"Yes, but don't make a big deal out of it. I think you created a monster when you told him we should be seen together as much as possible and tipped off the press on Saturday." She ate another spoonful.

"Tipped off the press? What are you talking about?"

"It's okay. He told me you guys had lunch Friday and you said I could use a break from work over the weekend and tipped off the press."

"We had lunch, and he told me he wanted to see you over the weekend, and I said you could use a break, but I also said good luck getting you to take one. I never said anything about seeing each other more or tipping off the press."

Leni's eyes narrowed, anger brewing inside her. "That son of a bitch lied to me."

Shea took the spoon and ate more ice cream. "Let me get this straight. He lied so he could see more of you and brought you your favorite food and dessert with an underlying hint of sugary sexual foreplay?" She picked up the can of whipped cream, wiggling it at Leni.

Leni grabbed it from her and tore off the top. "This is not *foreplay*." She piled it on her ice cream. "This is manipulation. I knew I couldn't trust him."

"Maybe I should've gone out with him after all. That's the kind of manipulation I, and half the single women in the world, dream about."

"Not this woman." Leni shoved more ice cream in her mouth, trying to drown out the little voice singing, *Liar, liar, pants on fire.*

Twelve

RAZ ARRIVED ALONE to the grand opening of Seth Braden and Jared Stone's restaurant, The Grill, Thursday evening. He smiled for the paparazzi as he exited his car, knowing the media would surely make shit up about him and Leni for showing up separately to the event. Leni had been dodging his calls and texts since he'd seen her Tuesday. She'd sent a brief message this afternoon saying she'd meet him at the opening. No greeting, no explanation, and no reply to his response. He wasn't thrilled with the arrangement, and being blown off didn't sit well with him, but he knew she was swamped at work and was thankful she could still make it.

The Grill was classy but not over the top, with dark hardwood floors, two-story brick walls lined with circle-head windows on one side, and elegant candle-style chandeliers illuminating tastefully set tables draped in white. There were three arched entranceways along the back of the restaurant. He knew from speaking with Seth that one of those entrances led to a large bar area and the other, to a private dining room and another room with several intimate and private booths.

Raz was greeted by a hostess, who explained that cocktails were being served in the bar. He headed that way and scanned the crowd for Leni as he walked into the bar.

"Hors d'oeuvre?" a waiter offered.

"No, thank you," Raz said, his eyes drawn to the auburn-haired beauty talking with Seth across the room. Leni looked classy and hot as hell in a tan suede miniskirt that showed off her legs and a black boat-neck top that clung to her curves, its gauzy sleeves adding a hint of elegance. Seth said something, and she put her hand on his arm as she responded. Raz felt a stab of jealousy, which made him feel like a dick. Leni wasn't his to be jealous over, and he genuinely liked Seth. The guy was about as laid-back as Patch, but he was also a brilliant investor, president of BRI Enterprises, a retail conglomerate, and he'd been named one of *Forbes* Most Eligible Bachelors twice. Beau's wife referred to him as having a hot-wealthy-nerd thing going on, because he often dressed in unmatched clothes, like a plaid shirt with a patterned sweater, his hair looked perpetually windblown, and he wore black-rimmed glasses. Raz saw nothing nerdy about the guy. He looked more like a hipster, with wavy brown hair and killer blue eyes, and he wore the hell out of those black-rimmed glasses, from behind which he was currently enjoying the woman Raz should have on his arm tonight.

Raz sidled up to Leni. "Sorry to keep you waiting, sweetheart." Putting a hand on her lower back, he leaned in to kiss her cheek.

She flashed a tight smile. "Seth is so entertaining, I didn't even miss you."

"Well, isn't that lucky? Nice to see you again, Seth." Raz held out his hand, and Seth shook it. "This place is fantastic, and it looks like you have a great turnout."

"Thanks. I appreciate you being here. The turnout is all Leni's doing. She's a world-class marketer, and Jared and I are lucky to have her on our team. She's handled several of our openings. I didn't realize you two were seeing each other."

"It's *new*," Leni said in a way that had Raz questioning her commitment to the ruse.

"Well, you found a good one," Seth said. "Raz is a great guy. I've known him forever. He's one of the few who haven't been tarnished by the industry."

"Thanks, man. I appreciate that," Raz said with a nod.

"Hey, it's true. You're no different now than you were when I used to kick your ass in basketball in Beau's backyard."

"You'll be glad to know he's still getting his ass kicked." Leni smirked. "Just don't take him golfing. It's not pretty."

"Babe, let me keep a *little* self-respect," Raz teased.

"Sounds like Leni is as ruthless on the course as she is professionally. She'll keep you on your toes. By the way, Leni, I spoke to my cousin Alyssa the other day. She really likes your vibe. She's excited to hear your ideas."

"I'm excited to work with her. I'll be touching base with her tomorrow to nail down a meeting time. Thank you again for the referral."

"My pleasure," Seth said. "I'll let you know if I head to Silver Island. If you'll excuse me, I think I'd better greet a few more guests."

As Seth walked away, Raz said, "He's going to Silver Island?"

"I believe he said *if*," she said, looking over the crowd.

Raz felt the air chill. "Rough week at work?"

"Not too bad." She still didn't look at him. "You?"

"My week was a little frustrating." He stepped in front of her so she had no choice but to meet his gaze, and despite her icy expression, that thrum of electricity hummed between them.

"Want to tell me why you blew me off all week?"

She lowered her voice, her keen eyes narrowing. "Want to tell me why you lied to me about Shea?"

Shit. He should've seen this coming. "Why don't we talk in private?" He guided her away from the crowd and around the corner to the hall that led to the bathrooms.

She crossed her arms. "You said Shea told you we should be seen together as often as possible, and she tipped off the paparazzi Saturday, but she said she never said either of those things."

"You're right. I wanted to see you, and I lied to get you to agree to it. It was a shitty thing to do, and I'm sorry. But you refused to see me outside the dates we originally set up, and I *like* being with you, Leni. Is that a crime?"

"Lying may not be a crime to some people, but it is to me," she snapped. "I don't appreciate being lied to when I'm putting my reputation on the line every time I'm seen with you."

"I understand, and I am truly sorry for misleading you. But I'm glad we got to spend the day together. Didn't you enjoy it?"

"Yes, but that's not the point," she said sharply.

"But it kind of *is* the point. Shea *did* say you could use a break, and I know I took advantage of the situation, but for good reason."

Her eyes narrowed. "What else have you lied to me about?"

It didn't make sense to him how angry she was. Had Wells scarred her for life with his lies, or was he just the first in a long line of lying boyfriends? That made him feel like shit for misleading her. "Leni—"

"I don't want to hear it. I will not spend another minute with you unless you are honest with me about *everything*," she seethed. "I don't play games, Raz, and I have no respect for liars."

"Babe, I get it, but cut me some slack. It was more of a friendly fib than a malicious lie."

"It doesn't *matter*," she said in a harsh whisper. "There's the truth, and then there are lies. Either you give me complete honesty, or this ruse is over."

"Okay, I'm sorry. If you want complete honesty, then that's what you'll get from now on. You want to know what else I lied to you about? The reason I didn't do the cologne campaign wasn't because I didn't care about it. I canceled because you booked it on the anniversary of my sister's death."

Her brows knitted. "Why didn't you just tell me that at the time?"

"Because I was pissed about not going home to be with my parents, and I didn't know you well enough to share that part of myself. I don't talk about my family with many people."

Her gaze softened. "I would have understood."

"Maybe. But you didn't know me then the way you do now, so I might have gotten an earful about not making commitments I couldn't keep, and honestly, with the frame of mind I was in at the time, I didn't need any more shit in my life."

Her jaw tightened. "That's fair, but I *hate* lies and I trusted you. You should know how I feel about lying from the things I told you that I haven't told other people."

"The last thing I want to do is hurt you in any way. I'm sorry I lied to you about Shea, and I promise, from here on out, I will not lie to you about a damn thing. But if you want honesty from me, it has to work both ways."

She scoffed. "I don't lie."

"Careful, Steele. I like that cute little nose of yours, and I'd hate to see it grow." Stepping closer, he gently uncrossed her arms. "We both know you lied every time you said you didn't want me or you didn't want to see me."

"You don't know that."

"*Mm.* But I do, and I'm pretty sure you do, too. I also know that you lied when we were naked and you said you were lost in thoughts that *weren't* about my body." Enjoying the crimson staining her cheeks, he closed the tiny gap between them. Their bodies brushed, and her lips parted. *Oh yeah, baby. You feel that zing of electricity, too.* "And a week later, when you texted and said you didn't remember getting down and dirty with me the week before? That was another stellar untruth."

She whispered, "Don't you ever forget *anything?*"

"Not when everything you do intrigues me. Although it *would* make my life easier if I could forget. Maybe then I wouldn't be thinking about how badly I want to drop to my knees and taste you again." Her eyes flamed, and he ran his hand down her hip. "And how incredible it felt to be inside you." He leaned in, speaking into her ear. "I can still hear those sexy pleas slipping through your lips." She inhaled a ragged breath, and he met her gaze again. "If only I could forget how sexy you looked on your knees while I fucked your mouth. That image alone has given my hand quite a workout this week."

The air rushed from her lungs, and she swallowed hard.

He slid his hand to the nape of her neck, tilting her face up. "If you tell me you haven't been thinking about all those things, *wanting* them, and that you aren't thinking about kissing me right now, we'll both know you're lying." He paused, letting that sink in. "So if you want honesty, now's the time to earn it."

"Shut up and kiss me." She pulled his mouth to hers, kissing him as hungrily as he did her.

Their tongues tangled, and a moan escaped her lips as she pressed her whole body against him. He wanted to take the kiss deeper, to let his hands and mouth wander, but he was acutely aware of their less-than-private surroundings, and although paparazzi weren't allowed in the restaurant, he didn't trust anyone with a phone. The animal in him considered dragging her into a bathroom and bending her over the counter, but there were too many reasons not to. The most important was that he had too much respect for her, and the least important was, with his luck, they'd get caught and she'd never speak to him again.

"Not here," he gritted out, and drew back, loving the lust brimming in her eyes. "I wouldn't want to tarnish your reputation." He ran his thumb beneath her lower lip, wiping a smear of lipstick. "You're so damn beautiful. I've missed you the last few days while you've been hating me. How's that for honesty?"

She blinked several times and blew out a breath, lifting her chin. "You missed sex."

"Before our spectacular night together, I'd gone months without it. I missed hanging out with *you*." She treated him like a regular person, and in his world, that was as rare as it was beautiful. "But don't get scared and lecture me about being your fake boyfriend. We both know this is temporary. In a few weeks, I'll be just an amusing memory of yours. Until then, I say we stop fighting our attraction and enjoy it."

"You mean have sex," Leni said flatly.

"I mean hang out and have fun, watch the games, make out if we feel like it, fuck ourselves senseless if we so desire, and not worry about whether we should be kissing for the cameras or holding hands, but doing whatever *we* want."

Her brows knitted, like she was thinking about it.

He cocked a grin. "I'm offering you free rein to these lips."

"And asking for free rein to mine," she pointed out.

"Tell me you don't want that, and I won't ask again. But remember…we're not fibbing anymore."

She crossed her arms again. "Fine. I'll go all in with this farce for *my* sexual satisfaction."

"Your satisfaction is my pleasure." He put his hand on her lower back, guiding her toward the crowd. "In the name of honesty, you should know that until I get you alone, I'll be thinking about you riding my face on your kitchen floor."

Her eyes widened. "How am I supposed to concentrate on anything else with *that* in my head?"

"Exactly."

LENI SPENT THE rest of the evening sidetracked by the lust that had seeded itself with his declaration and had been spreading like rampant vines, coiling inside her, hot and needy, thanks to Raz touching her under the table during dinner, whispering naughty things in her ear, and taking advantage of every opportunity to drive her out of her mind. She thought she'd get the upper hand by admitting she wanted all those sexy taunts and found there was an unexpected sense of freedom and power in letting her honest flag fly. But there was no upper hand to be gained. By the time they left, they were both ready to combust. Thank God there was a divider between them and the driver, because their mouths were fused, and Raz's hand was between her thighs, fucking her with his fingers as she stroked him through his jeans.

He growled against her lips, "Straddle me, baby. I can't wait another second to fuck you."

Just as he grabbed her hips to lift her onto his lap, the car pulled over. A whimper escaped before she could stop it, and Raz reclaimed her mouth, hard and possessive. When he tore his mouth away, he growled, "We *won't* be interrupted again."

He helped her out of the car and onto the sidewalk. She didn't recognize the building in front of them. "Where are we?"

"We're staying at my place tonight, so you can't kick me out." He flashed an arrogant grin. "Just being honest."

"But—"

He silenced her with another penetrating kiss, which sent her thoughts spiraling away, leaving her breathless.

After several panty-drenching kisses and tantalizing gropes in the elevator, they entered an enormous, chic two-story loft with hardwood floors and dark leather couches in a massive open living space that bled into a stainless-steel and black kitchen and a wall of windows overlooking the city.

"Wow, I didn't know you had a place here."

"It's my buddy Knox's. He's out of the country for a few weeks, but he doesn't use it often. He and his wife spend most of their time upstate."

Leni walked over to the windows. "This view is amazing."

"My view is even better." He came up behind her and tugged her blouse out of her skirt, pushing his hands beneath it to palm her breasts as he kissed her neck.

His mouth was hot, his tongue wicked as he kissed and sucked her neck, and groped and teased her nipples until she felt like a mass of live wires. "More," she begged, leaning her head back and to the side, giving him better access.

"That's it, baby. Let me take my fill." He sealed his teeth over her neck, sucking so hard she cried out and pressed her hand to the window for balance. "Too hard?"

"Never."

He did it again, sending scintillating sensations skating through her, and continued his moan-inducing taunts until she was trembling with need. He brushed his scruff over her cheek, sending prickles racing down her chest. He hiked up her skirt and tugged down her panties. His roughness electrified her. "Step out of them," he demanded, and she was quick to comply. Rubbing his hand over her ass cheek, he rasped against her neck, "This perfect ass taunts me every time I'm with you." He smacked it, and she cried out at the sting of pain, which turned to pleasure as it seared between her legs. "That's what you get for making me miss you all week."

It had been agonizing for her, too. She'd contemplated telling Shea she was done, but she'd had too much fun with Raz to walk away. "That's what you get for lying to me," she hissed.

"We're done lying." He nipped at her earlobe, sliding his hand over her hip and between her legs, teasing her clit. "Does it turn you on knowing someone could see you through the window?"

"I wouldn't let you do it if it didn't."

He bit her neck, and she sucked in a breath as he quickened his efforts, playing her body to perfection. She couldn't hold back the sounds of pleasure falling from her lips.

"Do you want to come, princess?"

God yes. *"No.* I'm just here for the view," she said sarcastically.

He spun her around. "That smart mouth of yours is going to look phenomenal wrapped around my cock."

"If I so choose." She arched a brow.

"Tell me you don't crave it as much as I do."

She was tempted to lie.

He must have seen that in her eyes, because he said, "Honesty, sweet girl, or this ruse is over, remember?"

"*Fuck*" came out just above a whisper. She narrowed her eyes and palmed his cock through his pants. "Does this answer your question?"

His eyes turned volcanic, and he crushed his mouth, eager and demanding, to hers. "Who knew honesty was an aphrodisiac?"

He stripped off her blouse and bra and used his knee to spread her legs. He dragged his fingers through her swollen lips, up to her clit, lingering with enough pressure to send her up on her toes as need consumed her. His fingers slid through her wetness again, then moved up again, and he continued teasing and taunting in a mind-numbing rhythm, hungry blue eyes boldly raking down her body.

"Look at you," he said gruffly. "My badass, sinful angel, legs spread, breasts bared, skirt hiked up around your waist, and those high heels giving me all sorts of ideas." He ran his tongue along her lower lip. She leaned forward to capture his mouth, and he pulled back, just out of reach. "I will think of you exactly like this, shaking with the need to come, every time we're apart." He slicked his tongue over her taut nipple, making her ache. "Your pussy is begging for me."

"Should we throw a parade? Or are you going to put that dirty mouth of yours to work and make me come?"

"Baby, if this were *work*, I'd become more of a workaholic than you are."

He dropped to his knees, using his talented mouth to set her body ablaze, his fingers heightening every sensation. She clung to his shoulders as he licked and sucked her clit and fucked her with his fingers, stroke after glorious stroke. *"There...don't stop..."*

Not only didn't he stop, but he intensified his efforts until her body shook, her legs flexed, and pleasure engulfed her, radiating from her core to the tips of her fingers and toes, and she cried out. He continued stroking and sucking until her knees buckled, and she dug her fingernails into his shoulders to keep from melting into a puddle at his feet.

He stood, holding her up and kissing her deeply. He tasted of sex and sin, his tongue sliding over hers, strong arms embracing her as he breathed a second wind into her lungs. He pushed one hand into her hair, tugging her head back as he took the kiss deeper. When he drew back, *"More"* flew desperately from her lips. He reclaimed her mouth, her inner muscles clenching greedily. How could she want him this much? She couldn't think clearly enough to find an answer, and she didn't care. He fueled her fire, and she needed more of *him*. She reached between them, squeezing his cock through his pants.

She tore her mouth away. *"Fuck me."*

He spun her around, and she pressed her hands to the glass, listening to the sounds of his pants coming off, the condom wrapper tearing. "Hurry," she urged, watching him roll on the condom in his reflection in the glass. He aligned their bodies, entering her with one hard thrust. She gasped.

"Fuuck." He pulled out and rammed in again, sending bolts of pleasure through her core. "You're so tight. It's *intense*."

"So *good*. Don't stop."

He grabbed her hips, driving into her again and again, every thrust taking her higher, drawing moans, gasps, and curses. The pleasure went so deep, she'd never felt anything like it.

"Come for me," he gritted out against her neck. "Let me hear you say Duncan."

Her chest tightened at the raw emotion in his voice and at how much she *wanted* to say his given name. But calling him Duncan felt intimate, which set off warning bells in her head. It was a lot easier to fake date Raz than to see him as the man behind the name and catch feelings for Duncan. But she *wanted* to say it in the bedroom. She could keep it there, couldn't she?

"Say it." He reached around her, stroking her most sensitive nerves as he pounded into her from behind, taking her higher, shattering her ability to think at all. She was entranced by the feel of him, the sound of his gruff voice, and the desire pulsing through her. He quickened his efforts, and she spiraled out of control. *"Duncan…Oh God…Duncan—"* Her body clenched and trembled as he pumped his hips, letting out a primal animalistic sound that spiked through her, heightening her pleasure. He pulled out, and she lost her breath as he turned her around and lifted her into his arms, and she sank onto his thick cock. He clutched her ass, moving her faster and harder along his shaft. *This* was what she craved, the brutal taking of uncontrollable lust. His jaw tightened with restraint, eyes blazing into her. She felt that pull deep in her chest that she'd been trying to ignore and closed her eyes, riding him faster, trying to chase away those unwanted emotions.

Her back hit the cold glass, and her eyes flew open.

"Look at me," he growled. "Don't run from it. Feel it. Let it consume you."

She held his gaze, his words burning into her, those emotions creeping in like weeds, taking hold as pleasure mounted inside her, pulsing beneath her skin.

"Your *mouth*," he demanded, desire raging in his voice.

Their mouths came together hard and feverish. She was addicted to his mouth, his taste, his *power*. She struggled to hold on to her sanity, but with his thick cock driving into her, his strong hands clutching her ass, and the cold glass at her back, the pleasure was too intense. The world spun away in an explosion of fiery sparks and erotic sensations as he gave in to his own powerful release, growling and groaning, unraveling her with his touch and the visceral sounds he made.

When she finally came down from the peak, she went limp in his arms, both of them panting. "*Jesus*, Leni. You destroy me."

I think you might destroy me, too.

RAZ AWOKE TO a *thud*, followed by Leni whispering, "Shit."

He propped himself up on his elbow and found her gloriously naked, hopping on one foot, holding her knee. She put her foot down, tiptoeing toward the door like Elmer Fudd sneaking up on Bugs Bunny. He glanced at the clock: *5:45*.

"Going somewhere?" he asked with amusement.

She stilled, shoulders creeping up. He imagined her silently cursing him for catching her sneaking out. She turned, hands crossed over her breasts. "I have to go to work."

He climbed out of bed, and her eyes went directly to his dick as he plucked his dress shirt off the floor and handed it to her. He stepped into his boxer briefs as she put it on. "It's early. Let's have a cup of coffee and ease into the day."

"I don't have time," she said, looking adorably sexy.

"It'll take two minutes. Come on, let's ring in the morning without stress or photographers or worries." He took her hand, leading her out of the bedroom.

She tugged her hand free as they descended the stairs. "I can't." She went into the living room and began gathering her clothes.

"Is that an honest answer?" He headed to the kitchen and

turned on the coffee maker. "Because we made a pact, remember? No more lies."

She shimmied into her underwear and skirt without answering and took off his shirt, draping it over the back of the couch. As she finished dressing, she said, "I can't have coffee with you, because coffee will lead to sex, and then I'll end up being late for work."

"I'm not an animal. I'm perfectly capable of having coffee with a beautiful woman and keeping my hands to myself." He added cream and sugar to their coffee and carried them into the living room, handing her one. "Or did you mean to say that if you stayed for coffee, you wouldn't be able to resist me?"

She rolled her eyes. "Do we really have to do this?"

"The honesty thing? That was your requirement, and I think it's a good one. I respect you, and hopefully you respect me." He pulled open the patio door. "You're going to get a three-day reprieve from me. I'm heading home for the weekend around noon."

"Oh." Her brows knitted. "I didn't realize that was this weekend."

Was that a hint of disappointment in her voice? "So, what do you say? Think you can keep your hands to yourself for five or ten minutes, so we can relax and enjoy this beautiful morning before you go out and conquer the world?"

"Think you can put some clothes on?" she asked with a small smile, and sipped her coffee.

"My, oh my, Lenore Steele. I am loving this honesty thing." He grabbed his shirt from the couch.

"Pants, *please*."

He laughed. "Anything for you, princess." He winked, and as he headed upstairs to get a pair of sweats, he said, "If you ditch me while I'm up here, I will show up at your office and do a striptease just so I can watch you squirm."

"That'll keep me here," she said sassily, and headed out to the balcony.

When he joined her, she was pacing. He set his coffee cup on the table, wondering if she ever fully relaxed or if she could only do that when she was asleep and that magnificent brain of hers finally turned off. Like last night, when she'd draped herself over him, as if she didn't want him to disappear, murmuring something about how good he felt. He thought about mentioning that to her now and telling her he slept better beside her as well, but if he brought it up, she'd probably deny it and make things weird.

"Okay, baby, looks like you need a little help relaxing." He took her coffee cup and led her to a chair. "Sit."

She lowered herself into the chair. "I don't have much time."

"I know." He set her cup on the table and moved behind her chair to massage her shoulders.

"What are you doing?" she asked skeptically but not angrily.

"Helping you relax."

"I don't need to relax. I need to gear up for wor—" She sighed. "That feels really good." She gathered her hair over one shoulder, stretching her neck.

"Everyone needs to relax sometimes." He rubbed at the knots in her shoulders.

"Ow, ow...*ooh*, that feels good."

"Sometimes it hurts a little to break up the knots. But if it hurts too much, just tell me. Now close your eyes and try to let your stress go."

"It lives in my bones." She laughed softly, and as he massaged deeper, she let out a long, appreciative sigh. "How did you get so good at this?"

"I played a massage therapist in a movie, so I asked a friend who was a massage therapist to teach me a few techniques. Haven't you ever had a massage?"

"Not like this. I don't like strangers' hands on my body."

"And yet you were on dating apps."

"That sounds a little judgy."

"Yup."

She tilted her head up, looking up at him. "Really? At least I got to know the few guys I met that way before I had sex with them. You have such a spotty dating history, there have to be a few strays in there."

"Strays? Sorry to disappoint you, but I've always been careful about who I let into my bed." His dating history was spotty by design. He'd never looked for a long-term, meaningful relationship. According to his therapist, he didn't let anyone get too close for fear of losing them the way he'd lost Tory. He didn't know if he bought that. Maybe there was something to it, but he believed it was more about being wanted for himself and not all he stood for. Either way, the last time he trusted a woman, he ended up in this media nightmare. That was enough to keep any man on the run.

"You expect me to believe that you didn't hook up with anyone you met at a party while you were in college, or a fan when you first got into the business?"

"Oh, we're going back to our college days?" He massaged across her shoulders and began working the muscles in her upper arms. "Okay, yeah, there were a few women along the way."

"See? You're no better than anyone else."

"I never said I was."

"Then why did you sound so judgmental about me being on dating apps?"

That's a good question. He gritted his teeth and stepped beside her chair, massaging down the length of her arm. "I think you're better than them, that's all."

"Nobody's *better* than them." She held his gaze. "They're just a way to meet people, like going to a bar or a party, and I don't have time for any of that."

He began massaging her hand, and her expression softened with pleasure.

"You are *really* good at that."

"Not a bad way to ring in the morning, huh?"

She smiled and sipped her coffee. "I don't hate it."

"See? You can make time for morning coffee, just like you could make time to meet men at parties or out on the town if you wanted to." He began rubbing each of her fingers. "Maybe you really don't want a man in your life."

"Haven't I already made that clear?"

"Quite. But why? Because a man might make you late for work too often?"

"*No,*" she said sharply, eyes narrowing.

"Afraid you might get attached and get your heart broken?"

"*No.* Have you not learned anything in the time we've spent together? I don't *need* a man."

"Sure you do. You're far too passionate to deny your sexual needs. Don't you want a man to fall crazy in love with you and tend to all your needs, in and out of the bedroom? Someone who looks at you like you're his everything, even when he's surrounded by a roomful of beautiful people? Someone to share your life with, who'll think you're perfect when you're dripping ice cream on your baggy sweats and will work around your busy schedule, accepting you for the workaholic you are?"

For a split second her expression looked almost dreamy, but it quickly morphed into one of a caged tiger looking for escape. "Why do you care what I want? It's not like you're putting yourself out there looking for a girlfriend."

"I'm currently trying to fix a media nightmare with a fake girlfriend, when I'd like nothing more than to disappear from the headlines." He didn't mean to say it so sharply, but fuck it. It was the truth, and they were all about honesty now. "But hopefully this scrutiny won't last forever, and someday I'll meet a small-town girl who likes Duncan more than she likes Raz and is looking to settle down."

"Well, good luck with that, and thanks for the coffee." She pushed to her feet. "I've got to go."

He pulled her into his arms, the irritation in her eyes scorched to ashes by the scalding heat between them. "Sorry for bringing that up. I didn't mean to hit a nerve."

"You hit a lot of nerves." Her tone was somehow seductive and annoyed.

Man, he liked getting under her skin, and he wanted to get even deeper. But they'd agreed to only one more date. They were attending the wedding two weeks from Sunday, and then he was leaving for LA. She claimed to be too busy to see him between now and the wedding, and though she probably was, it wasn't sitting well with him. He'd have to do something about that when he got back from seeing his parents.

"Thanks for sticking around this morning and for another great night. I really enjoyed both." He was hoping to earn another smile or hear her say she liked spending time with him, too, but she didn't say a word, and he felt her walls going up again. He held her a little tighter and went for levity. "Best sex of your life, right?"

She scoffed.

"Uh-uh. We're practicing honesty, remember?"

"I don't have time for this." She pushed out of his arms and strutted toward the door, grabbing her bag from where she'd dropped it last night.

"Your non-answer is a very clear indicator," he called after her.

She reached for the door. "Dream on, Duncan." She froze, her hand outstretched.

He was stunned silent.

She exhaled loudly, still facing the door, her shoulders dropping.

"Len—"

"I meant, *Raz*," she barked, and rushed out the door.

LENI ENDED A call with Alyssa Braden as she climbed out of a cab in front of the restaurant where she was meeting Abby for lunch. She zipped off a text to her assistant to get the meeting she'd scheduled with Alyssa in two weeks on the books and headed inside excited to see Abby. Abby's mother passed away earlier this year, and a few months ago Abby moved from New York back to the island to run her family's bistro, and she rarely made it into the city. Leni needed this time with her bestie, who knew all her secrets.

Or rather, who *had* known all her secrets before this fake-dating situation arose.

Abby waved from a table near the back of the restaurant, and Leni's mood brightened at the sight of her vibrant smile. Abby rivaled Jules with her positivity, and while she was a romantic, she was also real when it came to relationships, and Leni could use some perspective. She was used to thinking with her head, and her stupid heart was getting in the way. Raz giving her whiplash wasn't helping. He was sweet and intimate one minute, and the next he was making it clear he couldn't wait for whatever this was between them to end. *I'm currently trying to fix a media nightmare with a fake girlfriend, when I'd like nothing more than to disappear from the headlines.*

Even though they were on the same page with that, it had hurt to hear it.

"I'm so happy to see you," Leni said.

"Me too." Abby pushed to her feet to embrace her. Her golden-brown hair was as tousled and gorgeous as ever, cascading over her shoulders in gentle waves.

"How are you?" Leni asked as they sat down. "How are things? How's the Bistro?"

"I'm crazed but good. The Bistro is doing better than I ever could have imagined, and your aunt Faye is a godsend. That woman can cook me under the table."

"I don't believe that, but I knew you'd like working with her." Faye Steele had once been married to Leni's father's no-good brother, Jeffrey. They had six kids, including Shea. Faye was one of Leni's mother's closest friends, and after much urging, Faye had finally moved from Trusty, Colorado, to the island to get a fresh start. She'd been working with Abby ever since.

"She reminds me of my dad," Abby said. "She's got his warm, kind energy. I swear, moving back to the island was the best thing I've ever done, other than saying yes to marrying Aiden. I feel my father all around me in the Bistro."

Abby had been a daddy's girl until the day he passed away, when she was only nine. Her father, Olivier de Messiéres, had come to the island from France with a backpack full of money and a dream of owning a restaurant. He'd opened the beachfront Bistro, had fallen in love with Abby's much-younger mother, and had been a wonderful father to Abby and her older sister Deirdra.

"I'm sure he's watching over you with pride. I can still see him, with his long white ponytail, coming out of the kitchen to chat with the customers with that thick French accent."

"Me too." Abby blew out a breath. "But I'm not going to waste a second of our lunch getting all sentimental."

"Thank goodness for small favors," Leni teased. "Anything new with Deirdra or Cait?" Cait was Abby and Deirdra's half sister.

"Dee and Jagger are still traveling and loving life. They'll be back for the wedding, and Cait and Brant are madly in love, as you saw at their engagement party, and then there's my beautiful Aiden." Aiden Aldridge, a self-made billionaire who had raised his younger sister after they'd lost their parents, was her fiancé.

"How is your dream man?"

"Wonderful. He's so supportive. I can't wait to become his wife, even if he is driving me crazy with all his secrets about the wedding." They were getting married at the vineyard, and Aiden wanted to give Abby the wedding of her dreams. But he wouldn't share his plans with Abby or anyone else other than Jock's wife, Daphne, the vineyard's wedding planner.

"He loves you so much. He just wants it to be special."

"I know, but doesn't he realize that *he* makes our wedding special, not what he does for me?"

"He knows, the same way *you* know that he doesn't have any idea how to refrain from going all out for the people he loves."

"That's true," Abby said as the waitress arrived to take their orders.

After ordering, Leni said, "You *know* I'm thrilled for you and Aiden, but selfishly, I miss when we lived close enough that I could show up with a bottle of wine and we would commiserate about the trials and tribulations of life."

"I miss that, too. At least I get to see you on social media with your boyfriend. I feel like I should ask for your autograph or something."

"Shut up." Leni laughed. "You know I hate having my face plastered all over the internet."

"Yes, but I love seeing you, and in case your family hasn't mentioned it, people on the island are talking."

"I figured they might." Gossip spread faster than weeds on the island. "Tell them we're just having fun."

"They can *see* that. They want to know how Raz made the cut."

"What does that mean?" Leni sipped her water.

"That most guys piss you off during coffee dates and never get another shot, *and* you swore off anyone even remotely connected to Hollywood years ago, which means Raz must be pretty great."

If only he was as rotten as those coffee dates. Then Leni wouldn't be so drawn to him. "Trust me, he's not immune to pissing me off."

"No man is. It's in their genetic makeup to piss women off.

But you're still seeing him, so he must be worth it." She took a drink. "Then again, nothing fazes you when your mind is made up about something."

"Apparently *that's* no longer true." She still couldn't believe she'd called Raz *Duncan* when she was leaving. Using his given name outside the bedroom felt more intimate than sex. It was silly. It was just a name, but it felt much bigger, and the way he'd clammed up, she was pretty sure he'd been struck by it, too.

"Oh?" Abby arched a brow.

"He's getting under my skin, Ab, and a lot of things he says and does are affecting me. Like this morning. He basically accused me of hiding behind work to avoid getting my heart broken and ran through a litany of questions, like don't I want a man to fall crazy in love with me and think I'm perfect in baggy sweats and accept my busy work schedule. I mean, *Abby*, he's known me a few *weeks* and he acts like he *knows* me."

Abby tipped her head back and laughed.

"It's *not* funny."

"It's hilarious. He totally has your number."

"That's *why* it's irritating." The waitress arrived with their lunches, and Leni waited until she walked away to continue. "He's making me nuts."

"Why? Because he gets you? Come on, Leni. You have what most women would kill for."

"Yeah, if it were real and meant to be and all that jazz, but it's not. We're just having fun while he's in town, and sure, he takes my sarcasm in stride, giving me shit right back or being so damn charming, sarcasm becomes a game between us, but still."

"You're right. That's pretty awful." Grinning, Abby popped a cherry tomato into her mouth.

"You don't get it. You know what he did earlier this week? He lied about something Shea said so he could spend the day with me, and when I found out he lied, I gave him the cold shoulder. And what did he do? He texted every day, offering to bring me dinner at work or to walk me home so he would know I was safe, and other stupid thoughtful messages." She didn't mention that she'd read those messages dozens of times and had practically had to tie her hands down to keep from responding.

"I don't know how you stand it. You'd better get rid of him fast. That's horrible."

Leni laughed softly. "It's really hard to stay mad when he does shit like that. I actually felt guilty for binge-watching my favorite shows Wednesday night, because I *knew* he wanted to spend time with me." She ate a forkful of salad. "You know what he did when I told him I refused to be with a liar?"

"Oh God, what? Gave you a diamond ring? The jackass."

"Worse. He vowed never to lie again, and the bastard has not only stuck to it, he holds *me* accountable for every word out of my mouth." She couldn't imagine how Jacinda hadn't fallen madly in love with him.

"The bastard. I bet he's good in bed, too."

"*Good* doesn't even come close." Leni pushed the salad around with her fork. "He does things…"

Abby's eyes lit up. "Sexy things."

"*So* many sexy things. It's like he studied my fantasies and is determined to make them all come true." She leaned across the table, whispering, "He's a multiple-orgasm king. He should win an award for his talents."

"That's it," Abby said with feigned anger. "Now he's gone too far. You better dump his ass before you die from satisfaction."

They both laughed.

"You know you sound ridiculous, right?" Abby asked.

"I know he's kind of great," Leni admitted. "But I don't know where we'll end up." She tried to ignore the pang in her chest. She just had to get through a couple more weeks. This weekend while he was in Maryland seeing his family, she'd regain perspective, and by the time he returned, all those confusing feelings will have dissipated.

"I'll put you down for a plus-one at the wedding."

"No, don't bother. He's not even going to be here for your wedding. He's leaving at the end of the month to film a movie."

"Oh, that's a bummer. But it is his job. Then he'll come back and sweep you off your feet."

"*Abby*," she warned. "Put that romantic heart of yours away."

"Why? He could be *the one*."

"There is no *one* for me. Besides, actors' lives are full of drama and paparazzi and other headaches, and he lives in LA. You know how busy I am. The last thing I need is a guy complicating my life from across the country, complaining about how I don't have time for him because our schedules never line up." She leaned across the table, speaking quietly. "I'm kind of looking forward to when he leaves to get away from the cameras and the drama that goes with them." She tried to ignore the pinch in her chest as she said it, but it wasn't a total lie. She hated being followed and having her life out there for strangers to gawk over.

"Really?"

"Yes. Actors always hook up when they're on set, and I don't need that kind of worry taking my focus off work. Look at his ex."

"I guess I can understand that, but wasn't Raz the forever bachelor before Jacinda? I remember reading about him hooking up with a costar or two, but it wasn't like he was cheating on someone else, and I've never read anything about him being a player."

"Still. I don't want those worries."

"You know Remi went out with him a few years ago, right?"

Remi was Aiden's much-younger sister, an A-list actress whom Shea represented. Leni had met Remi several times, and a pang of jealousy slithered in, despite the fact that Remi was now happily married to her bodyguard, Mason Swift, and they'd not only adopted two girls, but she was pregnant with their baby. *Yup. I need to gain perspective sooner rather than later.*

"I forgot about that. Shea set them up."

"That's right. They only went on two dates. Remi said he's a great kisser, but they had no chemistry so they never took it further. But they've remained friends, and she has nothing but good things to say about him."

Leni tried to stop the visual from forming of Raz and gorgeous Remi kissing, but it plowed in like a runaway truck. She didn't like this jealous version of herself. It felt out of control and childish, especially since Raz wasn't her real boyfriend. "I can't imagine anyone not having sexual chemistry with him. It practically oozes from his pores when we're together."

"Maybe that's because he's with *you*."

"I don't think so. We're talking about a celebrity. A guy who can fake anything. A man who thousands of women lust after. Think about it, Ab. How long can it last with all that temptation out there?"

"I think you're being too harsh. Aiden travels, and I trust him."

"Aiden adores you. Raz and I are having fun while he's here. Neither of us is looking for a long-term relationship. He's just a great guy biding his time."

"Okay, but he obviously likes you, and it sounds like he's at least peeked over those iron-clad walls surrounding your heart. All I'm saying is maybe you should be open to the possibility that someone holds the key, and you never know who it might be."

"Well, it's not him, okay?" Her phone rang. "Sorry, I thought I turned it off." She pulled her phone out of her purse and saw Raz's name on the screen. Her stupid heart leapt. She was definitely looking forward to three Raz-free days to get her head on straight. "Speak of the devil. He's supposed to be on his way to see his parents for the weekend."

"It must be important. Go ahead and take it." Abby motioned for her to hurry up and answer the call.

She reluctantly put the phone to her ear and tried to sound like a concerned girlfriend. "Hi. Are you on your way to Maryland?"

"No. I've had a change of plans. My parents are here. They showed up while I was packing. They were out to dinner last night, and one of my mom's friends asked about my new girlfriend."

"Oh no." Leni's heart sank. She knew how hard he tried to protect his parents from the drama of his life.

"Yeah, it was a little unexpected. I thought I'd show them around the city tonight and take them to dinner and a show tomorrow. They'd really like to meet you. Do you think you could put off whatever work you have planned for tomorrow evening and join us?"

She didn't want to lie to his parents, but she couldn't say

that in front of Abby. "Are you sure you wouldn't rather have them all to yourself?"

"I'm sure, babe. My mom is *right here*, anxiously awaiting your answer."

Damn it. She didn't want to let him down. But if they met her, wouldn't it hurt them more after they ended the ruse? "Are you sure that's a good idea, given…everything?"

"Yes. I want you there, and they're excited to see me with a woman who actually adores me as much as I adore her."

He really was a good actor, and tomorrow night she'd have to be one, too. Maybe this was a blessing in disguise. It gave her a perfect excuse to do something nice for him without giving away her feelings. "Okay. Let me get the tickets and make reservations for dinner."

"You don't have to do that. I can get them."

"I have connections. I want to do this for you." She quickly corrected herself. "For them. Text me the details, what show they want to see, and if they have a preference for the type of restaurant, and I'll take care of it." Leni heard a woman say, *Well?* to Raz.

"She said yes, Mom."

"This is so exciting," the woman exclaimed. "Tell her I can't wait to get to know her."

Guilt swirled around Leni like a swarm of mosquitoes searching for a place to strike.

"Thanks, babe. My mom can't wait to meet you, and I can't wait to see you. I miss you already."

"Me too." Leni tried to sound excited.

After she ended the call, Abby said, "You sound happy."

"More like nervous. His parents came into town to surprise him, and I'm meeting them tomorrow night. We're going to see a show and out to dinner. *Ugh.* You know how I feel about Broadway shows."

"Oh, *please.* You used to love them when we were in college and we'd go with Indi to the matinees. Remember how fun that was? We'd look forward to it all week. What happened to *that* girl?"

"She got too busy for frivolous things like that. Besides, it was fun because I was with you and Indi."

"Maybe it's time to get unbusy. Seriously, Leni. You've got a great client base, and you're not going to miss anything by taking a little time off now and then."

"I'm *going,* aren't I?"

"Yes, and I'm glad, because it doesn't sound like Raz is thinking along the lines of a temporary relationship if he's introducing you to his parents."

"Don't get too excited. It's not like he told them about me. They found out through a friend."

"What do you mean? Pictures of you two are all over the internet."

"Yeah, but his parents don't keep up with social media or celebrity gossip, and Raz does everything he can to keep it away from their lives. He probably felt backed into a corner and didn't want to let them down."

"I'm not buying it. He could have made an excuse so you didn't have to meet them. I think he wants you to meet them because he thinks you're as magnificent as I do."

"Abby, don't get your hopes up." Wishing again that she could just tell her it was all fake, she lowered her voice and said, "We have fun together, but we didn't fall into each other's arms the first time *or* the last because we felt some soul-to-soul connection. We had sex because we'd both gone without for months. We enjoyed it, so we figured, why not continue while he's in town? It sounds horrible to admit it, but there's nothing real between us besides great sex, and don't you dare repeat that." It wasn't exactly true. They'd had some deep conversations, and there were plenty of times when she had to remind herself that the relationship wasn't real, like when she'd told him about her family and had cried in front of him. But those were even more reasons for Leni to pull herself together and protect her heart.

Which she was going to do, *after* tomorrow night. Because under the guise of the lie, she could let her true feelings come through and experience what it could be like to fall for Duncan Raz.

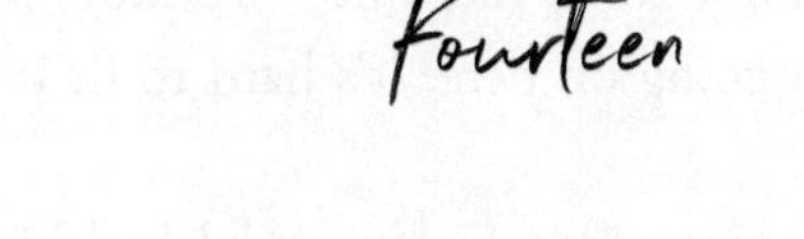

RAZ'S MOTHER, A thick-waisted, wildly likable brunette, looped her arm through Leni's on the way out of the theater Saturday evening, her bright hazel eyes dancing with delight. "I can't get over how good *Wicked* was. You think you know a story, and then someone adds a twist, and"—she lifted her hand, feigning an explosion with her fingers—"blows your mind."

Kind of like how I thought I knew exactly who your son was until he blew my mind. And my body...and my ability to concentrate. She glanced over her shoulder at Raz, walking with his father, who was tall and fit, with graying brown hair and the same electric-blue eyes as Raz. Raz met her gaze, looking at her the way he'd been all evening, like she was special and his to admire. Between holding her hand and pulling her closer to whisper funny, sweet, and sexy comments during the show, he was nailing the loving-boyfriend role, which made her a little nervous about letting her true feelings fly. She worried she might not be able to rein them in at the end of the night. But it felt oddly natural, and utterly enjoyable, to let her heart lead for the first time in years. It was scary, but a good kind of scary.

Raz winked, and Leni smiled before turning back to his

mother. "I'm glad you enjoyed it. I had forgotten how much I loved the theater."

"You mean you don't go all the time?" his mother asked. "I guess there's so much going on here, it's hard to fit it all in too regularly."

"Actually, I work more than I play, and I had kind of forgotten how fun this city is. But your son is doing a good job of reminding me."

"I'm glad to hear that. You're too young to miss out on all the wonderful things life has to offer. So…what's next?" his mother asked excitedly as they moved out of the way, letting people pass them on the sidewalk.

Raz was so protective of his parents, Leni had been nervous about meeting them, envisioning them to be serious and guarded. Boy was she wrong. His mother was a kindhearted elementary school teacher, and his father was a warm-natured businessman. They were sweet and funny and so loving toward each other and Raz and warm and welcoming toward her, they reminded Leni of her own parents. Although, now that she'd seen how close Raz was with them, she realized just how stressful it must be trying to buffer them from certain aspects of his life.

"Mom, why don't you ask your new best friend?" Raz teased, turning a sexy gaze on Leni.

"I made reservations at one of my favorite restaurants a few blocks from here."

"That sounds lovely," his mother said.

"Thank you for making the arrangements tonight," his father said.

"It was my pleasure." She'd enjoyed the process and had realized how long it had been since she'd put much thought into anything but work.

"We'll have to show you around when you come to Maryland." His mother gave Raz a hopeful glance.

When I come to Maryland? Guilt slithered in, and Raz must have noticed, because he nodded reassuringly and smoothly redirected the conversation with "I'll call for the car."

"Oh, honey, it's such a beautiful evening. Let's walk," his mother suggested. "If that's okay with you, Leni?"

"Absolutely."

"You're speaking Leni's language," Raz said. "She loves walking the streets."

"You make me sound like a hooker," Leni teased. "It's a good thing you're cute, or I might not keep you around." She reached for Raz's hand, and he pulled her closer, kissing her temple before heading down the busy sidewalk.

"This gal is something," his father said. "Reminds me of someone else I know."

"We girls have to keep them on their toes," his mother said as she eyed her.

"That's Leni's forte," Raz said.

"Just like Tory used to keep you on your toes," his mother said. "She would have loved Leni, and *Wicked.*"

"She sure would have," Raz said thoughtfully.

Leni was glad Tory wasn't a taboo subject like the rift between Archer and Jock had been. His parents had mentioned her a few times earlier in the evening, and she'd noticed how happy it made Raz to talk about her. She liked seeing that joy in his eyes and hoped to see more of it.

"Remember when Tory was in the middle school band and they played 'Defying Gravity'?" Raz asked. "I heard that song in my sleep."

"She played it incessantly," his mother said.

"I was so happy when she gave up the clarinet for cheerleading," Raz said.

"But she never gave up her love of music and arts. She wanted to teach kids both," his mother said. "And she would have been good at it."

Leni wondered if that was why the charity event they'd gone to was so important to Raz. "I wish I had known her. She sounds really special."

"She was," they all said in unison.

They stopped at the corner to wait for the walk signal, and his mother said, "I can't believe it took us so long to see the show."

"I can." His father glanced at Leni. "My wife is the epitome of a small-town girl. She'd never leave Pleasant Hill if she could help it."

"That's true for the most part, but once a year Duncan and his father force me out of my comfort zone to go adventuring," his mother said cheerily.

"Adventuring?" Leni asked.

"Honey, you haven't told her about our spin-the-wheel trips?" his mother asked.

"I haven't gotten around to it yet," Raz explained as they crossed the street. "Every year on Tory's birthday, I make a wheel like the one on *Wheel of Fortune*, and I write in a dozen potential vacation spots. Places we've talked about going, or Tory did. And then my mom spins it to see where we're going on our next adventure."

"I love that idea," Leni said.

"It's something we started when the kids were little, so they could get excited about our family vacations and we could figure out things they wanted to do and places they'd like to see along the way," his mother explained.

"We missed a few years after we lost Tory," his father said. "But not going made us miss her even more. It was Duncan who talked us into starting it up again. It was the best decision we ever made."

"I'm glad Duncan thought of it." His given name slid off her tongue like she called him that all the time, and the way his gaze warmed, she just might start doing it more often. "I guess you don't go skydiving or mountain climbing because *someone* is afraid of heights."

"Hey." Raz laughed.

"You know, he wasn't afraid of heights until he was fourteen, when he fell out of a treehouse trying to save Tory from doing the same," his mother said.

"We were helping Beau's brother Graham build his treehouse," Raz explained. "One side wasn't finished. Tory tripped and fell toward the edge. I grabbed her shirt, and as I shoved her back, I lost my balance and fell out."

"And landed on a branch that lodged in his chest," his mother said. "We got lucky that it didn't puncture his heart."

"That's how you got your scar," Leni said softly. "That was really brave of you."

He shrugged. "She was my baby sister. I couldn't let her fall."

"After that his sister tortured him about being afraid of heights," his mother said. "She'd call him into the kitchen when her friends were over and ask him to change the lightbulb, or she'd claim our cat was stuck in a tree and say he needed to save it."

"And did you?" Leni asked.

"I couldn't *not* do it when there were witnesses. I thought I was going to pass out the whole time," Raz said, and they laughed. "She was a brat when she wanted to be."

"In all fairness, Duncan isn't alone in his fear of heights. His father isn't too keen on heights, either."

"Dad's my hero," Raz said, and they chuckled.

"Do you take your trips at the same time every year?" Leni wondered how different Raz was on those vacations, when he was away from cameras and the stress that went along with being a celebrity. He was pretty laid-back when they were out, but she knew he was aware of being "on" for the cameras. She'd sensed an alertness in him that wasn't there when they were alone in her apartment.

"No. We go whenever we can all fit it into our schedules, which is no easy feat," his mother said. "This year we're going after Duncan finishes filming in February. Maybe you can join us."

That jerked her back to reality with a niggling in her chest. "I, *um…*"

"That's a little far out to think about, Mom, and Leni's schedule is always pretty busy," Raz said easily.

"Of course," his mother said. "Duncan told us you're in high demand in marketing and public relations, which must be exciting. He also said you're one of the best in the business."

"He's being generous."

"No, I'm not." Raz squeezed her hand as they turned down a street toward the restaurant. "You're excellent at what you do. Seth's opening was a testament to your hard work."

She didn't think he'd paid attention when Seth had complimented her, and his praise meant a lot, considering his views on her industry when they'd started this ruse.

"Duncan also told us how you two met." His father nodded approvingly.

"He did?" Leni glanced at Raz, wondering what story he'd made up this time, and caught him watching her in a way that made her insides warm and her pulse quicken.

"How could I not? The first time I saw you in your office is one of my favorite memories." He lifted her hand and kissed the back of it.

What was the universe doing to her? He was *too* good at this, and damn if she wasn't falling for it.

"We know the minute Duncan saw you, you knocked him off his feet," his mother said. "But I'm curious. Was it that way for you, too?"

Knocked him off his feet? It was one thing to play that up with his buddy at the bar, but these were his parents. Did he have to go that far with them? She looked at Raz questioningly.

He raised one shoulder. "I also told her that we took a vow of honesty."

Was there anything he *didn't* tell them? "In that case, I thought he was egotistical and too cocky for his own good. Obviously, Duncan is handsome, at least according to *People* magazine, but when we first met, he was Shea's most difficult client."

"Uh-oh." His father eyed him.

"He proved me wrong pretty quickly. We went to a charity event together, and I expected it to be a onetime thing." Leni smiled at Raz, remembering how antagonistic she'd been at the beginning of that fake date. "Then I got to know him, and he was funny and charming and smart, and while his ego isn't lacking, it doesn't lead the charge all the time."

His mother exhaled with relief. "That's good to know. We

didn't raise him to be difficult."

"I can tell. You raised a thoughtful, loyal son, and he had good reasons for acting the way he did." Leni would never forget the look in his eyes when he told her the reason behind his actions. She'd also never forget the way he was looking at her now, drawing the truth from someplace deep inside her. "He won me over that first night, and he's continued to win me over a little more each day."

RAZ HADN'T BEEN able to take his eyes off Leni all night. She was always beautiful, but tonight she was utterly radiant. As they ate dessert, she told his parents about her family, and she was just as open and carefree as she'd been all evening. Her laugh was untethered, her jokes playful, and her glances, well, they were seductive in the way real couples' inside jokes were. He liked her snark and her challenges, but this side of her was equally addicting. Was she giving him a glimpse of the woman she kept locked beneath her armor? Was this who she was at her core? Or was she an even better actress than he gave her credit for?

"Three brothers, two sisters, and you're a twin?" His mother shook her head. "I'm an only child, and Ron only has one sister. I can't imagine growing up with that many siblings."

"I can't imagine my life without them," Leni said. "Our house was loud and chaotic, with friends in and out all the time. My dad put a boxing ring in the garage and taught all the boys how to box, and my mom fed all our friends, telling stories and trying to keep her head on straight while my brothers pulled pranks on everyone."

"That sounds like fun," his father said. "What kind of pranks?"

"Just about anything you can imagine. My brothers are always trying to one-up each other, so the pranks get more outrageous every year. When we were young, they did things like setting up fake ghosts to scare us and putting all our underwear in the freezer. One time they told my twin, Levi, that it was free-candy-bar day at the store, so he'd steal candy bars and get caught. But they've ramped up since then and recently had Levi arrested by the Coast Guard. They even got my niece, Joey, Levi's daughter, in on the prank."

"Wow," his mother said. "They're really dedicated to their craft."

"Yes, they are, and sometimes they include all of us. Like when my older brother Archer fell in love with my friend Indi, we all pranked him. Archer is tough and gruff and not great at handling his emotions. He usually speaks and acts before thinking, so he and Indi came up with a safe word to pull him back to the moment and get him to calm down, and that safe word was *bananas*."

"Because he's like a gorilla?" Raz asked.

"*No*, because sometimes he goes bananas, and that signals him to stop."

"That's cute, as long as it's effective," his mother said.

"It is, because Indi is the one who says it, and his world revolves around her…"

Without her usual armor, the look in her eyes told Raz that she definitely wanted that in her life, though he knew she'd never admit it. And he also wasn't sure why he cared or noticed. They were nearing the end of their relationship. Not a budding beginning to some fairy tale. Fairy tales didn't exist in either of their worlds.

"Anyway, my other brothers got in touch with Indi's ex, who Archer had been jealous of at one point, and had him pretend to hit on Indi in a very public way. Archer was livid, and as expected, he lost it, but when he turned around to yell at my brothers, we were all eating bananas. You should have seen his face when he realized it was a prank."

"That's a little cruel," his mother said.

"I think it's brilliant," his father said.

"Brave might be a better word," Raz said. "You haven't met Archer. He's like the Hulk."

"With a big heart," Leni added. "One of these days, my sisters and I will come up with an epic prank to play on our brothers to get them back for years of torture."

"I can help you with that," Raz offered.

"I know you would if you could, but you're going to be a little busy for the next few months."

Raz thought he detected a hint of sadness in her eyes. She was the kind of woman he could go all in with, but he knew what was best, and that was sticking to the plan so no one got hurt.

"Silver Island," his father said. "Isn't that where Zev and Carly are diving?"

"It is," Raz said.

"Maybe we can get Clint and Lily to take a weekend trip there with us. Wouldn't that be fun?" his mother said.

"They're Beau's parents," Raz explained.

"What was it like growing up on the island?" his mother asked.

"It was great. As you can imagine, summers seemed endless,

and between holiday festivities and friends, there was always something to do. Silver Island is small, so it was like growing up with lots of extended family who weren't blood related but felt like they were. On the upside, we had lots of great friends. On the downside, everyone knows your business and wants to help in some way."

"Sounds like Pleasant Hill. You've got to love small-town life," his mother said.

"And I do. Maybe not the gossip, but the sense of community on the island is unbeatable."

"Do you miss it?" Raz asked.

"Sometimes. More now that Abby and Indi have moved there." She turned to his parents. "Indi and Abby are my best friends. Indi and I met in college, and Abby and I grew up together and eventually shared an apartment in the city. It's strange not living close to them."

"No wonder you miss them," his mother said.

"I do, but I am happy for them. Abby moved back home to run her family's bistro, and she's marrying a great guy soon, and as I mentioned, Indi is engaged to Archer. She has her own skincare and cosmetics line, called Indira, and she recently opened a boutique on the island."

"Wow, that's impressive," his father said.

"I *love* Indira products," his mother gushed. "I'll have to take a trip out to the island and check out her boutique."

"If you've never been there, you should plan your trip around one of the island events or holidays. There's nothing like them," Leni said. "All the towns decorate for the seasons, and there are parades, Easter egg hunts, flotillas, and a Christmas tree lighting. My sister Jules got engaged last year at the Christmas tree lighting, and she's getting married at this year's lighting."

"How beautiful," his mother said.

"I think it will be, and her fiancé's parents own the Silver House, where they're holding the reception. If you come to the island, that's where you'll want to stay. It's gorgeous."

"Leni's family owns a winery on the island," Raz added.

"Really? I wonder if they know Clint and Lily. They own a winery in Pleasant Hill," his father said.

"They might. I'm not sure," Leni said.

"Her brother Archer is an award-winning vintner, and very particular about his vines," Raz said.

"How do you know that?" Leni asked.

"I've done my homework."

"Spying on my family, are you?" she teased. "He is particular about his vines, but he allows our family to host the Field of Screams every year on Halloween weekend."

"That sounds intriguing," his mother said. "What is it?"

"It's one of my favorite events. We spend all day decorating the outside of the winery and creating a haunted walk through one section of the vineyards. My whole family dresses up for it. Last year my brothers and sisters and I were zombies, and this year's theme is classic horror movie characters. We hide in the vineyard and jump out to scare people as they walk through." She laughed softly. "It sounds awful, doesn't it? But it's really fun, and we have cauldrons full of candy and bobbing for apples and other games for little kids."

"That sounds amazing," his mother said. "And your family sounds wonderful."

"They are, but we have our moments."

Leni glanced at him with a knowing look, and he knew she was thinking about what had happened with Jock and Archer.

He reached for her hand, giving it a squeeze.

"Does your family watch that zombie show?" his father asked.

"*The Walking Dead?* Some of us do," Leni admitted. "I love it."

"Her guilty pleasure is binging horror shows. My girl is badass."

"You're pretty badass yourself. Except for the whole afraid-of-heights thing," Leni teased.

They left the restaurant hand in hand and climbed into the back of their waiting car with his parents. During the drive to Leni's place, they chatted amiably, but Raz felt Leni pulling away. The way she shifted in her seat so she wasn't pressed so tightly against him could have been his imagination, but there was no mistaking her faltering smile or that slight lift of her adorable chin. Why was she slipping back into her armor when they were having such a wonderful night? He wanted to tell her she didn't need it. That she was safe with him. The last few months of putting up a wall between him and the world to protect himself from the bullshit the media was printing had been exhausting. It was a relief to let go of that and be with Leni, even if only temporarily. He wished she would do the same, and enjoy the reprieve.

When they reached her apartment building, his parents got out of the car to say goodbye.

"I really enjoyed meeting both of you," Leni said sweetly.

"We did as well, honey. Will you be joining us for brunch and exploring Greenwich Village with us tomorrow?" his mother asked.

"I wish I could, but I'm tied up all day." She glanced at Raz with regret in her eyes. "Actually, I'm going to be really busy for the next few weeks until I head home for my sister's bridal shower."

He got the message loud and clear, and he didn't like it.

"Oh, what a shame," his mother said. "I was looking forward to spending more time together. It's nice to see my son smiling again."

"With you two around, he has every reason to smile. I'm sorry I'll miss it, but I know you'll have a great time." She hugged them both, then turned to do the same to Raz.

He wasn't going to let her get away that easily. "Mom, Dad, I'm going to walk Leni up. I'll be right down."

"You don't have to do that," Leni said.

"I know, sweetheart, but I want to." They headed inside. When they stepped into the elevator, he moved in front of her. "What just happened?"

Her brow furrowed. "What do you mean?"

"We were having a great time, and then you pulled away again."

"I didn't pull away *again*. I just…" Her expression softened. "Your parents are amazing, and they adore you, but it's all a lie, and on the ride over here, I realized how unfair that is to them." She pressed her lips together, a mix of sadness, regret, and something else swimming in her beautiful eyes. As if a switch had been flipped, she lifted her chin and schooled her expression. "It's bad enough that I have to lie to my family. It's really hard lying to yours."

Feeling too many things to decipher, he said, "It's definitely a fucked-up situation. I appreciate you coming tonight, and I'm sorry I didn't take into account how much playing this out with them would affect you. For what it's worth, I hate lying to them, too." Although it didn't feel like lying as much as he'd thought it would.

The elevator doors opened, and as they stepped out, she said, "You don't have to walk me to the door. I'm fine, and your parents are waiting."

"Leni—"

"Really, Raz, the sooner this is over, the better. It's a lot harder than I thought it would be."

No shit. But they were doing the right thing, no matter how drawn to her he was. And damn it, she was like a drug he couldn't get enough of. It wouldn't be fair to either of them to try to make something more of this before he took off for three months of filming. But he wasn't leaving for two weeks, and the idea of not seeing her until the wedding was eating away at him.

"Right. I'll try not to be too charming at Jay and Naomi's wedding."

She smiled. "I would appreciate that. Just dick yourself up a bit."

He waggled his brows. "We should get together a few times between now and then so I can practice."

"That's not a good idea."

"Let me show you how good an idea it is." He stepped closer and kissed her neck, whispering, "It's a *very* good idea."

She laughed softly. "Why do you have to be so fun?"

"You make me fun, baby. Think about it, okay?" He took her hand and kissed her lightly on the lips. "Good night, sweetheart."

Her fingers tightened around his, and she went up on her toes and kissed him. "Good night."

Fuck it. He tugged her against him, taking her in a deep, sensual kiss. As their lips parted, he said, "Damn, I like kissing you." She blinked longingly up at him, and he couldn't resist going back for more. She put her arms around his neck, hungrily returning his efforts, stumbling back against the wall with the force of their kisses. He drew back on a series of lighter kisses. "Your lips are dangerous." He kissed her again. "*Fuck*, princess. I'm addicted."

She laughed, pushing him away. "Get out of here. Your parents are waiting."

"Let them wait." He went in for another kiss, and she made a needy sound he knew he'd hear in his sleep. "*God*, I want you," he whispered, dusting kisses over her lips and cheeks.

"*Go*. Or your parents are going to file a missing-person report."

"Fine." He stepped back. "Look at you, so beautiful. I bet that dress would look hotter on the floor."

"Ohmygod. Would you *go*?" She laughed.

"I'm going." He pushed the button for the elevator. "But I'm never going to make it two weeks without seeing you."

"You'll be fine." She walked backward down the hall toward her apartment.

"I'll probably end up in the ER from withdrawal," he called after her.

"I'll make sure Patch knows where to visit you."

The elevator arrived, and he watched her unlock her door. She glanced over, that sexy smile hitting him like a ray of sunshine. She shooed him with her hand. He chuckled as he got into the elevator and watched her disappear into her apartment, leaving him as hot and happy as if he'd just come out of a summer storm.

Fifteen

LENI TYPED THREE more bullet points on the marketing plan for Alyssa Braden and glanced at her cell phone for the millionth time. It was Sunday afternoon, and Raz had been texting her pictures all day of his outing with his parents. Instead of focusing on the work she wanted to accomplish, she found herself anxiously awaiting his next text.

Irritated with herself, she turned the phone over and stared at the document on her laptop, struggling to concentrate. She glanced at her phone again, knowing she needed to stop this foolishness, but she was drawn to the stupid phone like a fish to water.

The heck with it. Just one more peek. Then it would be out of her system.

She picked up her phone and sat back, scrolling through the pictures again, taking in Raz's and his parents' smiling faces as they stood under the Washington Square Arch, in front of Hangman's Elm, the longest-living tree in New York City, and outside the restaurant where they'd had lunch. There were photos of them standing beneath the Bleeker Street sign, in the middle of MacDougal Street, and a dozen others. In every single one, Raz was holding what looked like a Popsicle stick with a big picture of Leni's smiling face attached to it. In several pictures, his parents pointed to her image with gleeful grins, and in others, Raz or one of his parents had their arm around Leni's invisible body, as if she were there with them.

She wished she were.

What was happening to her? She didn't recognize this girl who was wishing she was traipsing around Greenwich Village instead of working, and she didn't like it one bit.

This is ridiculous. She needed to restart her brain. Maybe a spin class would do the trick. She pushed to her feet and stalked into her bedroom to change her clothes.

On her way out of her building, her phone chimed several times. She dug it out of her bag, hoping for more pictures and annoyed at herself for it. She deflated at the sight of a family group text. Jules had sent several of the pictures that had been splashed all over social media of Leni and Raz holding hands on their way out of the restaurant with his parents last night with the accompanying headlines: *RAZ'S PARENTS MEET HIS NEW LOVE. IS THERE A WEDDING ON THE HORIZON?*

Jules: *Sissy is in LOVE! Time to plan another wedding!* Three celebration emojis popped up.

Archer: *He'd better put a ring on her finger.*

Jules sent a video of Beyoncé's "Single Ladies (Put a Ring on It)."

Jock: *Don't push her to marry a guy the rest of us haven't even met.*

Indi: *Don't worry. I'm revoking Archer's texting privileges.*

Archer: *Even the dirty ones, babe?* He added a devil emoji.

Indi: *Um…no…those can stay.* A blushing emoji popped up.

Grant: *Please remove me from this group text.*

Sutton sent three laughing emojis.

Levi: *I don't believe Leni is in love, and yes, please revoke Archer's texting privileges.*

Indi sent a laughing emoji.

Tara: *Is this real? Leni is getting married? I'm on a photo assignment and haven't looked at social. Jules?*

Jules: *It's true!* Pictures of Leni and Raz's mother arm in arm and Leni hugging Raz's parents outside her apartment building popped up, followed by about ten heart-eyed emojis.

Sutton sent a shocked emoji, followed by a face-palm emoji. *Leni???*

"God, really?" Leni said exasperatedly. "Do you want to buy a unicorn, too?"

Leni: *You can't believe everything you read. We're NOT getting married.*

Tara: *Shoot. I was getting excited.* A sad-faced emoji appeared.

Daphne: *Take it from someone who married the wrong man before I met the right one. Take your time, and be sure. You'll know if he's the one.*

Levi: *I'm just happy she hasn't booted him to the curb yet. I still can't believe someone made it past coffee.*

Jules: *But she met his parents!* Three fingers-crossed emojis appeared.

Pissed about having to keep up this ruse with her family and frustrated with herself for wishing she'd gone with Raz and his family, Leni furiously thumbed out, *I'm walking into a spin class. We have enough engaged family members. Stop trying to marry me off!* She silenced her phone and shoved it into her bag, needing the spin class now more than ever.

LENI LEFT THE spin class with a much clearer head and stopped on her way home to get snacks. But when she got back to her apartment, things went downhill fast. Raz sent more pictures, making it impossible for her to stop thinking about him, leaving her wondering what else they were doing this afternoon. If that wasn't bad enough, her mother called, wanting all the details about Leni's *new beau*, most importantly, how he treated her and whether she was as happy as she looked in the pictures.

Leni had reassured her, and even though that much was true, she'd been struggling to define the lines between fact and fiction for the past hour, staring at the same bullet points she'd written that morning. She grabbed another handful of Cheez-Its. Her phone rang, and as she reached for it, she put a quick and hard *stop* on the hope rising inside her that it was Raz.

She saw Levi's name on the screen, shoved the Cheez-Its into her mouth, and hit the speaker button. "Hey."

"Cheez-Its, chocolate, or ice cream?"

She took a drink. "Cheez-Its."

"Good choice. How's it going?"

"*Great*," she said sarcastically. "I was just on my way to look at wedding dresses."

He laughed. "Jules would love to have a double wedding."

Leni scoffed. "Not happening. What is wrong with everyone?"

"You have to admit, this is not the Leni we all know. Usually you see a guy once and call me to bitch about him. Or on the very rare occasion that you see someone more than once, you at least touch base with me and talk yourself out of liking him. But you're keeping your distance with this guy."

Levi had always been her sounding board, and she'd been his. When he found out he was going to be a father at nineteen, he'd come to her freaking out, and she'd helped him see that he could handle it. When Kip Jones had broken her heart, it was Levi's shoulder she'd cried on and his support that had helped her through. But what could she say now without divulging the ruse?

"You know you can trust me, Len. I might even have some good advice."

"You've been with Tara for five minutes and now you're a relationship guru?"

"*There's* the sister I know and love."

That made her smile.

"Come on, Len. You can level with me. You rarely make it past coffee, and after Kip screwed you over, you said you were done with long-distance relationships *and* you swore off actors. This guy is both, and suddenly you're meeting his parents. Are you pregnant?"

"Ohmygod. *No.*"

"Sorry. I'm just trying to make sense of it. We both know you wouldn't have met his parents if he wasn't important to you, so help me out here. I'm on your side, whatever side that is."

I'm confused about my fake-dating situation. Oh, how she wished she could say that to him. "His parents surprised him by coming into town for the weekend, and he asked me to go to dinner with them. It's not a big deal."

"It kind of *is* a big deal, and you of all people know that."

She closed her eyes, unable to believe she was about to blatantly lie to the only man she'd ever trusted with all her secrets. "Okay, you caught me. He's great, and when he asked me to meet his parents, I jumped at the chance. Now can you let it go?"

He was quiet for so long, she worried he might have sensed her lie, but when she opened her mouth to say something, he spoke first.

"It's good to hear you're finally thinking with your heart instead of your head."

"I don't know how you people live this way," Leni said. "It's painful and confusing."

He barked out a laugh. "It's much harder not to follow your heart. I denied my feelings for Tara for so many years, I didn't even know I was doing it. There was an emptiness and tightness inside me that I didn't understand, and it affected every decision I made."

"I know," she said softly. Everyone had known he had feelings for Tara. How could they not? He was a different person around her. Happier. *Like me around Raz.*

"I had wondered if Wells and Kip had hurt you so badly you'd never recover."

"They didn't break me," she snapped, hating the weakness his comment implied.

"I know. That's not what I meant. Nobody can break you, Len. You're stronger than me. But it's good to see you letting someone in, and for what it's worth, following my heart was the best thing I ever did."

Of course it was. Tara would have changed her entire life for Levi, as he would, and *did*, for her. But that wasn't in the cards for her and Raz, nor should it be. She'd never ask him to give up *anything* for her, and she'd worked too hard doing what she loved to change her life for any man. She just needed her family to stop talking about her and Raz. "Can you do me a favor? If Jules goes off on any more tangents, can you try to nicely shut her down?"

"Sure, but it won't work. Jules is going to spread her happy dust on everyone within reach."

Leni smiled at the image of her sister doing that. "You're probably right. But that's enough about me. How are things with you? Is Joey still loving her new school?"

"She is. But I'm having a rough time with it."

"Why? It's a great school."

"It's not the school. We met up with the Venting Vixens, and their boys are looking at Joey the wrong way." When Joey was an infant, Levi had met a group of moms that got together on weekends to commiserate and hang out, and he'd dubbed them the Venting Vixens. They'd been his sanity saviors the first year after Joey was born. After he and Joey had moved to Harborside, they continued getting together with the ladies and their children when they came back to the island.

"The *wrong* way?" She laughed. "She grew up with them. They know her like other boys don't."

"That doesn't make it any better. I know what happens with kids who grow up together. Look at you and Wells, and me and Amelia." Amelia was Joey's birth mother, and not a nice person.

"She's going to be interested in boys at some point, you know."

"No shit. I think thirty is a reasonable age for that to happen."

Leni laughed. "Trust me, you don't want her first sexual experience to be when she's our age. Guys have too much baggage by then."

"We are *not* talking about Joey's first sexual experience. As far as I'm concerned, even when she's married with children, she's still not doing that."

"Keep up that attitude, and she'll be running into boys' beds just to show you who's boss."

"Can we *not* talk about this?"

"You brought it up," she reminded him.

"And I'm shutting it down. Let's talk about something else."

He was so worked up, Leni couldn't resist teasing him. "Has she started sneaking out yet?"

"*Leni*," he warned.

"Oh, right, you wouldn't know. Maybe you should ask Grandma. She's in the know about everything."

They talked for a little while longer, and after ending the call, Leni put her nose to the grindstone. She managed to get a little work done, and when her phone chimed with a text from Raz, she was surprised to see it was after six. Trying to ignore her racing heart, she opened the message, and a picture of a jazz club appeared, followed by a picture of Raz and his parents sitting at a table. Raz's mother held the picture of Leni above the empty chair between her and Raz. He had his arm around the empty space, puckering his lips toward the image of Leni on that damn Popsicle stick, making her wish for the millionth time today that she'd gone with them.

LENI PUT ON her black Gucci power heels, slipped on her wide gold bracelet, and grabbed her phone from the bed. She told herself not to look at all the texts Raz had sent her over the last two days, but when it came to him, her willpower had a mind of its own. Clutching the phone in her hand, she struggled against the urge to scroll through the texts and pictures one more time.

The last two days had been full of a painful mix of happiness when she'd get a text or look at the pictures and self-loathing for pining after him. Leni had always believed that ice cream and a horror movie could make anything better. But late Sunday night she'd found out that eating a pint of ice cream while watching *The Conjuring* wasn't the cure-all she'd hoped for. She'd tested the theory again last night when Raz had asked her to meet him for drinks after her client dinner. She'd stuck to her guns to pull herself out of the all-consuming Duncan Raz vortex and had declined kindly. A pint of Cherry Garcia and another horror movie had left her wishing she'd met him for those drinks.

But today was a new day, and she'd woken up with renewed resolve. There would be *no* endless thoughts about the charming orgasm master.

Today she was all business.

She blew out a breath, shoved her phone into her leather bag, and took one last look in the mirror. She had a day full of meetings, and she looked sharp in an above-the-knee black skirt, belted at the waist, and a simple white blouse under a beige cashmere cardigan. Her Gucci heels added a dash of sleek sexiness. But Leni didn't wear them because they were sexy. In her world, everything had a purpose. They were her *I am woman, watch me soar* heels. They had thick heels, perfect for fast walking, showing her clients there was nobody she couldn't keep up with.

She headed out for work and found Raz leaning against the railing in front of her building, looking too damn fine in running shorts and a dark T-shirt.

"Good morning, sweetheart." He leaned down and kissed her cheek.

"Hi. I told you I couldn't go running with you." He'd texted her yesterday morning, asking if she wanted to join him for a run. She'd said she was slammed at work this week and was going in early every day. Luckily, that was true. She was trying to honor their honesty vows, after all.

"I know how busy you are, but I missed you, and I'm sure you're having withdrawals from seeing me, so I figured I'd walk you to work and then go running after."

Was he trying to make this more difficult? "*Raz*, that wasn't part of the deal."

"Like I said, I missed you, and I brought breakfast." He turned to pick up a bag and two to-go cups she hadn't noticed on the step beside him. "Coffee and strawberry muffins. We can have breakfast together while we walk and take in the sights, and you won't get off schedule."

She was momentarily stunned. "Sights?"

"Yeah. I know you're not used to checking out your surroundings, and your brain is probably racing in ten different directions, thinking about all the things you have to do today. I will try not to distract you as I point out the things you shouldn't miss. Like this." He flexed one arm, and she laughed. "There are many other sights we'll see along the way. None quite as nice, but definitely worth noticing."

She retracted her earlier thought. She'd need more than power heels to keep up with Duncan Raz.

WEDNESDAY MORNING LENI was surprised to find Raz waiting to walk her to work again, breakfast in hand. Thursday morning she woke up happier, with butterflies in her chest, hoping he'd be waiting for her. Not only didn't he disappoint, but he must have listened to every word she'd said the first day he'd walked her to work, when she'd mentioned having client dinners scheduled for every night this week except Thursday, because he was waiting to walk her home after work. He talked her into stopping for Chinese food, and they'd had a great time. He made her laugh more than any man ever had, and for a guy she'd thought had no respect for her industry, he asked endless questions and seemed more than interested in how her days went. She liked hearing about his days, too, the interviews he gave, the photo shoots he was in, and the scripts he was considering for future roles. When he'd suggested they hang out after dinner, every part of her wanted to jump at the chance.

But she knew they'd end up in bed, and that would make it a thousand times harder to walk away at the end of their ruse. She'd gone home and binged her favorite shows, wishing he'd been there with her.

"Wave to Zelda," Raz said Friday morning as they ate breakfast on the way to her office.

She lifted her to-go cup of coffee, smiling at the gray-haired woman who sat in her window every morning watching the world go by. Raz called her by a different name every day. Yesterday it was Clara, and the day before it was Suzette. "Do you think she ever gets bored?"

"No. She's remembering when she used to watch her husband walk to work in the morning. He'd look up from that spot where we just waved and wave to her. He passed away three years ago."

"Now you're a storyteller?"

"It's her story, and her name really is Zelda. I skipped running yesterday to bring her flowers."

"You did not."

"I sure did. She told me all about her husband, Charles. They met through her mother's friend when Zelda was eighteen and married a year later. They had three children, all of whom still live nearby, six grandchildren, and they'd been married for sixty-two years when he passed away."

Leni's heart swelled. "I can't believe you did that."

"Why? She looked lonely, and I had time before my appointments."

"I don't know. It's not something people usually do. Especially here. You just knocked on her door and she let you in?"

"Not really. To be honest, when I knocked on her door, I figured she'd tell me to get lost. But her son answered the door, and apparently he's a fan of my movies. I told him I'd seen her in the window a few times and wanted to make sure she was okay, and he invited me in."

She couldn't believe it. So many of the celebrities she knew couldn't be bothered to do things or make appearances they weren't paid for, and here was Raz, walking her to work and checking on a stranger. "You're really something. I bet you made their day."

"Actually, they made mine, and Zelda said we make her day every morning. She likes the way you look at me."

"*What?* How can she tell how I'm looking at you? She doesn't know me."

As they approached her office building, he said, "She can feel it, just like I can. Some people have an inescapable connection."

Warning bells went off as her resolve teetered, but the sight of Shea coming down the street pulled her back to reality. "It's only inescapable because you keep showing up."

"Damn right I do. Why not? We both know this is temporary. I just don't see a reason to deny the sparks, or chemistry, we feel."

"I never said I felt anything."

His eyes bored into her. "You didn't have to." The heat in his eyes dissipated, and he smiled casually as Shea approached. "How's it going, Shea?"

"Not as good as it is for you two. Raz, I heard you nailed yesterday's photo shoot."

"What'd you expect? Nailing things is what I'm best at. Right, sweetheart?"

Leni rolled her eyes.

He leaned in and kissed her cheek, then opened the door for

them. "Have a great day. I'll text you later."

They hadn't gotten naked again, but his texts had gotten progressively naughtier, making her wish they had. "Okay. Thanks for breakfast."

She followed Shea into the building, and when the door closed behind them, she wished he'd followed them in.

"No wonder you've been smiling all week. He took you to breakfast?" Shea lowered her voice as they headed for the stairs. "Like a morning-after breakfast?"

"*No*. He showed up Tuesday morning with coffee and muffins and walked me to work, and he's shown up every morning since. Last night he was waiting for me when I left the office. We had dinner together and he walked me home, but that was it."

"Okay, first of all, how cute is that? He *walks* you to work? I would kill for a guy who wanted to spend time with me enough that he'd walk me to work. Everyone I meet barely has time to have a real conversation."

"*Cute* doesn't even scratch the surface. I've been walking the same few blocks for years, and I've never noticed the flower pots on steps and flower boxes in windows or the gorgeous architecture of some of the buildings, much less the people who come in and out of them at the same time every day. Raz not only notices everything and everyone, but he says *hello* to people we see more than once whose faces had become familiar. Faces I've ignored for years. It was like I've had blinders on all this time. *And* he brought Zelda flowers."

"Who's Zelda?"

Frustrated at how unaware she'd been, she said, "It doesn't matter," and tried to change the subject. "Hawk makes time to talk with you."

"Only because it benefits him to spend time with me. I connect him with my clients. But why was that *it* for you and Raz last night? He's obviously into you, and we both know you wouldn't let him walk you to work every day if you weren't into him. You said you really liked his parents, so what's the problem?"

"How can you even ask that? Did you lose sight of the fact that Raz is with me to fix his reputation? That's pretty much equal to Hawk spending time with you for work. Plus Raz is basically on the rebound from Jacinda, and do I really need to remind you that this whole thing is a farce?"

"It started as a farce, but it looked pretty real to me just now."

"The line between real and fake is definitely blurring," Leni admitted. "And I don't like it."

"Why? He's been much easier to work with since you two started seeing each other."

"*Fake* seeing each other, Shea. You're the mastermind behind this ridiculous gig, so don't pretend it's not that."

"I'm sorry. Is it so bad that I was hoping it might be more?"

"*Yes*, it's bad. Neither of us wants a relationship, and it's getting harder to draw that line in the sand for me."

"Neither of you wants it? He really is a good actor. I'm sorry. I didn't realize that."

"It's okay. In a couple of weeks it'll all be over, and things will go back to normal." She didn't even remember what *normal* was anymore. Raz was always there, in her thoughts, in her texts, and in her fucking fantasies. But she'd deal with figuring that out when she got there. "Until then, I'm stuck trying to ignore the freaking butterflies he gives me and make it through that damn wedding next weekend without losing my mind." *Or my panties.*

Seventeen

Leni couldn't stop kissing Raz. She was obsessed with his mouth, with the feel of his wet, naked body rubbing against her. The warm shower water raining down on them made his every touch even more erotic. Her back hit the wall as they ate at each other's mouths, hands groping, bodies grinding. She'd tried so hard to resist him, but he'd shown up early Saturday morning, looking ridiculously delicious in his jogging clothes, and had coaxed her out for another run. After waking up wet and wanting for the past week, all their sexy taunts as they jogged through the park had gotten her riled up, and she was not going to give her vibrator another workout. She wanted the real thing—nine inches of Duncan Raz to make her scream.

"Fuck, I love kissing you," he growled, and took her in another spine-tingling kiss. His hands traveled all over her body as he tore his mouth away and began kissing her neck.

"*God*, that feels good." She stroked his cock as he sucked her sensitive flesh, sending heat scorching through her. "I can't believe we're doing this again," she panted out. "You have to stop doing this to me."

He laughed. "You nearly ripped my clothes off in the park

214

and lured me up here with the promise of sweet buns." He grabbed her ass with both hands, squeezing hard. "You're anything *but* sweet, my dirty little tigress."

"That's not what you said when you were on your knees eating *me* for breakfast five minutes ago."

"Your pussy is sweeter than cherry pie." He pushed two fingers inside her, and she moaned. "But that mouth of yours is as sinful as the devil."

He sank his teeth into her lower lip, and she gasped, going up on her toes. "Make me come again, and I'll show you just how sweet my mouth can be."

"Fuck yeah, you will."

He lowered his mouth to her breast, teasing her nipple as his thumb found her clit. Her head fell back as he licked and sucked and used his teeth in an act of cruel ravishment that had her entire body going up in flames. She clutched his arms, nails digging into his flesh. "Harder with your teeth, faster with your fingers," she pleaded, and he obeyed, sending a flood of heat and tingles up her core and down her limbs. Her vision blurred as pleasure stacked up inside her.

"That's it, baby, fuck my fingers good."

He moved his mouth to her other breast and grabbed her ass with his free hand, squeezing to the point of pain, hurtling her into ecstasy. She cried out, and he crushed his mouth to hers, grinding his hard length against her as her body bucked and clenched around his fingers. She hung on to him to combat her buckling knees as she hit the peak, sensations exploding inside her like fireworks. He tore his mouth away, eyes blazing into her. "That's it, baby, ride that high."

She clung to him, shaking, and he brushed his lips over hers as she came down from the peak, her mind hazy with lust. "I love watching you come." His mouth came coaxingly down over hers, kissing her slower, *deeper*, breathing air into her depleted lungs.

When their lips finally parted, she rested her forehead on his shoulder, her body quivering, aftershocks causing intermittent quakes. "That was outrageous," she panted out.

He laughed.

She should tell him to leave, but she wanted *more*. She wanted to be selfish, to make him think of her every minute the way he made her think of him, though she'd never admit that. She lifted her forehead from his shoulder, meeting his wicked stare. She loved the way he looked at her when he was turned on, like a panther ready to devour his prey. *Yes, please.*

"On your knees, baby. I want to fuck your mouth."

"I thought you'd never ask." She kissed his chest and dragged her tongue down his abs as she sank to her knees. He leaned his back against the shower wall, widening his stance, sinking lower so she could reach him. She licked him from base to tip, holding his gaze as she teased the head, and fisted his cock, stroking him.

He grabbed ahold of her wet hair. "Suck it."

She grinned, eyes narrowing, as she sank lower and sucked one of his balls into her mouth. *"Fuuck."* She stroked him as she teased his balls, loving the way his dick jerked in her hand. She moved higher, licking his length, teasing the broad crown. "Take it deep. I want to see my cock in your mouth."

"What a coincidence. I want to feel it there, and *don't* be gentle."

"Jesus," he hissed.

She lowered her mouth over his shaft, taking him to the back of her throat, stroking tight.

"That's it, baby. There's nothing sexier than seeing your luscious lips wrapped around my cock."

His dirty talk had taunted her all week, whispering through her dreams, ringing out in her head at the most inopportune times, like when she was in meetings with her clients. She craved it, conjured it each of the many times she'd been forced to make herself come just to take the edge off. She sucked him good and hard, his eyes flaming, but she wanted more. She grabbed his ass, quickening his efforts, and he caught on, thrusting faster.

"Touch your pussy," he commanded. "I want you to come when I do."

She reached between her legs as he fucked her mouth deep. She sank lower, taking him deeper with every thrust. "*Jesus.* You take me so well. Right down your throat," he growled. "Imagine those are *my* fingers teasing your clit, *my* mouth between your thighs, my tongue lapping at your pussy."

She closed her eyes as those images slammed into her.

"Eyes on me," he demanded.

The sight of his dark stare, his muscles rigid, abs flexing, had her sucking harder, stroking herself faster. Stings of pleasure coursed through her from the tug on her hair to the thrust of his cock down her throat. Those seconds of having her airway blocked sent spikes of heat racing up her core. Just as her orgasm crashed over her, he gritted out her name, hot jets of come hitting the back of her throat. The sounds of their pleasure echoed in the shower as they rode the waves of their passion until they both collapsed, spent and panting. He lifted her to her feet, holding her in his strong arms. Then his mouth was on hers, their tongues lashing, filling her with renewed desire hot as the desert, fierce as a tsunami.

He tugged her head back by her hair. "I can't get enough of you."

She couldn't either, and that was a problem. "You have to leave" came out breathless and half-heartedly.

"Hell no. I want to fuck you hard and deep and feel your pussy wrapped around my cock so tight, it's painful."

She wanted that, too, more than she cared to admit.

"You know you want it. You want to ride my dick until you have nothing left to give."

"Yes" came out as a desperate, panting plea. "But this is the last time."

"Last time." He sank his teeth into her neck, sending exquisite pleasure ricocheting through her, fracturing her ability to say another word. She stepped out of the shower, reaching for a towel. He swatted her hand away. "No towel. I want you wet all over." He slapped her ass, and she darted out of the bathroom, laughing.

He tackled her onto the bed, and as his mouth claimed hers, rough and hungry, she wondered how she'd ever make it through her typical Saturday mornings ever again.

AFTER THREE INSANELY intense orgasms and a second shower, Raz wouldn't stop kissing and touching Leni as they dressed. If she wasn't careful, they'd spend the whole day having sex, and she'd get nothing done.

As if he'd read her mind, he ran his nose along her cheek, his arms circling her waist. "Let's spend today together."

Her body begged her to agree, as if winning the orgasm

lottery wasn't enough. Why was he so irresistible? "I have to work."

"You know you'd rather hang out with me. How about tonight?"

"Get that smug look off your face, and *no*. You have already taken up too much of my time." She stepped out of his arms and headed for the bathroom before he could convince her to do anything else. "I'm going to dry my hair. Please close the door behind you on your way out."

Safely behind the bathroom door, she blew out a breath and focused on getting her head on straight. As she dried her hair, she toyed with the idea of spending the rest of the day with him. Her mind tiptoed down that make-believe path, imagining a lazy, sensual day of exploring each other's bodies, trying new and different positions she'd only read about, taking time out only to refuel with a light snack or a catnap before going back to their devious, toe-curling activities. She shuddered with the thought and realized her panties were damp.

What was wrong with her? That was the type of thing couples did. Lucky couples, real couples, not temporary, fake couples. She just had to make it through one more weekend, and then he'd be gone.

A wave of longing passed through her as she remembered the fun they'd had this week. Sad eyes gazed back at her from the mirror. What was she? A fucking schoolgirl?

She didn't have time for this nonsense.

She forced herself to think about the work she had to do, organizing it in her mind as she finished drying her hair. When she was done, she heard Raz talking in the bedroom. Why was he still there? She tugged open the bathroom door, ready to give him hell, and found him pacing by the window, talking on the phone.

"That sounds great. I can't wait to meet you." He lifted his chin in her direction. "Leni just got out of the bathroom. Hold on a second." He held out *her* phone, the gold case sparkling in his hand. "It's your mom."

Leni's heart nearly stopped, and his cocksure grin didn't help. She was sure she was breathing fire as she snagged the phone from him, hoping he was kidding. "Mom?"

"Hi, honey. What a nice young man Duncan is. I love him already. I can't wait to meet him next weekend."

She glowered at Raz, who looked even more smug than before. "Mom, that's not such a good idea." She scrambled for excuses. "I don't think we'll have enough room."

"Don't be silly. It's just you and Sutton, and wouldn't you and Duncan be sharing a room? Your father and I aren't old-fashioned."

Shit.

"Duncan is excited to meet everyone, too. I have to go, honey. I cannot wait to tell Jules. She's shown me all the pictures, and she's so excited that you're happy. Love you!"

The line went dead, and Leni stared at the phone, heart racing.

"I really like Mama Steele."

Leni met Raz's gaze with an icy one. "*Don't* call her that. I can't believe you answered my phone. You're *not* coming home with me."

"Your mom invited me. I'm not going to let her down. But don't worry. She assured me I'd have plenty to do while you're at the bridal shower with the girls."

Leni breathed deeply, trying to calm down. "I'll tell them we broke up or you couldn't make it."

"You can't tell them we broke up. I already added you as a plus-one for Jay's wedding that Sunday." He closed the distance between them, his expression softening. "It's only for a weekend. I'd like to check out the island anyway, and your mother said there's never any paparazzi there, so we can just kick back and have fun."

She softened, because that sounded nice. Everything was nice with him. *Nice* wasn't the issue. "Just because there's usually no paparazzi doesn't mean they won't follow us there, and I don't want to bring that chaos home with me on Jules's bridal shower weekend."

"I'll call Shea, and she can set up a decoy to get photographers off our scent."

"They're not *dogs*."

"The fuck they're not. They're media hounds. They make money off exploiting other people. Shea can get a couple who looks like us to take off on a private plane out of LaGuardia for the weekend. One leak about the destination, and the paparazzi will follow like flies to shit. It's an easy fix."

She knew he was right because they'd done it before for clients. "That's not the biggest issue. It's hard enough lying to"—*myself*—"my family over the phone. How am I going to do it in person?"

"You don't have to," he said reassuringly. "You like spending time with me, and you like kissing me. That's *real*, Leni, even if it's not forever. No need to lie about any of it. I'll tell you what. Treat me however you want to treat me, and I'll continue being the adoring fake boyfriend you can't resist. We've got this, princess."

Then why did she feel like she was careening down a hill that would most certainly end in a life-altering crash?

Eighteen

THE WEEK FLEW by in a whirlwind of all sorts of adventures with Raz, who rebutted her every half-hearted attempt to spend time alone. He walked her to work, and they'd brought Zelda muffins twice. Leni had found her as delightful as Raz had described. While he studied his lines and met his other commitments, Leni worked like a fiend and fielded messages from her family and friends about what Jules had enthusiastically deemed *Leni's boyfriend-reveal weekend*. Raz had gone shopping with Leni on her lunch hour to get Jules's bridal shower gift, and the evenings when her meetings didn't run too late, he either appeared to walk her home or was waiting on her doorstep, bearing boxes of Cheez-Its, ice cream, or takeout. On one occasion, he'd brought all three *and* had surprised her with sexy lingerie. They'd binged her favorite shows, which had scared Raz, and he'd forced her to watch a Rambo marathon, which made her want to be a Green Beret. They'd argued about characters and storylines, and despite Leni's continuous and emphatic *This is the last time*, they'd ended each of those nights tangled up in each other's arms and had woken the following mornings with Leni draped over him like a second skin.

The line between real and fake had gotten even blurrier,

which was why, as the ferry approached Silver Island, with its colorful cottages, cedar-sided homes, and lush landscape, a sight that usually brought the comforts of home, Leni's stomach twisted into knots.

A breeze swept over them where they stood by the railing. Leni pulled her jacket tighter over her sweater. She'd paired it with her favorite skinny jeans and knee-high leather boots. Raz had loved her boots so much, he'd said he wanted to see her wearing only them later.

She glanced at him, clean shaven and strikingly handsome in a navy sweater that made his eyes look even bluer, a black jacket, and dark jeans. She'd noticed he looked more relaxed lately, his smile more genuine than it had been when they'd started this ruse. Shea had said the same thing about Leni before she left the office today. Leni had brushed it off, but if the difference in her appearance was anything like what she saw in Raz, she was in big trouble.

"Cold, babe?" Raz drew her against him, rubbing his hand along her back.

Leni hadn't ever been a PDA type of person, but lately she'd melted a little every time he did sweet things like that, and when he called her *babe* or *sweetheart* or even *princess*. She didn't consider herself any of those endearments, but when he said them, she wanted to be every one of them for him.

"What a gorgeous island," he said. "We haven't even left the ferry, and it feels like we're a world away from the city."

"I know. Even after all these years, I still feel that way."

"What's that?" He pointed to the monument in the distance.

"Silver Monument." The stately monument resembled a turret from a castle. "It's in the center of the island, and it's surrounded by a brick-paved courtyard with iron benches. It's really pretty, and it's near the park where they light the Christmas tree."

"Where your sister is getting married?"

"Yeah, I can't believe you remembered."

"I told you I remember everything you say. It's like a curse." He laughed. "Can you go inside the monument?"

"Mm-hm. You can climb the stairs to the top. There are spectacular views." She remembered he was afraid of heights. "That *you* will probably never see."

He smiled. "Probably not. But I'd like to see the monument, and if we have time, maybe the towns you told me about, too?"

She'd been so nervous about the trip, she hadn't even thought about showing him around. "Sure, we can try. See the flags just down the hill from the monument? They're the winery flags. You can't see my parents' house from here, but it's next to the winery. My grandmother lives in the carriage house out back."

"Good. I want to have a chat with her about passing out condoms to innocent girls."

Leni laughed.

"Growing up next to the winery must have been something, huh? I bet the views are great."

"I don't think I fully appreciated how lucky we were to have grown up here until I moved away. My first apartment was like a shoebox."

"New York is pricey. How does it feel to come back here tonight? When I go home, I feel like I can let my guard down and just be me."

"It feels good to be home, but I never really let my guard

down."

"That's not true. I've made a little chink in your armor, haven't I?"

"*Well…*" She tried to stifle her smile.

"Come on, admit it, Steele. Just a little one?" He held up his finger and thumb about an inch apart.

She leaned into him. "Maybe a little."

"Are you nervous about introducing me to your family?"

"That's one way of putting it." There was more than just nerves in play. It had taken Leni a long time to get past the memories certain places on the island held because of her relationship with Wells, like where they'd had secret trysts or had spent special time together. With Wells, she hadn't felt anything close to what she felt for Raz, which made her wonder if she'd wrestle with even bigger ghosts after this trip.

"Don't worry about lying to your family. You like me too much to have to lie about anything."

She didn't try to deny it. He'd been calling her on her little white lies all week.

"Except for the future of our relationship," he said, looking away, his jaw as tight as the knots in Leni's stomach.

They didn't say much as the ferry docked, but she saw him scanning the surrounding area.

"Expecting someone to be here?" Leni asked.

"Paparazzi. I don't want those bastards interrupting your family's weekend or making you uncomfortable. I had Patch pay the guys who run the ferries on the mainland to give our security detail a heads-up if they spotted anyone suspicious, and we put a few security guys on both ends, just in case the decoy failed." He pointed to a guy sitting on a bench with his arm stretched across the back, ankle crossed over his knee, like a tourist, and two more guys walking the docks.

"That was really nice of you, but why didn't you take extra precautions when we went to dinner with your parents?"

"I had extra security. They were just discreet. It was a win-win. I got the evening with you, and the paparazzi got more of a story."

"But your security guys can't really do anything to stop them, can they?"

A slow grin split his lips.

"Never mind. I don't want to know."

Leni shouldered her overnight bag, and as they followed the crowd off the ferry, she spotted Sutton and Jules waiting for them. Sutton was smirking, her arms crossed. She knew just how nervous Leni was about bringing Raz home, and she was probably thinking, *Better you than me.* Beside her, Jules waved frantically, her golden-brown hair sprouting from a ponytail on top of her head like a fountain raining down on the long locks trailing over her shoulders. "There they are." Leni pointed to them. "The tall blonde is Sutton, and—"

"That has to be Jules. She's obviously happy you're here."

"I think she's happier to see you than me." They made their way toward her sisters. "I never bring guys home to meet the family."

"I'm honored, and I will do you proud."

"It's not like I had a choice in the matter," she reminded him.

Jules ran over and threw her arms around Leni. "I missed you!"

"I missed you, too, Jules."

Sutton hugged Leni, whispering, "He's even hotter in person."

Yup. "Raz, this is Sutton and Jules."

"Call me Duncan, please. I've heard a lot about you both." He flashed a winning smile and opened his arms. "Mind if I—"

Jules launched herself into his arms. "We're huggers, too! I'm so glad you're here."

Raz laughed, and Leni grabbed Jules's shoulder, prying her off him. "Okay, let the man breathe."

As he embraced Sutton, Jules said, "He's cute!"

"Yes, he is," Leni said with a sigh, catching Raz's very pleased grin.

"We're parked over there." Sutton pointed to Jules's Jeep.

Raz took Leni's hand as they followed her sisters. She saw Levi's Durango speed into the lot. "Was Levi supposed to pick us up?"

"No," Sutton said.

Levi's Durango stopped just ahead of them, and all four doors flew open. Jock, Archer, Grant, and Levi bolted out of the SUV. Levi exclaimed, "Welcoming committee!" Before Leni could process what was happening, they'd cable-tied Raz's wrists, and Jock and Levi were dragging him toward the SUV.

"Hey, Len, should I be worried?" Raz hollered.

"I don't know," Leni snapped. "What the hell are you guys doing?"

"Taking care of business," Archer said gruffly. He nodded to Grant, who put a sack over Raz's head.

"Hey! Stop it!" Leni grabbed Levi's arm, trying to tug him off Raz, and Sutton and Jules ran over to help. *"Levi,* cut the shit. Jock! Let him *go!"*

"What the hell, Archer?" Raz struggled to get free as they dragged him toward the SUV. "I thought we were friends."

Archer pulled the girls off, holding them back as they hollered threats, trying to fight their way past, while the guys shoved Raz into the back seat of the Durango. Jock and Grant flanked him and closed the doors as Levi climbed in behind the wheel. Archer shoved the girls away and climbed into the passenger seat.

Leni was shaking with fury. "You're going to pay for this!"

Archer flashed a big-ass grin. "Love you, too, sis."

As they sped off, Leni shouted, "We have to follow them!" They climbed into Jules's Jeep. "Hurry or we'll lose them."

Jules put the Jeep in reverse, and the telltale *clunk* of a flat tire had them all gasping.

"That doesn't sound good," Sutton said.

Leni jumped out to look for the flat and found a deep gash in the rear passenger tire. *Fucking Archer.*

"Oh my gosh, you guys, *look.*" Jules held up two one-hundred-dollar bills. "It was on my seat!"

"You're going to need that. Archer slashed your tire," Leni fumed, and pulled out her phone.

"Are you calling the auto shop to fix my tire?" Jules asked.

"No. I can put on your spare. I'm calling Dad so he can find his idiot sons and make sure they don't hurt Raz."

RAZ DIDN'T KNOW what was going on or why Leni's brothers and Grant were fucking with him, but no matter what he said, they didn't respond. When the SUV started rocking and pitching, he knew they were no longer on a paved road. He was sweating under the burlap sack. "How about taking this thing off my head?"

The truck stopped, and someone cut the engine. He heard the doors open, and then he was yanked from the vehicle, the burlap sack tugged off his head. He welcomed the cool air, breathing deeply, but before he could get a word out, they spun him around, and Jock and Levi dragged him toward the edge of a cliff. His heart slammed against his ribs. He struggled to get free and tried to plant his heels in the grass, but they were as big as he was and too determined to halt.

"Guys, seriously, what's going on? Why are you doing this?" He struggled harder as they neared the edge. Cold sea air blasted Raz's face, and he heard waves crashing against the bluffs below. "Seriously, put that thing back on my head. I'm not an action hero. I can't break free or not die when you toss me over the edge."

"No shit," Grant said with a laugh. "An action hero wouldn't have let us grab him in the first place."

They leaned him over the edge, and his eyes slammed shut. *Breathe. Just keep fucking breathing.* This was his worst nightmare, but he wasn't about to let them see that.

"What're your intentions with Leni?" Jock demanded.

"My *intentions*? I'm into her, man. She's amazing." What the hell? Was this some kind of test? He glowered at Archer. "I told you that."

"Yeah, after you sauntered out of her *bedroom* calling her Len Bug," Archer seethed. "You'd have said anything so I didn't kick your ass."

"Maybe you'd do that shit, but I wouldn't. I'm not afraid of you. So…*what?* You didn't believe me, so you got your brothers and buddy to do your dirty work? Pussy."

Grant chuckled behind him.

"*Dude*," Archer complained.

"What? It was funny," Grant said.

"I got plenty more where that came from," Raz snapped.

"Watch it," Levi warned, leaning Raz farther over the cliff.

"Whoa…*fuck*." Panic flared in his chest. "Pull me back! Pull me the fuck *back*!" He squeezed his eyes shut, but they flew open again. "I don't know if you're just messing with me, or what, but my parents already lost one kid. They won't survive losing another."

Their grips on his arms tightened. Jock and Levi exchanged confused glances and looked back at Grant and Archer.

"He's an actor. He's fucking with us," Archer snapped.

"I wouldn't lie about my sister! She was killed in a car accident during a storm. I swear it's true. You can ask Leni." *Jesus, Leni…*

"Fuck," Levi said as he and Jock yanked him back from the edge. "I'm sorry, man."

"Yeah, really sorry," Jock said, glassy-eyed. "I wouldn't wish that kind of loss on anyone."

"Seriously, dude. I've lost too many buddies to count. I'm sorry." Grant cut the cable tie.

Raz tried to catch his breath and turn to face Archer, but something heavy tugged at his waist. "What the f—" There was some kind of cable running between Raz, Grant, and Archer, and another one between Raz and the trailer hitch on the back of the SUV.

"In case you struggled free. We didn't want you to get hurt." Jock started unhooking the tethers.

"Leni would slaughter us," Levi added.

Grant scoffed. "She's going to do that anyway."

"Y'all deserve it. *Jesus*." Raz bent at the waist, hands on his thighs, trying to get a grip on his racing heart. "You nearly gave me a heart attack." Once free from the cables, he turned to Archer, whose bravado had dissipated. His face was a mask of regret.

"I didn't know about your sister," Archer said in a low, pained voice. "I'm sorry. We wouldn't have pranked you like that if we'd known. We've all lost people we loved."

Raz thought about the loss that had decimated Jock and Archer's relationship for years and had shattered the Steele family. "Leni told me about Kayla and Jock's baby. I'm sorry you all went through that."

Archer's and Jock's jaws tightened, and they exchanged a look Raz couldn't read, but their sadness thickened the air.

Raz trained his eyes on Archer. "I didn't lie to you when you came to Leni's apartment, and I'm not afraid of you. But I am afraid of hurting my family and Leni. So don't fuck with me like that."

Archer gave one curt nod.

He glowered at the others. "That goes for all of you."

"We got it," Levi said.

"I think he's earned a beer." Grant grabbed a six-pack out of the SUV and handed Raz a bottle of Fat Tire beer.

"Hey, this is my favorite beer," Raz said.

"Leni texted this morning and asked us to pick some up." Jock clapped him on the shoulder. "Congratulations. You passed our scrutiny."

Raz was still stuck on Leni thinking about getting him his favorite beer.

"Yeah, you passed," Levi said. "But listen carefully. Leni might be one of the strongest people you'll ever meet, but beneath that tough exterior is a soft-hearted woman who loves hard and hurts deep. So don't fuck with her, or I will personally make you pay for it."

"No wonder Leni gave up men," Raz said as they opened their beers. "You all are like the Silver Island mafia or some shit."

The guys laughed.

"The truth is, Leni doesn't need us to do her dirty work," Archer said. "If you hurt her, she'll deck you while she's crying."

Her brothers and Grant murmured their agreement.

"I have no doubt she'd deck me, but you must know a different Leni than I do. I get the feeling she doesn't let many people see her cry." Raz took a drink of his beer.

"No shit," Levi said.

"You've got that right," Jock added.

Raz should probably hate these guys for scaring the shit out of him, but how could he hate anyone for protecting their sister? "Please tell me you didn't let that asshole Wells get away with hurting Leni."

Grant lifted his chin, staring him down. "That asshole is my younger brother."

"Shit. Sorry about that."

"Nah, it's okay." Grant chuckled. "He was a dick back then."

"Not to worry. I handled Wells." Archer cracked his knuckles.

"Why am I not surprised?" Raz said, and they all laughed. He reached for his phone, but his pocket was empty. He checked his other pockets and looked around. "I think I dropped my phone."

The guys eyed each other, wearing troublemaking grins.

"All right, guys, give me my phone. I want to call Leni and let her know I'm still alive."

Grant coughed to cover his words as he said, "Pussy-whipped."

"Nah, man. I just don't want her to worry."

"She's too mad to be worried," Jock said.

"It's better to leave it as is until we see her," Levi added.

"Yeah, we'd like to live a little longer, so how about we enjoy our beers and deal with our sisters' wrath when we get back," Archer said. "We'll send Levi in first. He's got the best chance of survival, being her twin and all."

Nineteen

BY THE TIME Leni was done changing the tire, she was fit to be tied. The guys weren't answering their phones, and while Leni trusted them not to hurt Raz, she didn't know what kind of hell they'd put him through. She and her sisters had called their brothers' friends as well as their mother, Indi, Daphne, and Tara, none of whom knew anything about what had gone down.

If she had to listen to Jules say *Don't worry, Raz is fine* one more time, she was going to lose her shit. Even if he was fine, she was pissed at the way they'd manhandled him.

"I'm sure they're at Mom and Dad's, having a good laugh at your expense," Sutton said.

"They'd better be." Everyone was coming to their parents' house for dinner, and Leni hoped to hell they were there, but as they pulled up to her childhood home, with a gazebo anchoring one side of the wide front porch, disappointment set in. Only their mother's and the other girls' cars were there. The girls must have come over after hearing what the guys had done.

"Where could they be?" Leni asked as they climbed out of the Jeep.

"They're probably at Rock Bottom with Wells, and he's

covering for them," Sutton said.

"Wells wouldn't do that to Leni," Jules said as they headed up to the house.

"She's probably right. He knows I'd murder him."

They were greeted by the heavenly scent of a home-cooked meal and freshly baked *something*.

"Aunt Leni's here!" Joey ran out of the kitchen, her cinnamon hair trapped beneath a backward baseball cap.

Hadley toddled behind her in leggings and a cute pink sweater, clutching a cookie in one hand and her favorite stuffed owl in the other. "Auntie Leni!"

Joey threw her arms around Leni, and Hadley flew into Joey's back, giggling. "Had!" Joey said through her laughter, making Hadley giggle harder as she wiggled out from between her and Leni.

It was hard to stay mad with two adorable giggling girls hugging her. Leni held her grease-covered hands up, so as not to dirty their clothes. "I've missed you guys, but fair warning, your daddies are in big trouble when they get home."

"Why is Daddy Dock in twouble?" Hadley asked around a mouthful of cookie.

Sutton scooped her into her arms. "He absconded with Aunt Leni's boyfriend."

"What's absconded?" Joey asked.

"It means they kidnapped him, and Aunt Leni is mad and a little scared for him," Jules explained.

Leni wondered how Jules saw her fear through her anger.

Joey gasped. "For *real*, they kidnapped him?"

"No, honey. It was a prank, like you and your uncles did to your daddy on the boat," Leni said as they headed down the hall to the kitchen.

"Oh!" Joey cracked up. "That's a good one!"

"A pwank? I *love* pwanks," Hadley exclaimed.

The kitchen counters were littered with a feast's worth of food and cookies on cooling racks. Their mother and grandmother were making a salad at the counter, Daphne and Tara were setting the dining room table, and Indi was pouring several glasses of wine.

Their mother looked up with a warm smile and worried eyes, her auburn hair framing her beautiful face. "There's my girls."

"Someone's breathing fire," their grandmother said, as fashionable as ever, with her blond pixie cut, wearing black slacks and a black-and-white block sweater.

"Do you blame her?" Indi said, giving Leni a look that translated to *those dumbasses.*

Leni snagged a cookie and chomped on it as Tara and Daphne rushed into the kitchen from the dining room like the cavalry. The funny thing was, they were the sweetest, most gentle of all the girls.

"Mommy, Daddy Dock did a funny pwank on Aunt Leni's boyfwiend and she's mad and sad!" Hadley announced as Sutton set her down.

"I know, honey." Daphne, a curvy blonde, looked at Leni apologetically. "I tried calling Jock, but his phone must be off."

"I tried Levi, too, and got his voicemail," Tara said.

"Smart boys," their grandmother said.

"Have you heard from Raz?" Indi asked, blue eyes full of concern as she handed Leni a glass of wine.

"No, and I need about ten of those, but I have to wash my hands first."

"We called everyone, and nobody has seen them." Sutton

picked up a wineglass and took a sip.

"I haven't heard from your father, either," their mother said. "I called Margot and Gail, and they haven't heard from any of them." Margot Silver, Jules's soon-to-be mother-in-law, and Gail Remington were two of their mother's best friends.

"I can't imagine where they could've gone," Leni said as she dried her hands.

Their grandmother embraced her. "If they're smart, they're on their way *off* the island."

"*Mom*," their mother chided, and her grandmother chuckled. "Just breathe, baby." She hugged Leni, and Leni soaked in her comfort. "I'm glad you're here. I love you."

"I love you, too, Mom, but I don't love your sons very much right now."

She took Leni by the shoulders, giving her that boys-will-be-boys look. "You know they only did it because they love you, and I'm sure they're just bringing him into the fold. Showing him they have your back."

"Yeah? Well, I'm going to show them how my fist has their faces." Leni took the wineglass from Indi and downed half of it.

"*Leni*," her mother warned.

"What? They cable-tied his hands, put a sack over his head, and dragged him away like a frigging…I don't know what! God only knows what Raz was thinking. If I were him, I'd want to get the heck off the island." Which should make her happy because it would mean she wouldn't have to pretend to be his girlfriend when he was leaving in just a few days. But the thought of him leaving early made her stomach hurt even worse…and that annoyed the hell out of her. Her emotions were all over the place, and she hated it.

"I'll be sure to punish Archer," Indi assured her.

"Don't bother. He'd probably like it." Leni gulped more wine.

Her grandmother laughed. "You got that right. He's a chip off your grandfather's block, that one."

"I don't need to know that," their mother said.

"I'm sure he's fine," Jules said for the millionth time.

"He better be," Leni gritted out.

"Can you believe little Miss Prepared didn't warn him about their pranks?" Sutton shook her head. "If I ever bring a guy home, he'll be armed and dangerous, wearing full body armor."

Indi and the girls giggled.

"I was nervous enough about bringing him here." *And lying to everyone.* "I didn't think about their pranks."

"I don't blame you," Tara said. "I've known about the pranks for years, but the guys are so good at it, I totally believed Levi was being arrested when they pranked him."

"We got you so good!" Joey gloated.

Tara raised her eyebrow, giving Joey what Leni could only describe as a disapproving *mom* face.

"Um…?" Joey cracked an apologetic smile and climbed off the stool she was sitting on at the counter. "Come on, Had. I think we should go play."

As they ran out of the kitchen, Leni's mother went to Tara and touched her back. "Good job, Mama."

"I wasn't mad at her," Tara, who was only twenty-four, said sweetly.

"I know that," her mother said. "But you made it clear that gloating wasn't appropriate. You've gone from being her fun aunt to being a wonderful mom to her."

"Stepmom," Tara clarified.

"Call yourself what you will, honey, but *we* know you're the only mother she's ever really had."

The kitchen door opened, and they all spun around. Their father held his hands up. "It's just me." He went to Leni. "I went everywhere I thought they'd be, but no luck. I'm sorry, Bean."

Her heart squeezed at the childhood nickname. "Thanks for trying."

"I'll always do my best. You know that." He embraced her, holding her a little longer than usual. "Did you have any trouble changing the tire?"

"No, *she* didn't." Jules stomped over to them. "How come you taught Sutton and Leni how to change a tire and you didn't teach me?"

He raised his brows. "You had no interest in learning."

"How do you know?" Jules folded her arms over her chest. "You taught me how to use your woodworking tools, and I loved it."

"Yes, which is probably why when I tried to teach you how to change a tire, I believe you said *I know how to use enough tools, Daddy, and I'm never moving away, so if I get a flat, I'll just call you.*"

Jules cocked her head. "*Really?* That was ignorant."

He laughed. "Careful, now. That's my daughter you're talking about. You weren't ignorant. You were busy thinking about all the things sixteen-year-olds think about."

"You should've forced me to learn," Jules said.

"Baby, there was no forcing any of you into anything." He pulled Jules into a hug. "I'll teach you this weekend."

"Sutton and I already taught her." Leni finished her wine and set down her glass. "I wish they'd get back."

Jules's phone chimed. She pulled it out of her pocket, and

her eyes lit up. She bit her lower lip, texting feverishly. She'd gotten a text earlier that had made her grin like that, and she'd said Bellamy Silver, her maid of honor/bestie, had made a big sale at her gift shop.

"What are you so happy about?" Leni asked.

Jules put her phone behind her back, eyes wide. "*Um…new stock at my shop.*"

Leni and Sutton exchanged disbelieving glances.

"New stock my butt." Sutton snagged Jules's phone from her hand and read the text. "It's from Grant. *Hi Pix, we're on our way back. Miss you. Can't wait to…*" Her brows lifted, and she handed Jules back her phone. "You dirty little thing. Look at those naughty emojis."

Jules giggled.

"That's more information than I needed to hear." Their father went to their mother and pulled her into a kiss. "We don't need emojis, do we, sweet thing?"

Their mother giggled just like Jules had.

"Jules, do you know where they went?" Leni asked.

"No," Jules said.

"Then why did you lie about the text?" Sutton asked.

"I don't *know*," Jules insisted. "Because Leni's mad, and Grant sent me something sexy. I didn't want her to feel bad because she hadn't heard from Raz." She turned a syrupy sweet gaze on Leni. "I'm sorry. But I swear, if I knew where they were, I'd tell you."

"Who texted earlier?" Leni asked. "Was it Grant?"

Jules pressed her lips together.

"*Jules,*" Daphne exclaimed.

Leni glowered at Jules. "You have three seconds to tell me where they were."

"Uh-oh," their father said. "We might need to get our refer-ee outfits."

Sutton scoffed. "Might?"

"Jules," Leni warned.

"I don't *know*, okay? I asked where they went when he texted earlier, but I swear he didn't tell me."

Leni's eyes narrowed. "Then what *did* he say?"

"He said please don't be mad at him and that Raz was fine." Her cheeks flamed, and she turned her back to her parents, whispering, "And he wrote out all that dirty emoji stuff."

Leni fumed. "Don't you think you should have told me that?"

"I did! I kept saying he was fine and not to worry."

"I thought you were just being your peppy, optimistic self," Leni snapped.

The front door opened, and male voices filled the hall. Leni saw red and stalked out of the kitchen, hands fisting, barely aware of the others rushing after her. She set her eyes on the guys, all grins and joking around as they took off their jackets by the door. She could practically hear scary music following her down the hall, like in movies when the crazy person goes after their victims.

"Leni, *breathe*, honey," her mother called after her.

The guys turned and froze when they saw Leni, but her eyes shifted to Raz like metal to magnet, and something inside her snapped. Relief bowled her over, her legs propelling her forward without thought, and she threw her arms around him. "I'm so glad you're okay."

"I might need to change my underwear, but I'm fine, babe."

The guys laughed.

That snapped her brain into gear, and she turned on them,

glowering as she stalked closer, hands fisting. "You are all so dead."

"Relax," Archer snapped. "We just took him to see the view from Dead Man's Cove."

"The *view*?" she seethed.

Jock, Levi, and Grant exchanged uncomfortable glances and looked at Archer.

"*Jesus*," Archer gritted out. "So we held him over the cliff, but—"

"You did *what*?" She went after them, fists flying.

Archer, Jock, and Grant scrambled behind Levi, uttering something about it being a joke.

"Seriously, guys?" Levi held his hands up, a barrier between him and Leni.

"You think you're safe just because he's my twin?" Leni poked Levi hard in the center of his chest. "*You* betrayed me. I should have eaten you in the womb." He stumbled backward, causing the other guys to do the same.

"Please don't kill him," Tara pleaded. "I just got him."

"Thanks, babe," Levi said.

Leni glared at him, pushing past to get in Archer's face. "What the hell were you thinking? He could have fallen and died!" She shoved him with everything she had.

"What the fuck, Leni?" Archer rubbed his chest.

"Dude, little ears," Jock snapped.

"*Frick*. What the frick, Leni!" Archer fumed.

"I'll give you what the frick." Leni turned on Jock and Grant. "And you two—"

Raz grabbed her around the waist from behind, tugging her backward. "Whoa, babe, I'm fine."

"That's not the point." She struggled to get free. "They need to pay for this!"

"Don't let her go, dude," Archer pleaded, and the other guys pleaded the same.

"Okay, that's *enough*." Her father stepped between Leni and Archer. "Leni, it was a prank. Raz is fine. He said so himself."

"Yeah, seriously," Jock said.

"Really, chill, Len," Levi said.

Their father turned a dark stare on them. "You four. Outside. *Now*."

Her brothers and Grant hung their heads.

"I'm going with you," Leni fumed, but Raz locked his arms tighter around her, keeping her there.

"Babe, I love that you're defending my honor, but seriously, there are no hard feelings."

Her father pinned her with a serious stare. "Your boyfriend has been traumatized enough. I'll handle this."

Leni pointed at her brothers and Grant. "This *isn't* over. You'd better watch your backs."

Hadley toddled over, blinking sad eyes up at Raz. "Sorry you were napped."

Raz smiled warmly. "What, sweetie?"

"Sorry you were napped." Hadley handed him her stuffed owl and looked at Leni. "You don't need to be scared anymore." She took their hands, leading them toward the living room. Collective *Aww*s came from the girls and regretful *Damn*s from the guys as they headed out the door.

Leni glanced at Raz, who looked like he'd just won the lottery, while she wondered how she was going to survive the weekend without falling even harder for the man who had no idea he was about to break her heart.

Twenty

THE VISIT WITH Leni's family might have started like something out of a bad action movie, but as Raz sat at the dinner table joining their banter, it was like being in the best movie of his life, only better. This was *real*, and nobody treated him like a celebrity. Archer was gruff and ornery toward him and everyone else other than Indi, Joey, and Hadley, while Jock, a doting father and husband, seemed to be the peacemaker of the group, and Levi, though taking a stance at the cliffs, had been joking with him throughout dinner. He'd noticed that Sutton was quieter than the others, but she got her barbs in, and Jules reminded him so much of Tory, she was a welcome ray of sunshine. Leni's parents, Steve and Shelley, were a joy, volleying jokes, telling stories about everyone, and setting their adult children straight with parental glances he was sure they'd been using forever. Then there was Leni's grandmother, Lenore, queen of the Bra Brigaders. There was no question where Leni got her class or her snark from.

Around that table, he was just Leni's boyfriend. One of the guys. *Man*, he'd missed that. Just about the only time he ever felt like that was with his buddies back home in Pleasant Hill. Who would have thought that a fake date to a charity event could lead him here?

He glanced at Leni, and his chest felt tight. When he'd seen her storming down the hall with smoke barreling out of her ears, he was sure she'd say they were leaving. He'd been shocked by her embrace, and he knew by the looks on her family's faces, she'd shocked them with that show of affection, too. He had a feeling it had also shocked Leni, though she was so mad about the prank, it had been only a momentary slip. She'd been her bold self during dinner, doling out her usual sass and sarcasm, with an extra edge toward the guys. He didn't need protecting, but no woman had ever had his back like that, and that felt pretty fucking amazing.

"I love you, Unca Archer," Hadley said, pulling Raz from his thoughts as she went up on her knees to kiss Archer's cheek.

"Love you too, squirt," Archer said.

"Don't give Uncle Archer too much love," Leni said. "He's on the naughty list for kidnapping Raz…*Duncan.*"

"I forgot." Hadley's brows knitted. "What the fwick, Unca Archer?"

Everyone laughed.

"She is a sassy little thing," their grandmother said.

"Hadley, we don't say that word," Daphne chided.

Archer flashed a cocky grin. "Indi likes when I'm on her naughty list."

The guys chuckled.

"Usually that's true," the feisty blonde, who took no guff from her man, confirmed. "But I'm not happy with what you did, so you won't be getting any…" She looked at Hadley and Joey. "Extra dessert from me."

"I highly doubt that." Archer leaned closer to her, whispering something in her ear that made her blush, and Indi downed her drink.

Leni rolled her eyes. "I still can't believe you guys held him over the edge of the cliff."

"We had him tethered so he couldn't fall," Jock said.

"Besides, that's nothing as far as pranks go," Levi insisted. "I got arrested."

Raz laughed. "I heard about that."

"I was in on it," Joey exclaimed proudly, reaching over to high-five Archer and Jock.

"I wouldn't be so proud of that if I were you, kiddo," Levi said with a shake of his head.

"See, Steve? You got off easy," Shelley said. "All they did was steal your clothes."

"At the Christmas tree lighting," Steve reminded her sternly. He looked at Raz. "I had to walk around holding signs that said ADDITIONAL PARKING IN REAR over my privates while people threw money at me and whistled."

"That wasn't nearly as bad as when Jock and Archer shaved a…" Levi glanced at the kids. "An…*eggplant* into the back of my hair, and everyone at school saw it before I realized what they'd done."

Laughter erupted around the table.

"He loved boy bands and wanted them to dye his hair blond," Leni explained.

"Don't cast stones, sweet pea." Lenore eyed Leni with a mischievous grin. "I remember a certain young girl loving boy bands just as much, walking through the grocery store singing, *If you want it hot, find someone to hit the spot* and something about how people needed to rub you the right way."

Everyone burst into laughter.

Levi sang, "*If you want it good, you need a bad boy.*"

"I remember that," Sutton said. "I *told* her not to sing it, and she just sang louder."

"I wanted to gag her," Jock said.

"I had no idea what to say," Shelley said. "She was an innocent girl singing her favorite song."

"Innocent?" Archer scoffed. "Should we talk about her nighttime *swims* with Wells?"

Raz's ears perked up.

Leni's eyes narrowed. "We did go swimming."

"Naked," Archer barked.

"You went swimming naked with a boy?" Joey asked, wide-eyed.

"*No,*" Leni fumed. If looks could kill, Archer would be flayed and bleeding out. "Your uncle is just trying to stir up trouble." She set her napkin on the table. "Excuse me."

As she strode into the kitchen, Shelley glared at Archer. "Haven't you tortured your sister enough today?"

"Like she doesn't give me shit"—Archer's gaze darted to Hadley—"*crap* all the time?"

"I think I'll check on her." Raz headed into the kitchen and found Leni pacing.

She stopped, a small smile curving her lips as he went to her. "I'm sorry about my family."

"Why? They're awesome, and your brothers love you."

"They held you over a cliff."

"That's guy stuff. An initiation. They'd like to think they have a bigger dick than me, that's all."

She laughed. "You're a mess. Everything about us being here is a mess."

"Maybe, but it's fun. I love your loyalty toward me, but you should let your brothers off the hook."

"How can you say that after the way they treated you?"

"Because we talked out there on the bluff. I told them about losing Tory, and they shared their personal stories with me. That's what took so long. It was a good talk. They're good guys, Leni."

"You told them?" Her brows knitted.

"Yeah, it just came out. I didn't know they had me tethered, and I was pretty scared on that cliff, but not for myself. For my parents if anything happened to me." He didn't mention that he'd worried about the effect it might have on her, too.

"I didn't think about that," she said empathetically, but then anger rose in her eyes. "It makes me want to yell at them even more."

"I know, but let's just enjoy the weekend. So far, everything we've done together has been fun. I wouldn't have wanted to go through this with anyone else, and honestly, I wouldn't change a thing. Including their prank. I feel like I got a few good men as friends out of it. At least until the world hears about our breakup, and then they might want to toss me over the cliff for real. Luckily, I'll be far away by then."

"You think they won't hop on a plane?"

"I think you'd stop them." He slid his arms around her. "I feel like I should thank them for letting me see teenage Leni from a whole new perspective. Although I am wildly jealous that Wells got to go skinny-dipping with you."

She rolled her eyes. "We thought nobody knew."

"Siblings always know. But you know what needs to happen now, don't you?"

"I need to tar and feather Archer?" she said hopefully.

He grinned. "No. We're letting that go, remember? We need to go skinny-dipping. I've never been." He lowered his hands, grabbing her ass. "And I've also never gotten down and dirty in the ocean."

"As tempting as that sounds, it's October. Your beloved nine inches will shrink to three."

"Baby, where's the confidence?" he said with mock horror.

She laughed.

"One way or another, I'm getting you naked on the beach, and we're going to obliterate memories of you and Wells, or any other man on Silver Island."

"I haven't done anything like that with other guys here."

He brushed his lips over hers. "And when I'm done with you, you won't want to."

"I can't tell if this is part of your evil plan to ruin me for all other men, or if it's all about your ego."

"Aren't they one and the same? What guy wouldn't want you pining for him?"

"I have news for you. I don't *pine* for anyone."

"Okay, I'll confess. I just want to get you naked, lay you out on a blanket in the sand, and make you come so hard, they can hear you howling my name clear across the sea."

A smile darkened her eyes. "So you want to get me in trouble and give Archer a reason to kill you?"

"Damn. I didn't think about that."

"Obviously."

"Scratch the Neanderthal need for everyone to know I have ruined you, and replace it with a sweet, sexy night on the beach with a bottle of wine and mind-numbing pleasure."

"Now, for that, I think a moonlight beach walk can be arranged."

As he lowered his lips toward hers, he whispered, "You won't be disappointed," and took her in a slow, sensual kiss. She wound her arms around him, rising onto her toes. *That's it, baby, take what you want.*

"I told you they were making out," Sutton said, startling them.

Leni tried to step out of his arms, but he kept her close and said, "Sorry. I can't keep my hands off your sister."

"Yay!" Jules said, carrying a stack of dishes into the kitchen. "Go back to what you were doing. I told Mom I'd do the dishes while everyone gets ready for the bonfire, and kissing is way better than what I thought you were doing."

"What did you think we were doing?" Leni asked.

"Plotting Archer's murder," Jules said.

"Don't worry. I'm going to come up with a way to get back at *all* of them," Leni said.

Raz glanced into the empty dining room. "I'll do the dishes, but first, I have an idea about how we can get back at them."

"We?" Leni asked.

He pulled her into his arms again, because damn it, he couldn't resist, and pressed his lips to hers. "We're a team, princess."

"Princess Sarcasm, maybe," Sutton quipped.

"She's his princess, and he's her prince!" Jules exclaimed.

Leni looked up at the ceiling. "Please make it stop."

He laughed. "Okay, ladies, huddle up. It's time to plan our revenge."

Ten minutes later, Jules squealed. "I love this prank!" and began singing, *"Together, forever, together, all of us. Together, forever, we'll get them back, oh yes!"* She twirled through the kitchen and took Leni's hand, dancing as she sang, *"He's there for us and we're pranking together. Tonight's the night, we'll prank them right..."*

Sutton ran over and started dancing with Raz.

"I don't know this song," he said with a laugh.

"*High School Musical!*" Jules shouted.

"With Jules's lyrics," Sutton said. "Switch!"

Raz grabbed Leni before Sutton could and twirled her into his arms. "It's nice to see that smile again."

She gleamed wickedly. "Revenge is sweet."

So are you, babe. Dangerously sweet.

LENI FELT LIKE she was living someone else's life. Never in a hundred years could she have imagined she'd be sitting on a blanket by a roaring bonfire, snuggled up to Duncan Raz, while Hadley slept on his lap, clutching her owl, and her family chatted around them. She'd gone inside to use the bathroom earlier, and she'd found Raz waiting for her when she'd finished. He'd slipped into the bathroom and kissed her senseless and had been whispering dirty promises about a sexy beach tryst ever since.

They'd quietly clued in Indi, Tara, and Daphne about the prank. Worried the guys might pick up on their excited energy, she glanced at her coupled-off siblings. Levi and Grant had Tara and Jules on their laps. They were chatting with Raz, Sutton, and Joey, who was sitting on Sutton's lap. Indi was nestled between Archer's legs on a blanket, and beside them, Jock lay on a blanket with his head on Daphne's lap while she ran her fingers through his thick dark hair. Leni needn't have worried. They were obviously too happy to think past the moment. Even her parents looked extra cozy on the other side of the fire.

The funny thing was, Leni was happy, too, only she couldn't help *but* think past the moment.

"I can't believe my bridal shower is *tomorrow*, and soon I'll be marrying the man of my dreams," Jules exclaimed.

"I can't wait to make you my wife." Grant kissed her.

"You guys are so cute, and the shower is going to be perfect," Daphne said.

"We have some really fun things planned," Tara added.

"I'm excited to see what you and Bellamy have in store for us," Jules said. "I'm just so happy to celebrate with everyone tonight. I know how busy Sutton and Leni are, and, Duncan, having you here makes it even more special."

"What am I? Chopped liver," their grandmother teased.

"You know I love you, Gram. But he's Leni's boyfriend, and he's a movie star, so you know he's busy."

"I appreciate you letting me crash your special weekend," Raz said.

"You don't seem like a movie star," Joey said from her perch on Sutton's lap. "Are you really in movies?"

"Believe it or not, yes. Unless they've been fooling me this whole time and only pretending to film movies," he teased.

"Is it fun making movies?" Joey asked.

"Most of the time, but it can be hectic. I travel a lot, and it's hard work."

"Leni said you're leaving on Monday to make a movie in LA," her father said. "How long will you be filming?"

Leni had purposely *not* asked about his trip. The less she knew about where he was and what he was doing after he left, the better.

"If all goes well, about three months, but I won't be in LA the whole time. We're filming in several locations."

"Three months is a long time." Indi glanced empathetically at Leni. "Are you allowed to visit him on set?"

Leni didn't want to think about him leaving, much less talk about it. But she knew she had to and forced a casual tone. "I'll be too busy to take off work."

"Her schedule is crazy," Raz reiterated, giving her an I've-got-this look. "She doesn't need the pressure of flying across the country for a weekend."

"You should go, Aunt Leni. Maybe they'll let you be in a movie," Joey exclaimed.

"I don't want to be in movies," Leni said.

"Why not?" Joey asked, wide-eyed. "You could be a *star*."

"Leni isn't fond of the limelight. Do you want to be an actress, Joey?" Raz asked.

Thankful for the change in subject, Leni gave him a grateful smile.

"No. I'm going to be a professional skateboarder and a photographer, like Tara," Joey said. "But I think it's cool to be a movie star."

"I have a feeling you'll be a star at whatever you do," Raz said. "And you already have one star in the family."

"We do? Who?" Joey asked.

"Your aunt Sutton," Raz said.

"Oh *yeah*," Joey said. "But that's different. She's not in movies."

"Gee, thanks, Joey." Sutton tickled her ribs, earning giggles.

"She's not in movies, but she's on television, and that makes her a star. The camera loves her," Raz said.

Sutton eyed him curiously. "Have you seen my show?"

"Yes. Several of them. You interviewed a friend of mine, treasure hunter Zev Braden, and I liked that episode so much, I try to catch your show whenever I can. And like I said, you're great on-screen."

Sutton beamed with pride. "Thank you. That means a lot coming from you. I wish my boss thought that highly of me."

"Leni said he's been giving you a hard time. It was hard breaking into my industry, too. Just keep proving yourself. Keep showing up until he sees how great you are."

"I think I understand how this fine young man broke through my daughter's walls," their mother said.

She didn't know how right she was.

"You got that right." Raz hugged her against his side and kissed her temple, like she'd been his for years.

Part of her wished she had.

"Duncan," their grandmother said. "If Hollywood ever gets to be too hectic, my friends and I have an *in* with a fine entertainment establishment on the Cape. The fellas make great money."

"Grandma, he's *not* working at Pythons," Leni said. "He's an actor, not a stripper."

"Gram, are you hitting up strip clubs?" Raz teased.

Leni was struck by how easily *Gram* rolled off his tongue, just like *Mama Steele* had when she'd called last weekend, as well as the handful of endearments he'd been calling *her* since their first night together.

"Don't be silly," their grandmother said. "It's a ladies' club. We play bingo there."

"That cover was blown years ago, Mom," Shelley said.

Raz laughed, and Hadley woke up. She smiled at him and put her head back down.

"Let me take her off your hands and give you a break," Jock said, coming over to get Hadley.

"She's okay," Raz said.

"Tell me your legs aren't numb," Jock challenged.

"Maybe a little," Raz admitted.

"I figured as much." Jock picked up Hadley.

"Hug, Duncy!" Hadley reached for Raz.

He stood to hug her, and she wrapped her arms around his neck. "Thanks for sharing Owly with me."

"*'Kay*," Hadley said sleepily. "Love you, Duncy."

"Me too, Had," Raz said, looking directly at Leni.

She was sure she was looking at him as dreamily as every other woman around the fire was as he lowered himself to the blanket and draped an arm around her.

"You have Hadley's stamp of approval," Daphne said. "I know it doesn't seem like it, but she's not that comfortable with everyone."

"Well, I'm glad," Raz said. "I love kids, and I rarely get time with them."

"How many nieces and nephews do you have?" Joey asked.

"I don't have any," Raz said.

"Do you have brothers and sisters?" Joey asked. "I want a brother or sister. Daddy said maybe after he and Tara get married I can have one."

Leni's chest constricted, and she laced her hand with his.

He squeezed it appreciatively as he said, "I had a younger sister. Her name was Tory, and she was a lot like your aunt Jules, except she usually knew the right words to songs, and a lot like your aunt Leni, always giving me a hard time about something."

Joey smiled. "Where is she now?"

Raz shifted an approval-seeking gaze to Levi, who nodded. "She's in heaven."

Sorrow thickened the air around them.

"*Oh*," Joey said sadly. "I'm sorry. Do you miss her?"

"Yes, but she's still with me in here." He patted his chest over his heart.

Joey nodded. "Daddy says when people die, they watch over us."

Raz smiled. "I think your daddy is right."

"Oh, Duncan," her mother said. "I'm so sorry."

"Me too," Sutton said, and everyone else chimed in with condolences.

Jules got up from Grant's lap and knelt in front of Raz. "I'll be your surrogate younger sister." She hugged Raz.

Raz gazed at Leni as he returned Jules's embrace. "That'd be pretty cool, Jules."

She sank back on her heels. "I'll probably always get the lyrics to songs wrong."

"That's even better."

"Good!" Jules went back to sitting on Grant.

As she lowered herself to his lap, he said, "I love you, Pix," and kissed her.

"I think I'll head inside and grab a beer." Raz pushed to his feet. "Can I get anyone anything?"

There was a round of "No, thanks."

Raz touched Leni's shoulder. "How about you, princess?"

The only thing Leni wanted was more of his kisses.

"Princess?" Archer laughed.

Indi elbowed him. "Behave."

Leni glowered at Archer and turned a softer gaze on Raz. "I don't need anything, thanks."

He arched a brow. "Not even a little sugar?"

"*Well…*" How did he know?

He leaned down and kissed her.

"I have a sweet tooth," Sutton said.

Raz chuckled. "I'll get you a cookie."

As he headed inside, Joey went after him. "I wanna go with you!" Raz offered his hand, and she took it, smiling up at him. "Do you know Taylor Swift?"

"No, but I know people who do."

Joey gasped. "Tara and I *love* her! Could you get us her autograph?"

"Joey," Levi hollered. "Give the guy a break."

"It's all good," Raz called over his shoulder.

Sutton and Indi popped to their feet and hurried over to Leni, flanking her on the blanket.

"If you don't want him, I'll take him," Sutton said.

Indi looked at her like she was crazy. "Does she *act* like she doesn't want him?"

"Can't blame a girl for wishful thinking," Sutton said.

"He's incredible, Leni," Indi said. "I like him even more than I did when I first met him, and he won me over with his Archer-whisperer ways." She lowered her voice. "Archer said he was tough on the cliffs, too. I mean, as tough as he could be, given the situation."

"Oh, goodie, we're talking about Duncan!" Jules ran over, motioning for Tara and Daphne to join them. They formed a small circle with Leni and the others, and Jules said, "Are you madly in love?"

"You look so happy, and he's so attentive," Tara said.

"And really good with the girls," Daphne said. "He said he likes kids. Does he want them? Do *you*?"

"I think I need a beer after all," Grant said, pushing to his feet.

"Yeah, me too," Archer said. Jock and Levi agreed, and they all trudged inside like the girls had ruined their good time.

"Hold up!" their father yelled, and caught up with them.

"Good. They're gone. Tell us everything," Jules said.

"Yes, tell us everything," their mother said as she and their grandmother joined them.

They were all looking at Leni expectantly. "Nothing like a little pressure."

"We don't need all the sexy details," her grandmother said. "Our imaginations will suffice there."

"*Gram.*" Leni had never been the center of this type of attention before, and she was conflicted. As much as Leni would like to share in their unbridled positivity, she was smarter than that. She had to try to quell their enthusiasm for her sake as much as theirs, no matter how much she wanted to gush about Raz. He was the first man who made her *want* to rave about him to her family, even if he was only acting. That jolt of reality reminded her of why she didn't want a relationship, especially with an actor who lived across the country. She'd had her fill of believing in a make-believe world. But there was no harm in enjoying the benefits while she could or in gushing a tiny bit. It wasn't like she'd share that he was the best lover she'd ever had or that he infiltrated her thoughts even when they were apart.

"You've seen how wonderful he is," Leni said casually. "But I have to admit, he's the first man who has ever been able to get me away from work and out of my own head, which is nice." Nice? More like flat-out shocking, and she'd never had so much fun with a man.

"He *walks* her to work," Indi added in a hushed, excited tone. "And he takes her to dinner and brings her snacks and sexy lingerie."

"Hey, I told you those things in confidence," Leni complained.

Indi winced. "Sorry. I didn't know they were secrets."

"That's *so* sweet," Tara said.

"Don't get too carried away." *It's hard enough that I get carried away with him when I don't want to.*

"We're just happy because you're obviously crazy about each other," Daphne said.

"It sounds like Duncan knows just how to woo you," her mother said.

"You can say that again," their grandmother said. "The way they look at each other in public is proof of how well they take care of each other in private."

"Gram, can we *not* talk about my sex life?"

Sutton nudged her, smiling knowingly, making Leni regret sharing that information with her.

"I knew you'd found your one and only!" Jules exclaimed. "True love is magical, and I saw it in your eyes when you came off the ferry."

"You need to get your meter reader fixed. What you saw was me worrying that you'd do *this*. Can't two people date without everyone rushing them to the altar?"

"But you brought him home to meet everyone." Jules's brow furrowed. "You've never done that before. I thought that meant you knew he was your forever love."

"I brought him home because *Mama Steele*"—Leni shot a look to her mother—"swindled me into it by asking him behind my back."

"I'm sorry, honey," her mother said. "I just asked if he was coming with you. When he said he was, I assumed you'd planned it."

"It's okay, Mom. He obviously wanted to come, and knowing him, he'd have shown up even if you never said a thing. He's always showing up unannounced and against my wishes."

"I guess I'm a little surprised, too. You wouldn't have brought him with you anyway?" Sutton asked. "You two seem so into each other."

The guys' deep voices floated into Leni's ears. She looked over and saw them standing by the patio doors. Her father clapped Raz on the shoulder, saying something that made all of them laugh, cheer, and take a drink. Raz fit in so well with her family, it was easy to picture him as a permanent fixture. But as much as she'd like to think this perfect evening could lead to more, she knew better. If she'd had any doubts, Raz's I've-got-this look when he'd reiterated her reasons for not visiting him on set had solidified their reality.

"We are into each other, but…" *Things aren't always as they appear.*

"You don't need to explain yourself, honey," her mother said. "We all know you've never been on the prowl for a husband. You enjoy your independence, and there's nothing wrong with that."

"But love is good, even if you never want to get married," Jules urged.

"I never said I don't want to get married. It's just not the brass ring for me."

"Take it from someone who knows how fast life passes us by," their grandmother said. "Whatever this is between you and Duncan, whether it's just for now or the precursor to a beautiful life together, doesn't really matter. You're together now, and you of all people know that spine-tingling chemistry is rare, and the type you two have is a luxury. You should enjoy the hell out of that, sweetheart. You all should. If I had it to do all over again, *that's* what I'd focus on. The here and now, and all those incredible feelings that send you soaring higher than the sky."

"I thought you did that with Daddy," their mother said.

"I did, but it took a while to get there. When I first met your father, I wasted a lot of time wondering if we'd make it and trying to protect myself from falling too hard. I wish I'd put that energy into enjoying the moments we had together. I'd soak in every blissful second instead of worrying what anyone else thought or where we might end up. Because while I was trying to figure out a future, my present was passing me by." Their grandmother looked at Leni. "Don't let that happen to you."

"I didn't waste any time with Grant, and I've never been happier," Jules said.

"It took Archer and me some time to realize we were meant to be together forever," Indi admitted. "But trust me, we enjoyed our chemistry along the way."

"As much as I wish I could have been with Levi years ago, I think we came together at the perfect time," Tara said. "With everything we've been through with Joey and Amelia and my family, I know we'll stand the test of time."

"Of course you will, honey," their mother said.

"That's how I feel about Jock," Daphne said. "I wasn't in love with him as long as you were with Levi, but my daughter was. I'd been through one bad marriage. I had a lot of baggage and insecurities that came with the divorce, and Jock had to face all his demons to be with us. I have no doubt that when we're old and gray, we'll still be together."

And I know Raz and I won't be. Emotions clogged Leni's throat. She hadn't thought she'd wanted what they'd had so badly. But her rampant heart was telling her otherwise. Raz's voice came into focus, and as the guys joined them, all the girls jumped to their feet, and commotion ensued.

Raz went directly to Leni. He kissed her neck and whispered, "Do you think your family knows I'm picturing you naked right now?"

Leni's body flamed, and she grabbed hold of her grandmother's advice like a brass ring. "I don't care if they do." She went up on her toes and kissed him, soaking in every blissful second, anxious for more.

Twenty-One

THE REST OF the evening passed with an abundance of fun conversation and stolen kisses. They made plans to meet at their parents' house at nine the next morning for breakfast. The guys invited Raz to spend the afternoon with them while the girls were at Jules's bridal shower, and they all made plans to meet at Rock Bottom Bar and Grill after the shower.

By a little after ten o'clock, everyone had gone home except Jules and Grant, who were still saying goodbye. Jules embraced Leni, whispering, "I'll leave everything under the porch."

"If you tell Grant, I'll never forgive you," Leni warned.

Jules pretended to zip her mouth closed.

"What's that about?" their mother asked.

"Leni doesn't want me sharing our girl talk," Jules said.

"No worries, Len. I'm not into girl talk," Grant said. "Ready to go, Pix?"

"Yes." She took Grant's outstretched hand, calling out, "Love you guys. I'm glad you're here, Duncan," as they left.

"I am, too!" Raz hollered, and draped an arm over Leni's shoulder. "Mama Steele, Papa Steele, you have a great family. Thanks for letting me be part of it this weekend."

"We've been anxious to meet you," her mother said warmly.

"I haven't seen Leni this happy in a very long time, and I'm sorry about my boys and the kidnapping fiasco."

"That's okay. That's what big brothers are for."

He gazed thoughtfully at Leni, and she put her arms around him, knowing he was missing Tory.

"I gave them hell for what they did," her father said. "I don't think we have to worry about them pulling that kind of prank again."

Sutton shook her head. "You're dreaming, Dad."

"Probably so." Her father's eyes sparked with mischief. "Maybe it's time I get my buddies together and prank those boys into behaving."

Leni imagined his buddies Alexander Silver and Roddy Remington got into their fair share of trouble during their college years.

As their parents cleaned up around the bonfire, Leni, Sutton, and Raz headed inside to clean the kitchen. "We still have time before *you know what*. Do you want to hang out?" Sutton asked.

"Actually, if you don't mind, I was hoping to go for a walk on the beach with Leni." Raz put his arm around her.

"I believe that's called a *midnight swim*," Sutton teased.

"Really?" Leni deadpanned. "You, too?"

Sutton crossed her arms, eyes narrowing. "For your information, you abandoned me. So, yes, I'm going to give you shit."

"What are you talking about? I'm right here."

"While everyone else was coupling off, you and I were the single ones. I could always count on that, but now—"

"I came along and ruined your fun," Raz interjected.

"Yes," Sutton said. "Not that I'm mad at you, but suddenly my sister, who has never looked for a man on any serious level, shows up all googly-eyed over you, and I'm left to commiserate with the only other single Steele."

"Gram?" Leni asked incredulously.

"Yes. She spent all night trying to convince me to go to Pythons with her and her friends next Tuesday night."

"So that's a real thing?" Raz asked. "She really goes to a strip club called Pythons?"

"Yes," Leni said regretfully.

"Are you going, Sutton?" Raz asked.

"Hell no," Sutton exclaimed. "I don't need to watch her and her friends stuff money into G-strings."

They all laughed.

"What's so funny?" their mother asked as she and their father came inside.

"Grandma tried to get Sutton to go to Pythons," Leni said.

"Well, maybe you should," their mother said.

Sutton blinked several times. *"What?"*

"I'm not sure I want to know why you're suggesting that," their father said.

"I'm not saying she should go home with one of the performers. But she's young, Steve." Their mother looked thoughtfully at Sutton. "Between work and traveling, I doubt you get to have much fun, and if there's one thing your grandmother knows how to do, it's have fun."

Sutton rolled her eyes. "I don't want to talk about this. I'm going upstairs. Leni, text me when you're back."

"Okay."

As Sutton headed upstairs, their father said, "Back from where?"

"I thought Leni and I could take a walk on the beach," Raz said.

"That's a lovely idea, but it'll be cold," their mother said. "I'll get you blankets in case you want to sit and enjoy the view." She hurried out of the room.

"You can take my car. The keys are on the hook by the door," their father said.

"Thanks. We appreciate that," Raz said.

"Yeah, thanks, Dad."

Her mother returned with blankets and handed them to Leni. "Maybe you should show Duncan where Grandma took you for your first Bra Brigade outing." She lowered her voice. "It's nice and private."

"What happened to everyone's boundaries tonight? I don't want to hear this," her father said. "Good night, you guys. I'd say have fun, but…I'm your dad, Leni Bean. Be safe. Love you."

Leni had teased her siblings plenty of times about making out and had never given it a second thought. But even at thirty years old, being on the other side of having her family know what she was going off to do—what she'd been anxiously awaiting all night—carried a whole new type of embarrassment. As her father headed out of the kitchen, she said, "We're just going for a *walk*."

"That's what I'm telling myself." He waved without turning around.

"Don't mind him. We were young once, too. *Go*, have fun." Her mother ushered them toward the door. "And remember what I said."

"We're going for a *walk*, Mom. A *walk*."

"Yeah, a walk. Your dad and I used to go on lots of *walks* through the vineyard, on the beach, by the bluffs—"

"Now I need to bleach my ears!" Leni snagged her father's keys and walked out the door.

A LITTLE WHILE later, they made their way along the narrow path snaking between thick patches of dune grass and prickly brush to a sliver of a beach at Brighton Cove. Leni shivered against the cold salty breeze. Moonlight danced across the surface of the inky water as if beckoning them to follow its trail into the darkness.

"Is this where your grandmother took you?" Raz asked as they kicked off their shoes and spread out a blanket.

"No. But you wanted to erase my memories with Wells, so…" She felt her cheeks heating. She hadn't thought of being here with Wells since she left the island for college, but she liked the idea of replacing those memories with better ones.

A sly grin curved Raz's lips. He stalked toward her and wound his arms around her waist. "This is where he deflowered you?"

"Maybe I was the one doing the deflowering," she challenged.

He laughed softly. "Were you?"

"I'll never tell."

"Come on, princess. Your secrets are safe with me."

"No. You don't hear me asking about your first time."

"It was with Jessica Price, the summer before my senior year of high school. We met on the second day of my family's two-week vacation and spent all our free time together. She was hot, fun, and starting college in the fall."

"Look at you, with an older woman," she teased.

"I thought that made me super cool."

"I take it *she* instigated the deflowering?"

"Pretty much. I think I lasted almost a full minute the first time."

Leni laughed. "Really?"

"Unfortunately, yes. But I got better as the days went on, and I learned that there were benefits to jerking off before dates."

"I don't need to know that." Although her mind jumped to the image of him kneeling on her bed, stroking his cock before rolling on a condom, and her body flamed.

"Why? All guys do it."

"Seriously? Do you still?" She had to know.

"Depends who I'm going out with. Before a date with you? You're damn right I do. Otherwise we'd never make it out of your apartment. All it takes is thinking about getting my hands on you, and I'm ready to go." His eyes drilled into her, and her breath caught at the lust simmering between them. He took her hand and placed it over his zipper, squeezing her fingers around his erection. "Just. Like. That."

"*Raz*" slipped out like a plea.

He lowered himself to the blanket, bringing her down beside him. "Can you blame me?" He brushed his lips over hers. "You *know* what your lips do to me." He sucked her lower lip, tugging it between his teeth before releasing it, sending heat through her core.

"*Mm*," she moaned. "Tell me what they do to you."

"They make me want to suck them, kiss them, and feel them on every inch of my body." He slanted his mouth over hers, taking her down to her back. She'd been dying to kiss him like this all night, and when he intensified his efforts, she clung to him, rocking against his erection, aching to be closer. "I imagine your lips wrapped around my cock," he said seductively. "Sucking and licking until I nearly lose my mind."

He reclaimed her mouth and thrust his tongue deep. She sucked it as if it were his cock, earning a low guttural moan. He crushed his mouth to hers in a breath-stealing kiss that went on and on, leaving her panting and needy for more. "You drive me crazy," he growled, then slicked his tongue along her neck, sending shivers down her spine, and sank his teeth into the sensitive skin.

She inhaled sharply. *"More."*

He did it again, grinding his hard length against her center, and then his mouth came over hers, rough and demanding, his hand pushing beneath her sweater. He unhooked the front clasp on her bra, pushed up her sweater, and took her nipple into his mouth.

"Yesss."

He sucked it to the roof of his mouth, and she bowed beneath him, desire flooding her like lava. "I know I promised you a sweet, sexy night, but I need to feel your skin on mine," he said gruffly, reaching over his back to tug off his sweater. He quickly rid her of her shirt and bra, and they stripped off their jeans, shivering against the cold. He covered her with the extra blanket and went up on his knees to roll on a condom, all chiseled features and firm muscles.

"Hurry," she said through chattering teeth. "What were we thinking? It's freezing."

He climbed under the blanket with her, his skin chilled to the touch. "Another minute of that cold, and we might've been out of luck."

Their mouths came together as he sank into her, and their bodies took over. Their kisses turned fierce and desperate as their hips thrust and gyrated. She felt him everywhere—on her, inside her, in every breath she took—and it still wasn't enough. She wanted to burrow beneath his skin and brand his soul the way he'd snuck in and branded hers. She tore her mouth away. "I want to be on top." The lascivious grin that earned was sexy as hell.

He held her tight, and the blanket fell away as she rode him in the moonlight, cold air beating against her back, the sounds of the waves drowned out by their moans and his growls and praise. *So damn sexy…I can't get enough of you…You feel so fucking good.* He worked her clit to perfection, taking her right up to the edge of madness and holding her there. Her skin was on fire, the frigid air almost too much to bear, but it heightened her pleasure, making everything more intense. "Come on my cock, baby." His words had her riding him harder, faster. He added pressure to her clit and pinched her nipple, sending soul-drenching waves of pleasure crashing over her.

"That's it. Jesus…so tight…"

He stayed with her through every glorious second of her high, and as she came down from the peak, he rolled her beneath his big, hard body, and warmth engulfed her. She gazed up at him, broad and godlike in the moonlight, jaw tight, eyes dark with harsh control and greedy desire. His mouth covered hers roughly as he drove deeper into her. She wound her legs around his waist, reveling in his power, his *possession*, as the world spun away and they careened into oblivion.

He collapsed over her, his warmth seeping beneath her skin, his beautiful, filthy mouth placing tender kisses on her lips and cheeks as they tried to catch their breath. Tiny tremors shuddered through her. Raz pulled the blanket over them, but she was too euphoric, too lost in *them* to be cold.

He gazed at her with a sated smile. "That was insane."

"Yeah," she panted out. "Wait, the cold or the sex?"

"Both." His smile turned sinful. "Want to do it again?"

AFTER A QUICK and hilarious overzealous romp, during which they rolled off the blanket and into the sand, they picked up Sutton and headed to Jules and Grant's bungalow.

"How was your *walk*?" Sutton whispered as they snuck quietly through their yard.

"Fun but cold," Leni whispered.

"And sandy," Raz said.

"Got sand in your crack, huh?" Sutton teased.

"Among other places," Leni said.

Raz took her hand, pulling her into a quick kiss.

"Didn't you get enough already?" Sutton whispered.

Raz lifted his brows. "I don't think there is such a thing when it comes to your sister."

"It's about time someone figured that out—"

"There it is!" Leni whisper-shouted, then ran to the deck, pulling a box out from underneath it as Raz and Sutton peered over her shoulder. "Jules is freaking awesome. Paint, glitter, and *all* the goodies." She yanked another box out from under the deck and rubbed her hands together. "Let the pranking begin."

LENI WAS UP before the sun, and she was a bundle of nervous energy. She said she felt funny sleeping with him in her childhood bedroom while maintaining their ruse, but the thing was, she'd slept like a log. He dragged her out for a run, hoping to clear her head, and his own, because sleeping with Leni in her childhood bedroom with her parents down the hall had definitely fucked with *him*. He'd always had a hell of a lot of respect for family, and Leni's family deserved every bit of it.

They ran down Main Street in Silver Haven, a picture-perfect small town, with cute shops, flower boxes beneath massive display windows, and views of the water. They ran past Leni's favorite lunch spot, Trista's café, Indi's boutique, and Jules's Happy End gift shop, which was just as exuberant as Jules, with red-framed picture windows and two giraffe statues wearing sweaters and sunglasses flanking the door.

"See the park?" She pointed across the street as they jogged. "That's where we went sledding when we were kids."

"Do you still go sledding?" he asked as they jogged back toward her parents' house. She'd kept up pretty well.

She made a face like he'd asked her if she fought bears for a living. "No."

"You're missing out."

"Oh yeah? You do a lot of sledding in LA?"

"No, but I do in Maryland."

"Really?"

"Yeah. My parents do, too. Everyone sleds down a big hill by the elementary school where my mother teaches. I try to make it into town when there's going to be a big snowstorm. They've been few and far between the last few years, but my parents and I make an event out of it. My mom makes my favorite dinner, Bolognese, and we bake cookies the night before and spend most of the day at the hill with the kids."

"Do you actually bake, or do you lick the bowl and eat the cookies?"

"I *bake*. I'm more than just a pretty face, you know."

"Well, you do have other nice body parts."

"Now I feel objectified," he teased.

She laughed. "It's just that most of the celebrities I know only do things like that when they're getting recognition for it. Is that another tradition you had with Tory?"

"As a matter of fact, it is, and she loved it. When we were little, she'd sit between my legs on the sled, screaming at the top of her lungs as we sped down the hill. As soon as we were done, she'd say, 'Again!'"

"Is that why you still go?"

He liked that she knew him well enough to realize that. "Probably, but I do enjoy it."

They talked about Tory and winters and family traditions and relived their night of pranking as they jogged back toward her parents' house. They made it back to the bottom of their steep street around nine, but fifteen minutes later, they were barely halfway up the hill.

"My legs feel like rubber. Can we stop for a minute?" Leni grabbed the back of his shirt, bending at the waist as she trudged behind him. "Call an ambulance. I need a coffee IV. Stat."

He laughed. "Come on, Steele. We can see your parents' house from here. You're almost there. Let's show your brothers what you're made of."

She groaned.

"All right, princess. I've got you." He crouched in front of her. "Climb on."

"Yes!" She scrambled onto his back.

"I remember when you fought me on this." He reached behind his back, palming her ass as he rose to his feet, and she wound her arms around his neck.

"This is different." She rested her cheek on his head. "How do you still smell so good? That's so annoying."

He laughed, and ran the rest of the way up the hill, making her laugh.

"Show-off!"

"I prefer Superman." He carried her down the long driveway, stopping halfway to take in the vineyard to their left. He'd been so focused on Leni, and trying to deal with the guilt of letting her family believe they were a normal couple, he'd totally missed the cedar and brick winery and outbuildings, the covered pavilion in the back, and gorgeous vineyards as far as the eye could see. He set Leni on her feet. "What a magnificent sight."

"The vines are prettier when they're full of grapes, and the view from behind the vineyard is incredible. You can see halfway across the island."

"This view is pretty incredible, too." He pulled her closer. "How long has the winery been in your family?"

"Several generations, on my mom's side."

"And this is where you hold the Field of Screams?"

"Mm-hm."

He looked in the direction of the golf carts lined up in the side yard. "Is there a golf course around here?"

"No. We use those to go back and forth to the winery. Do you want to go over and see the inside and the courtyard out back? We can walk through the vines, too."

"At some point, but we're already late for breakfast, and it looks like everyone's here." He motioned to the cars and trucks in front of the house.

Leni's eyes lit up. "Come on!"

She ran down the driveway to her brothers' vehicles, pointing to the neon-pink, glittery tires and the windows boasting GLITTER PRINCE and I'M A BARBIE BOY in bright pink. They were cracking up when the front door flew open, and her brothers and Grant stormed out, their pink, glittery boots clomping on the walkway, which only made them laugh harder. They'd painted or dyed and glittered every pair of her brothers' and Grant's shoes.

"You are so dead!" Archer seethed.

"My work truck was bad enough, but my motorcycle tires, too?" Levi fumed. "And my leather riding boots?"

Raz moved closer to Leni as the other girls and Leni's parents ran out the front door, followed by Joey and Hadley.

Leni stood her ground. "What's the matter? Afraid your biker buddies won't think you're cool?"

Sutton and Indi ran to Leni, while Daphne, Jules, and Tara planted themselves in front of Jock, Grant, and Levi, all of them talking at once.

"A fuck—" Archer gritted his teeth when Hadley's voice

rose above the others as she rattled on about the pwank. *"Freaking* glitter bomb in my truck? That sh—*crap*—will never come out." He hulked over Leni, glitter sparkling in his hair and on his clothes.

Raz stepped forward, but Indi tugged him back, shaking her head.

Leni lifted her chin, holding Archer's stare like the petite badass she was. "Maybe next time you'll all think twice about messing with my boyfriend."

Raz puffed out his chest. "You tell him, princess."

Archer turned a dark stare on Raz, his gaze dropping to Raz's bright white sneakers. He scoffed. "Traitor."

"I'm as loyal as they come. Do you really want your sister dating a guy who'll put *anyone* else ahead of her?" He draped an arm over Leni's shoulder. "If my sister were still here, I'd want her boyfriend to be on her side no matter who she stood against."

"He's got a point," Grant said.

"Darn right he does, and I'm glad you see it." Jules wrapped her arms around him, and he leaned down for a kiss.

"We did start it," Jock added.

"What do you say, Archer?" Raz said. "Are you going to see the humor in it, or are you one of those guys who can dish it out but can't take it?"

Archer glowered at him, jaw clenched. "It doesn't come off."

"That's the point," Leni said.

Archer narrowed his eyes at her. She squared her shoulders, refusing to back down.

"So you have pink, glittery tires and a dozen pairs of pink shoes. Is that so bad?" Raz said. "They could have painted your boat, the outside of your truck, your vines, or any number of other things. Man up, dude. You held me over a frigging cliff, and you don't see me crying about it."

There was a round of chuckles.

"*Fine*," Archer bit out.

Leni flashed a victorious grin. "Truce?" She opened her arms.

"Get over here." Archer hauled her into a hug, and everyone laughed or sighed with relief.

"Love you, you big jerk," Leni said as he embraced her.

"Love you, too, you little shit. You girls better watch your backs."

"Now that things are back to normal," her father teased. "How about breakfast?"

As they headed inside, Raz took Leni's hand. "Don't worry, babe. If he wants you, he'll have to go through me first."

"You're lucky you're leaving town Monday. After this, he won't think twice about throwing you off a cliff."

AFTER HOW ANGRY Archer had been that morning, Leni was a little nervous about Raz spending the afternoon playing poker with the guys while she and the girls were at the shower. But Indi had snuck Archer out of the kitchen for twenty minutes, and he'd come back a much more relaxed and happy man. He'd even offered to give Raz a tour of the winery, which they did after breakfast. Leni rarely saw her brother in his element, and he was like a force of nature. The pride he took in the winery came across in droves as he showed off the wine cellar and grounds, proudly answering each of Raz's many questions. On the way out, he even gave Raz a royal-blue Top of the Island winery T-shirt.

Since the shower didn't start until three, Leni showed Raz a few of the other towns on the island, and he shared more stories from when he was younger, many of which included Tory. She didn't have to look far to understand why he was so different from most of the celebrities she knew. He'd lost the sister he'd loved, and it was clear that loss had driven home the importance of the thing that mattered most.

Family.

It turned out, she and the man she'd thought she had nothing in common with were woven from similar threads. How could she have been so wrong about him?

She tried to push thoughts of him aside and focus on getting ready for Jules's bridal shower with the girls. It was a Steele family tradition to get ready for big events together in Leni and Jules's old bedroom, the largest of the kids' rooms. Leni had always loved this part of the ritual. Their father had the uncanny ability to know exactly when they'd be ready. He'd get them, and they'd parade down the stairs one at a time, showing off their beautiful dresses, hair, and makeup for their brothers, as if they were some kind of royalty. While Sutton and Jules had always loved that attention, it had seemed silly to Leni when she was younger. But her father had explained that they weren't acting like *royalty.* They were acting like ladies who know they are special to the people who love them. He'd said it was as much for the people watching as it was for the girls and that one day they'd each meet someone special who would be excited to watch them make their grand entrance, and then it would all make sense.

She looked around the room, love and friendship practically painted into the wall. Indi was putting the finishing touches on Sutton's makeup, her long blond hair falling in glossy streaks down her back, as Sutton told her about her next assignment. Across the room, at a small round table, Joey, ever the tomboy in a cute black dress with colorful skateboards on it, black tights, and her black leather biker boots, was coloring with Hadley, who looked adorable in a fluffy pink dress with matching bows in her hair. Daphne and Tara were chatting with her grandmother, mother, and Jules about the shower. They were beautiful, with their hair and makeup done, in their fall-colored dresses. Leni was always the last to sit in the hair-and-makeup chair. She'd just as soon do her own, but she knew how happy it made Jules to have everyone look their absolute best for her party.

Jules was more vibrant than ever in a gold satin wrap maxi dress with thin shoulder straps and ruffled cold-shoulder sleeves. Leni's heart filled to the brim with love for her baby sister. If anyone deserved a lifetime of love and happiness, it was Jules. Leni's gaze shifted just beyond her, to the double bed that had replaced their old twin beds.

Those twin beds had held cherished memories of Jules whispering at all hours of the night. Leni could still hear her little-girl voice. *Sissy, are you awake?* If Leni had pretended to be asleep, Jules would sneak into her bed and lie as still as stone cuddled up beside her. But Jules had never been able to keep quiet for long, and on those nights, she would end up gabbing until Leni couldn't help but smile, laugh, or kick her out of her bed. But now the room also held memories of sleeping in Raz's arms and waking surrounded by his scent, the sound of his sexy murmurs thrumming around her like a heartbeat. She didn't have sexual hang-ups, but she felt guilty about her parents welcoming him into their home, and into their daughter's bed, when regardless of her burgeoning feelings, it was all a ruse.

"Okay, Leni, your turn." Sutton stood from the chair in a green maxi dress, drawing Leni back to the moment.

"She's busy daydreaming about Duncan." Jules made kissing noises.

Leni rolled her eyes and went to sit in the chair in front of the mirror. "I was just trying to decide how to wear my hair."

"Bologna and salami and a little bit of cheese," Jules said. "You always wear your hair down."

"Can't a girl change her mind?" Leni had no desire to wear her hair differently, but she didn't like to lose.

"Does that mean you're going to let me do something different tonight?" Indi asked excitedly.

"That depends. What do you have in mind?"

Indi stepped back, eyeing Leni's wine-colored V-neck dress. They'd bought it together a couple of months ago and had both loved the short pleated skirt and bell sleeves. "I have the perfect hairdo. I know the last thing you want is for your hair to be a hindrance. How would you feel if I made a messy fishtail braid into a side ponytail?"

Leni was skeptical. "Fishtail?"

"Let me show you." She grabbed her phone and began scrolling through pictures. "I'll leave a few strands to frame your face." She handed Leni the phone, and the girls hurried over to peek at the picture.

"That's perfect for you!" Jules said.

"Ooh, honey, that's beautiful," her mother said, looking beautiful herself in a burnt-orange wrap dress. Her signature style.

"And it'll give Raz access to your neck for smooches," her grandmother said, earning giggles from Joey.

"In *that* case," Leni said with not-totally-feigned enthusiasm. "Go for it."

Her mother and Jules stood beside her, watching in the mirror as Indi brushed her thick tresses and began braiding.

"Indi, thank you for making us all gorgeous for my bridal shower," Jules said.

"You guys make it easy and fun," Indi said.

"I can't believe my little Julesy is getting married," her mother said. "Our family is growing so fast." She looked at Daphne, Indi, and Tara. "We are so blessed to have you girls and Grant in our lives."

"Yes, we are," their grandmother said. "Now let's get to the good stuff. Who's getting married next? I want to put dates on my calendar."

"Are you that busy, Gram?" Leni asked.

"One never knows when I might decide to travel the world." Her grandmother looked stylish as ever in brown slacks and a cream blouse, with a colorful autumn-inspired silk scarf around her neck.

"Levi and I are thinking about getting married in the spring or summer," Tara said. Levi was going to lose his mind when he saw her in that clingy knit dress. It was strapless on one side and had a full sleeve on the other.

"I get to be Tara's maid of honor!" Joey chimed in.

"Aw," Jules said. "I love that."

"Me too!" Joey exclaimed. "They're planning their wedding around my school vacations. Grandma Shelley, can I stay with you when they're on their honeymoon?"

"Of course, sweetie."

"That's a gorgeous time for a wedding," Sutton said. "When you decide on dates, please try to give me enough notice so I can rework my filming schedule if I need to."

"We will," Tara promised. "We're still trying to decide where to have the wedding, but we're thinking about having it at our new house."

"That would be lovely," their grandmother said.

"How about you, Indi?" Daphne asked. "Are we putting a wedding date on the winery calendar next year?"

"Actually, Archer and I were thinking about having a small ceremony in the vineyard, with just family, but we don't know when yet." Indi looked at their grandmother. "He'd like to feel his grandfather around when we say our vows."

"Just like we did." Their grandmother touched the locket she wore around her neck. The locket Leni knew held a picture of their grandfather.

"Us too," their mother said.

"Maybe Leni will be next in line to walk down the aisle," Jules said hopefully.

"I told you to get that silly idea out of your head," Leni said. "I'm already weddinged out. I'm attending a wedding tomorrow in the city, and then Abby and Aiden's wedding is in November, and yours and Grant's is in December. I don't know how I'll survive the winter."

"Tequila, babe. Lots of tequila," Sutton said.

"Tequila gets me in trouble," Leni said, thinking about her first night with Raz. Although she didn't regret that tipsy night...or any other. It had been an amazing few weeks.

"Whose wedding are you going to tomorrow?" Daphne asked.

"A producer. Raz was invited. I'm his plus-one," Leni said.

"Jay Gold and Naomi Turner?" Indi asked, wide-eyed.

"Yeah, that's it."

"Are you kidding?" Daphne put her hands on the cinched waist of her coral dress, which accentuated her curves. "That's the wedding of the year."

"Yeah, I know," Leni said.

"Everyone who's anyone in Hollywood is going. It's going to be like the Oscars of weddings," Indi added. "I'm doing hair and makeup for some of the guests."

"I read they're having like five *hundred* guests," Daphne said.

"I bet they have a lot more than that. I'd give anything to see Naomi Turner in person," Jules said. "She's gorgeous."

"I would kill to get a photography gig like that," Tara said.

Leni shrugged. "It's just a wedding."

"This wedding is a really big deal, and you're just like"—Sutton shrugged—"Whatever...?"

"You know our girl has never been impressed by big, fancy *anything*." Her mother patted her shoulder, looking at her in the mirror. "That's why she's so good at her job. She sees past all the pomp and circumstance to the heart of who people are. Right, honey?"

Leni smiled. "Right, Mom."

"Since I'm going to be in the city, how about I swing by and do your hair and makeup, too?" Indi asked.

"You don't have to do that," Leni said.

"How are you Sutton and Jules's sister?" Indi was only half teasing. "They love getting dolled up."

"True that. You can do my hair and makeup anytime," Sutton said.

"Thank you." Indi looked at Leni in the mirror as she

worked on her hair. "How about I ply you with wine and Cheez-Its and convince you that you should look extra special to attend the wedding of the year with your new, spectacularly handsome and famous boyfriend?"

"You sold me at wine and Cheez-Its, but aren't you guys missing the bigger picture?" Leni looked at Jules. "The wedding of the year is taking place over the holidays right here on Silver Island, when our beautiful baby sister marries her dreamboat. That is the wedding you should be gushing over. Not a bunch of people you don't know just because they're famous. Jules and Grant are famous in their own right for Jules's perky personality and the way she and Grant give so much to others. *That's* worth celebrating."

"Aw, Leni." Jules got teary-eyed and came over to hug her.

"Love you, Julesy," Leni said.

"Careful of her hair," Indi warned.

"Leni's right. Jules is our star," Tara said, sparking excitement and conversation about how special Jules and Grant's wedding was going to be.

When Indi finished doing Leni's hair, Leni rose to her feet, and they turned all that girlie glamour chatter on her. She loved them for it, but she'd never understood why girls acted like a hairstyle, makeup, or a dress could be life-changing. *It's just hair* was on the tip of her tongue, but she didn't want to spoil their fun. Luckily, she was adept at redirecting. "Thanks, you guys, but it's not like I look half as good as Joey and Hadley."

"Nobody could look as good as them," Jules said, inciting more enthusiasm.

As they gushed about Joey and Hadley, Leni went to answer a knock at the bedroom door and found her father standing there. How did he know just when to show up?

"Whoa, Leni Bean. Look at you."

"Thanks, Dad. They made me do it," she said with a hint of annoyance, though she loved her new look.

"How many times did I hear *that* when you were kids? You look beautiful, sweetheart." He hugged her.

"Thank you."

"Gwampa, look at my pwetty bows and dwess!" Hadley patted her head and twirled.

"Who is this movie star?" He scooped her into his arms and kissed her cheek, earning sweet giggles. "You look beautiful, baby." He glanced into the room, letting out a low whistle. "I have a feeling we're going to have a heck of a time getting those men downstairs to let you ladies out of their sight tonight."

"Such a charmer." Their mother went over to him. "You're looking mighty sexy yourself, old man."

He looked down at his jeans and sweater. "It's all for you, darlin'."

As he pressed his lips to hers, Sutton said, "*God*, will it ever end?" making everyone laugh.

"The answer is *no*. Never," their father said. "Even after we're long gone, you're going to remember us kissing every-where we went."

"Aw, Daddy." Jules went over and hugged him. "I hope Grant and I will be just like you and Mom when we're older."

"You already are, sweetie." He set Hadley down. "Are you ladies ready to make your grand entrances?"

A collective "Yes!" rang out.

"Then how about it?" He held out his hands, and Joey and Hadley took them.

As everyone hurried toward the hall, Leni hung back with Sutton. "You don't think Raz is waiting down there like they are, do you?" Hopefully he'd wait off to the side, letting her family play out their tradition without getting involved.

"I *know* he is. That man looks at you like you're the star on the big screen."

"Oh God, really?" They were buying it, too. She didn't want to be affected if he brought out more of his charm in front of her family, but her stupid heart was already racing.

"I was putting it nicely. He looks at you like he's the big horny wolf, and you're his little red vixen."

"*That* I can handle."

Sutton took her arm. "I know. I've got you."

Leni waited anxiously as their father walked Hadley and Joey down the stairs, and Jock and Levi fawned over them. Jules went next.

"Grant looks like he wants to sprint up the steps and devour her," Sutton whispered, taking out her phone to snap a picture.

At the bottom of the stairs, their father was also taking pictures.

One by one, Daphne, Tara, and Indi descended the stairs, and Jock, Levi, and Archer looked like they were falling in love all over again with each of them. When their mother walked down, their father looked at her the same way, his love as genuine as ever. Their grandmother and Sutton walked down together, and the guys whistled and hooted. Leni was the last to go. She'd never been so nervous.

With a deep breath, she stepped up to the edge of the landing. She didn't see Raz, only her brothers and father. Relief swept through her. *This*, she could do. Drawing her shoulders back, she took her first step, and Raz appeared at the bottom of the stairs, holding a red rose in one hand, and *sweet baby Jesus*, the look in his eyes made her knees buckle. She grabbed the railing, unable to look away from him.

Maybe there was something to changing up her hairstyle after all.

She was vaguely aware of her father taking pictures as Raz reached for her hand, helping her off the last step and pulling her close. "*Wow*, Leni, you look…*Damn.*"

"He's speechless," their grandmother said. "That's a first!"

As everyone laughed, Raz said, "You look stunning."

Her throat thickened. Everything felt different surrounded by her family and so much love. It felt *real.* Panic flared in her chest. Did she want it to be real? In the space of a breath, she imagined trying to make their relationship work long-distance, but she knew herself too well. That would never be enough. If she was going to go all in with a man again, it would be forever, and her forever didn't include saying good night over video chat from across the country. She wanted more than that, and that could never be a reality for her and Raz.

Could it?

Her painful breakup with Kip came rushing back. *No.* She was a realist. Distance did *not* make the heart grow fonder. She was never going there again.

Raz whispered, "How'd I get so lucky as to land you as my fake date?"

As if she needed the reminder.

Was the universe stepping in to save her from herself?

"It wasn't luck," she said softly. "It was Shea." *And I'm going to give her hell when I see her at the shower.*

Twenty-Three

DAPHNE AND, SUPRISINGLY, Grant had turned the event room at the winery into a fairy tale come true for Jules. It was bursting with pink, white, and gold balloons, gorgeous flower arrangements, and special touches like tiny wooden lanterns Grant had made and painted fairies on. There were poster-sized framed pictures of Grant and Jules from the night of their engagement, at the flotilla, Easter, and a handful of other happy memories, on easels around the room. Eucalyptus sprigs added a splash of contrast to a massive balloon waterfall cascading around a rustic wooden sign Grant had made with BRIDE-TO-Be painted in white script across the middle.

If Leni were ever to settle down, that was what she wanted. A man who would go the extra mile to make her smile, even if he wasn't there to see it. And damn it, that wasn't Raz. Forty-eight hours from now he'd be on his way to LA, and she'd probably never see him again. It was better that way. He was a big distraction in her otherwise organized life, dropping in at all hours, and dragging her away from the work she should be doing. Her stupid mind wanted to manipulate everything he'd said and done to trick her into thinking maybe Jules was right, and he could be *the one.*

But she knew better, and so did he.

She filled out the note card Bellamy had given her and the other guests an hour ago, on which they were to anonymously jot down special memories with Jules. Jules would read them aloud before opening gifts, and the guests were going to guess who had written them. Leni didn't like to share her most special and private moments, so she went with fun memories instead.

She put the card on the gift table with the others and scanned the room for Shea. She hadn't been able to get a minute alone with her while everyone played party games. Leni was on a mission to make her cousin pay for the nonsense going on in her mind, but the place was packed with all the women who loved Jules, which seemed like half the island, and they were buzzing with excitement. She went up on her toes, feeling like she was at a concert, trying to see the main attraction. She spotted Jules with Tara and Bellamy and Randi and Tessa Remington. Jules was wearing a crown, a gold-and-white BRIDE-TO-BE sash, and the biggest smile Leni had ever seen. Just beyond her, Shea was talking with her sister, Fiona, Abby, and Abby's sister Cait.

Leni weaved through the crowd, trying to get to her.

"Leni!" Keira Silver, Grant's younger sister, pulled her into a hug. "Can I just say that Duncan is hella hot?" She owned the Sweet Barista, and Leni had introduced them during a coffee stop on his brief tour of the island earlier.

"You just did." She tried to sound light, but she didn't want to lose track of Shea, and it came out a little short.

"When you walked into the coffee shop with him, I just about died." Keira flipped her light brown hair over her shoulder, leaning closer like she was sharing a secret. "What's the scoop? Are you serious or what?"

"Let's go with *or what*. You know me, Kei. I'm all about a drama-free lifestyle, and dating a celebrity has its challenges."

"I figured as much. You're the last person I thought would ever date a celebrity. I wondered how you were handling all the attention, but you looked awfully into each other this afternoon."

"We are, and he's great, but you know how dating is. What about you? I saw a certain hot cop hanging around the Sweet Barista today. Is something going on there?"

"With Ryan?" Keira scoffed. "No way. He's always there asking me to make special treats for him to bring home for Ritchie. He sure loves that boy so much, but all I see is drama waiting to happen, and you know me." Ryan Lacroux was a police officer, and he was raising his drug-addicted brother's young son.

"Boy, do I ever." She was as drama free as Leni was. "Are you going to Rock Bottom with us after dinner?"

"Heck yeah."

"Great. Let's catch up then. I need to grab Shea and discuss a client."

"Girl, you never fail to amaze me with your work ethic."

It was that damn work ethic that got me into this predicament.

Leni headed for Shea. She didn't get far before Faye called her name. She turned and saw her big, beautiful blond aunt waving her over. She was with Leni's mother, Margot Silver, the chicest, and probably the wealthiest, woman on the island, and Gail Remington, a Glenn Close lookalike with curly gray-and-brown hair, trusting eyes, and a penchant for earthy fashion. Leni pushed down her irritation and smiled as she went to join the women who had always been like mothers to her. It wasn't their fault she needed to vent.

"Sweetie, where are you off to in such a hurry?" Faye asked, all rosy cheeks and kind brown eyes.

Before she could respond, Margot put her arm around her, drawing her to her side. She was tall and thin, her perfectly coiffed blond hair cut just below her ears, and she smelled soft and appealing, like expensive perfume that should be called *comfort*. "Love looks good on you, honey."

Leni glanced at her mother. "I don't know what my mom told you, but he's just a guy I'm dating. We're not in love."

"That glow you're sporting says otherwise," Gail said sweetly.

"And the new hairdo is gorgeous," Faye said. "I don't think I've seen you wear your hair any way but down since you were a little girl."

"And you only did it then because your mama did your hair," Gail added. "Remember how she'd leave for school with her hair in pigtails and ribbons and come home with her hair down in a tangled mess? You were so stinking cute."

"That's my girl," her mother said lovingly.

"Sorry to disappoint you, but I let Indi do my hair differently for Jules, not for Raz, and if I'm glowing, it's only because it's crowded in here and I'm hot." *Under the collar, that is.*

"We get it." Gail winked with a nod. "You're keeping your feelings on the down-low. We're cool, right, girls?"

"Cool as cucumbers," Margot said.

Her aunt whispered, "Our lips are sealed."

It took everything Leni had not to roll her eyes.

"We heard you got the boys good this morning," Margot said. "We've been waiting for you girls to take charge."

"I would've given anything to see Archer's face when that glitter bomb went off," Faye said with a giggle. "He's so ornery."

"Indi said it was priceless, and all the guys were furious about their tires," Gail added.

"It was pretty great, but I can't take credit for it. It was Raz's idea. Don't tell anyone that, though, or they'll probably drop him off that cliff."

"We heard about that, too." Faye frowned.

"I can't believe they went that far," her mother said. "But your father took care of it."

"Or so he thinks," Leni said. "If you'll excuse me, I want to catch Shea before Jules starts opening presents." She walked away before they could wrangle her into another conversation and made a beeline for Shea, who was still chatting with Fiona, Abby, and Cait.

"Hey, Len," Abby said as she approached. "I saw the matchmaking mob snag you back there. I guess now that you have Duncan, you're off their list."

"That *is* a benefit." *At least for now.*

"I heard them scheming earlier about finding Sutton a man." Cait shook her head, her raven hair swinging above her shoulders, tattooed arms on display in a pretty navy cap-sleeved dress. "Don't worry. I warned Sutton."

"I'm so glad our mom moved here. She needed their girls' club so badly," Fiona said. She pushed her long brown hair over her shoulder and looked at Shea. "She was wasting away in Trusty, Colorado, don't you think?"

"God, yes," Shea agreed. "I don't know how she didn't suffocate from all those bad memories of our father."

"Don't get me started on Uncle Jeffrey," Leni said about the asshat who had left his wife for a younger woman. "Everyone is thrilled that your mom moved here."

"I know I am." Abby nodded in the direction of Faye and the other ladies. "You know that'll be us in twenty or thirty years."

"I hope so." Cait smiled at Abby. They had a lot of missed years to make up for.

Leni said, "I won't be like them," and they looked aghast. "I mean, I want the friendships with you all, but if I ever have kids, I will stay *out* of their love lives. Are you coming to Rock Bottom after the party?"

"I am," Abby, Cait, and Shea said in unison.

"I'm not," Fiona said apologetically. "Jake has had Cannon all day, and I'm sure he'll need a break. I miss my little man…and my big man." She had reunited with her high school sweetheart, Jake Braden, after losing touch for several years. Jake was a top-notch stuntman, and an even better husband and father.

"Then I'll be sure to sit with you at dinner so we can catch up." Leni took Shea by the arm. "But if you don't mind, I need to borrow Shea for a moment to discuss work."

"Uh-oh, sounds like someone is in trouble," Fiona teased as Leni dragged Shea away.

"What's the matter?" Shea asked in a hushed voice. "Still got sand in your crack?"

"Sand in my…?" Understanding dawned on her. "I'm going to kill Sutton."

"So it's *true*. I guess you and Raz really are doing great. Gossip says you're practically engaged."

Safely away from prying ears, Leni said, "Cut the crap. Everyone is asking about him."

"That's not my fault. I told you to make it look real, not bring him home to meet your family. What were you thinking?"

"I didn't invite him. My *mother* did."

"Why didn't you just tell her he couldn't make it?"

"Because Raz answered her call on *my* phone and had it all planned before I finished drying my hair. I told him he couldn't come, but he was persistent."

Shea arched a brow. "We've been having more slumber parties?"

"Would you focus?" Leni took a deep breath, trying to calm down.

"Okay, ladies, grab a seat," Bellamy, a cute and petite brunette with cherubic cheeks, announced from the head of the room. "It's time to open presents!"

Leni spoke quietly as they followed the others toward the tables. "I'm off your fake-dating plate, and you owe me big-time."

"Technically, *he* owes you big-time," Shea retorted. "You did this to help him, not me."

Leni glowered at her. "I thought he was a jerk, remember? I did it for you, because you said I had to, and you're my boss."

"Okay, but you don't think he's a jerk *now*, and you're having fun. That's something," she said hopefully.

"Yeah, a whole lot of unnecessary confusion."

"I'm sorry," Shea said, grabbing a seat. "You just have to make it through the wedding tomorrow, and then you're off the hook."

"Right." Leni sat beside her and trained her gaze on Jules, beaming from her perch on a chair with balloons tied to it, between her dutiful maids of honor, Bellamy and Tara. Bellamy held the stack of note cards they'd collected earlier, and Tara had a notebook in her lap and pen in hand.

"For every gift Jules opens, she's going to read one of the

cards you filled out," Bellamy announced. "And then you can guess whose special memory it was. Every winner gets a prize."

Jules wiggled her shoulders. "I'm so excited you're all here, and I can't wait to see what you wrote!"

"Then let's get started." Bellamy handed Jules a card.

Jules sat pin straight as she read a card, looking like a pixie princess in her gold silk dress, crown, and bride-to-be sash. "My favorite memory of Jules is when she was seven. She made a bra out of one of her shirts and came outside naked as a jaybird, except for that hilariously cute bra, and said she was ready for the Bra Brigade."

Leni laughed along with everyone else and swore if she ever had any type of shower, nobody was allowed to share embarrassing memories.

"That had to be Grandma Lenore," someone called out.

"It wasn't me!" their grandmother answered.

"Mom?" Sutton asked.

"Nope," their mother said.

Everyone looked at each other, murmuring about who it could be. Leni saw her mother eyeing her aunt. Her aunt giggled, and her mother's eyes widened. "Faye?"

"You caught me," their aunt said. "It was our secret until today, Julesy, and the cutest thing I'd ever seen. Your mother and all her friends had gone with the Bra Brigaders, and you had pitched a fit about staying with Leni and Sutton, so I stayed with you, too, and said we'd have our own sunbathing party. Little did I know you were a streaker."

More laughter ensued.

Jules opened a present, gushing over a gorgeous silver serving platter, before reading another card and opening another present, a set of wineglasses with Grant's and Jules's names and wedding date on them. Bellamy handed her another card, and Jules read it aloud. "My favorite memory of Jules is when we compared notes on our moms' sex talks and realized we knew more than they did." Jules looked up and said, "Thank you, Google."

"Bellamy!" almost everyone called out at once, causing more laughter.

Bellamy stood and curtsied.

After opening another present, Jules read another card. "My favorite memory of Jules is taking her out of school early to get ice cream cones on Wednesdays."

"Mom, I thought you only did that with me," Sutton complained.

"What? She did it with you?" Leni snapped. "I thought that was *our* thing because I was such a good student."

"Is that what she told you?" Sutton asked. "She told me it was because I was such a good listener."

They looked at their mother expectantly, and she shrugged. "I guess I picked the wrong memory to share." More laughter ensued. "I just wanted special time with each of my kids."

"You did it for the boys, too?" Leni asked incredulously.

"No," she said emphatically, then softer, "I took them for burgers."

They had one laugh after another, followed by more thoughtful presents. Jules set down a gift and read another card. "My favorite memory of Jules was when Grant left for the military and she showed up on our front doorstep, suitcase and pillow in hand, and said Bellamy needed her there more than her family did."

There was a collective, "*Aw,*" and Keira said, "Mom? Was that you?"

"Yes," Margot said. "And I let her stay for a week."

"Best week of my life," Jules called out. "Well, until Grant and I got together."

"And she put that sex knowledge to use," someone called out, and everyone cracked up.

Jules opened another gift and held up the sexy lingerie Leni had picked out for her the day she and Raz had gone shopping together. Leni felt herself smiling as she remembered that outing and the playful things Raz had said and done.

"This'll go to good use." Jules giggled and read another card. "My favorite memory with Jules was playing office with her when she was my secretary."

Several people said, "Leni?"

"Yes, it was me," Leni admitted. "She used to follow me around, and I didn't want her to get into my notebooks, so I unplugged our dad's landline from his office and let her be my secretary."

"I loved it." In a high-pitched voice, Jules said, "Ms. Steele's office, how can I help you?"

"She told everyone I was busy," Leni said. "Including our parents when they called us down for dinner."

"She'd send Jules downstairs to get her 'takeout,'" her mother said with air quotes around "takeout." "Jules would pack Leni's dinner in Tupperware and bring it up to her room."

"She had her trained so well," Sutton said.

"You have to admit, Leni has always been innovative," Gail added.

As Jules opened another present, Shea whispered, "I feel really bad about you and Raz. I'm sorry I put you in this position. Do you want me to get you out of going to the wedding tomorrow?"

It would be easier to end things if they got off the ferry and went their separate ways instead of playing it up for another night in front of five hundred people. But the truth was, Leni didn't want to give up that time with him. "It's fine. I made a commitment, and I'll see it through. Then I can go back to my life and he can go back to his. But never again, Shea, and I mean it."

"I know." Shea flashed a coy grin. "It's not like anyone could measure up to him anyway."

Leni gave her the side-eye.

"*Sorry*, but it's true," Shea whispered. "He's Duncan Raz, America's heartthrob and orgasm master extraordinaire."

Tell me something I don't know.

Twenty-Four

RAZ SAT AT the bar in Rock Bottom Bar and Grill watching Wells Silver make his way around the room, stopping to schmooze with men and women alike. His wily eyes never slipped to inappropriate, which was commendable, given the attractiveness of the women who were eye-fucking him. But the extra touches on women's hands, arms, or backs did not go unnoticed. The guy was smooth. Raz had to give him that.

Wells looked nothing like his shaggy-haired, heavily muscled, brother Grant, who as far as Raz could tell, rarely smiled unless he was with Jules. Wells was lean and athletic, with perfectly manicured scruff as dark as his hair and eyes. Raz would never admit it to a soul, but he'd gotten curious and had googled the guy, whose real name was Wellington Silver. He had deep roots on the island and was born with a gold-plated spoon in his mouth. His ancestors were the original founders of the island, and his parents owned the Silver House, the only exclusive resort on the island. Wells was noted as one of the top one hundred restaurateurs on the East Coast last year in *Nation's Restaurant News*, and he had to be making a killing. How many restaurants offered dockside service to boaters? They'd eaten dinner in the restaurant before hitting the bar, and

Wells had stopped by their table long enough to say a quick hello, but Raz hadn't been formally introduced. He was fighting the urge to make his boyfriend status known, fake or not, and it bugged the hell out of him that he wanted to step in and put Wells in his place for hurting Leni. But fuck if he could stop it.

"Thinking about dropping Leni for Wells?" Brant Remington joked.

Raz looked at the laid-back, dimple-cheeked boat builder. Brant had joined them for poker earlier in the afternoon and cheered them on in the boxing match that had followed. Raz's jaw still smarted. "You think it's a bad move?"

Brant glanced across the room at Wells. "He's built, and he's good-looking, but I hear he's the love-'em and leave-'em type. I don't know about you, but I couldn't go there. I need my cuddle time."

"I believe you heard wrong," Levi chimed in from Raz's other side. "I heard he hooks his one-night stands up with breakfast in the morning."

"Fucks 'em and feeds 'em? That sounds more like Wells," Archer said, standing with Jock and Grant. "Always out to impress."

"Not a bad deal, if you ask me," Jock added.

"You're all out of your minds," Grant gritted out. "I wouldn't want to be the one to break the news to Leni that Duncan is swapping her for Wells. Those two have some rocky history."

"So I've heard." Raz took a drink. He'd had a great time with the guys. They might dick around and give each other shit, but it was obvious how much they cared about and respected each other, like he and Beau did. He could tell they cared about Wells, too, as they should. He might have screwed over Leni, but he was still a lifelong friend to the men Raz had only just met.

"This ought to be fun." Archer nodded toward Wells heading their way and tipped his glass to his lips.

"How's it going, gentlemen?" Wells flashed a grin at Raz. "You must be the actor who's got all the women on the island's hearts a flutter."

"Good thing Leni's already snagged mine." Raz stood and offered his hand. "Duncan Raz."

"Wells…*Silver*." He paused just long enough to let Silver sound important. His gaze dropped to Raz's bruised jaw, and he fucking grinned. "Want me to get you a steak for that?"

"No thanks. Leni will kiss it better when she gets here."

"Her lips make lots of things feel better," Wells said arrogantly. "You can thank me for that. I'm the one who taught her how to kiss…among other things."

"*Jesus*," Grant gritted out.

Archer took a step forward, and Raz shifted, blocking him with his shoulder. "Luckily, she got over that abysmal lesson and learned how to do things right." There was a lot of commotion at the entrance to the bar, and he heard Jules's name and knew Leni wouldn't be far behind, but he never took his eyes off Wells.

"They say a woman never forgets her first." Wells cocked a brow.

"Until she meets her last." Leni came into view over his shoulder. A fireball of dark, sensual energy blazing directly toward him, despite the irritated curiosity in her keen green eyes. He reached for her as the other girls hit the bar. "Hey, princess. I was just getting to know your good friend Wells."

She shot a warning glare at Wells. "I hope you're behaving

yourself."

"You know I only misbehave in the bedroom." Wells waggled his brows.

Rolling her eyes, she turned back to Raz. "How was your—" She gasped, anger and concern flaring in her eyes. "What did they do to you?"

"Nothing. I took all their money in poker, and Archer said he had to win it back in the boxing ring. Now I know where you got your competitive streak."

"Please tell me you knocked him out," she snapped.

Wells laughed. "Yeah, right."

Leni glowered at him.

Ignoring Wells, Raz said, "He only won half his money back. Take a look for yourself." He nodded to Archer. Indi was inspecting the purplish bruise on his cheek.

"Good," Leni said emphatically, then more compassionately, "Does your jaw hurt?"

"Not too much for a kiss."

She looked at him, as if to say, *Are you serious?*

He nodded, sure she would roll her eyes, but she surprised him by caressing his jaw and going up on her toes to kiss the sore spot. She batted her lashes, speaking in a dramatically breathy voice. "Is my big, strong man okay now?"

Laughing, Raz hauled her into his arms and crushed his mouth to hers. When she tried to pull back, he took the kiss deeper. Yeah, he was being a shameless ass, and he didn't fucking care.

"Get a room." Wells sounded irritated, but less so as he announced, "Serve up a round of drinks on me to celebrate my big brother marrying the sweetest girl on Silver Island."

There was a round of cheers, and only then did Raz pry his

lips from Leni's.

"Was that necessary?" she hissed.

"Yes. My ego was at stake."

She tried to stifle a smile. "*You* are in big trouble, mister."

"Good thing I brought that silk tie."

There was no hiding the flames igniting in her eyes.

Damn, he was going to miss that.

RAZ LAY IN Leni's childhood bedroom later that night, unable to stop thinking about Leni and Wells. He couldn't shake the feeling that her vehemence about not being cut out for love and Wells Silver were connected. But she'd said she hadn't ever been in love.

Why was he even thinking about that? He wasn't looking for love. He was excited to get back to work. It didn't matter how much she meant to him or how much he looked forward to seeing her, hearing her voice, and being close to her. He was sure all that would fade once he was gone. He told himself she was like a role he couldn't figure out, and he just wanted to understand the woman who slept draped over him like a human blanket nearly every night, as she was now. He added the way she slept to the growing list of things he was going to miss about her and ran his fingers through her hair, whispering, "What secrets are you hiding from me, sweetheart?"

"I'm not hiding anything." She peeled herself off his chest, gazing sleepily at him.

He was struck anew by how heart-stoppingly beautiful she was without makeup and how much he adored that sweet spray of freckles across her nose. She lowered her cheek onto his chest, her fingers lightly brushing his skin. He didn't know when she'd stopped trying to keep her distance. It had just sort of happened over time, and it was nice. He'd never had this level of intimacy, and with Leni he wanted more of it. That was fine a week or two ago, but the end of their time together was coming fast, and he had to keep those feelings in check.

He ran his hand down her back. "I hope I didn't wake you."

"You didn't. I was drifting in and out of sleep. That was fun tonight."

"Yeah, I enjoyed it, too. Your friends and family are great." They'd stayed at the bar celebrating Jules and Grant's upcoming wedding, and he'd enjoyed getting to know everyone better. When they'd gotten back to her parents' house, they'd hung out in the kitchen with Sutton, eating cookies and talking for a while before turning in for the night.

"Wells was in prime shape tonight," Leni said begrudgingly. "I hope he didn't annoy you too much."

"Nah, he was fine. I can't blame him for being rattled by a debonair movie star." He felt her smile against his skin and kissed the top of her head. "Just about everyone mentioned that you'd never brought a guy home before. Do you think Wells has been hoping to rekindle things with you for all this time?"

"Good God, *no*. He's just a needler. He likes to ruffle feathers."

"And flirt."

"Yes, he's good at that. He left with some blonde right before we did."

"I didn't notice." He was a little surprised that she had. "Can I ask you something about him?"

"Depends what it is."

"Ever the cagey one, aren't you? I know you said you've

never been in love, but now that you know my secrets and we've taken a vow of honesty, you can tell me the truth. Did you love him?"

She was quiet for so long, he wondered if she'd fallen back to sleep. But then she spoke, soft and thoughtful. "We were teenagers. I thought my world spun on his axis, and keeping our relationship a secret was exciting and dangerous, which I liked. But I wouldn't call it love."

"That sounds a lot like first love to me."

She rested her chin on his chest, meeting his gaze. "Trust me, it wasn't. Why does everyone think people fall in love with the first person they sleep with?"

"Maybe because most of us do. I was devastated when Jessica ghosted me."

"I thought she was just a vacation fling."

"I guess it was for her, but it wasn't like that for me. I saw us going back to that same beach year after year, long after she and I had a family of our own."

Leni wrinkled her nose. "Really? Are you a closet romantic?"

If anyone would know, it's you. She'd gotten closer to him than any woman ever had. "I don't know. Am I?"

"Most definitely. I'm sorry she broke your fragile heart."

He swatted her ass. "Don't make fun of my gullible teenage heart."

"Gullible is right. Did you really think a college girl would keep in touch with a high school kid?"

"*Yes.* She promised to stay in touch and said we'd see each other again during her fall break. She was very convincing, but she never returned any of my calls, and I never heard from her again until I became an actor."

"No way."

"You'd be surprised how many people come out of the

woodwork when you become famous."

"I hear about it all the time, but someone from a fling when you were teenagers? That takes big ones on her part. Especially since she hurt you."

"It's okay. I got over her a few months later with a cheerleader from another school."

"Of course you did. Why is it so easy for young guys to go from one girl's bed to the next?"

"It's not. I went out with that other girl for almost six months, until she cheated on me with the quarterback from her school's football team."

"*Ugh.* Is anyone faithful anymore?"

"The way your brothers and sister are with their significant others, I can't imagine any of them cheating."

"I don't think they would, either. It's like they won the love lottery."

"Let me ask you something. How do you know you weren't in love with Wells if you've never been in love since?"

"Because I knew he would never leave the island, and I still wanted to go to New York and eventually build a life there. When you love someone, you shouldn't feel good about leaving them."

"I don't know about that. I think two people can support each other while pursuing separate dreams, as long as they're faithful and finding ways to come together is a priority."

"You still believe that? Even after Jacinda? Because you said you weren't looking to get tied down."

"I'm not, but that has to do with the fucking press, not her. I wasn't in love with, or invested in, Jacinda. You know me better than she ever did, and I obviously didn't know her. Besides, a person can still believe in love and long-distance relationships without wanting them."

"I guess that's true, but they're not for me."

"How do you know? And don't tell me it's because you're not cut out for love."

"Why do you want to know so badly? You're leaving Monday."

"Because I care about you. You're an incredible woman, and a good friend, but you've got a chip on your shoulder about love, and I want to understand why. Your parents still paw after each other every chance they get, and your siblings are falling like flies. But you're on the other side of the field, casting darts to keep people at a distance, and that bothers me. You deserve to love and be loved."

She rested her cheek on his chest again and didn't respond.

"Who else did you trust with your heart, princess?" Whether or not she admitted to trusting Wells with it didn't matter. He knew the truth. Leni was not the type of person who would sleep with a guy she didn't trust, and he doubted she'd ever been any other way. Stroking her back, he pressed another kiss to the top of her head. "Why don't you believe two people can support each other while they're not in the same place?"

"Because I tried it once, okay?" she said sharply, lifting her face to look at him.

She looked so vulnerable, he ached to take away the hurt brimming in her eyes. "Who was it? Who do I have to kill, princess?"

She laughed softly. "You're no killer."

"Yeah, you're right. But for you I'd gladly go down trying."

"You did clock Archer."

"Damn right." He pushed her hair behind her ear. "Talk to me, Leni. I want to know what you've been through."

She looked as though she was debating answering for a moment. "It was my senior year of college. I was interning for

Shea, and he was bartending at an event we attended. We dated for a few months, and I was pretty crazy about him. He said and did all the right things. He wanted to be together for the long haul, and he asked about my work every day, cheering me on, and I did the same for him. He wanted to be an actor, so I used my connections to help him get an audition in Hollywood. He left New York, and two weeks later he dumped me over the phone to focus on his career. Six months after that, he married a pop star. I should have seen through it, but I was—"

"In love."

Her eyes narrowed in defiance. "Too swept up in him to see what was right in front of me."

"That's not on you. You know that, don't you? The guy was obviously a dick and a user. Hollywood is full of them."

"Yeah, no shit. That's why I swore off actors and long-distance relationships."

"And, eventually, the entire gender. Except for us fakies."

Her lips twitched into an *almost* smile. "Do you blame me? I'm a stepping-stone, not a forever girl. I'm too stubborn and sarcastic and hard to get close to. I get cheated on or used for men's personal gains. I mean, look at us. I'm your fake date so you can finally move on with your life after Jacinda."

"Leni—"

"*Don't.* This is what it is, and that's okay. I *accepted* this. It's different from what happened to me before. I was blindsided, but I think deep down I must have known he wasn't as all in as he claimed, because I never wanted to take him home to meet my family, and I never even talked much about him to Abby and Indi."

"Isn't that the way you are anyway? Protective of the people in your life?"

"Yes, but I *thought* I was crazy about him."

"You thought you were in love with him, Leni. You can admit it. It's not a weakness. It's part of life. First love is rarely real or smart. It's hormones and ego and a hundred other things that make us into a mess of bad decisions and false hope."

"Please don't ever tell Jules that. Grant is her one and only love."

"Their love is real. You could see it in their eyes, and even if it weren't, I wouldn't dare try to dull her shine. What's the name of the guy who hurt you?"

"Kip Jones."

"*Jesus.* I know that asshole. We were in a movie together before he got divorced. Everyone on set knew he was cheating on his wife." He had no doubt that Kip had never deserved Leni in the first place. No wonder she had her heart on lockdown. She'd *tried* love, and the two guys she'd trusted had given her every reason not to.

"That's par for your industry."

"Not all of us are like that."

"Maybe not, but I'll never put myself in that position again." She rolled onto her other side, facing away from him.

He put his arm around her, drew her back to his chest, and nuzzled her neck. "I'm sorry he hurt you." He didn't dare say another word, because he didn't trust what might come out. She'd gotten so deep under his skin, he couldn't help but wear his emotions on his sleeve. But he'd been hurt too. It was a different kind of hurt. The kind that he never wanted to go through again, which was why he'd become adept at knowing *when* and *how* to shut his feelings down when he needed to.

This was one of those times, because, for the first time in his career, he didn't have to work at the role he was playing, which made him wonder if Leni's adoring boyfriend was exactly who he was always meant to be.

Twenty-Five

LENI FOLLOWED RAZ downstairs Sunday morning, focusing on thumbing out an email to a client as he set their bags by the front door.

"Something smells delicious."

"My mom makes great breakfasts." Leni hit send, but she pretended to still be typing. "Go on in and eat. I just want to finish this email."

"I can wait."

She looked up from her phone, taking in his easy smile and scruffy cheeks. Scruffy-faced, dressed-down Raz was utterly irresistible, but she'd been having a hard time since they'd said goodbye to most of her family and friends last night. Jules had rattled on for ten minutes, hoping he'd be able to take the weekend off from filming to come to her wedding, and the guys wanted to know when they'd see him again, inviting him back anytime, even if their *workaholic sister* couldn't get time off. That was grueling enough, but it was small potatoes compared to how difficult it would be to watch her parents treating him like he was part of the family, while she and Raz were on the cusp of ending things.

"It's okay," she finally said. "I'm going to be a minute."

"Don't be too long. This is my last chance to make sure I'm always their favorite and ruin them for any future men you bring home."

He winked, and it felt like a knife in her chest.

He must have seen it in her expression, because he closed the distance between them. "I'm sorry. That was a bad joke. This isn't easy for me, either. Now I understand why you had such a hard time after we had dinner with my parents. In hindsight, the whole fake-dating thing was a terrible idea. But getting closer to you wasn't. I'm sorry we put you in this position with your family, but I can't say I'm sorry I met any of them."

A lump formed in her throat, and her gaze dropped to the bruise on his jaw, partially masked by his scruff. "Even Archer?"

He laughed softly. "Even Archer." He took her hand in his. "I know this is hard, but you've done harder things."

She wasn't so sure about that. "Yeah. I'll be fine."

"You truly suck at lying."

"*Ugh*. Shut up. Let me have my lies and go eat breakfast."

"As you wish, Lady Lenore." With a sexy grin, he headed into the kitchen, and she heard him say, "Morning, Mama Steele, Papa Steele. Something smells good."

Leni heard her father say, "Morning, son," and her mother say, "Hi, honey. I hope you like blueberry waffles. Oh my *goodness*. How did you get that bruise on your jaw?" Raz's voice floated into her ears. "Your daughter decked me when I refused to kiss her good night."

Leni laughed and looked up at the ceiling, whispering angrily, "What did I do to deserve *this*?"

"Would you like a detailed list?" Sutton said as she descended the stairs.

Leni spun around. "How long have you been there?"

"Why? Were you getting felt up by your boyfriend?"

Leni breathed a sigh of relief and glowered at her. *"No."*

"Too bad." Sutton smiled. "I know I said I didn't like being the odd girl out, but I kind of love you two together."

"Great, now I can buy that wedding dress," Leni said sarcastically, then quickly changed the subject. "Are you taking the ferry with us?"

"No. I'm meeting Keira and Randi after breakfast and spending the day with them." Sutton headed for the kitchen, looking over her shoulder. "Aren't you coming?"

"In a sec. I need to handle a few emails first."

"Okay. I'll just go tell Duncan all the horribly embarrassing things I know about you."

Leni hurried to catch up with her, but Sutton bolted into the kitchen, laughing as she said, "Duncan, did Leni tell you about the time I caught her practicing kissing with her pillow?"

AN HOUR LATER, her parents drove them to the ferry. Leni didn't understand the web of emotions tightening her chest as she shouldered her bag. She was never emotional when she left the island. She was usually too excited about getting back to work to think about anything else. But as she thanked her parents for driving them and hugged her mother, she felt on the verge of tears.

As she turned to her father, Raz said, "Mama Steele, I can't begin to tell you how much I enjoyed meeting you and your family. Thank you for inviting me, and"—he looked at Leni, emotions swimming in his eyes—"for raising such an incredible daughter."

Leni wanted to swat him for laying it on so thick.

"Oh, Duncan, get over here." Her mother embraced him. "I know you'll miss Field of Screams this year, but maybe next year?"

"You never know," Raz said.

As he chatted with her mother, Leni's father drew her into his arms, holding her tight. "Are you okay, Leni Bean?"

She closed her eyes, soaking in his comfort. "Mm-hm."

He drew back but kept his arm around her, guiding her a few feet from Raz and her mother. "You look like you did when Jock and Archer had their falling-out."

"I'm fine."

"I know Duncan is leaving tomorrow, and I'm sure it'll be hard to be away from him. But your mom and I dated long-distance while I finished college. It's doable."

Not for us. "I know, Dad. I'm fine, really. Just anxious to get my arms around a few new projects at work, that's all."

"Work. Right. Got it," he said tightly.

He might as well have said, *I know better.* Her father had a way of knowing just what she needed, when she needed it. She'd never told him how she'd felt about Kip, but late one night, when she couldn't shake the sadness, she'd called just to hear her father's safe, loving voice. The next morning he'd surprised her and shown up on her doorstep. They'd gone to breakfast, had watched a movie and a baseball game, and he'd never once pushed her for an explanation, taking her excuse of school and work being *a lot* at face value. But in her heart she'd known he'd somehow figured out what was really wrong.

"You know, if you need an extra hand with work or anything, you can call me and I'll be there, anytime, day or night."

"I know. Thank you," she said as they walked back to Raz and her mother.

Raz lifted his chin, brows knitted, a silent *Is everything okay* ringing in her ears. She nodded, loving that he cared enough to worry and hating that it meant so much.

"Papa Steele, I have a bone to pick with you," Raz said seriously.

"Uh-oh. What's that?"

Raz rubbed his jaw. "Did you have to teach Archer how to fight so well?"

They laughed.

"Actually, I have a favor to ask." He opened his bag and pulled several envelopes out of his pocket. "Would you mind giving these to the guys? They're labeled."

"Sure, of course," her father said.

"What's in them?" Leni asked.

"Money for new tires and shoes."

"That's awfully nice of you, but that's not how pranks work around here. Keep your money. They're big boys. They can deal with it." He handed the envelopes back to Raz. "It's not like they can give you back the minutes you were sweating bullets off the edge of that cliff."

Raz smiled, nodding. "You've got that right." He put the envelopes back in his bag and held out his hand. "Thanks for everything."

"I think we should be thanking you." Her father glanced at her briefly and took Raz's hand. He pulled him into an embrace, clapping him on the back. "Come back soon, son."

Her father's use of the endearment *son* tweaked her heart-strings.

As they made their way onto the ferry, Raz said, "Why couldn't you have shitty parents?"

Why couldn't you have remained the arrogant jerk I thought you were?

THEY DIDN'T TALK much on the ferry ride back to the mainland, each lost in their own thoughts. A car picked them up on the other side, and the stilted silence continued. Tension thickened around them. Leni worried he'd ask her to spend the day together before the wedding, and she tried to come up with an excuse not to.

When they got to her place, he got out of the car and put a hand on her back as they ascended the steps to her building.

"I was thinking—"

"I have to work," she blurted out.

"Okay." He looked confused. "I was going to say I was thinking I'd pick you up around five for the wedding if that's okay."

"Oh, sorry. I thought you might want to…Never mind." She felt like an idiot. A disappointed idiot. "Five is fine."

"Thanks for a great weekend. I'll see you then." He leaned down and kissed her cheek.

Her *cheek*? Not the lips he claimed to enjoy so much but her cheek, like she was a friend, and not the kind he got naked with? And he wasn't even walking her upstairs?

Sadness shrouded her like a cloak.

This was for the best. She knew it was. But what the hell had happened? He was always pushing for more time with her, not less. Maybe he didn't really like her family after all, or the guys had scared the piss out of him and he didn't want to deal with that.

Or maybe he didn't want to deal with her.

She tried to kick that idea to the curb, but she knew she wasn't an easy partner. She was bullheaded and sarcastic and hard to get close to. She was a stepping-stone, not a forever girl.

Holy crap. What am I doing?

Why do I care if he doesn't want to spend time with me? I didn't want to spend it with him, either. She *needed* this to end, and time apart would make it a whole lot easier.

She forced a smile. "Thank you." She headed inside, struggling against a lump in her throat the size of Canada.

RAZ HAD NEVER been affected by weddings before, especially over-the-top, black-tie affairs that felt more like a show than the start of an intimate life together. Sure, he'd been overjoyed for Beau when he'd married Charlotte, the woman who had helped him rediscover life and love again after losing Tory, but he hadn't felt drawn to be the one standing at the altar. Or in Jay and Naomi's case, beneath the chuppah. But as Jay prepared to break the glass, marking the final act before he and Naomi would be declared man and wife, Raz imagined standing before his family and friends with Leni draped in white satin and lace, her fiery hair trailing over her shoulders in sexy waves.

Shocked by the thought, a kernel of panic grew in his chest.

He'd gotten too close to her, too attached, and he'd thought the afternoon apart would help. But he'd fucking missed her in the hours before the wedding. It was crazy, and the minute he'd seen her in that shimmery forest-green gown with a sexy slit up one side, his heart had skipped to a new beat. Right then and there he'd known there was only one way to handle leaving tomorrow morning without losing his mind, and that was to give himself one more night to take everything he could possibly want from her and get her out of his system.

Or at least hold him over while he filmed. If that didn't do the trick, he could get lost in another woman for a night or two. He swallowed against the bile rising in his throat at the thought and glanced at Leni sitting beside him, trying her damnedest to blink away tears. The tug in his chest that had gone from foreign to familiar the last few weeks intensified. She'd been her snarky self when he'd picked her up, but she'd also been surprisingly cold toward him. Being the professional she was, that had changed the second they'd stepped out of the car at the hotel. She'd been all smiles for the paparazzi, and with a little encouragement, the sheen of ice she'd worn like a cloak had melted.

He reached for her hand, and she turned those beautiful glassy eyes on him, drawing his emotions to the surface. He lifted her hand to his lips, kissing the back of it, wondering if he'd tapped into a part of her these last few weeks that had been lying in wait, just as he suspected she'd done with him. Or if at a certain age, every man and woman became more emotional and started thinking about the future.

Jay stomped on the glass, and everyone yelled "Mazel Tov!" jerking him from his thoughts.

Leni dabbed at her eyes with a tissue, her smile growing as Jay and Naomi were pronounced husband and wife and made their way down the aisle.

Raz put his arm around Leni, pulling her closer. "Are you going soft on me, sweetheart?"

"*No.* They just look so happy."

"You can admit there's a squishy part of your heart hoping that'll be you one day."

She scoffed. "Hardly."

"Come on," he coaxed. "Your two best friends and your twin are engaged, and your younger sister is getting married. It would be natural for some part of you to want what they have."

She shook her head, not even gracing him with a response as they followed the other guests toward the grand ballroom.

He was impressed with her steadfast resolve to deny she wanted or needed a man in her life, even if he thought it was a decision born from fear and not the desire to be alone. Aching to peel back her layers one last time, he slid his arm around her waist, drawing her closer. "Did you know it's a Jewish tradition for the bride and groom to spend eight minutes alone and eat their first meal together as husband and wife after the ceremony?"

"Is that where they went?"

"Sure is, and I know what their first meal is." He waggled his brows. "I might need to find myself a Jewish girl to marry."

"If I ever get married, I won't need a tradition to make it okay to enjoy my husband on my wedding day. If I'm in love enough to say *I do*, it would only be to a man who would say, *The party can wait. I want you.*"

Why did the idea of Leni marrying some other guy bother him so much?

This wedding was definitely messing with his head.

Her eyes lit up as they entered the grandiose ballroom with its cream-and-gold decor, elaborate two-story coved ceiling, stately columns, and dozens of tables draped in gold with elegant white-rose centerpieces. "This is like a fairy tale. I bet the paparazzi are dying to get in here." There was security posted at every ballroom entrance to keep the reception private.

"It's nice that we're not the center of attention, isn't it?" he said as they made their way toward the bar.

"*Yes.* I could never live the life of a celebrity. I'd be caught flicking off the photographers too often."

"No, you wouldn't. You might want to, but you're too classy for that."

They mingled with other guests on the way to the bar, fielding questions about how they'd met and compliments about how great they were together. They *were* great together. Leni was charming and confident, and she played up their relationship so well, playfully teasing and gazing at him with adoration that felt as real as it sounded. Everything about them—talking, kissing, touching, joking, fucking. Hell, even arguing—had felt natural since the night they'd met.

"YOU COULD SELL condoms to a nun," he said as they walked away from Zane and Willow Walker and headed for the bar.

"I do marketing for a living. Besides, we're easy to sell. You're not bad to look at, pretty great between the sheets, and we have fun together. What else is there?"

"Not *bad?* Pretty great?" He stopped walking and looked at her. "Don't mind my ego as it skulks off to the corner to pout."

She laughed softly. "I don't need to shower you with compliments. You have millions of fans who do that for you."

"They don't know me. They *think* they know Raz." He stepped closer. "What if it's your opinion I care about?" *What the fuck am I doing?*

Her expression softened. "You know what I think of you."

"Do I? I know sometimes you can't keep your hands off me,

but you also have no problem kicking me out after spending a great night together."

"*Raz,*" she said softly.

"Sorry, princess, but it's our last date, and that name doesn't sound right coming from you anymore. It would mean a lot to me if you'd call me Duncan." Their gazes held, and he felt the familiar thrum of their connection burrow into his bones.

She opened her mouth to speak, but a familiar voice calling her name drew their attention to Jake and Fiona Braden, closing in on them. Jake had a few inches, and years, on Raz, and he was a hell of a guy.

"Hi." Leni embraced Fiona.

"You two know each other?" Raz asked.

"Fiona is my cousin, Shea's sister," Leni explained. "Do you know her and Jake?"

"I sure do. I didn't realize she was a Steele. Jake did my stunts in my last two movies, and we've hung out quite a few times. Nice to see you again. Fiona, you look as gorgeous as ever." Her long brown hair was twisted up off her neck, and she wore a sparkling blue gown. Raz hugged her and shook Jake's hand. "How's Cannon?"

"He's incredible, man. I highly recommend fatherhood." Jake leaned down to kiss Leni's cheek. "What're you doing with *this* guy?" he teased.

"*Jake,*" Fiona chided. "He's kidding. We love Raz."

"How could you not?" Raz reached for Leni's hand. "Honestly, I'm still trying to figure out what Leni's doing with me."

"Would you *stop?*" Leni straightened his lapel. "You know why I'm with you, Duncan."

His chest tightened at the way his name came out playful and intimate. He couldn't help but tease her. "The nine-inch thing, huh?"

They all laughed.

"Movies make everything look bigger," Jake added.

"Actually, the movies don't do him justice," Leni said thoughtfully. "But that's only part of his appeal. He's down to earth, driven, and he makes me laugh. But he can also be serious, and I have to admit, he looks pretty good in a tux."

Raz pulled her closer, eating up every word. "What is with this *pretty good* stuff?"

"Don't push it," she warned, making Jake and Fiona laugh. "You know you're like a caramel macchiato. Sweet and bold and hard to take in large doses. But you buy me ice cream, so I suffer through it."

He laughed, tugging her closer and whispering, "I'll give you a large dose of something hard."

"I never thought I'd see the day that Leni would let a man into her heart," Jake said.

"Oh, he's not in my heart," Leni said snarkily. "Too much of this guy can seriously knock a gal off her feet. We're just having fun. Right, Duncan?"

He wasn't sure what they were doing anymore, but he didn't dare pick it apart. "Something like that."

THEY WERE SEATED with Jake and Fiona, Aiden's sister, actress Remi Divine and her husband, Mason Swift, and a handful of other people during dinner. Leni had been surprised to run into Remi and had worried it might be uncomfortable since she and Raz had dated, but it wasn't. Raz was his charming, attentive self, making Leni feel special, and their last fake date feel very real.

Dinner was nothing short of spectacular. As their plates were cleared, Raz said, "If I hadn't been so intimidating to kiss on-screen, Remi and Mason never would have gotten together."

Jake's brow furrowed. "Somehow I don't believe that story."

"Because it's *not* true," Remi insisted. "I wasn't afraid to kiss Raz. We'd already kissed when we went out, ages ago. I've always had trouble with on-screen kisses, because kissing is intimate and hard to fake."

Even several months pregnant, the Natalie Portman lookalike was stunning, in an elegant black gown, and her bodyguard-turned-husband was just as handsome in his tux. His sharp eyes stopped scoping out their surroundings only long enough to admire his wife.

"I got her over that hump in time for your scene." Mason nodded at Raz. "You're welcome."

"Took a hit for the team, did ya?" Raz teased. "We nailed that scene, so thank you."

As they talked, Leni tried not to give any credence to the spear of jealousy slicing through her at the thought of Raz kissing Remi. She had been trying not to give weight to a lot of unexpected emotions tonight, thanks to Raz's heated glances, his taunting teases, sweet compliments, inside jokes, and dirty promises. The man could bring a dead woman back to life. Asking her to call him Duncan hadn't helped.

She hadn't expected his name to take on a life of its own. But it magnified everything they said to each other, every touch, and every kiss. She'd never had this problem before. Had never had such intense feelings for a man. As much as she needed their ruse to come to an end, she loathed—*and craved*—the way the ticking clock made her feel. When she thought about saying goodbye for good, desperation came over her, and she wanted to run into his arms. She hated that frenetic feeling almost as much as she loved the way he took control no matter how much she fought it.

The way he got her out of her own head, making her give in to having fun and *wanting* like she never had before, was almost enough to make her forget her *need* for control. She was determined not to dwell on the reality that the overwhelming happiness she'd felt these last few weeks was nearing its expiration date. She *needed* that expiration date. But sometime over the course of the evening, she'd given herself permission to let go of her control altogether and allow herself to revel in the urgency and desire that had rooted itself deep inside her. She was going to give and take with reckless abandon tonight, and she was going to enjoy the hell out of it. *Then* she could close the door on the ruse without any regrets and walk away with her heart fully intact.

The band began playing "Hava Nagila," and as guests rushed to the dance floor, Remi exclaimed, "The hora! I love this."

"Me too," Fiona said. "Let's go!"

As they hurried to the dance floor with Mason and Jake, Raz said, "Let's go, Steele."

He took her hand as he rose to his feet, pulling her up beside him. Dozens of guests were squishing together arm in arm, forming two giant circles as they danced and kicked. "I don't know how to do this."

"Stick with me, baby. I'll show you."

Hand in hand, they rushed to the dance floor, squeezing between Mason and Fiona. Leni tried to follow along, kicking when everyone kicked and chanting "Hava Nagila."

"I have no idea what I'm doing," she said to Fiona.

"It doesn't matter. Just have fun!"

She glanced at Raz's infectious grin, his joyous singing ringing in her ears, and she couldn't imagine ever *not* having fun with him.

A gaggle of men carried the bride and groom on chairs to the center of the circles, lifting and lowering them in tune with the joyous rhythm as everyone sang. The bride and groom radiated with love so strong, it was palpable. Leni got caught up in the excitement, singing and dancing, soaking in Raz's unbridled laughter and her own.

That happiness lasted for the next two hours as they danced to fast songs and slow and chatted with their friends and other guests. As the night wound down, the band began playing "Love Me Like You Do," and Raz led Leni out to the dance floor for the umpteenth time.

Leni wasn't a romantic, or at least she'd never been one. But as they swayed to the music, her cheek resting on Raz's chest, the lyrics wound around her heart like a ribbon. He was the only man who had ever set her heart on fire, and she definitely couldn't see clearly around him. She knew now that what she'd felt for Kip had been child's play compared to the way she felt about Raz. She looked up at him, and he gazed into her eyes with the warmest, most intimate smile she'd ever seen. *Be careful. Pull back*, whispered through her mind, but that whisper was no match for the shouts coming from the one place that hadn't spoken to her in years. Her heart.

As the chorus rang out about loving her like he did, Raz lowered his lips to hers, kissing her so slow and sweet, she felt like she was floating on a cloud. Somewhere in her head that whispered warning repeated, but tonight wasn't about denying herself the only man she truly wanted. It was about cherishing what they had here and now.

The song ended, and she thought he'd let her go, but his arms tightened around her.

"One last dance." His voice was low and soft, but it wasn't an offer or a suggestion. He was taking this dance whether she wanted him to or not, and that only made her want it more.

Their gazes held as they swayed to a nonexistent beat while guests made their way on and off the dance floor. When the band began playing, Leni recognized it as "Run to You" by Lea Michele. It was one of Jules's favorite songs. As the singer crooned about being safe in his arms and how he'd run to her if she called his name, it was Jules's lyrics that rang out in Leni's head.

'Cause I know I'm safe in your arms
If I call your name in the middle of the night
I know you'd run to me, and know I'd run to you

Leni's heart took a hit. Jules had that and more with Grant. Archer would take down an army for Indi. Jock fought unimaginable demons to be with Daphne and Hadley, and Levi left the life he'd built in Harborside for Tara. Part of Leni longed to be loved like that, and if she was ever going to consider opening herself up completely, the way they had, it would be with the man she was dancing with.

Fortunately, she knew the score and wouldn't fall prey to the fairy tale. Her heart had already suffered two painful breaks. A *chance* at finding true love wasn't worth the risk of a third broken heart. Not even with the charming orgasm king.

"Thank you for coming with me tonight," Raz whispered against her cheek. "Have you had a good time?"

Leni took a second to shore up the walls around her heart before meeting his gaze, but the second those ocean-blue eyes met hers, the walls that had always kept her safe chipped away beneath the heat of his stare. She tried to summon her snark to regain control, but she didn't have it in her, and she simply nodded.

"Me too, but now I want you all to myself." He brushed his lips over hers. "Will you give me that? One last night together?"

"What do you think?"

He pressed his lips to hers in a tender kiss. "I think I want to hear you say that you want me, too."

She looked at the man who desperately wanted, and deserved, to be loved for who he was rather than who everyone believed him to be, and she was pretty sure she'd already taken that plunge. "I want you, Duncan. All of you." She drew in a shaky breath, forcing those deeper emotions to remain at bay, and added, for both their sakes, "For one last night."

Twenty-Seven

RAZ'S ARMS CIRCLED Leni's waist, his warm lips descending on her neck in tantalizing openmouthed kisses as she pushed the key into the lock to her apartment. Desire pumped through her like blood in her veins. She closed her eyes against the butterflies swarming in her belly and chest. Everything felt different tonight. On the ride home, their kisses weren't feverish or savage, like they usually were. They were deep and sensual, heightening her arousal with every seductive slide of their tongues. Raz hadn't fisted his hands in her hair the way she usually craved. He'd threaded his fingers gently through it, cradling her face in his palms like he was cherishing her, savoring every second of their kisses, and she knew she'd forever crave that now, too.

He pressed his lips to her cheek, his hand closing over hers, which she hadn't realized had stilled holding the key in the lock. He turned the knob and pushed the door open, keeping hold of her as they went inside. She tried to turn around and face him, but with a strong grip on her hips and a commanding voice, he said, "Bedroom," and guided her down the hall.

He walked her over to a streak of moonlight cutting through the window, stopping when it cut a path across her breasts. She tried again to turn toward him, but he held her upper arms, keeping her back to him. "We're playing by my rules tonight, princess, so don't fight it."

A thrill shuddered through her. She had never fully submitted to any man, but with Raz she wanted to. That frightened her as much as it excited her. Not because she didn't trust him, but because in the bedroom, she trusted him implicitly, and she'd never felt that before. At least not to the point where she trusted a man enough to want to do *all* the things she'd never done before.

Standing behind her, he tossed his tuxedo jacket onto the chair. His bow tie followed. She closed her eyes as he gathered her hair over one shoulder and kissed the curve of her neck. "You were the most beautiful woman there tonight."

They'd been surrounded by some of the most gorgeous people in the world. Leni's knee-jerk reaction was to tell him he needed glasses. But the sincerity in his voice stifled her snark, making her a little nervous. As he unzipped her dress, she finally managed, "Thank you."

He pressed a kiss between her shoulder blades, sending shivers of heat down her spine.

"It was torture waiting to get my hands and mouth on you." He unhooked her bra and slid it off her shoulders along with the gown, kissing the skin he bared as her clothes slid to the floor, puddling at her feet. He ran his fingers down her arms. "While everyone else was eating dinner, I was thinking about laying you on the table and burying my face between your thighs until you screamed my name, letting everyone know that tonight you're *mine*."

Her sex clenched greedily. "Your arm was around me all night, and we kissed a hundred times. I think they knew."

"It wasn't enough." His hands moved down her sides, squeezing her waist as he dragged his tongue along the shell of her ear. "I wanted to possess you." He took her by the chin, turning her face so she could see him. "*All* of you." He crushed his mouth to hers, his mouth firm and insistent, his body hot and hard against her back. He fondled her breasts roughly, deepening the kiss, forcing her mouth open wider, thrusting his tongue deeper. She moaned at the sting of pain, which quickly morphed into agonizing pleasure. He pushed his hand into her panties, his fingers delving inside her like heat-guided missiles. She went up on her toes at the delicious intrusion.

He growled, and the hungry sound burned through her. He ate at her mouth, stroking that hidden spot inside her with his fingers, driving her out of her mind, and brought his other hand to the apex of her sex. Prickles of heat coiled low in her belly, spreading down her thighs and up her core like a ravenous animal. He moved one hand to her breast, and a swarm of sensations engulfed her. She tried to focus on his thick fingers moving inside her, his thumb playing over her throbbing clit, his mouth feasting on her, but she was lost in his touch. He squeezed her nipple, sending a shower of scintillating sensations raining down on her. Her knees weakened, and she tried to keep up, but it was too much pleasure to endure. Cries burst from her lungs into his, and he intensified everything—their kisses, the pace at which his fingers fucked her, the pressure on her clit—igniting her entire being like a flare. She clung to his forearms, hips bucking, pleasure roaring through her. He didn't slow down or let her catch her breath. He continued taking what he wanted, devouring her mouth as his fingers and thumb took her to unimaginable, breath-stealing heights.

When she went limp against him, light-headed, her vision

blurry, he kissed her neck and shoulder. "Still with me, beautiful?"

"Barely," she panted out.

He scooped her into his arms. She didn't have the energy to protest as he carried her to the bed and laid her down, taking a long, lascivious look at her. "*Mm-mm*. You are my gorgeous girl."

He spoke with such sincerity, she wanted to believe he felt that way, and just for tonight, she allowed herself the luxury of letting go of her doubts and soaking in every word.

He took off her heels and panties and pulled a string of condoms from his wallet. "There's more where these came from."

She laughed as he tossed them onto the nightstand. "Sounds like it's going to be a hell of a night."

"One I guarantee you'll never forget."

She watched him undress. The tip of his erection poked out the waistband of his boxer briefs. As he stripped them off, freeing the thick rod, her body flooded with heat. She squeezed her thighs together to quell the ache.

"Oh no, you don't," he growled, crawling over her and spreading her legs with his knees. "I want you wet and needy, and I want to see that slick pussy begging for my cock. Where's that silk tie I love so much?"

Giddiness scampered through her. "In my nightstand. You want to play Fifty Shades of Grey?"

"Fuck no. I want to play Fifty Shades of Steele." He nipped at her lower lip. "I'm going to make you beg me to fuck you."

God, he knew just how to push her buttons *and* her boundaries. "I don't beg."

"You beg, baby, and just for that, I'm going to make you

beg harder."

Oh, how she'd miss their sexual banter. "With a claim like that, you'd better not let me down."

"Baby, I'm going to fuck you so well, you'll never be able to have sex with another man without wishing he was me."

He covered her mouth with his, and there was nothing gentle about it. She moaned and writhed at the wicked assault. When he reached into the nightstand for the tie, she stroked his cock.

"You want my dick, don't you, sweetheart?"

"What do you think?"

Straddling her with a devilish glint in his eyes, he wound the silk tie around her wrists and then around a sprocket on the headboard. "I think I'm going to have fun making you want it even more."

"How will I *ever* survive?" she teased.

He secured the silk and ran his fingers lightly over her nipples and down the center of her body, bringing rise to goose bumps. "Where, oh where, should I start?"

She smirked. "I have some pretty good ideas."

"I'm sure you do, but I think we need to start with the thing you like to watch best." He reached between her legs, rubbing his hand through her arousal. "So wet for me. So ready to be fucked."

"*Yes*," she pleaded. "Fuck me."

"You don't want it enough yet." He fisted his cock with the same hand and began stroking himself. His shaft glistened with her arousal, and she moaned needily. His jaw tightened, abs rippling, and he stroked himself faster.

Her attention was riveted to his big, strong hand doing what *she* wanted to do. Lust ignited in her belly, scorching up her chest, bringing her nipples to painful peaks. "Let me lick you," she pleaded.

"I DON'T THINK so, sweetheart." Raz was always greedy for her, but tonight there was no holding back the beast she'd unleashed. He continued stroking his cock, tight and slow, loving the lust brimming in her eyes. "Remember how I said I'd ruin you for all other men? Let the ruining begin."

She closed her eyes, breasts heaving.

"Eyes on *me*."

She opened her eyes, immediately narrowing them in defiance.

She had no idea how much that turned him on. "*Mm*. Look at you eating this up, arms bound, pussy glistening." He reached between her legs, teased her, and a sighing moan slipped from her lips.

"I need to touch you." She tried to pull her arms free.

"In my head, you already are. It's your hand squeezing my cock, stroking it tight, and it feels fucking fantastic. Almost as good as when I fuck your mouth."

"You can do that now," she said desperately.

"Oh, I will, but as much as I want to do it now, that would defeat the purpose." He quickened his efforts, and a bead formed at the tip of his cock. "Look what you made me do." He rubbed his thumb over the bead of liquid, and her eyes followed with a hunger that got stronger every time they were together. He brushed his slick thumb over her lower lip, and her tongue shot out, lapping it up.

"More," she begged.

"You wicked little thing. You'll get more when I'm ready for you to have more." He dipped his head, teasing her silky breast with his teeth and tongue, purposely avoiding the taut peak. She bowed off the mattress, her wrists straining the tether. He blew cool air on her wet skin, and she gritted her teeth, writhing beneath him.

"Suck it, Duncan. *Bite* it. Give me *more*," she demanded.

"Now you're getting the idea." He memorized every seductive sound, every sensual move as he sucked and bit, earning needy whimpers and greedy moans. He bit, licked, sucked, and nipped his way down her body from her cheeks to her fingertips and toes, avoiding all her most sensitive spots. Her pussy was drenched, but he didn't touch it, refused to give in to what they both wanted. It nearly killed him, but with her he'd become a possessive bastard, and even though he knew they needed to walk away when this was done, he'd make damn sure she walked away a changed woman.

"Raz, please...oh God...I can't stand it...Lick me...Please touch me..."

He sealed his mouth over her inner thigh, inhaling her intoxicating scent, and taunted his way up her body again, pausing to rub his cock over her slick center. She whimpered. "You like that, baby?"

"Yes. Just fuck me already. I can't take any more," she pleaded.

"Is that begging I hear?" he teased, and she glowered. "You're almost ready."

"*Almost?* What the hell? This is torture."

He chuckled as he untied the silk from the headboard, leaving her hands bound.

"*Raz—*"

"*Duncan*," he reminded her firmly. "Turn over, gorgeous."

She rolled onto her stomach, and he lifted her onto her knees and elbows, her bound hands resting on the mattress. He kissed her ass cheeks, and her head dipped between her arms. He nipped at those soft globes, and she sucked in a sharp breath.

"Duncan, *please*."

His name came from her lips breathless and so full of passion, it was more of an aphrodisiac than anything he'd ever seen or heard. "You don't know what wanting is yet." He licked her slick center, and she moaned loudly. He did it again and again, continuing until she was panting desperately, rocking her hips back toward him. He dragged his tongue from her pussy to her forbidden entrance.

"*Fuuck.*" She whimpered.

"How many guys have you let do this to you? And don't you dare lie." He hated himself for asking, but he wanted to know.

"One," she snapped, and looked over her shoulder with narrowing eyes. "Only you, and if anyone ever finds out, I'll kill you in your sleep."

He couldn't stop his greedy grin. "Ah, you're going to let me sleep over. I'll take that as a win." He caressed her ass cheeks and grabbed hold of her hips, using his thumbs to keep those cheeks open as he licked her from one entrance to the other. Her hands fisted in the sheets, and a stream of indiscernible, sensual noises tumbled from her lips. He slid two fingers into her pussy, coating them with her arousal, and used them to tease her tightest hole. She moaned. "Like that, baby?"

"*Yes*," she panted out. She pushed back against his finger.

"This gorgeous ass is *mine* tonight." Moving his other hand to her clit, he slowly pushed his finger past the tight rim of muscles. Her loud, sensual moans filled the room. "That's it, baby, take what I give you. What a magnificent sight you are." He slid a second finger into her ass, and she moaned again. "Feel good?"

"Yes," she panted out.

"Time to feel even better." He brought his mouth to her pussy, while his other hand worked her clit, and he pumped his fingers into her ass fast and hard. His cock ached to get in on the action, and she was right there with him, wildly thrusting her hips back, until "*Duncan—*" flew from her lungs so loud, he was sure the neighbors heard it, and he fucking hoped they did. He continued devouring her clenching pussy and fucking her ass as her orgasm ravaged her. Never in his life had he ever wanted anyone so badly.

As she came down from the peak, he quickly sheathed his length, grabbed her hips, and drove into her pussy in one hard thrust. She cried out again, and he used one hand to breach her other entrance with his fingers as he fucked her.

"Your pussy is so tight with my finger in your ass." He pounded into her, bringing his other hand to her clit.

"*Oh God…Duncan…Oh—*"

The erotic noises she made and her body clamping around his cock and fingers like a vise as they rode out her second orgasm nearly took him over the edge. But she felt too damn good, and he was too fucking greedy to stop there. He forced himself to hold back as the pulse of aftershocks rippled through her. Withdrawing his fingers, he bent over her back, hugging her around her middle, his cock still buried deep, and kissed her spine. "Tell me to stop, sweetheart, or I'm going to fuck your ass with my cock."

"Don't stop," she begged. "Please don't stop. Just…go slow."

Jesus. He thought he could get through this without a flood of emotions overtaking him. But he was *too* into her to go there without the intimacy he craved and she deserved. He needed to see her face, needed to be sure he wasn't hurting her, and damn it, as much as he wanted to make his mark on her soul, he didn't want her to have any regrets.

He unbound her wrists and sat up against the headboard, handing over control to her. "Do it this way so I don't hurt you." The condom was still slick with her arousal as she straddled him, planting her hands on his shoulders. Her hair tumbled over her flushed breasts as she eased the head of his cock past the tight rim of muscles. Her brow furrowed, and she sucked in air between clenched teeth.

"Stop if it hurts too much, baby."

She shook her head, slowly sinking deeper onto him. He held tightly to her hips, not letting her drop too fast. The trust in her eyes was as excruciating as watching her take him where no man had gone before, stoking the inferno of emotions searing him from the inside out. The feel of her body stretching for him was unlike anything he'd ever felt, and from the emotions glowing in her eyes, he knew she was as overwhelmed as he was. When she sank all the way down, their breath left their lungs in a rush. Neither one said a word, emotions thickening the space between them. He wanted to tell her how special she was, how he'd never done this with anyone else, and damn it to hell, he knew he'd never be able to, because while he was ruining her, she'd already ruined him.

But he kept all that to himself because it wouldn't be fair to say when he was only hours from flying across the country. "You okay, princess?"

She nodded and began moving along his shaft. He drew her mouth to his, drinking in the passion that practically dripped from her pores. Her mouth was sweet and hot. He wanted to kiss her for days as she rode his cock. But she felt too good. He wasn't going to last, and he wanted her to come with him. Her head fell back with a moan, fingernails digging into his shoulders, luscious lips parted, and those gorgeous auburn locks bouncing against her breasts and over her shoulders. He took her nipple into his mouth, working her clit as she moved along his shaft faster, *rougher*. Her ass was so tight, her arousal soaking his skin. Heat pounded through him, but he needed to feel closer to her. He needed *more* of her.

"This mouth is mine," he growled, tugging her mouth to his.

Their tongues lashed erotically, and he wrapped his arms around her. *This* was what he needed, to taste the emotions she'd never admitted to. Pressure mounted inside him, and their thighs flexed in unison, as if their oncoming orgasms were two trains riding the same rail. Her inner muscles squeezed around his cock, sending heat shooting down his spine, and they surrendered to the power of their passion. The pleasure was merciless. As their growls and cries echoed off the walls, he knew those sounds, this moment, and this woman would be etched into his heart, into his *soul*, forever.

When the last of their climaxes subsided, she climbed off him, and he drew her into his arms, unable to speak for the emotions swamping him. She buried her face in his chest, and he assumed she was feeling the same way. "I didn't hurt you, did I?" he whispered.

She shook her head, and without a word, she slipped out of bed, heading into the bathroom. He went to use the hall bathroom. When he returned, Leni was sitting on the far side of the bed wearing a T-shirt. Her shoulders were rounded forward, head bowed, hair curtaining her face. He pulled on his boxer briefs, and as he went to her, she said, "You should leave."

His chest seized. He was sure he'd heard her wrong. "Leave?"

She nodded.

"No." He went around the bed and knelt before her.

She averted her eyes.

Running his hands along her thighs and around her back, he pulled her closer. "I'm not leaving after what we just did. Did I do something wrong? Did you not want to do that?"

"I *wanted* to," she said softly. "I just can't believe I went through with it. I've never done that before."

"Neither have I."

Her brows knitted.

"That's us, Leni. There's a fire between us that refuses to go out."

"I can't…" She shook her head.

"We don't have to talk about it, but I'm not going to walk out the door like it meant nothing. Like *you* mean nothing."

She closed her eyes, whispering, *"Please go."*

He gritted his teeth against the pain that brought. "Is that what you really want?"

Her eyes opened, but she didn't say a word. She didn't have to. He saw the answer in her eyes and felt it in his heart. This was it.

This was goodbye.

He thought he'd have one last night to hold her in his arms, one last morning to wake up with her wrapped around him like an octopus. He was bereft, unprepared for the sudden loss. There were so many things he wanted to say. "Len—"

"*Stop.*" She held up her hand, pleading eyes telling him to leave.

Fucking hell. "Are you sure?"

She nodded and closed her eyes again.

Her eyes remained closed as he dressed. When he knelt before her again, she didn't move a muscle. His chest was so tight, it was hard to breathe. He tucked her hair behind her ear, and her eyes finally opened, brimming with both sadness and determination. He took her beautiful face between his hands and pressed his lips to hers. "You're a special woman, Leni Steele. Don't you ever forget that."

As he pushed to his feet, a single tear slipped down her cheek, gutting him to the core as he walked out of her bedroom for the last time.

Twenty-Eight

LENI SAT ACROSS the conference table from Alyssa Braden, a sharp, dimple-cheeked brunette, trying like hell to focus on their meeting and not the endless abyss inside her. It was Wednesday evening, three days since Raz walked out the door. Three days since she'd heard his voice or received a text from him.

She *hated* how it felt like he'd taken a big part of her with him. The part she liked most, it turned out. The part she hadn't even known existed before their stupid fake-dating drama. She'd done a good job of holding herself together in public. She had to. The fucking paparazzi were taking pictures of both of them on opposite coasts. She wouldn't give them the satisfaction of seeing how shattered she was, and she refused to look at any pictures of him. If she could be off his mind so quickly, then she'd find a way to do the same. She'd kept herself busy with spin classes, nose-to-the-grindstone workdays, and as many client meetings as she could pile on, with the goal of falling into bed too exhausted to think every night. It was the only viable option. Left with energy to ponder her thoughts brought a rush of memories that played like a movie starring Duncan Raz on repeat in her mind, and *that* was excruciating.

But she was determined not to let this break her, and she smiled at Alyssa, ready to put on her own Oscar-worthy performance. "I reviewed your previous marketing strategies, and I noticed you've shied away from any mention of the festival having been founded by your parents."

"Yes. We were advised to change up our marketing three years ago, to make the festival appear bigger and more prestigious. But I'm not happy with the new direction. It feels *off*. I was hoping you might come up with a way to shift gears."

"There's always a way to redirect. Unfortunately, you fell prey to a trend, and not one our company encouraged. Many of the family-owned businesses who followed that path fell short of their goals."

"So you think we should go back to our old strategies?"

"No. You tried something new for a reason, and your marketing is working. The festival is known for, and prides itself on, the hand selection of vendors, which makes those slots highly sought after."

"Yes, and tickets to the event usually sell out within two or three hours."

"Which is spectacular, but when reviewing the demographics of the attendees at your last three events, I noticed you've lost a good number of the people who have bought tickets in the past, but you've gained an equal number of older attendees from markets that suggest the broader business strategy holds some weight. I've come up with a plan that includes both."

Leni pushed the proposal across the table. "Let me show you exactly what I'm thinking."

Two and a half hours and one commitment later, Leni shook Alyssa's hand. "You won't be disappointed."

"I have no doubt. You're a keen businesswoman, and I like that." Alyssa gathered her things. "If you weren't with Duncan Raz, I'd try to set you up with one of my brothers."

Leni tried not to let her smile falter despite the bone-deep ache rising from the dredges where she had adeptly buried it. She drew her shoulders back, steeling herself against a wave of sadness threatening to break her. "That's sweet of you, but I'm sure there are plenty of other women out there."

"You have no idea how slim the pickings are for men and women."

"Oh, I have a good idea."

"Well, if you happen along any other guys like Duncan, please pass them my way."

If Leni were in a better mood, she might suggest one of her handsome cousins from Harborside, but she couldn't play matchmaker in her current frame of mind. "Will do."

She grabbed her copy of the proposal and walked Alyssa out, locking the office door behind her, and strode directly into Shea's office. "Alyssa is on board." She slapped the signed proposal on her desk.

"Is she gone?" Shea asked.

"It's seven fifteen. Yes, she's gone, and the door is locked."

"Yes!" Shea got up and hugged her. "I *knew* you'd nail it." She pulled a bottle of champagne out of her desk drawer.

"No champagne for me. I've got another few hours of work to do."

"You can take a break, Len. You just solidified a huge contract, and you haven't left the office before ten o'clock this week."

"How do you know?"

"Because…" Her brows knitted. "I know *you*."

Leni narrowed her eyes. "You're worse at lying than I am, but it doesn't matter. When are you leaking the breakup to the press?" She'd asked Shea first thing Monday morning after another client had made a comment about her and Raz, and Shea had said she was working out the details.

"I don't know yet. I'm still working on the best way to do it."

"What is there to work on? Just leak that we had a fight and broke up and we're both doing fine and want our privacy."

Shea set the champagne bottle on her desk. "What's the rush?"

The rush? Was she serious? Every room in her apartment held memories of him. She had to practically boil her sheets to get rid of his scent, and she'd thought the emptiness in the pit of her stomach would go away after a few hours, but it was still there, waiting to swallow her from the inside out. She'd tried to fill that void with ice cream and Thai food, but she couldn't even look at them without sadness rushing in. When Abby and Indi had texted to see how she was holding up without her *boyfriend*—a term she now despised—she'd nearly caved and told them the truth. But sharing her heartache would not quell the longing. It would only bring an onslaught of girlie comfort, and she did *not* need that.

She needed to throw axes at Raz's picture, which he'd so generously left on her fridge their last night together, on which he'd written, *Best Fake Boyfriend Ever*, in black Sharpie.

She wondered, momentarily, if they could do a heart transplant for a broken heart.

"Hello, Leni...? Are you going to tell me why you're in such a rush?"

Leni blinked several times. See? That's what Raz did to her.

He made her think with her heart and not her head. He made her stupid. "I just want my life back."

"What do you mean? Are you interested in dating someone else already?"

"You're not serious. I'd rather gouge my eyes out with a spoon." *Than endure this type of unending heartache again.*

"Then you miss him?" she asked hopefully. "I knew you were falling for him!"

"*No*, I don't miss him." *And he obviously doesn't miss me.* That reality was like a kick in the gut. "I'm happier without him. I'm better alone, damn it."

"Okay, geez. Sorry. I just don't see what the rush is. I want to be sure we handle it right so it doesn't come crashing down on either of you, and that takes finesse."

"Then start finessing, because if one more person tells me how great we are together or asks how I'm holding up since he's filming for the next few months, I might deck them."

As she stalked out of the office, Shea said, "Please don't punch any clients!"

Leni hollered back, "Then end this nightmare!"

LENI WORKED UNTIL eleven, had Cheez-Its for dinner, watched *Supernatural* until her eyes felt like they were bleeding, and finally went to bed. As soon as she crawled beneath the covers, her phone chimed with a text. Groaning, she cursed herself for not remembering to silence it and snagged it from the nightstand. Her heart sprinted at the sight of Raz's name on the message bubble. She stared at it for what felt like an hour but was probably only a minute or two before opening it. A picture of a refrigerator covered with photos popped up. She zoomed in and saw they were pictures of Raz and his family.

Another message appeared. *You've inspired me to make my house homier.*

She zoomed in on the fridge again, studying the pictures. There was not a single one of her. Closing her eyes against the sting of tears, she refused to let them fall. She was not going to lose herself because she'd been too weak to keep her head on straight and not fall for him. She silenced her phone and set it on the nightstand, rolling to the other side of the bed and curling around a pillow, *I'm better off alone* playing like a mantra in her head.

Twenty-Nine

RAZ PACED THE living room Friday night, glaring at the unanswered text he'd sent Leni two days ago. He was considering sending another, telling himself all sorts of ignorant shit, like she'd lost her phone or hadn't seen the text. But he knew better. He'd been stupid enough to think a text might spark a conversation and hearing her voice might help ease the gut-wrenching ache of missing her. It was better this way. Hearing her voice would have slayed him anew, and that wasn't what he needed to move on.

He was gazing out the window when his phone rang. Beau's name flashed on the screen, and he was glad for the distraction. "Beau, my man. How's it going?"

"Great. How are things with you? How does it feel to be back in LA?"

"It feels like fucking LA."

Beau laughed. "I hear ya. How did it go with Leni's parents?"

Too damn well. "They're great. Her brothers are a trip." He told him about the prank they'd pulled and how they'd gotten them back.

Beau laughed. "A cliff? Did you piss your pants?"

"Luckily, no. I wouldn't have ever lived that down. The funny thing was, I wasn't scared for myself. I was worried about my parents and Leni."

"Funny how quickly that changes, isn't it? How's filming?"

"Slow. I'm so far off my game, I can't even spell the word."

"Well, you left your girl behind. That's got to weigh on you. I couldn't do it."

Raz wished he could tell him the truth about the ruse and get all the horrible feelings off his chest, but since he couldn't, he tried to thwart any conversation about Leni. "Yeah, I remember. You gave up a big-time deal out here to be with Char."

"None of that shit mattered. I gained a life with the woman I love, and I still wake up every day wondering how I got so lucky."

Raz woke up wondering how he'd get through every fucking day without his snarky princess by his side. How fucked up was that? He rubbed a pain that had been nagging at the back of his neck all week. "Char's a good one, and she sure loves you. How's she doing?"

"Well, that's kind of why I'm calling. We haven't told the family yet, so keep this between us, but I've got to tell someone. Char is pregnant."

"No shit? That's incredible. I'm so happy for you."

"Thanks. It's surreal. I never thought I'd be able to love anyone after Tory, and now I'm going to be a father. A *dad*. How wild is that?"

Raz looked up at the ceiling. The future was all he'd thought about since leaving New York. "You'll be a great dad, Beau. You've got it all, buddy. Enjoy it."

"I am blessed. What about you? You and Leni seem pretty

serious. When will you see her again?"

"I don't know." He paced again. "Can I ask you something?"

"Anything, you know that."

"Do you worry that you'll lose Char like we lost Tory?"

A long silence passed before he spoke. "Yeah. All the time. I didn't know how to handle my grief with Tory before meeting Char. But your sister taught me how to love. It was young love, and we both know how different that is. Not a day goes by that I don't miss her. But I treasure every moment I had with Tory, and I'll do the same with every minute I get with Char. This might sound strange, but I believe Tory guided me here."

"Like she was sick of you wasting your life alone?"

"Something like that. It was pretty coincidental that Char and I came together around the anniversary of Tory's death, don't you think?"

"Who knows? But that is something my sister would do. Talk about unselfish. That was Tory through and through."

"How about you? Any thoughts on settling down?"

He had a hell of a lot of thoughts on that subject. More than he cared to pick apart. "Maybe one day, but I have a lot to figure out."

"You know, not everyone has to give up what they have to get what they want."

"I hear ya. But sometimes you just have to make do with what you have to stop thinking about what you don't." His doorbell chimed, and he glanced at the clock. *Right on time.* "Hey, man. I've got to go. Congratulations again. Give Char my best."

"Will do."

He pocketed his phone as he crossed the room and answered the door. His gaze trailed over Jacinda's sultry smile. "Hey."

"I'm glad you were free. I've missed you," she said as she came inside, and he closed the door behind her.

Thirty

WHEN LENI LEFT to catch the first ferry to Silver Island Saturday morning, she'd never been so thankful for Halloween. She needed to get out of her apartment and away from the city. Spending the afternoon decorating for the Field of Screams and the night running around scaring people would be a great distraction from the sadness that had been swamping her. Shea still hadn't staged their breakup, and if she didn't do it soon, Leni was going to do it herself. It wasn't even about other people's well-intentioned comments anymore. She needed a clean break to save her sanity. She still felt bound to Raz in her thoughts, and worse, in her heart. His essence lingered in her apartment like a ghost, appearing when she least expected it. She heard his voice when she watched TV, saw him walking into the bedroom with the damn Cheez-Its box and a coaxing grin. When she finally got to sleep at night, all the sensual things they did together returned in heart-thundering, toe-curling detail.

It was exhausting.

Time on the island was supposed to cure her of all of that. But the minute she stepped onto the ferry, the fun they'd had on the island and their nearly silent ferry ride home rushed in.

Raz had imprinted himself in every part of her life. *Why couldn't she forget him?*

Forget the heart transplant. She needed the neuralyzer from *Men in Black*. One bright flash and her memories would be wiped clean. Wouldn't that be great? Much to her irritation, the thought made her sad, and that pissed her off.

Hell, all of it pissed her off. Why was she wasting any thought on him when he clearly hadn't thought about her? Frustrated with herself, she did the one thing she knew would distract her from the man who wasn't there. She pulled out her laptop and got to work.

She didn't come up for air until the ferry docked.

Her father was waiting with open arms as she came off the ramp. "How's my girl? Ready for the Field of Screams?"

"Yes." She was going to be Freddy Krueger, which was perfect. Nobody would recognize her, which meant she wouldn't have to field questions about Raz. "Is everyone decorating?"

"They sure are." As they headed to the car, he said, "How's Duncan's filming going?"

"Great, I think." It wasn't a lie. He was a great actor, after all.

"I remember when your mother and I were apart," he said as they settled into their seats. "We spent hours on the phone every night."

"Yeah. It's pretty crazy," she said, silently cursing her cousin for forcing her to keep up the ruse.

"Did your mother tell you he sent us the nicest thank-you card and a box of Ghirardelli chocolates?"

Irritation clawed up her spine. *You get chocolates, and I get a picture of his refrigerator without so much as a "Hey, how are you?"* "That was nice of him."

"He's a class act."

"He's something, all right," Leni said tightly, and looked out the window as they left the parking lot.

When they got to her parents' house, her father took a golf cart over to the winery, and Leni headed inside. "Hello?" she called out, inhaling the scent of banana bread. Every year her mother spent hours baking for the event while the rest of the family decorated.

"In the kitchen," her grandmother called out.

Leni left her bag by the front steps and went to join them. "It smells delicious in here—" She nearly tripped over a crate of bananas.

"Careful, honey," her mother said as she decorated cookies.

The counters were covered with pies, cookies shaped like ghosts and witch hats, loaves of banana bread, and dozens of other goodies. There were two more crates of bananas by her mother's feet.

"Was there a sale on bananas?" Leni asked.

"*No,*" Archer snapped as he and Indi walked into the kitchen carrying boxes of decorations. "You can tell your boyfriend he's going down. The bastard sent me a fucking *truckload* of bananas."

"A literal truckload," her grandmother said with a grin.

"*What?*" Leni asked. "When?"

"This morning," Indi said. "He had it delivered to the boat. It was hilarious."

"It was *not* hilarious," Archer hissed.

Leni couldn't believe Raz had found a way to get Archer back and hadn't at least clued her in. If he were there, they would have laughed about the prank together. She tried to push past the reality that *out of sight* really did mean *out of mind* for him.

"He's a keeper, that Duncan," her grandmother said, earning a scowl from Archer.

The hell he is. Leni never would have imagined being on the same side as Archer when it came to Raz.

"At least nothing will go to waste. Tonight every guest will go home with a bunch of bananas," her mother said. "And as you can see, we've got banana pies, cookies, bread, bars, and muffins."

"And milk shakes." Her grandmother held up a frothy glass.

"Keira is having a sale on everything banana for the next week, and Scoops is featuring buy-one-get-one-free banana splits," Indi added. "All the local restaurants are going to feature banana dishes."

"Nobody will be able to stand the sight of bananas after this," Leni said spitefully.

"Like I said, he's dead meat." Archer brushed past Leni and walked out the kitchen door.

Leni glowered at him, and immediately regretted it. Why was she standing up for a guy who didn't give a damn about her?

"I'm loving Raz's pranks way too much," Indi said. "Len, I'm taking the decorations over. Want to ride with me?"

"Yeah." Leni grabbed a cookie, then turned to her mother and grandmother. "See you later."

"Have fun," her mother called after them.

"So, catch me up," Indi said as she climbed into the passenger seat of the golf cart, holding the box of decorations on her lap. "Is the orgasm master just as skilled over the phone and on video chat?"

"How would I know?" she said without thinking, and

quickly added, "I mean, he's busy filming and I'm slammed at work, so, you know."

"He doesn't film all night, does he?"

Leni grabbed that golden excuse and ran with it. "Yeah, super late. I'm usually asleep by the time he's done."

"That's a bummer. Do you miss him?"

No. I love having my heart ripped out of my chest. "Not really. I'm too busy to miss him much."

"That's how I was with Archer. Until I wasn't. I swear, I got to a point where being apart physically hurt."

"I remember." She also remembered not understanding why Indi would feel that way. She wished she still didn't understand. "But like I said, we're not you and Archer. I don't need all that togetherness."

Leni parked by the back of the winery, and they headed over to the courtyard, where there was a flurry of activity going on. Jock was on a ladder securing zombies to the back of the winery. Levi waved from where he and Hadley were setting up a fake graveyard in the grass, complete with skeletons climbing out of the graves. Sutton's voice carried across the courtyard as she argued with Archer, and Tara, Daphne, and Jules were chatting as they set up tables and chairs. A few feet away, her father was hanging cobwebs and ghosts in a tree with Joey.

This was what Leni loved most about Halloween, everyone pulling together to give the community something wonderful. In a few hours they'd change into their costumes and gather in her parents' house, joking around, eating snacks, and goading each other while Indi did their makeup. Leni was determined not to let her state of mind ruin her night, but it wasn't as easy as she'd hoped.

Indi set her box on a table and started sorting through decorations.

"Who needs help?" Leni called out.

"Aunt Leni." Joey waved her over. "Come help me and Grandpa!"

Leni headed that way.

"Do you like my new jacket?" Joey asked, handing her grandfather a ghost. She looked cute in orange leggings with black pumpkins on them and a denim jacket with sparkling embellishments on the sleeves and front pocket.

"It's beautiful."

"Duncan sent it to me. He got it from Taylor Swift! Look!" She turned around. Written across her shoulders in pink letters outlined with sparkling embellishments was SWIFTIE, and in the center of her back, written in what looked like black marker, was TO JOEY, MY FAVORITE SILVER ISLAND FAN. LOVE, TAYLOR SWIFT. "He sent Tara an autographed picture of her, too."

Leni's heart stumbled. "That was nice of him to send you such a special jacket."

"It's not just *any* jacket," Joey insisted. "It's *from* Taylor. She sent me a handwritten letter and everything! Tara framed it for me, and Daddy hung it up in my room."

"It was the real deal," her father said. "Taylor said when she's back on the East Coast she'd give Duncan a call and maybe she and Joey could have lunch."

As Joey handed her grandfather a cobweb and directed him to put it on the other side of the tree, Leni wondered why the hell she couldn't escape Raz anywhere. Was this a game to him? *I'm going to ruin you for all other men.* Was he purposely making it hard for her to forget him while he did God only knew what in LA?

She pulled out her phone and began thumbing out a text to

Shea. *End it with Raz today or I—*

"I can't believe it. It's not true. It *can't* be true." Jules sounded upset.

Leni looked over, seeing the panic on Jules's face, her text forgotten, and went to her sister. "What's wrong?"

Jules continued staring at her phone. "I just can't…I don't understand."

"Pix, what happened?" Grant strode over to her.

"*Jules,*" Leni said sharply. "What is it?"

Jules looked up with tears in her eyes and shook her head. "I'm sorry, Leni." Her voice cracked as she handed Leni the phone.

Leni's throat felt like it was closing, making it hard to breathe as she took in a sequence of pictures of Raz and Jacinda, showing Raz holding open the front door of a house as she walked in, time-stamped with last night's date and 11:30 p.m., and the two of them walking out of the house at 4:00 a.m., embracing on the porch at 4:03 a.m. His hair was tousled, and he was wearing sweats and the winery shirt Archer had given him. Jacinda was bare-legged and barefoot, her coat covering her to midthigh, heels dangling from her fingers. The headline read, RAZ AND JACINDA'S MIDNIGHT RENDEZVOUS.

Leni handed Jules the phone, trying to drag air into her lungs, and realized some of the others had gathered around to see what was happening. They huddled around the phone.

"Why would he do this to you?" Jules cried, and Grant pulled her into his arms.

"Maybe it's not what it looks like," Daphne said.

"Yeah. It could be nothing," Tara said.

"It looks like a fucking booty call," Levi gritted out.

"Leni, are you okay?" Indi put her arm around her.

Leni couldn't breathe. Was this how Shea *finessed* the situation? Would she do that to her? Would he? *I'm going to ruin you for all other men.* Was *this* what he meant? She'd told him her deepest secrets, and *this* was what he did with them? Her heart felt like it was being shredded, piece by painful piece.

"Maybe it's an old picture," Sutton said.

"Yeah, you know how the media is always stirring up trouble," Jock said.

"It's not. That's the shirt Archer gave him," Indi said.

"Why would he cheat on Leni? I *hate* him," Jules declared, tears streaming down her cheeks. "Grant, you have to give back the donation he made to your charity."

"Don't worry, Pix. I don't want his guilt money," Grant said.

"What the hell is going on?" Archer stalked over and grabbed the phone, the muscles in his neck bulging. "I'm going to kill him."

"It's *fine*," Leni managed. Anger and hurt warred inside her, stacking up on top of all the emotions she'd been holding in all week, making her feel like she was going to explode.

"The hell it is," Archer seethed.

"He's going to pay for this," Levi said.

Her hands curled into fists.

"Levi, you and me. We'll handle this," Archer said. "I'll call Tessa and have her fly us out to Logan Airport." Tessa Remington was a local pilot.

"*Stop*," Leni fumed. "You're not going anywhere. It's *fine*. It's not real."

"Leni, look at the fucking picture," Archer snapped.

"No. *Us*. Me and Raz. *We* were never real. It was all a stupid ruse to fix his reputation." She didn't mean to yell, but she couldn't stop. "It was all fake! I'm sorry for lying, but—"

"Fake? Leni Bean, there's no way that was fake."

"There *is*, Dad. He's an actor. He was playing a role," she seethed.

"The fucker played us all," Archer barked.

"I can't…" Leni gulped for air, searching for…*what?* She had no car. "I can't do this. I have to get out of here. Levi, can I borrow your keys?"

"I'll go with you," Indi and Levi said at the same time.

Leni shook her head, fighting against tears. "No. *Please.*"

Levi handed her his keys, curling his hand around hers. "Are you sure?"

She nodded and sprinted toward his Durango, shaking as she climbed behind the wheel and peeled out of the parking lot. *Don'tcrydon'tcrydon'tcry.* Her phone rang, and she pulled it out of her pocket, seeing Shea's name on the screen. She answered on speakerphone. "This is the most fucked-up way you could have ended things!"

"It wasn't *me*. I just saw the news, Leni. Are you okay? I can't believe he'd do this to you."

Leni couldn't speak, pain gutting her anew, twisting like knives in her chest.

"I can't reach Raz. Patch said he hasn't been able to get ahold of him all day."

"Fuck him. I gotta go." She ended the call, white-knuckling the steering wheel as the dam broke and tears flooded her cheeks.

Twenty heart-wrenching minutes later, cold air whipped against her skin, making her eyes sting as she stepped onto the sliver of beach at Brighton Cove. She pulled her flannel shirt tight around her and sat on the sand with her heart racing, knees pulled up to her chest. She stared absently at surfers farther down the beach until her tears turned to sobs, and she could do nothing more than bury her face in her arms and surrender to the agonizing misery of her broken heart. But the pain consumed her like sharp heavy boulders, making it hard to breathe. She was drowning in it. *What did I do to deserve this? How could I have misread him so badly?* The questions echoed in her head, battling the devil on her shoulder. *You let him in. You knew better, and you still gave him the power to destroy you.*

Her chest constricted.

He was a charmer, not a destroyer.

No, she thought angrily. That was an act, and she'd bought it hook, line, and sinker. She'd always known he'd hurt her. That was *why* she'd told him to leave the night of the wedding. But she never expected him to be so ruthless. Now she knew the truth. Duncan Raz was a charming *destroyer*. But she wouldn't give him the satisfaction.

This wasn't who *she* was. She didn't cry over men. She didn't question herself because some guy couldn't keep it in his pants. She sat up straight, gulping the cold, salty air, trying to pull herself together, but the picture of Raz embracing Jacinda flashed before her like a neon billboard.

A fucking disgusting neon billboard.

Sobs stole her breath, and she pulled her knees up and crossed her arms over them, burying her face again. Sobs racked her body like waves crashing against the shore. She cried for her own stupidity, for the hope she'd allowed to grow inside her despite her denials. She could fool others, but her stupid heart knew the truth, and this was how she paid for it.

Her tears ebbed and flowed, coming in brutal waves, then easing long enough for her to think she might be okay, and then another memory slayed her. She didn't know how long she sat there in the cold, crying too many tears, thinking about all the things he'd said and done. The way he'd shown up at her office with ice cream and Thai food and the fun they'd had that first day he'd dragged her out for a run, had kept her out all day, and ended up at the comedy show. She thought about the way he looked at her, the comfort she took in his arms, and—

"Leni?"

Her head shot up, and she swiped at her tears, bringing Wells into focus. He was wearing a sweatshirt, his wet suit hanging at his waist. "Go away, Wells."

He looked down the beach, but he sank to the sand beside her.

"What part of go away don't you understand?" she snapped.

"I understand every word, but I heard what happened. Grant texted. Everyone's worried about you."

"I'm *fine*."

"Clearly, because you always cry at the drop of a hat."

She deadpanned. "I'm not crying."

He looked out at the water. "Okay."

"Please go away."

His jaw ticked, and he met her gaze. "I've let you send me away for years. I'm not leaving this time."

"What is *wrong* with you? I don't want you here. Can't you see that?"

"I'm sorry about Duncan. The guy obviously has issues."

She scoffed. "That's rich coming from you. At least with him it was fake to begin with." Shit. She shouldn't have let that slip. Fuck it. If Raz could screw her over like this, let the world know the truth.

"What is that supposed to mean?"

"My relationship with Raz was fake. It was made up. Not real."

"Bullshit. Nobody can fake the way you two looked at each other. You were happy, Leni. Happy like I haven't seen you in years."

"*It. Wasn't. Real,*" she seethed.

"I'm not buying it. You protect your heart with an army of Uzis and AK-47s. You'd rather be alone than open yourself up to a relationship. But you let him in."

"Because I'm stupid," she snapped. "I'm not cut out for relationships. There's something about me that makes men cheat or run. Is that what you want to hear? I get it. I'm a fucking asshole magnet. And he's an actor, Wells. That's what he does for a living. We faked a relationship for the press. I lost my mind and got carried away, and he *didn't*. That's all there is to it."

"You are not an asshole magnet, and nobody can fake the way he looked at you. The only other place I've seen that look was on my face when you and I were together."

She half scoffed, half laughed. "Don't start. I don't have the patience for your nonsense. Please just go away and let me be miserable by myself." She lowered her forehead to her arms.

"*No.* You have never let me explain myself, and damn it, Leni, you need to hear it, because this bullshit he's pulled is not because of you."

"Please *go*," she said without lifting her face.

"Do you know why I went out with Abby all those years ago?"

"Because you're a dick."

"Because I was in love with you, and my own parents couldn't hold a relationship together. If they couldn't do it, I knew I couldn't, either, and that scared me. I was terrified and had no idea what to do with my feelings, so I ended things the only way I was sure you'd never want me back."

"Real noble of you," she said sarcastically.

"I'm serious, Leni. I loved you with everything I had before we even slept together."

"You convinced Abby not to tell me, so don't pretend it was some big plan."

"I told Abby not to tell anyone, not *you* specifically. You were her best friend. I assumed she'd run straight to you."

Her thoughts stumbled over that.

"I have no idea why she waited two weeks, and when you found out about her, I realized how stupid I'd been. It was one thing to think I wanted, or needed, to break up with you, but when it actually happened? I was devastated. I tried to tell you why I'd done it and make things right, but you couldn't even look at me. I wanted to explain myself then, and I tried a hundred times after that, but you wouldn't listen. It took me a fucking *year* to get over you, and I have never once cheated on a woman since then, because the hurt I caused you was about half as bad as the hurt and guilt I caused myself."

The sincerity in his voice drew her eyes to his. "You're serious?"

"Dead serious. You're the whole package, Leni. You're beautiful, smart, strong, and you respect the hell out of yourself. My biggest regret was not being man enough to tell you I was scared and end things differently. I know I scarred you by breaking your trust. I was a fucking idiot, and I'm so sorry. If I could take it back, I would, a hundred times over."

"You hurt me a *lot*."

"I know. I'm so sorry."

She swallowed against the lump lodged in her throat. "But I didn't love you the way I love him."

"I know that, too," he said softly. "I knew back then that you didn't love me as much as I loved you. You had big dreams that didn't include me. That was a tough pill to swallow, and I didn't handle it well."

She held her legs tighter against her chest and looked out at the surf pounding against the shore. "I thought it was all a lie, that I wasn't hot enough or fun enough or…*something*."

"I meant everything I said to you back then and every word I've just told you."

"I'm sorry I didn't love you more."

"Don't be. We were kids. We didn't even know who we were yet. I'm sorry Duncan cheated on you. It was nice to see you happy."

"Well, he didn't technically cheat on me. I sent him away. He can do whatever he wants with his ex or any other woman." *It just hurts.*

"You sent him away? Why doesn't that surprise me?"

She arched a brow. "Really? Are we going there?"

"No. But know it's not you, Len. I thought the guy was cool, but he must be a douche."

"Don't call him that. Only I can call him that." She managed a smile. "This fucking hurts."

"I know." He put his arm around her, and she rested her head on his shoulder. "If it's any consolation, I think your brothers are putting together a SWAT team to take him down."

She laughed softly. "I love those idiots."

"They sure love you."

They sat in comfortable silence, watching the waves roll in as old wounds healed and burned bridges righted themselves.

"You want to grab a drink or something?" Wells asked.

"No, thanks. I just want to be alone."

"Are you going to be okay?"

She nodded. "Aren't I always?"

"Yeah." He pushed to his feet, giving her shoulder a reassuring squeeze before heading down the beach.

"Hey, Wells?"

He looked over his shoulder, brows raised in question.

"Thanks."

With a nod, he turned and walked away.

Thirty-One

LENI SURVIVED THE afternoon, and that evening, as they got ready for the Field of Screams, she made it clear that discussing Raz was off-limits. Her family had been walking on eggshells around her ever since. Now the Field of Screams was in full swing. She stood in the shadows eating Cheez-Its as shrieks and laughter rose around her. She was dressed as Freddy Krueger, which was fitting since she felt as burned as his face looked. Indi had done an epic job on Leni's makeup. Her face was mapped with deep grooves and disfigured tissue. She wore a brown fedora, a red-and-green striped sweater, and a metal-clawed brown leather glove on her right hand.

Leni clung to the Cheez-Its box, listening to the sounds of fast footfalls, whispers, and giggles mingling with the music coming from the courtyard. The melodic murmurs of children playing, people dancing, and friends chatting hummed through the night. A teenager ran past, then stopped. Leni held her breath as he backtracked until he was standing before her in a Dracula costume.

"Hey," he said with an annoyed expression.

She shoved her hand into the box of Cheez-Its. "You're not supposed to be in this aisle."

"Aren't you supposed to scare us?"

"*Boo*," she said, and popped a handful of Cheez-Its into her mouth. "Now get out of here."

"That was lame."

"No shit. Now, get going before I sic someone with a chain saw on you."

The kid took off, and Leni looked at her phone to check the time. She and her family were taking shifts in the vines. Thankfully, she had only a half hour left. Then she could fill her pockets with candy, grab a bottle of wine, and hole up in her room watching a horror movie. She was taking the first ferry out in the morning and planned on burying herself in work until her life went back to normal.

Whatever the hell that was.

She felt a pang of guilt over the waiting texts from Shea and Abby. She didn't have it in her to discuss what had happened in any further detail.

She thought she heard someone call her name and tipped her ear up, listening intently as she ate another handful of Cheez-Its. The music stopped, and what sounded like a dozen people were calling her name. *Damn it.* If that teenager ratted on her, she was going to give him hell. Can't a girl have a broken heart in peace?

She walked to the other end of the aisle, the voices becoming louder, and peered around the last vine. There were people a few aisles up, calling her name.

"Leni Steele! Where are you, princess?"

She froze, her stupid heart beating faster. Her gaze skirted the darkness to the edge of the courtyard, where the guys had stacked hay bales ten feet high and positioned zombies climbing up them. She squinted at the silver ladder leaning against the towering hay, gleaming in the moonlight, and saw Raz standing near the top, clinging to it for dear life.

"I'm not leaving until you come out here, Leni!" he hollered.

She stumbled across the grass, sure she was delirious from all that crying. She blinked several times, but he was still there. Her heart slammed against her ribs, and she shouted, "I have *nothing* to say to you."

"That's fine. All you have to do is listen. Those pictures aren't what you think!"

"I don't *care*."

"Yes, you do. And if you don't, I care enough for both of us!"

His voice dripped with sincerity, determination, and emotions that couldn't be real. Not after what he'd done. "You don't even have me on your fridge, so I don't *care*!"

"First of all, your face is all over my fridge on the half I didn't send you because I didn't think you wanted me. And second of all, you are a terrible liar, and we made a vow of honesty."

That lump in her throat returned, but she managed, "You don't deserve my honesty."

"Yes, I do. I messed up, sweetheart, but not in the way you think. Jacinda came over to apologize, and we talked. Mostly about *you*. I never touched her beyond that embrace the cameras caught, and that was a thank-you hug. How could I touch any other woman when my heart belongs to you?"

A collective *Aww* rose around them, and tears burned Leni's eyes.

"I should have fought for you that night you sent me away. I should've refused to leave and told you exactly how I felt. It killed me to walk out that door, but you said you didn't want a long-distance relationship, and I thought I didn't, either. I thought I could just return to my life in LA, and things would go back to normal. But there is no normal anymore. There's only life with you and life without you."

Tears slid down her cheeks.

"Baby, my life is nothing without you in it. I joked about ruining you for all other men, but what I didn't realize was that you had ruined me for all other women the first time I set my eyes on you in that heart-stopping moment in your office when the whole world stood still. I saw you in slow motion, your hair blowing over your shoulders, every sway of your hips pronounced. When you looked up from your phone, our eyes connected, and that lightning bolt was real."

Her breath left her lungs with a laugh.

"But you didn't stumble, and I didn't catch you. Your evergreen eyes did find mine, and I was *done*. Meant to be yours from that moment on, despite the fact that you were throwing visual daggers."

There was a rumble of laughter.

"I remember that," she said shakily, walking closer. She saw her brothers standing at the bottom of the ladder, and then she saw that bastard paparazzi, Ken Singer, watching them through his camera lens. Anger exploded inside her. *"Hey! Singer!* Get out of here!" She ran toward the cameraman.

"I invited him!" Raz hollered, stopping her in her tracks.

She looked up at him with disbelief.

"The media humiliated you with lies, and I'm setting that straight. I gave him an exclusive to make sure that the world knows nothing happened between me and Jacinda, and nothing will *ever* happen between me and any other woman, because I love you, Leni Steele, and I will do whatever it takes to win you back. I know you think you're a stepping-stone, not a forever girl, but you're *my* forever girl."

Leni tried to see through the blur of tears.

"I love that you're a stubborn, sarcastic, snarky, workaholic, and yes, getting close to you, the real you, was harder than breaking into Fort Knox. But you're worth it, baby, and I will fight for you until you let yourself love me wholly and completely. I miss us. I miss my sinful angel. The woman who sees beyond glamour and glitz, who fought to bring her family back together no matter how many times she hit a brick wall, and who loves so deeply it terrifies her."

"You say that like you think you know me," she teased, grinning like the lovesick fool she was, and swiped at her tears.

Chuckles rose around them, and Raz's smile hit her in the center of her chest.

"Knowing you will take a lifetime, and I'm here for that. I know you don't want a long-distance relationship, and you worry about being distracted from work, but *I* know we can make this work. I'll move to New York as soon as I'm done filming, and I'll have to travel and film on location and all of that, but I'll *always* come home to you. I can't sleep worth a darn without you lying on me like a second skin, so what do you say, princess?"

More tears wet her cheeks. "I want you to distract me from work."

He laughed. "I'm good at that."

"I'll take time off to visit you when you're filming, because I love you, and I want to be with *you*, Duncan, here, in LA, Maryland, or anywhere else you want or need to be. Now get down here and kiss me, you fool."

He clung to the ladder and glanced down at her brothers. "I think they put my name on one of those graves over there."

"Get your ass—" Archer glanced at the children running around. "Get your butt down here and seal this deal, or I *will* put you six feet under."

Raz climbed down the ladder, and Leni launched herself into his arms, the two of them kissing and laughing, murmuring *I love you* as cheers rang out around them.

He drew back. "Hold on one sec. I'm sorry." He pulled a bottle of cologne out of his pocket and held it, facing Ken Singer's camera. "Fans and friends, be sure to pick up Rugged for Men cologne. It'll get you your girl. Or a monster, if you're into that." He pulled Leni into another kiss, inciting more cheers and whistles. "I can't believe I'm kissing Freddy Krueger."

She laughed. "I can't believe you climbed a ladder."

"I had to. Your brothers were out for blood. Not that I blame them, but Levi swung at me, and I ducked, then swung back and clocked him in the jaw. They all came after me, and I would've let them take me down if you'd sent me away."

"I still can't believe you came back," she said through fresh tears.

"Believe it, baby, and know in your heart that I always will."

RAZ'S CELL PHONE rang as the car pulled away from LaGuardia Airport. Leni's name flashed on the screen, and he felt himself smiling. Long-distance was hard for both of them, but there was nothing they couldn't get through for each other. They talked every night and texted as they were able, but he hadn't been with her since Thanksgiving, nearly three weeks ago. It had taken some doing, but he'd finagled two nights off from filming to attend Jules's wedding. They were taking the ferry to Silver Island tomorrow morning, but tonight he'd have Leni all to himself.

"Hey, princess. I should be there in about an hour and a half, depending on traffic. How was your day?"

"Crazy. I was hoping to be home by the time you got there, but my client had to bump our meeting. It's not starting for another forty-five minutes. There should be some leftover pizza in the fridge if you're hungry. I'm really sorry I have to work late. Do you have your key?"

He didn't think it was possible to love her more than he already did, but every time he heard her voice, that love grew by leaps and bounds. "Yeah, I've got it. Don't stress about being late. Focus on your client, and I'll see you when you're done."

"Okay. I love you."

"I love you, too, sweetheart. I'll see you soon."

He'd never tire of hearing, or saying, those words. Letting their true feelings out had changed both of them. Leni was still as adorably snarky and challenging as ever, but she left no question about her feelings for him, sharing them through words and the special things she did. Like surprising him at Thanksgiving when they hadn't taken a break from filming for the holiday. Leni had not only come to LA, but she'd flown in his parents as well. She'd also secretly filled his freezer with strawberry ice cream so he'd have it to eat when they binged their shows together on opposite coasts. He watched her horror shows, and she watched his action movies. But they did more watching each other than the shows. She missed him as much as he missed her and held nothing back during their sexy video calls. It couldn't replace having her in his arms, but he'd take what he could get while they were apart.

A little more than an hour later, he was heading down the hall to Leni's apartment. The last time he walked that hall was the night she'd sent him away after Jay and Naomi's wedding. He hadn't thought he'd survive that night. He'd finally woken up from that stupor when Jacinda came over to talk. He'd realized he'd stayed up half the night talking to the wrong woman. It had taken hard negotiating and forfeiting a good chunk of what he was being paid to make the movie in order for the filming schedule to be reworked so he could get time off at Halloween to go get his girl, but he'd have given up everything to get back to Leni that night.

He unlocked her apartment door, breathing in the scents of honeysuckle and caramel. The scents of his sweet love. As he set his bags by the door, his gaze moved through the living room, taking in a Christmas tree in the corner, not yet decorated, and several new framed pictures decorating the walls and furniture. On the end tables were pictures of them the paparazzi had taken, like the one of him giving Leni a piggyback ride and the two of them holding hands as they left the restaurant the night his parents had surprised him in New York. A picture of his mother with her arm looped through Leni's in front of the theater and a few others hung on the walls. Interspersed with those pictures were photos of his family, including Tory, from when they were younger. He swallowed hard. Where had she gotten them? He peered into her office, and on her desk he saw the picture she'd texted to her family from her bed the night before Archer had stormed into her apartment. They had love in their eyes even then.

Leni came out of the kitchen, gorgeous in an emerald-green dress. "Duncan, I didn't hear you come in." She threw her arms up. "Surprise!"

Hearing his given name coming out of her mouth was another thing he'd never tire of. "Hi, beautiful." He drew her into his arms and kissed her. "I thought you were working late."

"I only said that so I could surprise you, but then you snuck in like a ninja."

He laughed and kissed her again. "God, I've missed you. You've been busy. You got us a Christmas tree, and where did you get all these pictures?"

"I thought we could decorate the tree tonight." Her parents had invited his family to join them for the holiday. "Your mom gave me some decorations that she said were special to you, including a clay Christmas tree Tory gave you for your eleventh birthday."

Unexpected tears stung his eyes. "You're amazing to think

of that for me. This will be the best Christmas ever."

"I was hoping you'd say that. Your mom also gave me all the pictures of your family. I hope that's okay, and Ken got me most of the others." Ken Singer had done right by them. Their Halloween reunion had been the hottest topic on social media for weeks, and sales of Rugged for Men cologne had shot through the roof, as did inquiries for events at the winery. "I also tried to make your favorite dinner," she said a little tentatively. "I got your mom's recipe for Bolognese, but when I was putting in the chili flakes, the top popped off the shaker, and I ruined it."

His heart overflowed with love for this woman who stepped so far out of her comfort zone for him. "You *cooked* for me?"

"I *tried*. I wanted to do something special for you since you came all this way for two nights. And even though we're not moving your stuff in until you're done filming, and we might look for a bigger place, this is your home, too. I wanted it to feel like home when you got here."

"Baby, I'd cross the country for an *hour* with you, and I love that you did all this for me, but I hope you know that *you* are all I ever need. Wherever you are is home for me. Anything else is just whipped cream on my Leni Steele sundae." He gathered her in his arms and kissed her smiling lips. "But I have to admit, domestic Leni is damn sexy."

"Domestic Leni sucks. She ruined dinner."

A slow smile spread his lips. "She sucks, huh? I think I'm going to like her a lot."

"Oh yeah?" Her eyes darkened.

He kissed her again as he unbuttoned the front of her dress and lowered his mouth to the swell of her breast, sucking and licking until she was moaning and fumbling with the button on his jeans. "We have to hurry," she panted out. "I ordered delivery. It'll be here in thirty minutes."

"Just enough time for me to have my favorite appetizer."

He took her in a passionate kiss, and they both went a little wild, leaving a trail of clothes down the hall and barely making it to the bed before he sheathed his length and buried his cock deep inside her. "God, I've missed fucking you."

"Stop talking and show me." She pulled his mouth to hers, and he loved her with everything he had until they were both too spent to move.

ALL OF SILVER Island was decorated for the holidays, with twinkling lights in trees, streetlamps wrapped in gold tinsel, and wreaths on shops and house doors alike, but love was in the air at Majestic Park. They'd set up two hundred chairs decorated with red and green ribbons for Jules and Grant's wedding, but the park was full to the brim. People had come from clear across the island to celebrate the happy couple. They'd lit the Christmas tree earlier in the evening, and now, beneath a clear starry sky, lanterns illuminated a red-carpeted aisle that led to a wedding arch draped in white silk, red roses, green vines, and tiny golden lights. Leni and the other bridesmaids stood on one side in gorgeous crimson gowns with white fur shawls, holding bouquets of white and red roses. Grant and his groomsmen, striking in black tuxedos with red boutonnieres, stood on the other side, and photographer Hawk Pennington moved stealthily in the background, catching it all on camera.

Grant looked anxious, his eyes glued to the aisle, where Hadley and Joey were making their way toward the altar in adorable white faux-fur coats over beautiful white gowns with puffy tulle skirts that had green and red moons, stars, and starbursts embroidered on them. They carried wooden lanterns filled with sparkling confetti, tossing handfuls with every step.

Hadley threw it as high as she could and twirled beneath the showering confetti, shouting, "Look, Daddy Dock! It's pixie dust!"

Everyone laughed.

"Had, no, you're supposed to sprinkle it on the ground," Joey said, but Hadley did it again and again, giggling wildly, and Joey gave in, joining her younger cousin's confetti-tossing twirlfest.

They were adorably entertaining, but Leni's gaze returned to the boyfriend she couldn't get enough of. Duncan was sitting with her mother and aunt, beyond gorgeous in a dark suit and tie. He was watching her with so much love in his eyes, she swore she felt it wrapping around her like an embrace. To an outsider, her life probably looked the same as it always had. Her days appeared to revolve around work, but in reality, her entire world had changed. Work was still a priority, but it wasn't her top priority. Duncan was. He was always on her mind, and even though they were thousands of miles apart when he was filming, it didn't feel that way.

Jules was right. There was something magical about true love. It left no room for doubt or second-guessing. She and Duncan had encountered bumps and bruises, like all couples, with miscommunication here and there and juggling schedules, but at the end of the day, it was his voice that soothed her soul, and she hoped she did the same for him.

The "Wedding March" played, drawing Leni's attention to the aisle as Jules and her father stepped up to the red carpet. Jules looked like a princess shimmering in the moonlight, holding a bouquet of red roses. Her gown was a dreamy combination of pearled beading, sequins, and lace appliqués sprinkled over shattered glass sparkling tulle, with a basque bodice and sweetheart neckline. Her white faux-fur trimmed wedding cape added a dash of small-town charm, and when Jules pushed the secret button on her gown, dozens of white lights burst to life along the neckline and spilling halfway down the skirt in jagged sections, making her look like a fairy-tale pixie.

The crowd gasped, and it was so perfectly Jules, tears welled in Leni's eyes. Jules looked at Grant, and her smile leapt through the air, bringing tears to his eyes, and probably everyone else's, too.

Their father was so handsome in his tuxedo, pride shining in his eyes as he walked Jules down the aisle. Leni couldn't be happier to see the girl who only ever wanted to make others happy blossom before her eyes into a soon-to-be wife to a man who adored and protected her, and have all *her* dreams come true. Leni's gaze was drawn to Duncan again, and she wasn't surprised to find his eyes trained on her. Two and a half months ago, she'd sworn off men, and tonight, as her sister stepped up to the place where she'd say her vows, Leni couldn't take her eyes off the man who made her want to do the same.

HOURS LATER, THE reception was in full swing in the banquet room of the Silver House, one of the most sought-after wedding destinations on the East Coast. Built on a bluff overlooking Sunset Beach, every room had a commanding view of an expansive stone patio, meticulously manicured gardens, intricately designed arbors, and blissfully beautiful Silver

Harbor. The heartfelt toasts had brought many to tears, Jules and Grant's first dance was as magical as their ceremony, dinner was incredible, and the band was spectacular.

Duncan spun Leni in his arms for the hundredth time and gazed into her eyes, stirring those butterflies that were still taking up residence in her chest. Surrounded by music and love, in the arms of the man she never expected to win her heart, Leni wanted this moment to last forever.

"I'm glad you were able to get this time off," she said softly.

"I missed Abby's wedding. I wasn't about to make you go solo to Jules's, too."

"You did miss a fabulous wedding." Aiden had gone above and beyond Abby's wildest dreams, bringing in a chef from her father's hometown in France and her favorite band from the UK.

"I know, and I was jealous of every guy who got to see you in the sexy dress you wore. There was no way I was going to miss seeing you in *this* one." He brushed his scruff along her cheek, speaking low and seductively. "Or miss stripping it off you later."

A shiver of heat trickled down her spine. "How long do we have to stay?"

He chuckled and lowered his lips to hers as the song came to an end.

"A'right, you two, that's enough." Archer grabbed one of Duncan's arms, and Levi grabbed the other.

"This guy hasn't had enough shots yet," Levi said.

"If you do anything to him, I will make it my mission in life to ruin you both," Leni warned.

"Who needs a bodyguard when I have a badass princess?" Duncan winked.

As they dragged him off, Leni headed over to Sutton, Shea, and Indi at the edge of the dance floor. "Indi, should I be worried about Archer and Levi absconding with my man again?"

"No. I already thwarted the worst prank ever," Indi said.

"Oh God. Do we even want to know?" Sutton asked.

"I came home early during their poker night last week and caught them planning to rip holes in the butts of our bridesmaid gowns."

Leni's jaw dropped. "I would have slaughtered them if they'd ruined Jules's wedding."

"Don't worry. I told Archer if they pranked anyone tonight, I'd give him his ring back." Indi sipped her drink. "The only fabric being ripped off tonight is going to be my panties."

"I don't need to picture my brother doing that," Leni said.

"Yeah, I'm with you," Sutton agreed.

Shea sighed, watching Hawk take pictures of the guests. "I really need some panty-ripping options, or I'm going to make some very poor choices."

"Fitz and Wells are single," Sutton said.

"They're hot but a little too young for me and a little too *good boy*, right?" Shea said.

"Um, *no*," Indi said.

Leni and Sutton exchanged curious glances.

"What do you know that we don't?" Leni asked.

Indi lowered her voice. "I overheard a couple of women in my shop talking about them, and it sounded like they'd had a *very* good time."

"I don't need to hear this." Leni was thankful that she and Wells had cleared the air, but there was only one man whose sex life interested her, and he was at the bar with her brothers,

Grant, and Brant, laughing about something. "Why don't I start handling Hawk? Then you can let him do your panty ripping."

"Tempting offer, but no thank you," Shea said. "I wouldn't hand off a business associate just so I could…do *that*."

"If you're into bearded bikers, Levi is still a member of the Dark Knights in Harborside, and they have some hot members," Sutton said.

"Yeah, and it's run by two of my brothers." Shea sipped her drink. "That would not go over well. What's happening with your boss?"

"Nothing good. He's being sketchy. I think he's testing me," Sutton said.

"Why?" Shea asked.

"Because he said we're going to have some major assignments in Mongolia, the Amazon Rainforest, and Antarctica, but he's only giving me the bare minimum about what we'll be reporting on and hasn't told me *when* for any of them. It's really hard to prepare."

"Well, the travel sounds exciting, no matter when you go," Indi said.

Leni cocked a brow. "At least you know you'll either be packing a parka or a bikini."

"I don't think I'd wear a bikini in the rainforest," Shea said. "You might get bugs in your cooch."

They laughed.

"Can I have your attention, please?" the lead singer of the band announced. "We'd like to invite all the single ladies to the dance floor for the tossing of the bouquet."

There was a flurry of activity as women rushed to the dance floor.

"That's us!" Shea said excitedly and grabbed Sutton's and Leni's hands.

Leni yanked her hand free. "I'm good over here." Catching a bouquet led to expectations of proposals, and as much as she wanted forever with Duncan, he didn't need that type of pressure.

"Oh, no, you're *not*." Jules flew to her side like a vulture and dragged her toward the dance floor. "It's tradition, and I want you in every part of my wedding."

Leni didn't bother arguing. This was Jules's special day, and she wasn't going to put a damper on it. "Fine." *I'll just stand in the back.*

Jules planted Leni between Shea and Sutton. "Don't let her run away."

"What am I, five?" Leni said as Jules ran to the head of the dance floor.

Their aunt Faye joined Leni and the others. "This is so exciting!"

"I know, right?" Shea gushed.

Jules stood before the crowd and said, "Okay, ladies, who's ready to be as happy as I am?"

Cheers rang out around Leni as she silently cheered, *I already am!*

Jules turned around and said, "One. Two. *Three!*"

She threw the bouquet, and as Leni looked up, it almost hit her in the face. Jules spun around and squealed, and everyone clapped and cheered.

"Wait! I didn't try to catch it," Leni said. "Here." She shoved it toward Shea.

"You can't give it away," Shea said, pushing it back and then scurrying out of reach.

"It's fate!" Jules did a happy dance, and everyone laughed.

Leni scanned the room, looking for Duncan, and the band started playing "If You Want It to Be Good Girl (Get Yourself a Bad Boy)." She spun around and saw Grant, Jock, Archer, Levi, Duncan, and her father *strutting* across the dance floor. They lined up, doing a hip-grinding, shoulder-shaking dance. Leni took a step back, laughing.

Grant danced toward Jules, stripping off his tuxedo jacket and singing, "If you want to hit it good, girl, jump on my wood, girl."

Everyone howled with laughter. Sutton covered Joey's ears.

"I think I just got pregnant." Jules fanned her face, inciting more laughter.

Archer strutted toward Indi, stripping off his dress shirt, singing, "If you want to make my boat rock, come jump on my hard—" He covered his mouth, eyes wide, feigning shock, and gyrating his hips.

More laughter rang out as Jock did his own sexy dance toward Daphne, who was blushing a red streak as he sang, "If you want your muffins hot, girl, you know I'll hit the spot, girl!"

Daphne squealed and covered her face.

Levi strutted toward a very embarrassed Tara like he'd done it a hundred times before, singing, "If you want me wild, girl, just give me a dial, girl." He wiggled his hand with his pinkie and thumb out, as if saying, *Call me.* Tara doubled over with laughter.

Their father didn't miss a beat, snapping his fingers and shaking his hips as he closed in on their mother, who was dancing toward him as he sang, "If you want to get to slammin', girl, let's get to jammin'!"

"Dad!" Leni and her sisters complained through their laughter as everyone cracked up.

Duncan danced toward Leni like he was on *Magic Mike*, sexy and seductive, singing, "I know you want me bad, girl, and you know I love *my* bad girl."

Ohmygod. Leni covered her mouth, unable to stop laughing, but he didn't stop there, singing, "If you want dirty fun, girl, I'm your *only* one, girl." He grabbed his shirt with both hands and tore it open. Buttons went flying, and the crowd went wild, howling and whistling, as he stripped it off and dragged it across Leni's shoulders, circling her as he sang, "I want it to last, girl, so I have to ask, girl." He strutted back toward the stage, then ran toward her and slid on his knees, stopping at her feet as applause rang out. He propped himself up on one knee, holding up a stunning princess-cut diamond ring with a double band, and sang, "I want you for life, girl. Will you be my *wife*, girl?"

The entire room seemed to gasp with Leni as tears streamed down her cheeks and her heart tried to climb out of her chest to get to him. *Yes!* screamed through her head, but "This is crazy" came out with a laugh. "We haven't even lived together yet."

The room went silent, save for the music.

"I know we haven't, but it's not crazy, baby. Our love is monumental. It doesn't matter if we're thousands of miles apart or in the same room, it only gets stronger. I have fallen deeper in love with you every single day since we met, and I know you feel the same."

She nodded, sniffling. "I do."

His smile grew. "We both know how quickly the people we love can be taken away. I don't want to wait for some mystical perfect time. I know I want to spend the rest of my days building a life with you, watching horror movies that scare me and action movies that make you want to head out to the jungle and eat bugs."

Chuckles rumbled through the room, and Leni's heart beat so hard, she feared she might pass out.

"I want to walk you to work and come home to ruined dinners and laugh as we eat ice cream at three in the morning. I want silk ties and dirty showers, challenges that I rarely win, and maybe, one day, when we're both ready, we'll raise feisty girls who put boys in their places and secretly romantic boys who set girls' hearts on fire."

Leni opened her mouth to say she wanted that, too, but she was too choked up to speak.

"I want our kids to talk about how ridiculously in love we are, like we do about our parents. But most of all, I want *you*, baby. All of you. Your stubborn, loving heart, your die-hard loyalty, and your sweet, sensual side you hide from everyone else. We're meant to be together. It's that simple. So what do you say, princess? Will you be my forever girl, and let me be your bad boy?"

She laughed and cried. "You're too charming to be a bad boy."

"He's got a mean right hook," Archer called out, earning more chuckles.

Duncan arched a brow, waiting for an answer. "What do you say, princess?"

"I say *yes*, so get up here and kiss me before I change my mind."

He was on his feet and crushing his mouth to hers so fast, he nearly knocked her over. Cheers rang out, and he slid the sparkling diamond ring on her finger. "Now you're stuck with me."

"How will I ever survive all that Raznick charm?"

The crowd converged on them as they kissed, said *I love you*, and kissed some more. Moments passed in a blur of happy tears, embraces, congratulations, and sheer elation as they were torn in different directions. When they finally landed back in each other's arms, the band started up again, and Grant's father announced, "This calls for more champagne."

"I can't believe you hijacked Jules's wedding."

"I didn't hijack it. I asked Jules and Grant if it would be okay, because you're not a quiet proposal girl, even if you think you are. You're a grand gesture, let the world know I love you girl, and you're all mine."

"You think you know me," she teased.

"Tell me I'm wrong."

"I can't. We took a vow of honesty."

He laughed and pressed his lips to hers.

"Get a room," Shea said as she walked over with two glasses of champagne for them. "I couldn't be happier for you."

"We kind of owe you for setting us up," Leni said.

"That reminds me, I want to send a thank-you gift to the actress who broke her tooth and canceled," Duncan said.

"About that," Shea said tentatively. "There wasn't really a date with an actress."

"What do you mean?" Duncan asked.

"*Well...*" Shea's brow wrinkled. "I saw the way you looked at Leni when you came to my office, and if I had to watch her work herself to death one more Friday night, I was going to lose my mind. So I figured I'd try my hand at matchmaking to see if it worked."

"*You...?* I can't *believe* you did that," Leni said incredulously. "You let me go through hell."

"Hey, now," Duncan said with a grin.

"It was *so* hard falling for you and feeling like I shouldn't."

Shea backed away. "I think I'll go get some more champagne."

As she hurried away, Leni said, "It was worth the torture, but I'm totally going to get her back."

A sly grin slid across Duncan's lips. "I look forward to helping with that."

After many more toasts, Jules and Grant cut the cake, and Leni and Duncan joined everyone on the dance floor, swaying to "Still Falling for You."

"Hey, lovebirds," Abby said, dancing with Aiden beside them. "The Silvers are extending the party and having a bonfire on the patio after this."

"Great." Leni tried to sound enthusiastic, but all she really wanted was to be alone with Duncan.

They danced to a few more songs, and Duncan twirled her across the floor. When they reached the back of the banquet room, he took her hand, hurrying out a door and into a hallway.

"What are you do—" Her words were silenced by the insistent press of his lips.

"The party can wait. I want *you*." He took her hand, leading her to the elevator. "I got us a room for the night, so we wouldn't have to be quiet."

Her heart swelled. "God, I love you."

"I love you, too, sweetheart. Today, tomorrow, and forever."

"You *better*."

He lowered his smiling lips to hers and kissed her senseless.

About the Love in Bloom World

Love in Bloom is the overarching romance collection name for several family series whose worlds interconnect. For example, *Lovers at Heart, Reimagined* is the title of the first book in The Bradens. The Bradens are set in the Love in Bloom world, and within The Bradens, you will see characters from other Love in Bloom series, such as The Snow Sisters and The Remingtons, so you never miss an engagement, wedding, or birth.

Where to Start

All Love in Bloom books can be enjoyed as stand-alone novels or as part of the larger series.

If you are an avid reader and enjoy long series, I'd suggest starting with the very first Love in Bloom novel, *Sisters in Love*, and then reading through all the series in the collection in publication order. However, you can start with any book or series without feeling a step behind. I offer free downloadable series checklists, publication schedules, and family trees on my website. A paperback guide for the first thirty-six books in the series is available at most retailers and provides pertinent details for each book as well as places for you to take notes about the characters and stories.

See the Entire Love in Bloom Collection

www.MelissaFoster.com/love-bloom-series

Download Series Checklists, Family Trees, and Publication Schedules

www.MelissaFoster.com/reader-goodies

Download Free First-in-Series eBooks

www.MelissaFoster.com/free-ebooks

LOVE IN BLOOM SERIES

SNOW SISTERS
Sisters in Love
Sisters in Bloom
Sisters in White

THE BRADENS at Weston
Lovers at Heart, Reimagined
Destined for Love
Friendship on Fire
Sea of Love
Bursting with Love
Hearts at Play

THE BRADENS at Trusty
Taken by Love
Fated for Love
Romancing My Love
Flirting with Love
Dreaming of Love
Crashing into Love

THE BRADENS at Peaceful Harbor
Healed by Love
Surrender My Love
River of Love
Crushing on Love
Whisper of Love
Thrill of Love

THE BRADENS & MONTGOMERYS at Pleasant Hill – Oak Falls
Embracing Her Heart

Anything for Love
Trails of Love
Wild Crazy Hearts
Making You Mine
Searching for Love
Hot for Love
Sweet Sexy Heart
Then Came Love
Rocked by Love
Falling For Mr. Bad (Previously *Our Wicked Hearts*)
Claiming Her Heart

THE BRADEN NOVELLAS
Promise My Love
Our New Love
Daring Her Love
Story of Love
Love at Last
A Very Braden Christmas

THE REMINGTONS
Game of Love
Stroke of Love
Flames of Love
Slope of Love
Read, Write, Love
Touched by Love

SEASIDE SUMMERS
Seaside Dreams
Seaside Hearts
Seaside Sunsets
Seaside Secrets
Seaside Nights
Seaside Embrace
Seaside Lovers

THE WHISKEYS: DARK KNIGHTS AT REDEMPTION RANCH

The Trouble with Whiskey
Freeing Sully: Prequel to For the Love of Whiskey
For the Love of Whiskey
A Taste of Whiskey

SUGAR LAKE

The Real Thing
Only for You
Love Like Ours
Finding My Girl

HARMONY POINTE

Call Her Mine
This is Love
She Loves Me

THE WICKEDS: DARK KNIGHTS AT BAYSIDE

A Little Bit Wicked
The Wicked Aftermath
Crazy, Wicked Love
The Wicked Truth
His Wicked Ways

SILVER HARBOR

Maybe We Will
Maybe We Should
Maybe We Won't

WILD BOYS AFTER DARK

Logan
Heath
Jackson
Cooper

BAD BOYS AFTER DARK

Mick

Dylan
Carson
Brett

HARBORSIDE NIGHTS SERIES
Includes characters from the Love in Bloom series
Catching Cassidy
Discovering Delilah
Tempting Tristan

More Books by Melissa
Chasing Amanda (mystery/suspense)
Come Back to Me (mystery/suspense)
Have No Shame (historical fiction/romance)
Love, Lies & Mystery (3-book bundle)
Megan's Way (literary fiction)
Traces of Kara (psychological thriller)
Where Petals Fall (suspense)

Acknowledgments

I hope you enjoyed Duncan and Leni's journey to their happily ever after, and I cannot wait to bring you more Silver Island love stories. My Silver Harbor series is also set on Silver Island and features the de Messiéres family. As with all my series, characters from each story cross over to other series. If you'd like to read more about Silver Island, pick up *Searching for Love*, a Bradens & Montgomerys novel featuring treasure hunter Zev Braden. A good portion of Zev's story takes place on and around the island, as does *Bayside Fantasies*, a Bayside Summers novel featuring billionaire Jett Masters.

Writing a book is never a solo process. I'd like to thank my stand-up comedian friend Tyler Roderick for a particular stage joke about how long men last and my friend and assistant Lisa Filipe for brainstorming other jokes with me. Oh, the fun we had!

I'm blessed to have the support of many friends and family members and cannot name them all, but I am so grateful for each of you and for my hawk-eyed editorial team: Kristen, Penina, Elaini, Juliette, Lynn, Justinn, and Lee.

If you'd like to get to know me better and haven't joined my Facebook fan club, I hope you will. We have loads of fun, chat about books and hunky heroes, and members get special sneak peeks of upcoming publications and exclusive giveaways. www.Facebook.com/groups/MelissaFosterFans

Meet Melissa

www.MelissaFoster.com

Melissa Foster is the *New York Times*, *Wall Street Journal*, and *USA Today* bestselling and award-winning author of more than 100 novels. Her books have been recommended by *USA Today*'s book blog, *Hagerstown* magazine, *The Patriot*, and several other print venues.

Melissa enjoys discussing her books with book clubs and reader groups and welcomes an invitation to your event. Melissa's books are available through most online retailers in paperback, digital, and audio formats.

Shop Melissa's store for exclusive discounts, bundles, and more. shop.melissafoster.com

Melissa also writes sweet romance under the pen name Addison Cole.